Praise for Mick Farren

"Mick Farren's writing is pointed, truthful, and amazingly funny."

—*Village View* (Los Angeles)

"Farren is a true creator."

—*New Times* (Miami)

Enjoyable and inventive."

—*Time Out* (London)

"Mick Farren has had a long, illustrious career as an infamous editor, journalist, and English rock star....[He] has important points to make about the times we live in."

—*New York Paper*

The Time of Feasting

MICK FARREN

TOR®

A Tom Doherty Associates Book
New York

THE TIME OF FEASTING

A Tor Book
Published by Tom Doherty Associates, Inc.
175 Fifth Avenue
New York, NY 10010

Tor Books on the World Wide Web:
http://www.tor.com

Tor® is a registered trademark of Tom Doherty Associates, Inc.

ISBN: 0-812-53874-9
Library of Congress Catalog Card Number: 96-22943

First edition: December 1996
First mass market edition: September 1998

Printed in the United States of America

0 9 8 7 6 5 4 3 2

This book is for Susan in gratitude
for her love, support, and tolerance
through this daytrip to the heart of darkness.

The Time of Feasting

Prologue

Victor Renquist slowly rose from his chair as the two men came into the room. "So what is it to be, gentlemen? The wooden stake? Drive it deep into their hearts and burn the bodies? Isn't that the traditional remedy?"

Renquist had heard criminals talk of how, after months, even years on the run, the instant of capture brought an illogical sense of peace, despite all the punishments that might await them in the future. A similar calm seemed to settle on him as he faced these two intruders who had invaded his domain. "I assume that you're here to stake and burn?"

The two men seemed nervous, cautious as they entered. McGuire, the detective, even had a pistol in his hand, although the limitations of using firearms had already been more than adequately demonstrated. Their expressions were those of people who believed that they were entering one of the inner circles of Hell—which indeed, in their own terms, they almost were.

Renquist half smiled. "After all you've been through, you now have nothing to say to me?"

As he spoke, the men's nervousness grew and expanded to a

poisonous aura of loathing and fear. Their eyes were still adjusting to the gloom and they moved with the hesitancy of the partially blind. Humans observed their short, wretched lives on such a narrow spectrum. Fortunately, Renquist and those like him had no such limitations. The *nosferatu* perception ranged from infrared to ultraviolet and way beyond. They saw not only heat and light but also Kirlian images of mood and emotion.

"I really expected more of two intrepid vampire hunters."

Outside, the city was bathed in cool morning sunshine after a night of rain. The easy-listening radio stations would be playing Frank Sinatra's "Autumn In New York," in optimistic anticipation of an early fall. Within the Residence, however, the darkness was as comfortable as night itself. In more placid times, Renquist and the others went about their business with only the most minimal reference to the passage of days. It was when they emerged into the streets of the city that they had to take such matters into account. And at that point, day and night had to be treated with deadly seriousness. Sunlight killed. That was fact, no product of any human storybook, nightmare, or folklore.

The two men seemed uncertain as to what to do next. What had these fools expected to find? The whole colony sleeping, helpless in neat rows of coffins, like some funeral parlor dormitory. Humans clung to a wealth of misconceptions about Renquist's kind, compounded down the years by fiction, fantasy, and culture. As if to confirm Renquist's thoughts, Kelly, the crazy one who had once been a priest, raised his arm with a desperate, dramatic flourish. "Approach us not, foul abomination!"

Kelly was holding up a cross, a small cross of black wood with a silver figure of Christ nailed to it by the feet and hands. Renquist shook his head and laughed. "And now they bring out the trinkets, the gewgaws of superstition. This is New York City at the end of the twentieth century, gentlemen. Are you still unable to separate fact from fancy? Do you expect me to cringe and cover my eyes like some creature on the television late show?"

As he spoke, Renquist took a cursory reading of the two men's exposed thoughts. Kelly was dark crimson hate, old and deep-seated. Hate had eaten at him through most of his life, as familiar and ingrained as a chronic disease. Most of the time, Kelly hated himself and the imaginary, patriarchal God that was the personified extension of his own guilt. In Renquist, how-ever, he had finally found what he saw as a sufficiently power-ful external evil to provide him, at least temporarily, with the sanctuary of another target.

Renquist took a step forward. Kelly held his ground although obvious terror pulsed through him. "In the name of the Father, the Son, and the Holy Ghost, I order you to stay back."

Renquist halted. Too much pressure too soon might cause Kelly to panic, and panic on the part of either of the humans would add too many random factors to an already perilous sit-uation. "Is that whiskey I smell on your breath?"

A flush of guilt suffused Kelly's aura. Clearly the man con-tinued to feel shame over his drinking. Renquist glanced at McGuire, the policeman. "Did you really think it was a wise move to form an alliance with this drunken buffoon?"

McGuire's thoughts were less driven, more confused. He didn't share the obsessive sense of divine mission that allowed Kelly to suspend all of his natural doubts and disbelief. The de-tective was walking the edge of a chasm, horror and unreality held in check only by training and an iron will. That was why he still clutched the gun. It served as a talisman, solid and re-assuring, something he could cling to from what he thought of as the real world, a source of comfort more akin to Kelly's cross than a practical weapon. He had accompanied Kelly to the Residence, through all that had gone before, but he still had difficulty accepting the idea that he was confronting a being from myth, legend, and low-budget movies.

McGuire was a trained peace officer and his profession was

regulated by rules of behavior. His problem was that the codes, protocols, and conditioned reflexes, the book by which he operated, in no way covered an eventuality like the one that now faced him. Renquist could also sense McGuire's open dislike of Kelly, whom he blamed for much of his current inner conflict. Renquist recognized this conflict and dislike as the twin psychological wedges that could be driven between the two humans.

Kelly squared his shoulders and brandished the cross at arm's length, still apparently expecting Renquist to cower away from it. "Look upon the Holy Cross, fiend, and tremble!"

Renquist made a curtly dismissive gesture. "You can put that thing down. It really has no effect."

The ex-priest's lip curled. "You'd like that, wouldn't you? You'd like me to be defenseless."

Kelly was holding an old-fashioned leather bag in his other hand. The man's mind was like a murky crystal, flawed and bloodshot, but still transparent enough for Renquist, even in his present weakened state, to read the contents of the case without effort. The club hammer and the sharpened stakes were the source of an excitement that was close to sexual. Kelly couldn't wait to swing the hammer and feel the stake penetrate a body. He wanted the violent release so badly that the desire smoldered like a dark beacon in the hellswamp of his psyche. The destruction of Renquist and the others would be the orgasm of triumph, the final redeeming climax of a life spent in fury and frustration, the act that would bring him back to the grace of his irrational and sadistic God.

For Renquist, the danger lay in that Kelly was absolutely right about the stakes. Unlike the cross, the sharpened stake, symbolic as it might be, was no handed-down figment of a human horror story. Used correctly, it could kill even more swiftly than direct sunlight. The nosferatu's capacity for instant regeneration, which could protect them from the most ghastly wounds inflicted by sword or firearm, was of no avail when their oversized hearts were pierced by a sharp, organic instrument. The penetration of the stake broke the seal of immortality. The life-force dissipated in a screaming rush like escaping vapor, and the victim was projected across the divide into the unknown dominion of true death.

Much would have to happen, though, before Kelly had the chance to bring his hammer into play. Renquist would first have to be rendered helpless, and he wasn't about to allow that to happen. He hadn't lived for a thousand years merely to brought down by a New York City cop and drunken, defrocked whiskey priest. Renquist turned slightly and focused on McGuire, using only the very minimum of his power to control and cloud human minds. "Your friend wants to kill me. He wants to kill me very badly."

McGuire's expression was guarded. He was still holding the pistol, a compact 9mm automatic, down by his side. "Do you blame him?"

Renquist raised a questioning eyebrow. "But can you allow him to kill me?" He slightly raised the level of the hypnotic influence. The question was crucial, the start of the essential dividing of the two humans.

McGuire didn't answer, and Renquist smiled as he sensed an increase in the policeman's unease. "Wouldn't that be murder, Detective McGuire?"

"I doubt any jury would convict him."

"That's not really the point, is it?"

Kelly glanced quickly at McGuire, as though afraid to take his eyes off Renquist. "Don't listen to him. Remember that he's clever. He's terribly clever. We have to finish it."

Renquist had placed the first thin tip of the wedge between Kelly and McGuire. It was his own pointed stake and his task was now to hammer it home. "Think about it, McGuire. You're sworn to uphold the law. Can you really, in good conscience, become an accessory to murder? Can you be a part of what amounts to vigilante justice?"

"Are you really suggesting that I take you in? That I arrest you like any normal criminal?"

"Can you really do anything else?"

Kelly's voice took on a desperate edge. "Don't listen to him. He's the Devil and he'll try to confuse you with a lot of talk."

It was plain that McGuire was torn. The policeman was wrestling with conflicting emotions. Renquist kept the front of his mind, the immediate temporal level, centered on McGuire and Kelly and the situation at hand, but, with an almost willful conceit in his ability to think on any number of simultaneous planes, he allowed his memory to move back, along the sequence of events that had brought him to this confrontation, to the point where it had all started, to the moment when the nosferatu colony had realized that the Feasting was upon them and, despite all their powers, they could do nothing to prevent it . . .

chapter *One*

It was one month earlier.

Renquist walked slowly down the length of the long windowless room. His footsteps on the polished hardwood floor were a series of hanging punctuations in a brittle shroud of silence. The eyes in the paintings followed him as he paced. They watched him without remorse, without even interest; they watched because watching was the only thing left to them. He halted in front of the big Rembrandt. The standing portrait showed a somberly dressed man in self-satisfied middle age, grown weighty in wealth and ponderous in authority. Renquist had known him when he had cut a very different figure, lean and swift with a wild hunger for everything the world had to offer, and no inclination to count the cost.

"Although you balked at one thing, didn't you, Bent Van Leyden? You lacked the nerve to make the ultimate transcendence. You came to the very edge, but in the final moment you retreated. And now you're dead these three hundred years and I still haunt this frightened world. Which of us, would you say, was the better off, my old friend?"

The long paneled room was respected by all in the Residence

as Renquist's private space, a place of uninterrupted retreat where he would shut himself away when his thinking grew too complex for distraction, or if he simply needed to return to some facet of the near-infinite past. They accepted that when Renquist closed himself in the gallery, he was not to be disturbed. Thus it came as something of a momentary surprise when the door of the gallery opened and Cynara quietly entered carrying a tray covered by a black cloth.

"Victor . . ."

Renquist sighed. He was suddenly weary. "Is it that time already?"

The open door created a triangle of yellow light across the floor. Renquist needed no light, even to stare into the face of the Rembrandt. The single candle that burned in the tall iron candlestick was from habit rather than necessity. When he tired of the paintings, he might simply sit and stare into its flame. The candlestick had originally been placed in the cold marble fireplace as a slight nosferatu parody of the more robust human fires that had once burned there. It had remained there for so long, though, that it had eventually become something of a Residence tradition.

Cynara moved soundlessly down the length of the gallery. A high-backed chair and a small end table stood beside the fireplace. When she reached them, she set the tray down on the table, then straightened and faced Renquist. "If you put it off any longer, you'll start to grow weak."

Renquist nodded and turned away from the Rembrandt. "I know, I know."

The truth was that he already felt weak, but with the weakness came a certain numbness that he welcomed, along with a stifling disinclination to do anything but drift aimlessly in the energy-drained void that was the nosferatu equivalent of human depression.

When he got in that frame of mind, Cynara tended to become brisk and curt, as though dealing with a petulant child.

"If you don't feed now, Victor, you'll start to look old, and you know how that upsets your vanity."

A sudden irritation gripped Renquist. Cynara may have once been his concubine, but that hardly entitled her to speak to him as though she was his nurse or some human mother. "At certain times, you do rather tend to stretch our bonding."

"It's for your own good and you know it."

Renquist gave up. He didn't have the strength for an argument he could only lose. He moved towards Cynara, slowly rolling back the sleeve of his white ruffled shirt. As he approached, Cynara removed the cover from the tray.

No less than four paintings of Cynara hung in the gallery. The oldest was the ornately decorated nude that had been painted in Vienna in 1906 by Gustav Klimt, back in the days when her hair had been flaming red. Since that time her hair color had changed at least annually, but her body had remained exactly the same. She still had the same narrow hips and small high, young-girl breasts, the long slender legs and dancer's muscle tone. The second portrait was from her time in Weimar Berlin, by an artist named Jacob Berg, whose life and creative spark had been abruptly snuffed out by the coming of the Nazis. This one showed a fully clothed Cynara. With hair now black, scraped back and severe, she stared grimly across a desolate, mist-shrouded landscape, as though anticipating the misery and suffering that would so shortly overtake the world.

The third painting of her was a psychedelic piece from the late sixties that showed a strangely smiling Cynara, dressed up in white lace and standing on the surface of the moon, amid rocks and craters, with a vibrant rainbow rising from beyond the lunar horizon. She and Renquist had found the picture in a headshop on Haight Street in 1969, and immediately bought it. The store owner had been too acid-damaged to remember the name of the artist and, despite a great deal of detective work, they had never been able to locate him or discover how he had obtained Cynara's image to use in his picture. Normally Renquist would never have hung this work. It hardly made the grade in terms of quality and Renquist certainly had no taste for sixties psychedelic kitsch, but it had struck a chord somewhere in Cynara's psyche and she insisted that it should join the rest of the portraits.

The final painting was by Renquist himself, with Cynara very much as she was right then, dressed in black satin, with sculpted white blonde hair. Although a product of his super-realist period, it showed Cynara as only another of her kind would see her, with diamond-hard, predatory eyes, incapable of hiding a carefully controlled and enduring savagery.

During the years when the graphic arts still held his interest, Renquist had painted many of his own kind, and a number of these portraits hung in different rooms in the Residence. He had, however, never allowed himself to be painted and his image featured nowhere in the collection.

Cynara carefully folded the black cloth that had covered the tray and set it to one side. The tray held all of the paraphernalia of the modern way, the plastic pack of whole blood, the clear tubing, the needle, the swabs, Band-Aid strips, and a bottle of surgical spirit. As Renquist settled himself in the chair, the soft red leather of its upholstery sighed against the silk of his shirt. Cynara fitted the needle into the end of the tube. "You look pale."

Renquist's head turned and he permitted himself a weary smile. "I'm supposed to look pale."

In the last few weeks, the space for humor around the Residence had been minimal. The future hung like a thunderhead over everything, smothering all but the darkest flippancy.

With the deftness of a trained nurse, Cynara swabbed his arm with surgical spirit, located a vein, and slid the needle through the skin and into flesh. Renquist experienced a momentary catch of anticipation as she taped down the needle with a Band-Aid and connected the blood bag. The excitement was slight, however—a sterile instant, as sterile as the whole clinical procedure.

The tube turned crimson as the blood began to flow. The blood came from St. Vincent's Hospital, the result of a long-standing deal with a senior orderly with a need for money as all-encompassing as his capacity for corruption. Deals of this kind were now the new way of the nosferatu.

The fresh blood entered the cold labyrinths of Renquist's metabolism like an insinuation. This artificial substitute was no more than a whimper when set against the primal scream of true feeding. No matter how many times he told himself that the plastic and the cold needles were the mechanics by which the nosferatu had come to terms with human civilization, he could never overcome his contempt for the process or his soul-hunger for the old rage. He was cursed by memory. The furnace-red, roaring exultation of the hunt and the natural kill, the feeding upon a living victim, could never be forgotten. The glory days of absolute freedom were too ingrained in his makeup for him ever to let go of the ancient desire, or for the visions ever to fade. Even as he clenched and unclenched his hand, feeling the tentative infusion of new energy spreading up his arm, specters of the past surrounded him, closing in, refusing to be denied, mocking him with all that had been lost in the name of survival.

In his mind's eye, prey-blood spurted, rich and pungent, vigorous and purple-dark, vibrating with the lifeforce, the power of moon-howling, primitive connection. The bloodheat steam would rise and billow under a clear midnight, and he would feel the racked, body-to-body shudder as the victim died. Then he, the *wampyr*, fangs still fully extended, would rise from the ravaged throat of the white, drained corpse and stretch to his full height, arms raised in triumph to the moon. His very cells were imprinted with the recall, the way the surge of stolen energy would explode through his entire being to send him risking and racing, shooting death's dice with a false winter dawn, so charged and omnipotent that he would even flirt with the fatal agony of the rising sun.

He looked up at Cynara and spoke from the heart. "I hate this."

"We all hate it."

In the departed times of freedom, when the nosferatu owned the night, no one had talked of caution or counseled compromise. Even secrecy had been a halfhearted matter of arrogance and mockery, the castle on the mountain and the name the humans would dare not even whisper. Those nights had become the stuff of history in the short span of that terrible summer. The Slaughter of 1919 had changed their world into a fearful, furtive place of whines, whimpers, and excuses, where the weak talked of their "disease" and their "affliction," and dull cowering replaced proud passion.

"We can't continue like this."

Cynara removed the needle from his arm. "We are all very aware of that. The Feasting cannot be postponed indefinitely. Very soon, the pressure to feed normally will become intolerable."

Renquist massaged his forearm where the needle had left a small red mark. Cynara was dropping paraphernalia into a disposal plastic bag with a label that read "Danger—Blood Products."

"When will you talk to the others?"

A cramp knotted his stomach as he rose from the chair. Cramps were the natural aftermath of transfusion, but this one may well have been partially triggered by the reminder of the pressing need for him to address the problems that confronted the colony. "I'll talk to them tonight, before the dawn."

Cynara sealed the disposal bag. "They need leadership at a time like this, and you are the Master."

The implication was obvious. If he wouldn't assume the leadership, it would give the young ones just the excuse they needed to challenge his authority. That it should come from the steadfastly loyal Cynara made the suggestion carry all the more weight. "I'll talk to them before the dawn."

Cynara seemed satisfied by this. "I must attend to my own feeding."

"We all know what is coming. We all knew that sooner or later it would come again. In a world as timeless as ours, it is all too easy to create the illusion that the future will attend to itself. Illusion, however, is nothing more than illusion, no matter how well crafted, and reality must be faced."

Renquist paused, allowing himself the emphasis of silence. With two hours remaining before the dawn, the whole colony was assembled in the large drawing room. The ten who comprised this New York City enclave and made their primary homes in the Residence were all present. The impression might have been of a relaxed, even casual gathering, but if that was the case, the first impression would have failed to include the eyes. Ten pairs of nosferatu eyes, infinite and unblinking with their hooded hypnotic power, capable of bending any human will, were fixed on him, watching for the slightest nuance of weakness, uncertainty, or hesitation. If he faltered now, the new bloods, led by Carfax, would be at his throat. Literally at his throat.

"The nosferatu cannot be held back and forced to live this shadow life forever. The Feasting is upon us. Very soon, it will reach the point of an uncontrollable rampage. This could be weeks in coming or happen in a matter of days."

Despite, or perhaps because of the individual power of its members, a nosferatu colony was a fragile thing, held together by the willpower of its Master and the self-interest of its members. If either of these failed, it could easily fragment, or worse still, turn in on itself in devastating internal conflict. The New York colony was particularly vulnerable. Had it been one of the old-fashioned groups in which a single Master lorded it over a subservient coterie of his own creations, this meeting would never have taken place. The Master would have spoken and the followers would have obeyed. Like the city in which it had made its home, however, the New York group was diverse and sophisticated, a deliberate banding together of lone hunters and bonded pairs who had sacrificed a measure of their independence in return for the advantages of mutual support and protection.

"I am far older than most of you, and it has been a long time since I've made a warm slay. You can believe me when I tell you that I feel the craving as strongly as any of you. I am very aware that we all grow sickened by the unsatisfactory substitute of the blood bag and the needle, and I am also aware that some have covertly disregarded the rules of prey and made discreet kills among human derelicts in Tompkins Square Park and the prostitutes on Tenth Avenue and around the Port Authority. Since those victims are never missed and their deaths in no way threaten the colony with exposure, I have thus far turned a blind eye to these infractions. With the Feasting upon us, though, this laxity can no longer continue. The condition of Feasting, even with the most stringent compliance to whatever orders I may see fit to give, will still produce stresses that may press us to the very limits of our endurance."

Renquist was strictly confining himself to the flat unvarnished facts. Any attempt to deceive a gathering of nosferatu or try to blind them with oratory would be worse than pointless. They were not only listening to his words, but also reading his aura, and the aura of the liar or dissembler was all too obviously tainted by deception. He also made no attempt to use the power voice or any hypnotic influence. Had he done so, it might have swayed a few of the younger ones, but the older members of the group would have immediately detected what he was doing and treated the ploy with the contempt that it deserved. The nosferatu code of manners was as cold as it was intricate, and had no pity for fools and charlatans.

"We should not be surprised by the feelings stirring inside

us, or try to pretend that they will either fade or retreat. Quite the reverse, they will grow and intensify until they become an unbearable bloodrage. I cannot minimize this or suggest otherwise. We have learned the hard way that the transfusions can only hold the craving and slake the thirst for a finite time. We once imagined that they might be a permanent substitute for warm-kill and would enable us to merge gradually with the humans. This quickly proved to be a false assumption. The first Feastings that broke out in colonies using these substitute means proved, beyond doubt, that we are what we are, and no devices exist to make us otherwise. Eventually, we must take prey, or be destroyed by our own deepest needs. We are compelled by our own complex DNA to stalk and subjugate and then make the glorious thrust to deep drinking."

Renquist briefly scanned the aura of Carfax, the young one. It was already suffused with a tentative but visibly growing magenta. The very thought of warm-kill was exciting the boy, and an excited nosferatu was volatile and highly dangerous. Renquist, however, decided that he would briefly play with him and the other young ones who had grown sufficiently arrogant in their newfound strength to resent Renquist's authority. A human might have viewed such a decision as foolish and reckless, with such a crisis bearing down on them, but Renquist was not human. He might be Master and responsible for the colony's survival, but he was also nosferatu and possessed of the overwhelming nosferatu pride. The colony would hardly respect him if he totally sacrificed that pride to merely doing the right thing. However, the chance also existed that he might goad one or more of the young ones into some rash and premature move.

He started slowly, keeping his voice and aura bland and unassuming. "To those of you, the young and newly transformed, who have not experienced the urge to Feasting, who have only heard the stories, all I can say is that they are not exaggerated. If anything, they tend to understate the fury of the experience."

Renquist looked directly at Carfax. He knew that the young one had sneaked out and killed on a number of occasions during the last few months but he pretended to be ignorant of the fact. Carfax was very proud of his secret kills, so to talk at him as though he was a neophyte was a calculated insult to his pumped-up, juvenile self-image. The young one stared back at Renquist from behind insolent sunglasses, but his aura was already registering a tracery of anger.

Renquist continued. "The danger in the urge to Feasting lies in that it robs us of our reason and makes us vulnerable to the humans. Our only advantage is that these first stirrings can serve as warnings, so we can heed them and act accordingly."

"Accordingly? What do you consider acting accordingly?"

Carfax had made his first move. The words were more of a challenge than a question. Renquist was tempted to smile, but a smile would have been too much at that point in the game. He remained stiff and formal. "Would you repeat the question, Brother Carfax?"

"I asked what you meant by acting accordingly."

Carfax sat indolently in one of the drawing room's dark leather armchairs, legs crossed and a lighted cigarette between two languid fingers. His small group of followers surrounded him, providing the stage set for what Renquist half hoped would be some ill-considered power play. To Carfax's right stood Blasco, the tech-obsessed young one who made things in the cellar out of plastic, scrap metal, and electronic circuitry. On his left sat Julia, albino white with Nordic blonde hair that hung, dead straight, clear to her waist. Slightly behind Carfax was the fourth of what Renquist thought of as the dangerous quartet. Segal, the hairless grotesque with the misshapen features, the total lack of hair, and long corkscrew fingernails, whom Carfax treated as a virtual body servant. Renquist observed the four carefully as he measured his words. Carfax and Julia had recently taken to playing an elaborately perverse game of twins. On this particular night, they had decided to affect the same somber bohemian costume, right down to identical sunglasses and motorcycle boots.

Again Renquist was tempted to smile. Let them flaunt their black clothes and their hunch-shouldered rebellion. He had once met the young Marlon Brando and Carfax was not him. "Early recognition of what is happening to us is our primary advantage. It allows us to plan for the Feasting and put systems in place to protect ourselves before the fury is upon us. The worst thing we could do is to deny our nature and pretend that nothing is amiss until the dam inevitably bursts and we run amok, driven by nothing but blind beast savagery. In that moment, we become totally vulnerable to the humans, and, since no way exists for us to circumvent the moment, our only viable option is to plan for it and be thoroughly prepared."

Now Carfax rose slowly from the armchair. Male competitiveness flashed around him like emerald sparkles. "You are talking control, Renquist. All I hear in these clinical times is control and fear of humans. What has happened to us, Master Renquist? Were we not once free beings? Didn't we range wild and unrestrained while humans hung garlic on their doors and cowered in their verminous beds? What has become of us, Master Renquist? What has become of our self-respect?"

Renquist noted that Carfax was using a small measure of the voice on him and, as a result, some of the older ones were stirring uneasily. To use the voice at an exclusive gathering of the colony, and, moreover, to use it on the Master, was a serious breach of the code. Carfax's inappropriate use of the voice had brought trouble down on him before. In his human life, he had been the leader of a not-altogether successful musical group called Love in the Time of Cholera, who had gained a certain local notoriety for their cultivated gothic decadence. It was even whispered around the Residence that Carfax's completely voluntary and wished-for transformation had been more of a gesture to impress than any weighed decision to assume the burden of immortality. Julia was the one who had brought him across, and Renquist, among others, suspected that her initial intention had been simply to acquire a lasting plaything, a body-creature that would unquestioningly do her bidding. The irony was that Carfax had adapted to the wampyr state with unbelievable swiftness and resource, and the plaything had quickly assumed the dominant role in the pair-bond.

For a while after the transformation, Carfax had continued to perform with Love in the Time of Cholera. No one, not even the other musicians, noticed the change. To their bleary, junkie perception, he was still the Kurt Carfax that they had always known, except that with his new nosferatu energy and ability, the group actually began to prosper. Record company executives became the unknowing targets of his power to cloud human minds and willingly offered him lucrative recording contracts where once they had shown him the door and refused to take his calls. By the same process, he was able to arrange a prestigious showcase concert for the band at the Brooklyn Academy of Music.

The concert had all but proved to be Carfax's downfall. The spurious show business buzz that had come to surround the group attracted a capacity crowd, among which were a number of prominent art-rock celebrities—David Bowie, Lou Reed, Lydia Lunch, and the fading Madonna. At the climax of the show, Carfax, carried away by his electric potency, had actually screamed out loud in the nosferatu voice of power. At full stretch and through a massively amplified sound system, its effect was nothing short of devastating. In a matter of seconds, the entire crowd was thrown into full mental trauma. Some fled the hall in screaming panic. Others went catatonic and remained that way for a number of hours before they could be revived. Unable to explain the incident without revealing his true nature, Carfax announced his retirement from music and had never performed on the public stage again. This forcible removal from the spotlight might well have been a contributing factor in his current obsession with fomenting unrest and creating factionalism within the colony. A troublemaker attracts an audience just like an artist.

Renquist knew that simply to ignore Carfax's use of the voice at the gathering, and to overlook the implicit disrespect, would constitute a severe loss of face. It would be seen as little short of backing down before his rival. Renquist slowly stroked his chin as though contemplating his next move, and then, with a slight shrug of his shoulders, he allowed the full force of his own aura and his own potential for anger to be seen. Although the blaze of clear white light lasted for no longer than a brilliant millisecond, it produced resonances through the drawing room and beyond. The lights briefly dimmed, the temperature dropped, and for an instant, the air was filled with negative ions and the smell of ozone. Outside, a single clap of thunder rumbled across Brooklyn. A quietly spontaneous whisper of approval was drawn from the older members of the colony. Renquist had shown them what amounted to a near-perfect peacock display both of his power and his infinite appreciation of grace in conflict.

When all had returned to normal, Renquist smiled coolly at Carfax. "Perhaps I should also give you a brief instruction in our history, Brother Carfax."

For an instant, Carfax seemed genuinely awed, but then he regained both his composure and bad attitude as though nothing significant had happened. "History? We live under the yoke of history. What happened to the wild present? Humans are our rightful prey and yet the once proud nosferatu seem now to live in fear of them. Will you tell me what's wrong with this picture, Master Renquist?"

Renquist had to give the young one credit for a powerfully stubborn resilience. A lesser being might have staggered under the impact of the blast he had unleashed. "I won't insult you with any reminders of how undigested history repeats itself. I must, however, disabuse you of the idea that there was ever a golden age when we were totally free and unfettered. We have always, at best, lived and hunted in the margins created by human ignorance and fear of the unknown. Those of us who have survived tend to forget the countless thousands who fell victim to the stake and the fire. We survived because we were organized and we used our intelligence to conceal ourselves from the ravening human mobs. Those who perished were the feral and the stupid, the deranged and the crudely brutal. They ran wild, driven by the urge to feed, with no thought given to camouflage or protection, and the humans took them easily in their sleep. We are only here because we tempered our wildness with a level of caution. It may not sit well with your sense of romance, but it is unfortunately a fact."

Carfax acknowledged Renquist's words with a slight, mockingly deferential bow in the Japanese manner. Carfax was doing his best to make up the ground he had lost, but Renquist noticed that some of the other young ones, including Julia, were noticeably distancing themselves from him. Renquist pressed his advantage.

"We have always protected ourselves, and many times that protection has come from the human's own propensity for carnage. Our kind have ridden with their Huns, Mongols, and Cossacks and shared campfires and victims with their legions. We have marched with Agamemnon, Alexander, Darius, and Tamerlane. The huge leap in our numbers in Eastern Europe, the greatest increase since the Creators made us, came during the constant religious and political slaughter of the Thirty Years' War. We have haunted their battlefields and lurked in the shadows of their revolutionary terrors. We followed their pioneer wagons across this country, picking off the stragglers and discovering our red-fanged Native American cousins. We infiltrated the Nazi SS and masqueraded as guards at the death camps, and some of us walked through Hiroshima on that first night, while the fires still burned and the air crackled with hard radiation. Others followed the Khmer Rouge into Cambodia for the mass murder of the Year One. It's lucky that our way of life effectively puts us beyond any sense of shame."

Carfax was now seated again. "Are you saying we have to leave New York before the Feasting comes and go in search of war or genocide?"

Renquist shook his head. "There is no need to change our lifestyle in any radical manner. You, Brother Carfax, speak ringingly of the pride of the nosferatu. Think also of the cunning of the nosferatu. Once again, the humans have unwittingly provided us with the concealment we need. This time, in their current epidemic of random aberrant homicide. Lonely people, beset by demons, are moved to stalk and kill their own to quiet the voices. The humans seem to view these serial murderers with a perverse mixture of fear and fascination, and we will exploit that."

Carfax affected an unconcerned drawl. "You make them sound just like us."

Renquist stared coldly at Carfax. "They are nothing like us. Any resemblance is purely superficial. You can be assured of that. We do what we do because it is our nature. We kill to survive. It has been that way for fourteen thousand years. These human killers are defects, driven by crippled genes, injured minds, and tainted flesh. They can, however, provide the cover for our Feasting. The period of our Feasting will come, and, at each dawn, the humans will blanch in horror at our leavings, as their world-weary policemen place the blood-drained carrion in the black body bags. And yet the policemen and the medical examiners who probe the corpses will never suspect that something like us is responsible. We will mark and mutilate the bodies, and arrange their limbs in configurations that the human forensic experts will assume are the desperate demented signals of some poor tortured soul begging to be stopped before he kills again. Oh, yes, my friends, when the humans find our leavings, they will assume that one of their own is loose in the city. We will know the full raging joy of our Feasting, and with a little care and attention to detail, the security of this colony will never be compromised."

Renquist allowed himself to smile. He had accomplished a small triumph of persuasion. The older ones showed him by their auras that they fully approved of the way that he had approached the problems. Even Julia, Segal, and Blasco remained noticeably neutral; only Carfax sat sunk in a black hole of resentment. Renquist took a deep breath. "I repeat, Brother Carfax, the cunning of the nosferatu."

The time had come to sleep. Renquist slipped off his shoes and his velvet jacket, then removed the silver links from the French cuffs of his ruffled evening shirt. Faint sounds of early traffic, the first buildup to the full-blown rush hour, penetrated even the sealed windows and heavy drapes of the bedchamber. He took a cigarette from the silver box on the table beside the bed, Russian tobacco, rolled in black paper with a gold foil tip, and lit it with a Dunhill lighter. The cigarette brought an instant recall of St. Petersburg in the days of the last Czar, when snow fell on Cossack patrols around the Winter Palace and the very air throbbed with the heady pulse of pent-up revolutionary violence. White uniforms and Bolshevik overcoats circled in cumbersome Slavic intrigue. The mad monk Rasputin maintained his hold over the Czarina and his peasant-mystic suspicions of Renquist. When, all too late, they decided to rid the world of Rasputin, he refused to die even though he was full of enough poison to kill a brace of oxen. In the end, they had been forced to shoot him in the head and push his body under the ice of the frozen river, where it wouldn't surface until the spring thaw. Renquist remembered the cigarette smoke in the subzero air after that deed had been accomplished.

He slipped off his shirt and flexed muscles stiff from the tension of the night just passed. The meeting had gone well for him. Better, in fact, than he had expected. Unfortunately, the hardest part of his task was still in front of him. A bottle of vodka in a bucket of ice and two chilled glasses also stood on the bedside table. Renquist selected a glass and poured himself a generous measure of the clear spirit. He drank it down in one, Russian style, and an alien heat flared briefly inside him. The nicotine and alcohol had no lasting effect on his undead metabolism, which was far beyond such crass stimulants. The truth was that he used them primarily to summon memories. When life extended infinitely, memories tended to become thin and unreal, with the insubstantial quality of fading dreams. They were prone to drift in and out of any set sequence and simply float as random images. The taste of a drink, a cigarette, or the sound of a piece of music helped to give them a temporary solidity.

Renquist removed the rest of his clothing and stood for a moment naked at the foot of the big, ornately carved four-poster bed. His body was hard and lean, to all outward appearances that of a healthy, athletic human male in his mid- to late thirties. For a human to maintain such a body would require a constant regimen of workout and strict dieting. Renquist, on the other hand, took very little exercise and his diet was quite beyond the comprehension of any human nutritionist. His body was the way it was simply because he willed it to be so.

His toes curled for a moment, kneading the rich pile of the Persian carpet beneath his feet. Both the bed and the carpet had been part of his life for a very long time, and had moved with him across continents and down centuries. Contrary to the fondly held human belief, the nosferatu were not compelled to sleep in their original coffins, although a few did, purely out of a sense of tradition. A consistent sleeping place did, however, provide a certain continuity in lives that tended to follow strange and convoluted paths. Renquist had formed an extended attachment to the great bed of dark wood. It had been the mute witness of some his most intense passions and greatest triumphs, and sometimes in the isolation of the day he fancied that he could detect the ghost-shadow imprints of those who had passed through it over the years.

He had no time, though, to conjure phantoms. If he was to preserve the colony effectively, his memory had to become a finely honed weapon instead of an album of ancient photographs. He had to use his centuries of experience to protect those in his charge from what he saw as the twin dangers, the humans without and the possible internecine conflict within.

The colony had survived undetected in New York City for almost thirty years. This had been greatly helped by Lower Manhattan's long-accepted bohemian underground. So many of its human inhabitants cultivated a taste for black clothes and never seemed to come out in the daylight. By local standards, the colony was nothing remarkable. A thousand human nonconformists who frequented the downtown bars, cafes, and nightclubs lived in exactly the same way. The colony had found a place where even their kind was able to blend effortlessly into the natural cover.

The periods of Feasting had been a little more difficult. Feasting had become the nosferatu's great Achilles' heel in the twentieth century. Approximately every seven years, it would fight its way to the surface, as primal and irresistible as the imperative that caused birds to migrate or salmon to swim upriver to spawn. Every time, it posed the problem of how to disguise the presence of ten or more murderously deranged wampyren who had lost all concepts of discretion or caution.

The Feasting that was almost upon them would be the fifth they had experienced since the establishment of the colony, and the first since Renquist had become Master. Back in the days when Dietrich had ruled the colony, they had always left the city at the first signs of the primal urge, taking what amounted to a bizarre and bloody communal vacation in some place where death was so commonplace that their depredations went entirely unnoticed. For the last Feasting, they had gone to Haiti, where the attaché gunmen, the successors to the Tonton Macout, had been slaughtering everyone and anyone who gave the impression, real or imagined, of opposing the military junta. The time before that they had travelled further south to El Salvador, where they had shadowed the military death squads on their nightly kill sprees and left the bodies of their own victims in the same quarries and roadside dumps that were the last resting place of those slain in the course of that nation's grisly political process.

Renquist had decided that, this time, they were not going to flee the city. Dietrich was gone and his methods had gone with him. The previous Master had moved on to the next stage, succumbing to the need for isolation that was the curse, or maybe the blessing, of the incalculably old. He had made his home in North Africa, in an isolated cave, high in the Mountains of the Moon, where he now lived in timeless and unimaginable solitude like some distracted nocturnal hermit, rarely feeding, and staring at the sky through countless hours of countless nights, as though he could perceive the motions of the stars and hear the singing of galaxies.

Even when Dietrich had ruled, resentment had been growing among the young ones. That they should have come through the pain of the transition to nothing more than blood bags, needles, and a shabby pretense of being human, seemed like a theft of their essential birthright. They now looked to the Feasting as a means to assert themselves. They would finally hunt in the old way, in their own city, on their own turf. Had Renquist insisted that the Feasting should take place under cover of some far-flung outbreak of ethnic cleansing or in a sorry third-world nation where life was cheap, he would have faced more than just Carfax's public insolence. The young ones would have simply revolted. The colony would have been split before the madness was even fully upon them.

Renquist drew back the bed's fur cover. Now that he was alone, he had to admit to some of the deep-seated doubts that troubled him, primarily as to whether he actually measured up to the task in front of him. He sighed and lay back on the bed, assuming the wampyr position of rest, flat on his back with his arms straight at his sides, putting all doubts aside until the next sunset. Nothing would be achieved by depriving himself of rest.

The sun had set beyond the New Jersey horizon, and undead life was again starting to stir within the Residence. After the blurred moments that followed first waking had passed, Renquist slipped into his silk robe and climbed the back stairs to the attics of the Residence that had become, over the years, chiefly Cynara's domain. Now he entered the white room, the one with the sloping ceiling, right under the eaves of the building's mansard roof. The only piece of furniture in the room was a big Moorish divan. A dozen or more lighted candles threw flickering shadows across the strange angles of the walls and dripped wax onto the bare floor. Cynara and the young one called Sada lay naked together on top of the covers, and discarded clothing formed a trail to the door. Two thin, marble-white bodies entwined, moving one against the other with a slow somnambulistic languor, mouths slack, eyes heavy-lidded, like depraved children at forbidden play. Although rampant sex, the thrusting drive of brute creation, died with their humanity, some nosferatu, particularly the women, could still abandon themselves to a hypnotically tactile sensuality.

Renquist halted in the doorway, aware that he had intruded on a private moment. "I'm sorry, I'll come back later."

Cynara partially disengaged herself from Sada and raised herself on one elbow. "Did you want something?"

Renquist nodded. "I need a car. It's time that I went out into the world again and took a look at it."

Cynara stared at him doubtfully. "You know how long it is since you went outside?"

Renquist pursed his lips. It was the nurse/mother act again, and hardly plausible in Cynara's current state of erotic disarray. "I am perfectly well aware how long it is since I last emerged from the Residence. I believe I can calculate it to the very day. All I need is a car and possibly your companionship when I first venture out."

Cynara half smiled. "If that's all you want." Sada made a soft mewing sound and Cynara leaned forward and gently kissed the young one's breast. Sada arched her back like a contented kitten. Cynara looked back up at Renquist. "I will arrange a limousine for you directly I am finished here."

Renquist and Cynara rode down in the Victorian wrought-iron elevator with its smoked glass and ornamental cherubs. Renquist hesitated at the street door. Cynara glanced at him questioningly. Renquist spread his hands in a deprecating gesture. "It's been a long time. The minds of the humans, they make too much noise . . ."

"You don't have to go."

"I'm afraid I do, either now or later."

Almost two years had passed since Renquist had ventured out of the Residence. Back then, he had reached a point at which he could no longer deal with the human world's haste and temptation. It was so full, so overflowing with crude energy and vulgar life that it brought out the worst in him. It encouraged cravings for unreasonable excess and fanned the flames of black-night desires. To be in the midst of such a packed density of scrabbling, desperate mortals had become altogether too much for him. His control had started wavering and he'd known that it was only a matter of time before it cracked and hurled him spiraling into a flamboyant but ultimately self-destructive blaze of unrestrained wilding that would not only seal his own doom but that of the entire colony.

With a significant finality, Renquist snapped back the deadbolts that secured the street door. Like every other dwelling in Manhattan, the Residence had taken on aspects of a fortress. "Either now or later. And this hardly seems the time to be putting things off."

The sunset glow had all but faded behind the towers of the West Side and the night air was heavy with humidity, pollution, and the stench of humanity, refuse, and gasoline. The last wave of commuters coming from the subway looked wilted and half-dead. He had also forgotten how filthy it was on the outside and the very grime was a shock. Even though the nosferatu took little account of extremes in temperature, the Residence was fully and aggressively air-conditioned.

He glanced at Cynara. "Was it always like this?"

Cynara shrugged. She went out all the time. "Only in the summer. In the winter, it freezes."

Renquist noted how good Cynara looked in the context of the street. It was like seeing her with fresh new eyes. She was wearing a man's tuxedo jacket over a short black dress and dark stockings. Her white hair was piled up in a loose yet elaborate confection that allowed a couple of stray strands to fall in front of her face. Renquist couldn't remember seeing anything like it since the sixties, the heyday of Sharon Tate and Jean Shrimpton. Cynara didn't appear to be a day over twenty-five and it was hard to imagine that she had watched the epic battles of the Civil War, and been present at the burning of Atlanta. Cynara and Renquist, both as a bonded couple and as members of the same colony, had run and dwelled and hunted together for a very long time. She was so totally loyal to him that he fervently hoped he wouldn't make any slip in the coming weeks that would betray such devotion.

The driver was holding open the rear door of the limo but, before stepping inside, Renquist glanced back up at the Residence. To anyone walking by, it looked just like any other downtown townhouse and the casual observer might have been forgiven for assuming that its inhabitants were the usual well-to-do followers of fashion who had taken over the area during the 1980s. Nothing about its Victorian façade, blank, blind windows, or ornamental stone suggested that anyone passing beyond the imposing front door would be entering a frightening and alien environment.

In his more cynical moments, Renquist actually doubted that, should anyone have suspected the true nature of the Residence and its inhabitants, they would have bothered to do anything about it. The level of indifference and detachment was now so high in the city that it seemed quite possible for a nest of predatory undead to pass without comment. Hadn't that psycho-killer in the East Village kept the dismembered body of his girlfriend in his apartment with the full knowledge of other people in the building, people who had only called the cops when the smell of the decaying corpse had become unbearable?

As Renquist stepped into the car's womblike interior, with its TV, bar, and concealed mood lighting, he quickly read the driver and found nothing more than a routine resentment at having to chauffeur around one more pair of the wealthy and worthless. The driver was a fleshy Armenian from Astoria and he seemed particularly to resent the fact that the two of them were so slim and pale and wearing dark expensive clothes. They looked to him "like a pair of fucking . . . vampires." Renquist hated the word so much that he could hardly bring himself to repeat it. The ugly thought was mercifully fleeting, however, and the driver quickly moved on to his own preoccupations. The Armenian was seemingly cheating on his wife, a practice that filled him with both considerable guilt and considerable excitement. Renquist received a fast, unfocused image of an equally fleshy, bleached blonde in cheap purple lingerie, stockinged legs spread wide and offering a red lipstick smile of invitation. He presumed this was the mistress rather than the wife, and swiftly withdrew from the man's mind, leaving him to his fears and fantasies.

The limousine was underway and the driver was wanting to know where he should go. Cynara supplied the answer. "Section Eight."

Renquist glanced at her. The name meant nothing to him. "What's Section Eight?"

"A restaurant. It's current."

"I've never heard of it."

"That's because you haven't been out in two years and you refuse to read the gossip columns."

"Will I be recognized?"

"Almost certainly."

"I'm not sure how I feel about that."

The maitre d's reaction as Renquist and Cynara entered the restaurant was nothing short of a classic double take. He stood beside the small lectern that carried the reservations book like a sentinel, the guardian of the fashionable exclusivity of the establishment. None came to a table but through him. The restaurant was already full, with every table taken and the bar crowd standing three deep. They had arrived at the peak of the early evening crush when the humans assembled to eat and drink in the aftermath of the workday, before consuming culture and or consummating liaisons, and a line of a half-dozen people waited on his attention and recognition. Without even thinking about it, Renquist took Cynara by the arm and walked to the head of the line. He had always done it that way. Renquist remembered the maitre d'. His name was Michael, and two years earlier, before Renquist had gone into seclusion, he'd been nothing more than a lowly bartender at another place that had long since fallen from favor. Michael's first reaction was one of cool outrage. How dare this couple come sauntering to the head of the line? They weren't valued regular patrons and therefore merited no select position in the front area of his professional memory. It took him a couple of seconds to pull Renquist from his deeper recall. Outrage changed to a look of genuine surprise. "Mr. Renquist, if you'd called first, I . . ."

Renquist waved away his confusion. "It is not a problem. We

can wait. A booth in the back, though, please Michael. Where I can watch without being a sideshow."

Renquist's celebrity status was a phenomenon that even he was at a loss to explain. It had started in the early eighties, apparently by accident, although at times he would blame himself for underestimating the human capacity for self-delusion and believing anything that they saw on TV and read in *People* magazine. He had certainly never courted any measure of notoriety. For a nosferatu as long-lived and cautious as himself, such a courtship would have run counter to every ingrained instinct of self-preservation. The undead survived in the shrouds of smoke and mystery, and the glare of the spotlight was almost as much of an anathema to them as the sun itself.

When the young and brash became infected with the idea that they might do otherwise than live out their immortality in the discreet shadows, it usually resulted in some debacle like Carfax's disastrous concert. The only analysis of his public reputation that Renquist could offer was that the very smokescreen of mystery that he had so carefully cultivated had turned on him. Humans loved mystery, and the mystery itself had drawn them like moths to a flame, causing him to become one of those odd eighties beings who were only famous for being famous.

At the time, Renquist had been presented with few other options. Through the final years that Dietrich had been Master of the colony, it had been clear that he was phasing out. He would spend long hours, sometimes entire nights, in the other space, locked in silent contemplation. Renquist had known that before he assumed the Mastership, he would need to spend a good deal of time out in the human world, upgrading and modernizing the financial infrastructure that was ultimately the colony's best defense against intrusion and exposure.

For most nosferatu, the amassing of a large personal fortune was a comparatively easy business. The profitable manipulation of human markets and monetary systems was simple in the extreme when one was never interrupted by death or taxes and had the capacity to cloud human minds. In the old days, it also hadn't been hard to keep and protect a fortune. All it took was a substantial stronghold, some ironbound chests and a retinue of armed retainers—boyars, Cossacks, or musketeers, depending on the location of that stronghold.

In a reality populated by entities like the IRS, the FBI, the SEC, and the international banking system, where computer records of a person's cash or consumption could be effortlessly maintained, individuals who lived forever, never ate, had no contact with conventional medical care, and conformed to absolutely none of the basic statistical patterns, had to be extremely careful if their secrets were to remain secret. Devious moves had to be made to avoid triggering alarms and inviting investigation.

Renquist had thus ventured into the twilight zones of New York City high finance. Using a network of contacts that included junk bond salesmen and cocaine dealers, dubious lawyers and overt criminals, Renquist had multiplied and channeled the colony's considerable assets in a manner that could never be traced under anything but the most exceptional circumstances. Some of these contacts, from John Gotti at one extreme to Roy Cohn at the other, courted high profile lifestyles. While weaving his penetration-proof financial web, Renquist would often find himself at dinner or attending nightclubs in the company of the rich, famous, and influential. To conduct business during the hours of darkness obviously suited the limitations of his nature, but unfortunately it had also meant being noticed. New York society, and the gossip columnists who danced attendance on its vanity, began to ask who this Victor Renquist was. He had come out of nowhere, but appeared inordinately wealthy and well connected. Head waiters began to treat him with deference, heads turned when he entered restaurants, and attempts were made by the paparazzi to photograph him. As much as possible, he made use of his almost atrophied shape-shifting ability to make such pictures unusable. On a number of occasions, though, he was taken unaware and the results were used to illustrate speculative stories about his imagined background. This strange role in which Renquist had found himself cast, virtually that of a wampyr Jay Gatsby, didn't sit well with him. When his work was finally completed, he found himself profoundly relieved to retire to the Residence and not emerge for a very long time.

As Renquist and Cynara followed the maitre d' to one of the restaurant's rear booths, Renquist found that it took him several moments to adjust to being in close proximity to so much humanity in one enclosed place. They all but overwhelmed him before he recalled the art of tuning them down. In a crush like this, running at the full social flood, he didn't have to make any effort to read them. Their emotions came at him like a wall of white noise, noisy minds and tiny thoughts—petty, paranoid, inane and venal, an unpalatable cocktail of lust, greed, and insecurity. The semicircular booth was positioned in such a way that it allowed its occupants a full view of the main area of Section Eight, while at the same time making it difficult for anyone to see them. He sank into the leather of the banquet with the sigh of someone who has just undergone an ordeal.

Drinks were brought, chablis for Cynara, straight vodka for Renquist. At Section Eight, they served their vodka elaborately, in a tall narrow shotglass that fitted into a glass sleeve containing ice to keep the spirit chilled to the last drop. Renquist sipped it tentatively. All across the room, auras flickered from minds affected by various quantities of alcohol. Renquist was reminded how much humans resembled a flock of sheep, playing their games, making their noises, while two wolves watched and waited, unobserved and unsuspected. Then he saw that possibly he and Cynara weren't totally unobserved. Two men by the bar were staring in the direction of the booth and the aura of one of them, a smooth, balding man dressed in an expensive blue suit from an exclusive London tailor, showed flashes of intense anxiety.

Renquist recognized the man immediately. Anthony Ferrari called himself a financier, a fairly accurate description insofar as he bankrolled an array of enterprises on both sides of the law and earned a not so modest percentage on the returns. Some, who neither feared him nor owed him money, dismissed Ferrari as an upper-class loanshark, but Renquist had found him uniquely useful as an organizer of deals that should receive little or no attention. A typical example of Ferrari's usefulness had been when Cynara, curing her boredom with a computerized frenzy of literary output, had written the series of ludicrous homoerotic vampire novels under the name Charlotte Mayze. Ferrari had arranged their publication, and when, to Renquist's surprise, the first of them had sold close to a million copies in three printings, he had even arranged for a bohemian, out-of-work, and valium-addicted actress, who looked the part, to pose as Charlotte Mayze for publicity purposes.

The anxiety flashes coming from Ferrari had nothing to do with the man having any knowledge of Renquist's true nature. Quite the reverse, in fact. The knowledge that Renquist had about Ferrari was what scared him. When Renquist had first become involved with the man, he'd subjected him to the deepest and most intense mind reading, and had immediately hit such a solid vein of perversion and decadence that it surprised even him. At weekends, Ferrari's Montauk mansion was the scene of homosexual orgies of extreme violence and depravity, and Renquist quite literally knew where the bodies were buried. It gave Renquist a hook in Ferrari's brain that the human would never be able to remove. Ferrari both knew and hated this.

Renquist used the influence to draw the man to his table. If he was going to return to the human world, it wouldn't hurt to have a few subservient creatures to do his bidding. In a place as crowded as Section Eight, however, it wasn't always possible to use the influence with pinpoint accuracy. A number of other humans in the same area as Ferrari also turned in Renquist's direction and some even rose from their tables without realizing exactly why. Ferrari, under the full influence, quickly took leave of his companion and came towards Renquist's booth, moving in a stiff and slightly robotic manner. Wide-eyed and apprehensive, he halted in front of the booth. Renquist did not invite him to sit. "You seem surprised to see me, Anthony."

Ferrari swallowed hard. "It's been so long. I thought you'd left the country or something."

Renquist's smile was neither pleasant nor humorous. "If that was the case, Anthony, you should be delighted to see that I am back."

"You seem uncomfortable, Anthony."

Ferrari avoided Renquist's eyes. "It was a surprise to run into you like this, Victor."

Renquist gently forced Ferrari to look at him. "It goes deeper than that, doesn't it?"

"You know rather a lot about me."

Renquist used just a whisper of the influence on him. "And are you still doing all those shameful things?"

The whisper was more than enough. Ferrari almost choked on his drink. "Of course not."

Ferrari's aura indicated that, as far as it went, he was telling the truth. The party boys were dead, gone, or grown mortally cautious. In this modern world, the old sins were all but impossible.

"Perhaps you'll be a little more at ease with yourself now?"

"Perhaps."

But Anthony Ferrari wasn't at ease with himself at all, and the unease went a great deal deeper than just his surface nervousness at suddenly seeing Renquist again after so long. The man's previous lavish vices had been replaced by something shrunken and even darker, more intimate and fearfully clandestine. Renquist was sufficiently intrigued that, had they been alone, he would have instantly subjected the man to the most intense of readings, to the point of having him thrashing and convulsing on the floor as his mind gave up its secrets. Unfortunately, not even Renquist had the power to turn one human's mind inside out in front of a hundred or more others without anyone noticing.

"Or perhaps you'd be happier if we adjourned this conversation until a later date, and I let you get back to your friend?"

Ferrari was doglike in his eagerness to get away. "The guy I was with . . . we do have some things that we need to talk about."

The second man was still waiting on his own by the bar, repeatedly glancing in the direction of the booth to see when his companion intended to return. Ferrari's latest lover? Renquist couldn't be bothered to scan for an answer. He could make this Ferrari his creature any time that he needed him. "Go ahead. I didn't mean to detain you. We'll be in touch."

"Lunch maybe?"

Renquist shook his head. "I never eat lunch."

"Nothing changes?"

"Not in that respect."

Ferrari was already retreating. "We'll be in touch."

"We will indeed."

Shortly after Ferrari had arrived at the table, Cynara must either have sensed that Renquist had plans for the man or simply didn't find Ferrari in the least entertaining. Either way, she excused herself, claiming that she had spotted some human with whom she was acquainted on the other side of the restaurant. Despite her age, Cynara still seemed to enjoy human company and courted the same kind of society that Renquist had grown to shun. With the departure of Ferrari, Renquist now sat alone. He eased back his perception of the physical world. The restaurant and its human clientele receded, becoming wraithlike and insubstantial. The waiters and table hoppers turned into drifting ghosts and people in the surrounding booths were almost transparent to his adjusted vision. He was seeing on a spectrum of emotional response that was really a heightened version of his aura perception. The restaurant was now filled with a roiling swampwater blue-green that was the color of pointless small talk between people who didn't especially like each other. Here and there, small patches of dull emerald glowed through the general murk where an individual suffered from a specific tension—unrequited love, unfulfilled lust, the anxiety of the uncompleted deal, or the unease of social nonacceptance. Brighter areas of excitement showed where a couple knew that, sooner or later, they were going home to bed with each other, or an individual was confident that he or she had prevailed over a rival.

In contrast, Cynara, way across the room, blazed with a pure and splendid orange light. She was in conversation with a handsome young male who flamed brilliant green in response to her attentions. Renquist saw that Cynara was also heating up herself. As he watched, her orange glow rapidly developed a white hot core. The hunger was on her and the need to kill was growing stronger. Renquist frowned and hoped that she could resist taking this contact to its natural conclusion. Be careful, Cynara. She was one of the strongest, but the need was building. Her control had to hold. If they all started running amok as early as this, the colony was almost certainly doomed.

Renquist was surprised to see more orange flares appear in the entrance to the restaurant, and surprise turned to a momentary, unguarded flash of anger when he recognized them as Carfax and Julia. What did the two young fools think they were doing? They had made no attempt either to conceal or camouflage their strangeness. Quite the reverse, in fact. They seemed to have gone out of their way to draw attention to themselves. They were dressed identically and actually wearing capes, flowing black capes thrown over their shoulders, and they stalked through the humans like it was a Halloween parade.

Renquist felt his anger building and had to exercise an iron control not to reveal it through his aura. Was it pure happenstance that had brought them there? Renquist didn't think so. Where nosferatu were concerned, he put no trust in happenstance. Carfax had come to Section Eight because he, Renquist, was there. It was another challenge, another move against his leadership. Renquist had counciled caution and Carfax was responding by flaunting his recklessness. And, as a result, Renquist's control was being taxed to its limits.

To confront each other in the safety of the Residence was one thing, but to bring their conflict here, out among the humans, was unforgivable. The arrival of Carfax and Julia was made even more galling by the awareness that they were deliberately counting on Renquist's own restraint in order to thumb their noses at him. Renquist could too easily imagine what might happen if he simply allowed his anger to take over. He had the power to destroy the young ones, but he was bound by his sense of responsibility. The horror and the shrieking panic among the humans that would result from two nosferatu going head to head, right there in the restaurant, could threaten everything for which he had worked since he had become Master of the colony. The incident would probably make the TV news, pictures at eleven.

Renquist watched powerlessly as Carfax and Julia joined Cynara and her human at the bar. Had Cynara known that this was going to happen? Had she told the young ones that she and Renquist were coming to this place? He could hardly believe that someone with Cynara's experience and cool intelligence would betray him to side with a hothead like Carfax, and yet the three of them were standing together, conversing unconcernedly, apparently oblivious to the stares they were drawing from the other diners and drinkers. And then, just as Renquist was considering his immediate options, a human voice interrupted his thoughts and added a fresh factor to the equation.

"Do you remember me?"

* * *

"Do you remember me?"

Renquist's transition back to normal was entirely seamless. Sometimes he surprised even himself. "Of course I remember you."

Why did humans have such little faith in the capacity of their memories? Their minds were weak but not that weak. Renquist remembered the woman very well. Her name was Chelsea Underwood and they had spent a night together that, even by the standards of the most degenerate human, should at least have been memorable. The night in question had been back in the days before he'd retreated into seclusion, and, indeed, it had been too many nights of that kind that had contributed to his decision to exit the human world.

Back when Renquist had first met Chelsea Underwood, her hair had been wild red, retro-styled in the manner of Rita Hayworth, the movie star of the 1940s. On that night, she had been wearing a red knit dress that showed off her legs and much of the upper portion of her ample breasts. In keeping with her scarlet woman image-of-the-evening, her sexual overtures had been immediate and blatant. During the time that had elapsed since their last encounter, however, she seemed to have become withdrawn and somber. She had darkened her hair to a deep chestnut, and was now dressed in a fairly conservative outfit of bottle-green leather. Where previously she had been brash and overt, she now showed a distinct nervousness as she looked down at him seated in the booth. "It must be two years since we saw each other."

The very last thing that Renquist wanted was to enter this woman's mind. As he recalled, it had been an uncomfortable, disorganized place. Even without going inside, though, he could easily detect a second emotion, a kind of projected reproach beneath the anxiety. Did she blame him for the changes that he'd observed? Renquist nodded, wondering where all this might be leading. "That's right. It's over two years."

"I called you a number of times."

"I was told."

"But you wouldn't speak to me."

"I was going through a very difficult time."

"And then you vanished from sight."

"That was the end product of the difficult time."

"But now you're back?"

"I think so."

"You're not sure?"

"I'm back. The question is how long I'll stay."

"You're about to leave again?"

"I'm not sure."

"I see you're still wearing black."

Renquist smiled politely, continuing to avoid directly reading her thoughts. "I fear I've become a little narrow in my preferences."

"That's not what I remember."

Renquist avoided the path that Underwood seemed to be indicating. "You seem a lot less flamboyant yourself."

"Maybe these are less flamboyant times."

Renquist didn't quite know what to do with her. The conversation had reached its limit as a mere exchange of pleasantries, but she seemed unwilling to take her leave. She appeared to be waiting for some move on his part. He glanced at the bar. Cynara, Carfax, Julia, and the human seemed to be deep in conversation. Renquist could see no harm in entertaining a companion of his own for a brief time. He gestured to the banquette beside him. "Would you care to join me for a drink?"

She hesitated. "I'm with some people . . ."

Renquist shrugged. "That's too bad."

"I suppose they wouldn't miss me, just for a short time."

Without further urging, she slid into the booth beside him. Now Renquist didn't need to read her mind. His own memories were vividly returning. Two years ago, Renquist and

Chelsea Underwood had met at a short-lived nightclub called Encounter. After a courtship of no more than a half hour, the two of them had left and taken a cab back to her apartment in the east seventies. He clearly recalled how, even in the back of the cab, the hunger had been building inside him. He hadn't hunted or fed in a very long time, but he knew he was on shaky ground with this woman. She had appeared to know a lot of people in the club and many of had seen her and Renquist leave together. If he made her a victim, she'd be missed and the trail would lead too obviously back to him. For that reason alone, she had been less than suitable.

A waiter came to the table. Underwood ordered a double screwdriver and then smiled at Renquist. "When I saw you and your girlfriend sitting here, I wondered if it was appropriate to come over and speak to you. I didn't want to cause you any embarrassment."

"My girlfriend?"

"The woman you were sitting with, she wasn't your girlfriend?"

Renquist didn't have to read minds to realize the motive behind Underwood's question. He decided spare her any further need to probe. "Cynara isn't my girlfriend."

"She isn't?"

"A business associate."

"I see." Her delight at this piece of news was transparently evident. Renquist decided to reroute the conversation. "Do you still live at the same place?"

Her apartment had been large and expensive, part of an exclusive Upper East Side co-op. This had been another reason that Renquist hadn't gone all the way and killed her that night. Their arrival together and his eventual solitary departure had probably not only been noted by the doorman but also recorded by least one security camera. She was also clearly very wealthy, either in her own right or through ties of family, and he knew from experience that the rich made dangerous victims.

They were always missed, if only by their bankers.

Underwood nodded. "I'm still there. I own the place and, in New York, you can't just move on a whim. I've redecorated, though, since you were there."

"You became bored with art nouveau?"

Underwood beamed. "You remembered."

Renquist, at his most deadly charming, returned the smile. "Of course."

She sipped her drink. "You also remember that it was quite a night we shared?"

"You think I could forget?"

Underwood all but purred. On that night two years ago, he'd thought, when they'd reached her apartment and he'd explained that he was unable to make love to her in the conventional manner, it might have produced an immediate cooling of her ardor. In fact, quite the reverse turned out to be the case. He didn't have to read her to feel the rising excitement at the idea of the unconventional. When he scanned the menu of her fantasies, he found that she had a definite bias in the direction of degradation, debasement, and even pain. No quarter and no prisoners. She would submit to the limit and if she cried or begged for mercy it would only be for effect or to push him to further cruelty. She was positively devilish in the convolutions of game-power that she had woven around the simple sex act, and the pride that she took in her potential to derive pleasure from virtually anything that two people could do to each other. If he wanted to whip her to orgasm, urinate on her upturned face, suspend her from the ceiling, or drip hot wax on her breasts, she would eagerly position herself to receive the abuse. Ice cubes, black pepper, a riding crop—she would happily find them for him and bring them to him on her grovelling hands and knees. All she reserved was the right to remain the ultimate manipulator. Her deepest core of satisfaction was derived from observing, with a detached calm, as she drove a man, or in some instances a woman, to discover the worst in themselves and lose control over that dark side. Of course, in Renquist, she had not the slightest clue with what she was dealing, or for how long he had walked an infinitely more twisted path.

Where no quarter is offered and no prisoners are taken, retreat is also impossible. Renquist simply read her scrolling fantasies and made them real—slowly, deliberately, and with great attention to detail—until she moaned and sobbed, strained against the bonds that held her, cursed obscenely and tore at the silk sheets with her long customized fingernails. Once he had brought her to peaks that were verging on insanity, he'd added one or two refinements of his own, causing her quiver with involuntary spasms. Her breath came in agonized shudders as she all but lapsed into mindless incoherence. Renquist had taken the redheaded woman called Chelsea to the outer reaches of her own not inconsiderable imagination and on into a new dark universe that she had never visited even in her most fevered dreaming.

Much of what Renquist had done to her hadn't even been physical. With her mind unknowingly wide open to him, he had only to float a suggestion into her unconscious and her hyperactive nervous system would grab and run with it, quite convinced that it was really happening, sending her body into those shuddering convulsions. At the end, she had simply stared at him in mute shock, too far gone to be either disgusted or adoring. He'd shown her erotic landscapes that she hadn't the vocabulary to describe, even to herself. He'd brought her to the point of truly believing that, if he didn't carve a fresh violent experience on her soul, she might not be able to survive to the dawn.

It was then that he made his own move and appeased his own desire. He had taken the small and very sharp steel spike from its ornate silver sheath and, while she watched, silent and wide-eyed, he had opened a vein in her neck. She'd moaned as he'd put his cold lips to the crimson flow of her blood.

"Oh, Victor, yes . . ."

He had fed from her, but not to the point of death. She would recover after a few days of sleep and desperate haunted dreams. Probably she wouldn't know exactly what had been done to her. Her mind would reject the glorious, monstrous finale of their encounter, telling herself that it was a matter of delusion and bad drugs. After the feeding, he had slipped away, leaving her dazed amid the torn satin and the ruined and bloody silk, her mind whirling in a deranged kaleidoscope of confusion that was equal parts delight and fear. Later she'd feel shame, but she wouldn't quite know why.

Such half-measures had been his way, back in those final days of his last time in the world. Much of the reason he had withdrawn was that he had suspected each contact of this kind was another stop along the road to eventual madness. Better the cold transfusion and the solitude of the Residence than to be so near the focus of his hunger and yet so far away.

In the present, Underwood put out a tentative hand and touched his. Now he couldn't help reading her mind. She was nervous again, afraid of feelings that were threatening to overwhelm her. As he'd expected, she didn't completely remember everything that had transpired through the course of that night two years ago, but she wanted to revisit the dark places in the worst possible way. Nothing to compare had happened to her before or since and she craved again it with such intensity that she scared herself.

"Your skin's so cold."

Renquist nodded and half smiled. "Maybe yours is just warmer."

"It made me very unhappy when you didn't call me."

"I'm sorry."

"It was as though you'd planted an idea inside me that I wanted to know more about."

"It was unavoidable."

"I missed what you did for me."

"I had to leave New York quite suddenly."

"Are you a gangster or something?"

Renquist laughed, but under the guise of picking up his drink, he withdrew his arm so their hands were no longer touching. "What I do is much more complicated."

She was intelligent enough not to press the point. "I'd really like for us to get together again. Is that possible?"

Renquist solemnly nodded and, with the most sincere of expressions, lied like a politician. "It would be infinitely possible."

The very last thing he wanted was to get together with Chelsea Underwood one more time. With the Feasting coming on, he might not be able restrain himself from killing her.

"Will you call me?"

"I will."

He perceived that from the other side of the room, Carfax, Julia, and Cynara were watching him and the woman. They could certainly read her mind as easily as he could and Renquist didn't like that. It was a mind filled with passionate, razor-edged shards of their night together, if anything made sharper and more painfully demanding by the passage of time. He could feel the heat inside her and the effort with which she pulled herself together and reasserted her control. "I really should be going back to my friends."

Renquist was aware of his own needs starting to burn, but he forced himself to be coolly charming. "Really, so soon?"

Before easing her way out of the booth, she took out a pen and wrote her number on a cocktail napkin. "It would make me very happy if you called me."

"I'll do that."

He had no intention of doing that. In fact, he wanted out of the restaurant, right there and then.

"I think you should see this."

Cynara held out a copy of the *New York Post*. The major part of the front page was taken up by a large grainy photograph of a group of police officers in thigh-length rubber boots and scuba suits lifting a woman's naked body from the water. The screaming banner headline read: NAKED BODY IN CENTRAL PARK LAKE. Renquist looked at the headline and then up at Cynara.

"So? It's hardly a classic headline, hardly as memorable as 'Headless Body in Topless Bar.' "

Cynara didn't smile. "Read the story."

Renquist did as she suggested. It seemed that early-morning joggers had spotted a white shape floating in Central Park Lake and called the police. He still didn't see why Cynara was showing him this. Murders were commonplace and she knew he could go for weeks without reading a paper or watching a TV show. Then it suddenly became clear and a chill spread through him.

> Forensic experts stated that, as far as they could as-
> certain, the body had been completely drained of
> blood and they were of the opinion the victim had
> been killed elsewhere and the body dumped in the
> lake. The victim has been identified as 31-year-old
> Chelsea Brewer Underwood, a resident of East 76th
> Street in Manhattan.

The story continued on an inside page and was accompanied by a small picture of Chelsea Underwood laughing, with a champagne glass in her hand, and looking very like she had the previous evening at Section Eight.

Renquist slowly put down the newspaper and looked at Cynara. "Where are Carfax and Julia?"

Cynara shook her head. "I don't know."

"They didn't return at dawn?"

"They have other bolt-holes around the city. They don't have to sleep here."

Renquist tapped the newspaper. "They were responsible for this?"

Cynara avoided his eyes. "I can't be certain of that."

"But you suspect as I do?"

"It would seem probable."

"Were you with then?"

Again she shook her head. "Of course not."

"What happened after I left the restaurant?"

Cynara shrugged. "I saw Julia in conversation with the woman and later the three of them left together."

"Julia, Carfax, and the Underwood woman?"

"That's right."

"What about the other human?"

"What human?"

"The man that was with you."

"I'd sent him on his way long before that."

"And now the Underwood woman is found floating in Central Park Lake, drained of her blood."

Cynara's face was blank. "It does look bad."

"Is your human also going to turn up drained and dead?"

Cynara almost hid her anger, but Renquist knew her too well. "Have you stopped trusting me, Victor?"

Renquist immediately regretted what he had said. "I'm sorry."

"You should have more faith in me."

Renquist closed his eyes and lay back on the bed. "I do. It's just that this is very bad. They have deliberately flouted my wishes. Feeding in public like this, in a way that can be so easily traced, is pure insanity."

"What are you going to do?"

Renquist sighed. He had been wakened too early and his mind was slow and sluggish. "I don't know. I have much to think about. If Carfax and the others refuse to be contained, if they insist on going against me, the colony will be split."

Outside, a hot, hazy afternoon was coming to its close in a blaze of glory, but no damaging light penetrated the safety and comfort of the Residence. In their private gloom, it was all too easy for the colony to succumb to the illusion that they had the world shut out, that the humans couldn't hurt them. It was easy to forget that their comfort and safety were fragile bubbles that could be burst by a single act of willful carelessness. Renquist flashed on a swift, furious vision of burning Carfax with a deadly all-consuming fire until the upstart was reduced to nothing more than ash and atoms.

Cynara's eyes were dark and guarded. "Perhaps we should leave the city . . ."

"That would also split the colony."

"Maybe that wouldn't be the worst thing that could happen."

"It would make us all vulnerable."

"Carfax seems to be doing his best to make us all vulnerable right now."

Now Renquist was experiencing a second vision, Chelsea Underwood and her oh-so-tempting willingness. He could have had her himself. She had offered herself to him, and she would at least have died in ecstasy. He quickly thrust away the image, though. It was hardly the time to be gnawing on the bones of what might have been. "As I said, I have much to think about."

Gideon Kelly sat in his dirty underwear on the narrow unmade bed with its stained sheets, single threadbare blanket, and hard thin pillow, and stared at the photograph on page one of the *New York Post*. A slut was dead, a harlot had reaped the whirlwind of her iniquity, dead in the park, drained of her tainted lifeblood. He knew she'd been a slut. That was beyond question. A whore, a tramp, a licentious wanton, woman of the night-filth, a thing of the streets, evil in her corruption, beyond redemption, drawn to the magnet lights of Babylon, the slack-faced, perfume-reeking sextoy of venal and diseased men, to be used and degraded and ultimately consumed, henceforth consigned to burn for howling eternity in the same Holy Agony that awaited him. Oh yes, they were brother and sister under that weak leprous flesh, kindred in shame and flaccid desire, the only difference being that she had gone before, along the path of doom and damnation to her infinitely deserved punishment.

Without even the need for thought, Gideon Kelly's hand reached down for the pint of Queen Anne scotch that stood on the floor beside the bed. The guilty burn of cheap whiskey was the only thing in his miserable life that momentarily muted the awful fear of the fires of Hell and provided a brief forgetfulness of his fall from Grace.

Gideon Kelly had been staring at the photographs in the *Post* for a very long time, turning from the one to the other and then back again. The sun was already going down and soon it would be time to return to the purgatory and evil temptation of the streets. The two pictures told the whole of the story. On the front page, burly officers lifted the whore from the lake in all her deadwhite, fishbelly nakedness, revealed and exposed. On the inside of the newspaper, she laughed at him from the smaller picture, hot and painted with a glass in her hand. He could all but smell her corruption and imagine the rancid gloss on those red lips, the dirty and defiling mouth and the bright calculating eyes that could seduce a man's very soul. He had tasted of those bitter deceitful kisses and known that poison flesh. He had paid the wages of sin and known the infection of women. Whores had delivered him to this place, shunned by his God and cast out by his Mother Church without forgiveness, hope of redemption, or comfort in his wretchedness. Sweet innocent Jesus and all of the saints, but he'd like to shake the hand of the man who had cut down this whore, laid her low, and left her floating on the waters as an example to the rest of her foul sisterhood.

It was whores and pride that had brought him to this cell in the Dupont Hotel on 26th Street, in the devil city of Manhattan. Whores, pride, and his own weakness, such was the Unholy Trinity that had delivered him to this ghetto of the damned, with only a bottle for a friend, and only the *New York*

Post to remind him that, even in this city, the Sword of Retribution could still fall upon the fornicators and the Justice of the Lord of Hosts would not be denied.

Gideon Kelly held the whiskey in his mouth before he swallowed it, letting the amber spirit find the cavities in his teeth and sear the roof of his mouth. Then he swallowed and winced as his throat burned and ultimately the pain hit his stomach like a fist. Months earlier, the charity doctor had told him that he had a pre-ulcerous condition and a liver like a worn-out sponge, but he had never followed up the diagnosis or sought any kind of treatment. He would endure whatever the Lord God visited upon him, and suffer the Divine Will without pleading for mitigation. Soon the burn would reach his blood and the pain would abate. Blood and fire, fire and blood, such was the Axis of the Universe—and who was he, loathsome sinner that he was, to question the Axis of the Universe.

In the foreground of the photograph on the cover of the *Post*, he could see the painted toenails on the slut's left foot. He wished that he had the courage to go to the lake in the park and be near the spot where the whore had been cast into the waters. He wished, but he knew that he wouldn't. He didn't have it in him to brave the dangers and the Spawn of Satan that lurked in the defiled bushes and amid the haunted trees. In daylight, he might have gone, but already the darkness was gathering beyond the dirty window.

chapter Two

The large eighteenth-century grandfather clock that stood just inside the front door of the mansion, the one on which carved wooden demons scaled a carved wooden tower, had just chimed midnight. Almost immediately Renquist heard the voice of Carfax coming up from the floor below. The doors of the elevator slid and slammed, and Renquist moved like lightning to the stairwell and peered down. Carfax was coming out of the elevator, followed by Julia, the misshapen Segal, and another woman, a young human with too much make-up and green streaked hair. The human looked like one of the lost tribe of young women with negative self-esteem who hung around with a particular kind of musician and downtown drug dealer. Right at that moment, she seemed hardly able to walk and had to be helped by Segal. As she stepped out of the elevator, her high heels went out from under her and she sprawled like a rag-doll, hiking her short and very tight leopard print dress almost to her waist and spilling small objects from her oversized shoulderbag. Segal reached down, grabbed her arm with one of his massive hands, and lifted her bodily to her feet. It was seemingly not the first time that the woman had fallen. Her fishnet stockings were torn and her right knee was freshly grazed. Directly she was on her feet again, she started to complain in an irritating New Jersey whine.

"I'm telling you. I lost my jacket."

Julia shot her a dangerous look. "Shut up about your jacket. You aren't going to need a jacket."

"It was leather. I need it."

Carfax abruptly turned and looked as though he was about to strike her. "Will you shut the fuck up about your jacket?"

"You don't give a fuck about my jacket, do you?"

Julia moved between Carfax and the human. "No, he doesn't give a fuck about your jacket, but he will undoubtedly hurt you if you don't be quiet."

The woman pouted. "I don't like him."

"That's okay. He doesn't like you either."

The unlikely quartet moved away from the elevator. They appeared to be on their way to what the young ones referred to as the playroom, the soundproofed area at the rear of the house that was fitted out with state of the art recording and projection equipment. Renquist could too easily imagine what Carfax and his companions had in mind for the girl. He moved to the head of the stairs, determined to put a crimp in their intended frolic. "I'd like to talk to you if I may, Brother Carfax."

Carfax looked up, saw Renquist standing at the top of the stairs, and an insolent sneer spread across his face. "I don't think this is quite the right time." He indicated the human. "We're kind of busy right now . . . Victor."

Renquist only kept his temper with great difficulty. That's exactly what I want to talk to you about."

Julia arched an equally insolent eyebrow. "You could always join us. How long has it been, Victor?"

The human suddenly giggled and put a hand on Segal's shoulder to steady herself. She pointed to Renquist. "Who's he? Is he your father or something?"

Julia laughed nastily. "Sometimes he thinks he is."

Renquist angrily fixed his gaze on the human. Drunk as she was, her words stung him. He had given up a lot when he'd assumed the Mastership, including much of his freewheeling spirit. He actually did sound like some Spencer Tracy father waiting up for an errant Elizabeth Taylor. He didn't look that old, damn it, and, if he did, he was going to do something about it. "Who the hell are you?"

The girl swayed forward as though she intended to climb the stairs to where Renquist was standing, but then swayed back again, clearly thinking better of it. "I'm Lana. As in Turner. Why don't you do like she said and come down here?"

Julia smiled evilly. "That's right, Victor, come on down here."

Lana appeared to be having trouble focusing her eyes. "We're all here to have a real good time." She squinted at Carfax. "That's what Kurt here told me: 'a real good time.' "

Julia looked amused. "You hear that, Victor? A real good time? How long's it been since you had a real good time?"

Renquist said nothing. Lana, meanwhile, thought about the concept of a real good time for a moment. "I got a problem with this."

Renquist eyed her coldly "What's that?"

"I really don't think I like Kurt."

Renquist half smiled. "Many of us have a problem liking Kurt."

"He doesn't care about my jacket."

Renquist looked directly at Carfax. The boy's eyes were hidden behind the usual black sunglasses. "Kurt doesn't care about a lot of things. In fact, I believe you could fill a book with things that Kurt doesn't care about."

Lana solemnly nodded. Her attention span seemed to have run out on the subject of Kurt. Now she was peering at Segal. "Christ, but you're weird looking."

Renquist shook his head at the absurdity. This drunken human fool was swaying and giggling while three cold nosferatu, with the agreed intention of killing her, stood around encouraging her pitiable antics. Carfax and Julia were still dressed as they had been the night before. Presumably they hadn't been able to change since Renquist had seen them at the restaurant. Segal was wearing a very conservative dark suit, a white shirt, and a narrow tie which made him look like a deformed FBI man. Had they really taken him out on the streets? He was one of a small percentage of their kind who came out of transition malformed and hideous. Even in New York, a face and a figure that rivaled the Elephant Man was still able to stop traffic. Usually he only left the Residence on the rarest of occasions; if Carfax and Julia had invited him along with them on one of their nighttime excursions, it was another symptom of their suicidal determination to throw all caution to the winds.

Lana was now looking around with the delayed-action curiosity of the very drunk, obviously wondering when the "real good time" was going to roll. She'd only come with these three weirdos because they'd promised her that she'd be getting into something way cool. Her mind was so fogged by vodka, valium, and cheap amphetamine that her thoughts were scarcely coherent. Her primary motivation was an infantile desire for more. She wanted more, but, if anyone had asked her more of what, she would possibly have had trouble telling them. The focus of the need shifted constantly and, right at that moment, it had fixed on more alcohol.

"Who do I have to fuck to get a drink around here?"

Renquist wanted no more of this and he quickly and arbitrarily shut her down. He hardly even had to perceive her drab aura as he collapsed it to nothing. The woman's arms dropped limply to her sides. She continued to stand, but otherwise she was catatonic.

With the outsider witness immobilized, Renquist advanced down the stairs towards the three young ones. "Now we can talk."

He could feel the three of them drawing together. That was reassuring. At least they hadn't grown so arrogant that they'd ceased to fear his power. Carfax removed his dark glasses, and Renquist wondered if it was a sign of compromise or just the gloves coming off. Then he saw that Carfax's eyes were suffused with fresh blood. The young one hadn't been just feeding, he'd been gorging mindlessly, far beyond any physical or spiritual need. Carfax had something to prove and his first question more than confirmed this. "Are you going to make an issue of this, Victor?"

Renquist reached the foot of the stairs and halted a couple of paces from the three young ones and the inert human. "You don't think it's an issue already?"

"Is following our nature an issue?"

"Flaunting your nature is just plain stupid."

Carfax replaced his sunglasses. "You are making it an issue."

Renquist took a deep breath. "I think you made it an issue when you left the body of the Underwood woman in Central Park Lake."

Carfax and Julia glanced quickly at each other. They reminded Renquist of guilty children and he made his displeasure plain. "Did you really think I wouldn't connect it?"

Julia pouted slightly. "You fed from her."

"That was two years ago and I was careful."

Carfax stiffened slightly. "We've finished with being careful. We're going to be free."

"There's a difference between free and making the cover of the *New York Post*. How many more bodies are out there waiting to be discovered?"

"That depends on how hard the humans care to look."

Renquist was not about to tolerate any more of this bombast. Carfax had to be so gorged from overfeeding that he'd lost what little reason he'd ever possessed. In his own way, he was as drunk as the dysfunctional Lana. He turned to Julia. "Are you as overstimulated as he is?"

Julia avoided looking directly at Renquist. "What he does is his own business."

Clearly she was the more rational of the two. Renquist focused all of his attention on her. "You may think that bucking my authority is a game, but the truth is you're putting everyone in the colony at risk. When the others start to realize this, they may have less patience than I do. There's a history of colonies turning on groups that threatened their collective security. It's always very ugly and very violent."

Julia said nothing. Feeling himself pressed, Carfax looked quickly around. "Isn't it a little ridiculous to be standing here in the hall discussing this? Shall we go into the playroom?"

Carfax obviously wanted to move the game onto his own turf, and away from the rest of the colony. That at least indicated that he wasn't completely without a shred of caution. Renquist decided to go along with the move. "By all means."

They all turned to go. Renquist was just indicating that Carfax should walk in front of him, when Segal gestured to Lana. His speaking voice was a hoarse, unearthly rasp that was as disturbing as his physical appearance. "What about her?"

Carfax didn't give the catatonic girl a second glance. "Bring her along; she'll keep."

Segal nodded, effortlessly swung the woman over one massive arm, and followed the others in the direction of the playroom. Renquist smiled to himself. So that was the deal here: The girl was a reward for Segal. Carfax was maintaining the loyalty of the grotesque by bringing live prey to him. Segal, like most grotesques, was possessed of immense physical strength, and Carfax almost certainly relied on it for a form of feudal muscle. Renquist made a note to dismantle that transactional relationship as soon as he possibly could.

The playroom had changed a good deal since Renquist had last been in there. The young ones had totally taken over. The floor was strewn with huge, black, kapok-filled cushions and one wall was entirely filled with state-of-the-art electronics, sound and computer equipment, two big projection TVs, and maybe a dozen or so smaller monitors—the toys of the modern world. Perhaps the strangest of all was a life-size red leather rocking horse. Diffused lighting panels, set in the ceiling at discreet intervals, gave Renquist the impression that they were entering a dim aquarium, and he didn't find the effect at all pleasant.

Some much older toys were displayed on the wall facing the electronics. Elaborate arrangements of chains and manacles hung from heavy iron rings welded to the building's structural supports. Presumably the young ones used them to restrain the live prey they brought back there for their games. Renquist hardly shared their enthusiasm for this sado-gothic kitsch. As art, it was too depressingly passé and, in practical terms, it should have been redundant. If nosferatu couldn't immobilize their prey without resorting to shackles and tacky bondage devices, they hardly merited the name. On the other hand, as Master, he wasn't expected to be the arbiter of colony good taste. The centerpiece of the room was a low table created from a massively solid block of granite that resembled an anonymous tomb. More chains were attached to more rings set in the sides of the slab, confirming that games of wampyr cat-and-mouse had become a part of the playroom's function and menu. Further confirmation came when Segal immediately dumped the shutdown Lana on a cushion and routinely secured her to the wall by manacles and a length of chain.

While Segal shackled the human, Julia walked to the racks of electronics and turned on a DAT player. The room was filled with a low, white-noise drone that may well have been one of her own compositions. Renquist wasn't sure that he liked Julia's music. For one who had known both Mozart and Jim Morrison, the atonal monotony was hard to take. For that matter, though, he wasn't sure he liked Julia. A strange, incestuous thread ran through the present conflict within the Residence. Julia had created Carfax, but, almost sixty years earlier, Renquist himself had created Julia.

The relationship between a young one and the elder who brought him or her to transition was never easy. Anger and rejection were the first reaction. Only a tiny minority of new arrivals in the dark world came willingly or were ever consulted as to whether they wanted to make the transition at all. Most started their new life with a poisonous hatred for the individual who "killed" them. Quickly though, as the possibilities and almost limitless potential of the new and strange life started to sink in, hate was replaced by an almost slavish love, the devotion of the novice for the teacher.

In time, that love would also change. When the young ones started to feel their strength, the adoration ceased and the relationship entered a period of competition and challenge, the breaking of the original bonds and ties of blood. At that point, depending on the natural strength of the young one, a number of things might happen. If the young one was weak, the creator might drive him or her away, to survive or perish as best he or she could. When the newcomer's strength was approximately equal to the elder's, an accord might be reached. Creator and creation forged new ties and new alliances, as in the case of Julia and Carfax, still running together, but in a freshly resolved dynamic.

The most usual outcome, however, was that the young would break with the old, severing all links to the ones who made them and taking a lone path of discovery that might not bring them back in contact with their creators for decades, even centuries. This was how it had been with Renquist and Julia.

Renquist first met the still-human Julia in Berlin in 1935. At the time, she had been one of the stable of pretty blonde starlets that Josef Goebbels, as Hitler's Minister of Propaganda, maintained as a facility for the newly formed National Socialist film industry. She played Aryan maidens and fluffy chorus girls and, according to rumor, also consummated a number of sexual liaisons among the Nazi hierarchy. When he'd first encountered Julia in a fashionable café on the Unter Den Linden, his distaste for the Nazis and their baleful philosophy had triggered the idea of transforming one of the playthings of these uniformed thugs and allowing her to run amok among them, a wampyr cat among fat, unsuspecting Nazi pigeons.

Julia had seemed like the ideal subject for this covert act of moral vengeance. She was spoiled, vain, conceited, totally self-centered, and capriciously promiscuous. She would thrive as a nosferatu. Best of all, she was perversely attracted to Renquist from the first moment they met. About the only stumbling block had been Cynara. Cynara had been his companion in Berlin and hadn't seen the point of going to all the trouble of transforming a human for no reason other than what she saw as some quixotic gesture on Renquist's part.

Despite Cynara's objections, Renquist had gone ahead and brought Julia across. To his surprise, the vapid starlet had taken to her new condition with vicious enthusiasm. She had reached the stage of breakaway independence in an alarmingly short space of time, possibly spurred by Cynara's open hostility. Unfortunately, Renquist never had the chance to observe first-hand what havoc Julia had wreaked among the Nazi leaders. At approximately the same time as Julia had gone out on her own, he and Cynara had been forced to flee Germany and seek refuge in the United States. The last news he had heard of her was that, at the end of the war, she had vanished into the madness of Stalin's Russia.

Renquist had received no word of her for almost 20 years, to the point where he'd become convinced she must have fallen victim to the sun, the fire, or the sharpened stake. Renquist knew from bitter experience that the Russians had a way with these things, and that the old knowledge hadn't been totally buried by dialectic materialism. He considered Julia a very minor loss, though, and had rarely thought about her until she suddenly appeared in New York City in 1966, seemingly out of nowhere, lurking and presumably feeding on the periphery of the Warhol Factory crowd, talking in a smoky German accent and gathering a reputation for audio collages, erotic pop lithographs, and as an organizer of "happenings." By that time, Segal was already with her, kept strictly in the background, filling the role of servant and bodyguard. Neither Julia nor Segal ever discussed the origins of the misshapen giant, but a theory existed among the other nosferatu that Segal was actually her own botched creation, and she kept him with her out of some peculiar sense of shame.

When the colony had been set up in 1968, both Julia and Segal had been proposed as founding members. At first, Cynara had objected quite strenuously to their inclusion. Cynara saw Julia as a potentially disruptive factor, but the majority dismissed this as jealousy over a possible new relationship with Renquist. In the end, Dietrich had overridden Cynara. Julia and Segal had become part of the colony.

In the playroom, Julia now moved from the racks of electronics and curled catlike on one of the huge floor cushions, waiting to see what would happen next. Lana, the human, hung limp from arms pulled above her head by the chains that secured her. Segal squatted beside her as though staking out his claim. Carfax walked over to Lana, passed a hand in front of her blank face, and then looked at Renquist. "Did you have to close her down so completely? She might have learned something from watching this."

Renquist scowled impatiently. "Don't be ridiculous. We don't need any witnesses."

Carfax shrugged as though it was a matter of no importance. "She'll hardly be in a position to tell her story to anyone."

Renquist noted that Segal had been watching Carfax with glaring distrust ever since he'd come near the girl. Perhaps the grotesque wasn't the complete idiot-slave that Renquist had always assumed. "You think it was an intelligent move to bring casual prey to the Residence, under the current circumstances?"

"We were discreet."

"Like you were discreet with Chelsea Underwood?"

"What about Chelsea Underwood?"

"You deny that you killed her?"

Carfax flopped down on a cushion. "I think I've fed too much. I feel strange."

Renquist stood over him. "You deny that you killed the Underwood woman?"

"No, but . . ."

"You were trying to send me a message?"

Carfax gathered his senses as best he could. "Why should we want to send you a message?"

Julia's voice from the cushion was like a nicotine-stained icicle. "That's right, Victor. Why should we want to send you a message? All we have to do is walk upstairs and talk to you. I mean, you're our leader—isn't your door always open?"

"You both know exactly what I'm talking about."

Carfax managed to get his sneer back. "We do?"

Renquist nodded. "Of course you do."

"Actually we were only following one of your suggestions."

"What are you talking about?"

Julia lay back and stared at the ceiling. Renquist knew that the two of them were coming as close to taunting him openly as they dared. "You told us when the Feasting comes, we should make our kills look like a human serial killer."

"So?"

"We did exactly that. The media are already saying it's the work of a psycho."

"I was seen talking to the woman at Section Eight and you two were seen leaving the place with her."

Julia folded her arms behind her head. "Are you sure you're not just jealous?"

"Jealous?"

"We had her and you didn't We saw what was in her mind. She was crazy for you, Victor. You really know how to show a girl a good time."

"You're being absurd."

Segal's hissing rasp cut through the exchange. "Do the three of you have to talk all night? You brought me the woman and I am tired of waiting."

Carfax glanced at Segal. "I think our Master wants to lecture us on our lack of responsibility for a while longer."

Renquist allowed his disgust to show. "I have no more to say to you. You know the risks you're running."

Julia slowly sat up. "It's a pity we didn't bring another drunken human slut for you, Victor. Then you and Segal could have fed together."

For two nosferatu to feed together was an act of great intimacy, and for Julia to suggest that Renquist should casually feed with a deformity like Segal was nothing short of a calculated insult. The conversation went totally over Segal's head, however. He growled deep in his throat. "I want the woman."

Julia pulled her legs up under her so she was sitting cross-legged. She smiled at Segal. "Then take her, my darling; Victor has no more to say to us."

This didn't seem to be enough for Segal. He turned a questioning face to Renquist. Julia immediately stood up and moved between them. "You don't need his approval. He doesn't own us."

Renquist shook his head. He wanted no part of this. He could barely keep his fury in check. Did they think he was a fool? "What about the body?"

Julia seemed to sense that Renquist was close to the edge and backed off a little in her attitude. "Don't worry. It won't be found."

"Just make sure that it isn't. Your antics have received enough media attention already." He moved quickly to the door, where he turned and, with a fast hand gesture, lifted the block from Lana. He grinned at Segal. "Take her, kid, she's yours."

Lana's reanimated eyes grew as large as saucers as, for the first time, she saw her chained hands and Segal leaning towards her. She let out a cry of alarm and outrage. "What the fuck do you bastards think you're doing? I didn't come here to . . ."

Renquist closed the soundproof door behind him, cutting off the start of her screaming.

Renquist found himself being shaken awake out of a sleep so deep and deathlike that the dreams were untranslatable. He opened his eyes and found Cynara leaning over him. Fingers of pain extended up from his shoulders, gripped the back of his neck, and probed his brain.

"Wake up, Victor. This is important."

Renquist blinked, trying to focus both his eyes and his thoughts.

"It can't be sunset yet."

"It isn't."

"So what are you doing up? Is something wrong?"

"Two policemen are downstairs. They want to talk to you."

Renquist sat up, trying to clear his head. A nosferatu wakened while the sun was still up could be a wretchedly disorganized thing. "Did they say what they wanted to talk to me about?"

"No, but they asked for you specifically."

"I think that qualifies as something wrong. Is the place fully sealed against the light?"

Cynara took a dark blue silk shirt from the rack in the closet and handed it to him. "Would I be walking around if it wasn't?"

"I'm Detective McGuire, Mr. Renquist, and this is my partner, Detective Williams."

Renquist nodded, doing his best to appear affable and not in the least sinister. "I'm sorry I kept you waiting, gentlemen. I was taking a nap. I don't exactly keep regular hours these days."

Renquist had instructed Cynara to show the two officers into the reception area on the first floor of the Residence that was always used when a member of the colony had to conduct conventional business with humans. The area had been specifically decorated to be as nonthreatening as was plausibly possible and to give no clue as to the nature of the rest of the building. Although the windows had, by necessity, to be sealed, the room was painted white and furnished with bright, functional office furniture, and the ceiling-mounted track lighting gave the illusion that it was light and airy. A David Hockney sketch and a Robert Mapplethorpe photograph of an oiled and naked black man hung on one wall, while four of Julia's bondage lithographs were arranged in a group on one of the others.

McGuire was white, pure Brooklyn Irish, while Williams, the older of the two, was black with the brawny build of an ex-athlete running to fat. As Renquist entered, Williams was examining the Hockney. "Is this real?"

Renquist nodded. "Indeed it is. Hockney and I were quite close friends back in the sixties."

McGuire was more formal. Probably the result of a Catholic upbringing. "We'd like to ask you some questions if we may, Mr. Renquist."

"How can I help you?"

McGuire looked Renquist directly in the eye. "There's been a murder, Mr. Renquist."

Renquist looked directly back at him. "You mean Chelsea Underwood?"

"That's right. Do you have something to tell us?"

Renquist shook his head. "I only know what I saw in the papers and on TV."

McGuire raised an eyebrow. "Why did you immediately think of her?"

"She's the only person I know who was recently killed."

Williams was now studying the Mapplethorpe with a disapproving expression. "You may have been one of the last people to see her alive."

"I've been thinking about that."

"I believe you were with her at a restaurant called Section Eight on the evening of the murder."

"To say I was 'with her' is stretching it a bit. I talked to her for a short while. I talked to a lot of people that night. It was the first time that I'd been out in a long time."

"How long did the two of you talk?"

Renquist shrugged. "I don't know. Not long. Certainly not longer than five or ten minutes. She was with some other people."

"So it was just a casual conversation?"

"That's right."

"And you didn't see her again?"

Renquist shook his head. "Not to speak to. I saw her in the distance but that was all the conversation we had. In fact, I left quite soon after that. The crowd started to get to me."

"You don't like crowds, Mr. Renquist?"

Renquist, for his own protection, hadn't read either of the policemen. He didn't want to risk raising their suspicions by inadvertently reacting to something he saw in their minds rather than what they said. He was starting to get the impression, however, that this was little more than just a routine inquiry. "No, I don't like crowds."

Williams turned and faced Renquist, treating him to a probing stare. "But you used to be quite the socialite, didn't you?"

"Things change."

Williams looked back at the artwork and McGuire once again took the ball. "How well you did you know Chelsea Underwood, Mr. Renquist?"

Renquist answered carefully. How much did they know? "Not that well."

This time Williams didn't look round. He just gestured to the third print in the series. The lithographs, done in the late seventies, were highly realistic works based on photographs from hardcore S&M and bondage magazines. They showed both men and women secured in painfully contorted poses by chains, ropes, and straps, and were executed in tones of cool grey, ice blue, and black, with the occasional vibrant highlight of red or orange. The particular one Williams was staring at showed a young, dark-haired, Oriental woman in stockings and a garterbelt tied down across a metal bedframe. "Why would anyone paint a thing like this?"

Renquist stiffened. He wasn't about to defend the function of art to a couple of policemen. "It isn't a painting. It's a lithograph print."

"Whatever."

Renquist was becoming irritated. "I believe the artist was making a comment on the nature of society and its response to erotica."

"You think so?"

"I'm only guessing. Maybe she was just attracted to the image."

"It looks like porno smut to me."

As the gloves came off. Renquist suddenly saw the room in an entirely new light. What seemed pleasantly normal to him might appear sinister and perverse to a pair of humans from a different, more conservative background. Living too long in Lower Manhattan could totally divorce one from the prejudices of the majority. He also saw the game that the two cops were playing. Williams put him off balance and then McGuire moved in with the sandbag. "We heard you slept with her, Mr. Renquist."

Renquist still resisted the temptation read the men. He knew that he was being teamed by experts and it was starting to become a challenge. "Who told you that?"

McGuire answered with a half-smile. "Nobody told us, Mr. Renquist."

Williams continued to study Julia's print. "I still don't see why anyone should want to paint a thing like this."

Renquist was anticipating the game. He glanced coldly at Williams. "The series was very well received by the critics."

McGuire's voice was quite casual. "You like to tie up women, Mr. Renquist?"

"I didn't make those prints."

"You hung them on the wall though, didn't you?"

McGuire stepped in for what he thought of as the kill. "Did you tie up Chelsea Underwood, Mr. Renquist? Did you tie her up that night you slept with her?"

"Do I have to answer that?"

It was McGuire's turn to shrug. "That's up to you, pal, but I think I should warn you that we have her diaries, and you figure in them quite prominently."

"That's ridiculous. I spent one night with the woman. It was over two years ago and I didn't see her again until the night before last." He glanced at Williams. "And yes, for your information, I did tie her up. It's not something that I normally do, but she seemed to want it. Does that settle the matter? I also didn't kill her, if that's what you really want to know."

Renquist realized that he'd been backed into a corner by nothing more than his own overconfidence. This wasn't a high-stakes chemin de fer game or some abstract mathematical puzzle. This was serious. It was time to look into their minds. He read them hard and fast and, to his relief, discovered that he wasn't a serious suspect, and that they knew absolutely nothing about what really went on inside the Residence. The two detectives were looking more for a picture of the world in which Chelsea Underwood lived and conducted her affairs, and how Renquist might figure in that world and in those affairs. Apparently her diaries had been a luridly uninhibited release for her, and they were trying to find out how much of the solitary confessional outpourings were fact and how much were fantasy.

The two men played their double act very well. The way they meshed, like a finely tuned machine, was a product of both training and long experience. Without realizing the truth, they had a surprisingly accurate grasp of the situation. They saw Renquist as a prominent and possibly powerful figure in some kind of perverse downtown art subworld, and they guessed that Chelsea Underwood had been a thrill seeker on the margins of that world. They didn't think Renquist had killed her, but they were working on the possibility that the killer was someone close to him. He was surprised to find that they knew a good deal about the private life of Anthony Ferrari, not enough to press charges or even start a serious investigation, but enough to be following a theory that the woman's killer came from the same general circle of people.

Delving deeper, he came to the bedrock of the two detectives' characters. Williams, close to the end of his 20 years with the NYPD, was a straight-arrow, uptight, church-going family man who believed in the principles of God, morality, and the rules. All of these had been beaten into him through the first 15 years of his life by a father with a strong arm, a leather belt, and a determination that his kids were going to do better than inner city Newark. At 15, Williams had lied about his age and shipped out to Vietnam as a private in the Marines. A couple of years after his return, he had joined the police department and more or less satisfied the angry ghost of his father.

Williams despised Renquist and his art and the kind of people with whom he imagined Renquist associated. He saw them as a boil on the face of the earth that, if his hands weren't tied by a lot of lawyers and bleeding hearts, he would have been happy to lance. And yet a deeply hidden part of Williams would have liked nothing better than to tie a nearly naked woman to a metal bedframe. Renquist detected a deep scar from some heavily suppressed wartime incident that had taken place outside of Nha Trang and involved four Marines, including Williams, and a teenage Vietnamese girl. Renquist couldn't see the details through a thick callous of time and guilt, but the girl had died as a result of what they'd done to her.

McGuire was a good deal more reasonable. He'd long ago

THE TIME OF FEASTING   77

given up making value judgements about people. After 16 years
in the police department, he pretty much treated all of humanity
with a uniform dislike. His marriage had failed when his wife
had taken to drink, no longer able to handle the job, the hours,
and her husband's deepening misanthropy. He wanted to nail
the killer of Chelsea Underwood, not out of any real sense of
outrage, desire for justice, or even to protect the city from a psy-
chopath. It was simply his job, and apart from sadly following
the Mets, and an on-again/off-again relationship with a woman
who worked for the phone company, doing his job well was his
only real source of satisfaction. McGuire lived in a world of deliberately diminished expectations. Mainly he stayed alive because the vestigial Catholicism in his make-up wouldn't allow
him to commit suicide—what cops called "going down on his
gun"—although he regularly considered it.

Williams walked slowly to where Renquist was standing. "For
your information, Mr. Renquist, we don't think that you killed
her either, but we do believe it's possible one of your group of
friends, associates, and hangers-on did. I don't like you, Renquist, or anything you stand for. I believe it's people like you
who are pumping poison into this country in the name of so-
called art and culture, but unfortunately that isn't something
we can arrest you for."

Now both cops were facing Renquist, crowding him,
McGuire on one side and Williams on the other. McGuire
leaned closer. "You seem to have had quite an effect on Chelsea
Underwood. You may have thought of her as nothing more
than a casual one-night stand for your pervert fun, but her diaries are full of you. She seems to have been obsessed with you,
Renquist, and I have this feeling in my gut that obsession had
something to do with her death."

Renquist took a step back. McGuire was, in his own way, too
damned close to the truth for any kind of comfort. "I don't see
how I can be held responsible for the fantasies of an unstable
woman."

Williams lip curled. "That's what your kind always say. You ain't responsible for shit."

McGuire moved towards the door, but Renquist knew the encounter wasn't quite over. Halfway there, the detective stopped and turned, in the manner of Peter Falk playing Columbo. "You have a Kurt Carfax living here, Renquist?"

Renquist blinked. Somehow the cops had both managed to keep their knowledge of Carfax hidden from him. He nodded. "Yes, he sublets a part of the building from me."

"Could we talk to him?"

Renquist moved to the desk at one side of the room and pressed the talk button on the deskset intercom. "Cynara, is Kurt in the building?"

Cynara's voice sounded tinny and distorted through the small speaker. "No, he's not. He went out a little while ago."

Renquist turned to the detectives with a gesture of helplessness. "I'm sorry, gentlemen. I'm afraid if you want to talk to Carfax, you'll have to come back later."

McGuire nodded. "I think I should tell you something about the police department, Mr. Renquist. Our job is to protect the city by arresting and locking up criminals. The way the system works is that we only arrest someone when we think we can make a case against them. We don't arrest anyone because we don't like their patterns of behavior. That doesn't mean, however, that we don't notice things and remember things. I personally don't like your relationship with Chelsea Underwood, but I can't do anything about that unless solid evidence turns up that you were responsible for her death. In the same way, I can't arrest your friend Carfax because he's been observed in a number of places where no respectable person ought to be. Your sub-tenant has been associating with some very dubious and dangerous people, Mr. Renquist, and his behavior patterns have been noticed. You might like to pass that along to him."

Renquist looked from one officer to the other. "Thank you

for the lesson in civics, gentlemen. I will certainly pass the gist of your remarks along to Mr. Carfax. I take it that will be all for now?"

Williams treated him to a hard look. "All for now, Mr. Renquist, but we'll be back, you can count on that."

With that grim assurance, the two men made their exit. When they were gone, Renquist walked slowly back to the desk. A terra cotta statue of a Mexican jaguar god stood beside the phone and intercom. Without any change of expression, he picked it up and hurled it very hard at a spot on the wall about 18 inches to the left of the Hockney, with enough force to shatter it into several hundred pieces.

"I'm afraid that isn't all." Once again, Cynara was holding a newspaper. This time it was *Newsday*. "You made Liz Smith's column."

Renquist sighed. "I did."

Cynara passed him the newspaper without further comment. The item was subheaded: MURDERED WOMAN WAS RENQUIST PAL. Renquist read it quickly and then lowered the paper. "This is getting out of hand. Is it after sunset yet?"

Cynara nodded. "Yes, the sun's gone down. Also Lupo wants to see you."

Renquist nodded. "Tell Lupo to come to the gallery."

"These are difficult times, Don Victor."

Lupo took the concept of leadership very seriously. Renquist was Lupo's leader and his don, and, as such, he must be shown the ultimate in respect. Lupo was a squat man with the shoulders of a bull and the massive lined face of a Roman senator. Renquist sat erect and formal in the tall wing chair by the fireplace. Lupo had pulled up a second chair so he was facing him. The single candle burned, and the two of them spoke with slow Old World formality. After Renquist, Lupo was the second most long-lived member of the colony. Although he rarely talked about his origins, he was reputedly created in the time of the Borgias and the warring Italian city-states of the fifteenth century. Some stories, which had never been confirmed or denied by Lupo, claimed that he had been deliberately created by a master necromancer in the employ of Cesare Borgia. The apparent intention had been to use him as a satanic secret weapon, an unstoppable assassin in the employ of popes and princes.

Lupo was by far the most withdrawn of all the members of the colony. He largely kept to himself, living in semi-isolation in a small room at the top of the building, constantly reading as though he wanted to absorb all the knowledge of the world. He only ventured out to make his discreet and private kills. His sense of tradition was so strong that he continued to sleep in a huge and ornate coffin and had never allowed the removal of his large retractable canine fangs.

"You should not be worried that the police come to visit you, Don Victor. These things happen, but these things also pass. Our protection is that the police live entirely in this modern world. They do not believe in us and cannot threaten what they don't believe in."

Renquist slowly nodded. "You are a wise man, Lupo, but the Feasting is almost upon us, and I fear for the security of the colony."

Lupo thought about this and Renquist allowed him the time. Except when hunting, Lupo lived on a much slower timescale, one from the days when courtesy and respect were valued more than speed and the instant decision. Lupo didn't come to Renquist like this very often, but when he did, Renquist listened with grave attention. Lupo was unique. Of all the nosferatu Renquist had ever encountered, Lupo was the only one who had turned his need to kill into a highly profitable profession. Indeed, Lupo, with his murders, had contributed almost as much to the common finances of the colony as Renquist had with his speculation and financial manipulation.

"I am not saying that there are not dangers, Don Victor.

When the Feasting comes, we will be vulnerable. The worst danger, however, is not from the police or the common population of this city. It will be from those who still believe. The ones who still have roots in the ways of the Old World are the truly dangerous. The ones who know we're something more than a fairy tale with which to scare the young girls and make them scream. A handful of normals have always had the power to sense us. Such powers may grow weak in these scientific times, but those who have them still exist. Should one of these get wind of us in the heat of Feasting, we would have reason to fear."

Lupo was a legend among the nosferatu of New York many times over. In the twenties and thirties, he had performed executions for Charlie "Lucky" Luciano and other Mafia chieftains of Prohibition. Back in those days, he'd been known as Joey Nightshade because no one ever saw him in the daylight. Such was Lupo's care and secrecy that none of his gangster employers ever suspected his true nature. They simply saw him as a shadowy but absolutely reliable contract killer. A shadow in a world of shadows, Joey Nightshade could be counted on to do the seemingly impossible. Even today, he continued to maintain ties with the contemporary New York underworld, and had advised Renquist in his dealings with various mob figures who had featured in his financial schemes.

"You counsel caution, Don Victor, and in this I agree with you, but caution is hard when the wolf is loose. At Feasting, we not only kill, we also sleep much and we lose our reason. If those who remember the old ways should come against us, we would be hard pressed to defend ourselves."

"You think this is likely."

Lupo nodded. "It's likely if we leave corpses all over the city. Someone will realize the truth and they will come. This business of the woman in the lake is no good. There must be no others like this."

"Carfax is a hothead."

Lupo shrugged. "The young are young. They have a sense of drama and they want to make their bones. We were like them once."

Renquist stroked his chin. "I'm still very tempted to push him out into the sunlight after what he did."

Lupo smiled. "I know how you feel, Don Victor, but you must not do that. It's not fitting that our kind should fall upon each other with an intent to kill. We leave that to the humans."

Renquist knew Lupo well enough to understand that he wanted something, but he also knew Lupo well enough not to ask him what that might be. Lupo was never direct. Already he had relayed one very important message. His constant use of the title "Don Victor" told Renquist that Lupo was confirming his continued and unreserved loyalty in the coming crisis. That was reassuring, but Renquist suspected there might be more to come. Neither Lupo nor Renquist would be so disrespectful as to read the other, but the old one smiled again as if he knew what Renquist was thinking.

"Tonight I hunt, Don Victor. The hunt is not only for my pleasure but also for a modest profit. Mr. Taglia of Elizabeth Street requires the removal of some Colombians who lack even a rudimentary sense of honor." Lupo made a cutting motion with his right hand. "Perhaps you would care to hunt with me?"

Now Renquist smiled. Mr. Taglia of Elizabeth Street was the famous Vincent Taglia, a highly placed lieutenant in what had once been the Gambino family. The Colombians were clearly as good as dead. "I would be honored to hunt with you, Brother Lupo, but I fear this is not the time for me to be away from the Residence."

Lupo made a sympathetic gesture. "It is as I expected. Such is the burden of leadership. I therefore ask your permission to take Segal with me. He's strong and could benefit from the experience."

So this is what Lupo had really come to see him about. By forming a hunting bond with Segal, a supreme honor for the young grotesque that not even he could fail to appreciate, Lupo would also be taking him away from Carfax's influence. The removal of Segai and his physical strength would greatly reduce the power of Carfax and his coterie. Lupo was not only making a gesture of support and loyalty but offering serious practical assistance. Renquist knew that he owed Lupo his thanks, but, with Lupo, the form was never to be that direct. "Segal is also very ugly."

Lupo laughed. "In a hat and coat, his looks will not show too much. We're not going to the Stork Club."

Renquist smiled. "No bodies floating in lakes though, my friend."

Lupo's grin was pure robust evil. "No bodies at all, Don Victor. That's why Staten Island has landfills."

Lupo rose and Renquist rose also. Lupo inclined his head. "I thank you for your time, Don Victor."

Renquist put a hand on the man's shoulder. "I thank you, Lupo. I always enjoy our conversations."

As Lupo opened the door to take his leave, Renquist raised a hand. "Uh, Lupo, I wonder if you'd mind taking care of something for me?"

Lupo was silent. If his don asked him for something, it went without saying that he would do it. That was how it worked in Lupo's world.

"On the subject of bodies, Lupo. I would appreciate it if you could keep an eye on the young ones and see that they never again flaunt their leavings as they did the other day. They grow more careless as the Feasting comes closer."

Lupo nodded. "I'll see that they put their toys away when they've done with them, Don Victor."

The time was a little after midnight and the lights of the Chrysler Building and the Empire State had already had been turned off, but the rest of New York City shone like a treasury of gleaming jewels. Cabs, cars, and limousines moved up and down the glowing canyons of the streets and avenues. Beneath those streets, the subways endlessly rolled and rumbled. The cafés, restaurants, and bars were still open and thronged with customers. People strolled along sidewalks or staggered drunk or drugged. Thieves, prostitutes, and hustlers plied their trades. Women danced naked for the benefit of men, men postured and preened for the benefit of women, or, in some sections of the city, for the benefit of other men.

Behind the curtained windows of a million apartments, human beings stared at the flickering screens of television sets, read, fought, made love, or just sat immersed in their thoughts. Some exulted, others despaired. At that very moment, someone was dying, someone else was giving birth, and a third was quite possibly committing murder. The whole of the dirty, unkempt city throbbed with inescapable human life. Perhaps not altogether healthy, and with a decided flawed beauty, New York was, despite everything, a breathing, organic thing, vibrating with thoughts of hate and love, greed and charity, prejudice and pragmatism. It could never stop and seemingly never die.

Standing alone on the roof of the Residence, the city's very life filled Renquist with a profound and hollow sadness. Like the city, he could live forever, but, unlike the city, he would never be part of such vibrancy, except maybe in the few fleeting moments immediately after he had made the kill and fed. He had traded the warmth, the haphazard contact, and the eventual angry death for the chill eternity of the nosferatu. But he was far too old to be feeling sorry for himself, or getting sentimental over city lights. He was a thousand years old and undead, and that more than outweighed any organic might-have-been. He needed to live in the present because the present required all of his attention.

An almost full, dirty yellow moon hung low in the sky over Queens. Renquist felt like raising his head and howling aloud to it. He spent all his time preaching control and restraint, and yet, buried deep, he was hungering as badly as any of them. At certain times, his flesh crawled and spasmed as though worms were burrowing under his skin. He had to climb down and admit that he wasn't immune to the madness. If he was going to function, he had to feed, and if he was going to feed, it might as well be tonight. With the rationalizing taken care of, the tension immediately fell away. His breath quickened in anticipation. He knew it was tonight. He had put in enough time taking responsibility for the colony. He owed at least one night to his own welfare and creature comfort.

Renquist turned, ready to go back down into the building and prepare himself for the hunt, but he saw that someone was standing in the doorway that opened onto the roof, an instant reminder that the colony and its demands were still there. The figure of a woman was silhouetted against the light.

"Cynara?"

The figure shook its head. "No, not Cynara."

The deep husky voice was unmistakable. "Julia?"

"You're surprised to see me?"

"Are you looking for me?"

"Who else comes up to the roof for solitary introspection?"

Evidently Julia was up to something. Even the simple act of stepping out into the light was a theatrical entrance. Renquist observed that her thoughts were cloaked but everything else about her was overt and dramatic. She floated across the flat central section of the roof, trailing a nightgown that could have belonged to Jean Harlow. The draped and extremely low-cut scarlet satin clung and shivered as though alive. Long matching evening gloves covered her arms, and a necklace of large rubies that actually had once been owned by Elizabeth Taylor was around her throat. Her spike-heeled mules with tufts of ostrich feathers above the toes hardly made a sound as she approached.

Renquist sighed, wondering what game this major costuming portended. "You look very elaborate."

Julia reached the parapet rail that ran around the flat center of the roof, and stood a short way off from Renquist, looking out at the city. "We can't wear black all the time."

"Is the scarlet woman outfit intended for my benefit?"

Julia pouted. "For who else, lord and Master?"

"Surely we're way past anything that would require you to vamp me with satin, high heels, and a half-million dollars in rubies?"

Julia raised a quizzical eyebrow. " 'Vamp'? That's an odd verb for you to use."

"It was the first verb that came to mind."

"Is there any reason why I shouldn't 'vamp' you?"

"I would have thought you reserved all your vamping for Carfax."

Julia turned and stretched languidly against the parapet rail. "You've never really understood about Kurt and me, have you, Victor?"

Renquist watched a pleasure boat moving up the Hudson. A party seemed to be in progress on the deck. "I didn't know there was that much to understand. I imagined that you'd simply created a companion for yourself. Although possibly he didn't quite turn out as you expected."

"Kurt can be amusing, but essentially he's a fool."

"So why choose him as a constant companion?"

"Because you will never make yourself available."

Renquist slowly shook his head. Even with satin and rubies as accessories, the idea was a little farfetched. "Oh no, Julia, I really can't believe that. Are you seriously telling me that you only created Carfax because I wouldn't bond with you?"

"You're denying your own magnetism, Victor."

"Are you forgetting that I created you?"

"Who would understand your power better than your own creation?"

Renquist raised a warning hand. "Whatever this game is, Julia, it isn't going to work."

Julia ignored Renquist's rejection and moved along the parapet rail so she was closer to him. He voice became soft and breathy. "Who better than your own creation to understand your strength, and the way that you misuse it on all this hiding and subterfuge?"

"Unfortunately, in a situation like ours, someone has to take control."

"You'll end up withering away, Victor. You'll control yourself out of existence."

She moved even closer to him, and Renquist wished that she hadn't Although he totally suspected her motives, she was stirring feelings inside him, and his feelings were quite complicated enough already. "If it wasn't so patently absurd, I'd say that you were trying to seduce me."

Julia positioned herself so the gloss on her lips and the rubies around her throat caught and reflected the light. The rubies were like bright drops of blood at her throat. "Maybe I am."

"Then you will fail."

"I'm not so sure about that." Her perfume was all but overwhelming. It spoke of hot airless nights, heavy with the scent of jasmine, wisps of cloud drifting across an indigo sky and wolves with lolling tongues lurking in the shadows. The worms started crawling under his skin again, and he only fought them down with the greatest effort.

Julia sensed his discomfort and smiled. She ran her hands down her body, smoothing the scarlet satin across her hips. "I'm trying to lure out the beast in you, Victor. Think of it as me doing my part for the survival of the colony."

"How do you come to that conclusion?"

"If you don't let go and give in to the wilding now and again, you'll crack under the strain."

"Perhaps it's you who's underestimating my power."

"You've never liked me, have you, Victor?"

"Why should that matter?"

"I think it's because you made me. You think I'm just some kind of pretty but lethal doll that you created for your own short-term amusement."

Renquist held up his hands in protest. Enough was enough. "I don't think I believe any of this encounter."

Julia, however, was relentless. "When you left me in Berlin, you believed you'd seen the last of me. I was a temporary creation and you were glad to be rid of me."

"Is this some strategy designed to throw me off balance?"

Julia ignored him. "When I survived, and turned up in New York, and even became part of Dietrich's original colony, I think both you and Cynara felt guilty. You and Cynara, so neat, so bonded, so well adapted to living in the human's world, and suddenly your wild creation was back as a permanent reminder of a time when you weren't so controlled, when you still did things on raw impulse. Did you ever consider why Cynara was determined to deny me membership of the colony?"

"There was some talk at the time about . . ."

Julia angrily interrupted him. "It wasn't just talk. She was terrified that I'd lead you back to the old ways."

A slow smile spread over Renquist's face. "So that's it. That's what this is all about. The object is to drive a wedge between myself and Cynara. Am I right?"

Julia responded with a smile of her own. "You're absolutely right, Victor. I'm trying to drive a wedge between you and Cynara."

Now Renquist was really surprised. "You admit it?"

"Of course I admit it."

"You're incredible."

"And you're so blind."

"I am?"

"You're too blind to see that I'm only driving a wedge between you and Cynara because I want you for myself."

Renquist took a deep breath. Julia's seduction was beginning to work. A heat was building inside him, and only the persistent belief that he was being lured into some kind of trap stopped him from surrendering to it. "After all we've been through, I really can't believe you."

Julia's eyes closed and her lips parted. Her voice became the velvet growl of a wolf in heat. "I want to hunt with you, Victor."

"And what about Carfax? What about your bond with him?"

Julia's eyes flashed angrily. "Carfax is a boy! You have a thousand years on him."

Renquist took a firm grip on the parapet rail. "This isn't going to work."

"You don't think so?"

"I really don't think so."

Julia leaned even closer, until her face was just inches away from his. She slowly undulated her body. "I'd be good for you, Victor. Cynara has drawn your fangs. She's made you small. She's diminished you."

Renquist said nothing. Tempting and primitive images were invading his thoughts. He and Julia bonding together, right there on the roof and then going down into the city to run and hunt.

"Why don't you kiss me, Victor?"

Renquist could feel the warmth of her breath. Beneath the perfume it had a uniquely sweet, carnivore smell. Julia had fed in the last twenty-four hours. When was the last time that he had smelled fresh blood on the breath of a female?

"Why don't you kiss me, Victor? Taste my lips. They'll convince you."

Renquist was off balance. He couldn't pretend otherwise. He was nosferatu, a creature of cravings and desires. Even a Master couldn't be expected to exert limitless control. Julia reached out and touched his chest. Her hand slid inside his shirt, and her teeth gleamed white in the moonlight. Her voice sunk to a low purr. She was using the power on him. "Kiss me right now, Victor."

Her hand suddenly ripped downwards, tearing the buttons from his shirt, baring his naked chest. "Don't resist, Victor. You will kiss me."

Renquist was overwhelmed. He didn't even want to resist. The call of blood was too strong and too passionate. He was in a vortex of scarlet. His hands gripped her shoulders, pulling her to him. Her mouth rose to meet his and fuse their hunger.

And then the second voice came from the doorway to the roof.

"Victor? Are you out there?"

Cynara!

The spell was broken. The scarlet place collapsed in on itself. Renquist lurched back against the parapet rail as Julia spun around to face the intruder with a furious hiss. "What do you want here, female?"

Cynara must have realized in an instant what she had interrupted and, in her own fury, she spat back at Julia. "You dare to put your hands on him?" Then she glowered at Renquist. "Are you really that vulnerable, Victor?"

Renquist tried to frame some kind of an answer or explanation, but Cynara didn't allow him the time. The blast of her disgust hit him like a physical force. He sagged against the rail, his shirt hanging open and his head spinning, caught in the vice of conflict between what he was and what he was expected to be. Renquist was, however, merely a bystander in the confrontation. He may have been the trigger, the catalyst, even the cause, but the dislike and hostility between Julia and Cynara ran old and deep. The rage of the two women boiled over, burning and swirling in front of him, like angry liquid fire, clashing maelstroms of unchecked energy, surging across the roof.

As Renquist tried to compose himself, both Cynara and Julia started to change. Their outward resemblance to twentieth-century human females fell away before his eyes. Their shoulders hunched, their muscles tensed, hands turned to claws and teeth became bared fangs. Julia stood her ground, half-crouched, ready to do battle as Cynara advanced across the room towards her. For a fraction of an instant, it almost seemed that Cynara had somehow used the lost art of shape-shifting to turn herself into the snarling wolf form, but then Renquist realized that it could have been an illusion created by the backwash of frenzy.

And then the women were on each other and that was no illusion. They became two beings of pure blazing hate, nothing remaining but the primeval desire to tear each other limb from limb. Teeth flashed and clawed hands slashed, seeking eyes and flesh and hair to rip and rend. Power and loathing cloaked them like angry clouds, while Renquist stood, temporarily paralyzed. He knew that two nosferatu using all of their awesome strength in naked combat were more than capable of destroying each other, and maybe him along with them, but at the moment they fell upon each other he was powerless to intervene, mesmerized by the concentrated spectacle of unholy violence.

With an almost unnatural effort, Renquist pushed himself away from the parapet rail. Something snagged his torn shirt and pulled it from his shoulders. For a second, it hung like a defeated banner, then fluttered down to the street below. Renquist, however, had no time to think about shirts. He was doing his best to shut out the mayhem and focus on recovering his own power. If only Lupo was in the Residence. Together, the two of them might have had the strength to halt this madness, but Lupo was somewhere out in the night, hunting the enemies of Mr. Taglia of Elizabeth Street. Gradually, though, Renquist felt a fresh energy growing inside him as necessity tapped into his deepest resources. He waited for as long as he dared, allowing this final flare of power to reach a temporary peak, while Julia and Cynara wrestled and staggered, hands round each other's throats, each looking for the killer opening or the murderous advantage.

As Renquist's strength returned, so did his confidence. He took a step forward and used the voice at median force. "Will you both stop this?"

The women hesitated for a split second, then went at it again. Julia even used the brief respite to hurl herself at Cynara, carrying her to her knees with savage momentum. Now Renquist put all the power that he could summon behind the voice, letting it roll out like thunder. *"I said stop this!"*

Cynara and Julia froze in mid-conflict. Although Renquist didn't know it at the time, humans were also halted in their tracks for two full blocks around the Residence, minds momentarily washed blank by the shout he had loosed. Cars came to a sudden stop and were immediately rear-ended by other drivers who hadn't blindly braked as their minds were seared by Renquist's nosferatu primal scream. The next day, the whole of downtown would be rife with stories of freak tornadoes and rogue earth tremors, and TV news items on the mysterious shockwave would air on channels Five, Nine, and Eleven and be picked up by CNN.

Cynara was the first to recover. She got slowly to her feet attempting to pull together her shredded clothing. "Victor, I . . ."

Renquist's voice dropped to an angry hiss. "Silence!"

"I didn't . . ."

Renquist bared his teeth in a snarl. "I told you to be silent."

Julia was gathering up Elizabeth Taylor's rubies, which had been scattered by the violence. For a moment, she looked as if she was about to say something, but then thought better of it. The satin nightgown had been entirely ripped away, but the vivid slash marks Cynara had inflicted on her body were already fading as her nosferatu metabolism worked its miraculous damage control.

Renquist looked from one woman to another, breathing deeply as the shock of using the voice at full stretch slowly dissipated. He stood shirtless, Julia was naked, and Cynara in rags, a graphic demonstration of the fragility of their civilized veneer.

"Have you both succumbed to total insanity?"

Cynara straightened her spine, reasserting as much dignity as she could with her clothing torn and her hair disordered. She fixed Renquist with a glacial stare. "Were you really about to bond with her?"

Julia picked up the last of the rubies and also got to her feet. "Tell her, Victor, were you about to bond with me? I'd be interested to know myself."

Renquist experienced a moment of guilt, but he angrily thrust it away. "I am not about to be questioned like some errant human husband. I am the Master of this colony. The time was when one in my position might bond and hunt with a dozen of the opposite gender. I don't recall being informed that the rules had changed."

Julia moved so she was standing slightly behind Cynara, and flashed her rival a look of triumph. She held the rubies in her cupped hands. "So perhaps you don't own him after all?"

Renquist glared at Julia. "I suggest that you remain silent until I tell you to speak."

Julia opened her mouth to protest, but then abruptly closed it. She seemed to realize that this was a radically different Renquist. Apparently Cynara didn't make the same connection. She turned on her heel and started walking towards the door to the roof. "I don't have to listen to this."

Renquist's voice snapped after her. "Stay exactly where you are."

Cynara turned and stared at him in complete amazement. "You dare to speak to me like that?"

"I believe it's high time that everyone in this colony learned the meaning of the word Master. If the two of you want to fight like alley cats, why shouldn't you be treated as such?"

Cynara could scarcely believe what she was hearing. "Victor . . ."

"Why did you come up here?"

Cynara still seemed at a loss for words. "I . . ."

Renquist gestured impatiently. "Yes?"

"I came up here to tell you about a videotape that I discovered in the playroom."

"A videotape?"

Julia pursed her lips. "I can imagine what videotape that is."

Renquist glared at her. "I told you to be silent." He looked back to Cynara. "What is this videotape?"

Cynara motioned towards Julia. "She and Carfax made a tape of the death of Chelsea Underwood."

Julia looked bleakly at Cynara. "Actually Blasco made the tape. Kurt and I were merely two of the performers."

Cynara was about to say something but Renquist cut her off. "I want to see this tape."

Both women looked shocked. "Now?"

"Right now."

"After what happened? You expect us to watch a video?"

Renquist nodded. In a strange way, he was actually starting to enjoy himself. Just to issue orders rather than to be constantly considering the correct path of diplomacy came as a heady relief. The conflict was now out in the open and Renquist could only act accordingly. "That's exactly what I expect. You're neither of you actually harmed, are you?"

Both women shook their heads. "No, but . . ."

"Then go and put on fresh clothing. I will be waiting in the playroom."

The screen flickered and a grainy black and white close-up of Chelsea Underwood appeared. The lighting was harsh and amateurish, and she stood against a wall of unfinished brick. At first, the camera held on her face in tight closeup. Her eyes were heavy-lidded and half-closed, as though she was either drugged or under some hypnotic influence. After about five seconds, the presumably handheld camera pulled back, wavering and unsteady, to reveal that she was still wearing the dark green leather jacket and skirt that Renquist had seen her in at Section Eight.

As the camera moved, she frowned and squinted, apparently dazzled by the lights and unsure as to what was happening to her. Her diction was slurred and she appeared to have difficulty forming words. "What . . . are you people doing?"

In total contrast, when Carfax's voice came from somewhere offscreen, it was mockingly assured. "Nothing that you have to worry about."

"But I don't know where I am."

"You're with us, Chelsea. And we're going to have fun."

In the playroom, Renquist turned from the screen and looked at Julia. "Where is this tape being shot?"

Julia at least had the decency to shift uncomfortably. "In a loft in the west twenties."

"One of the little homes away from home that you, Carfax, and the rest of the gang maintain around the city?"

Julia nodded. "You know about those?"

"I'm not completely out of touch."

On the screen, Chelsea Underwood raised a hand to shade her eyes. "What are you doing back there?"

The offscreen voice of Carfax answered. "We're making you into a movie star."

Underwood giggled and shook her head. "I don't believe you. You just want to make amateur pornography." She swayed slightly. "And after that, you'll probably try and blackmail me with it. Except you can't blackmail me, because everyone knows I'm a slut and will do just about anything with anyone to prove a point."

"So why don't you take your clothes off for the camera?"

Even reproduced on tape, Renquist could tell that Carfax was now using a low power voice on Underwood. A side effect seemed to be that it caused her to shake her head as though trying to remember something she couldn't quite dredge up through the murk that was clouding her brain. At one point she muttered to herself. "I swear I've heard that before . . ."

Then Julia's own throaty rasp came from the speakers, cut-

ting her off. "Of course you've heard it before, darling, probably hundreds of times. So why don't you just do as you're told
and take your clothes off?"

Underwood gave a final, helpless shake of her head. The
memory was gone. Renquist suddenly realized that he was the
only person, either in the playroom or present at the obscene
videotaping who knew what she was talking about. She had
heard Carfax using the nosferatu power voice and, somewhere
in her fogged memory, it had triggered a reminder of the time,
two years ago, when he had used the voice on her. She wasn't
remembering the tone or timbre of a voice but the effect it had
had on her.

The video camera closed on Underwood's hands as she fum-
blingly started to unbutton the leather jacket. Carfax mockingly
encouraged her. "That's right, Chelsea, take it off."

She slipped out of the jacket and dropped it to the floor. Now
she stood framed from the waist up, clad only in a black bra.
One strap dangled loose off her shoulder. As if in a trance, she
unzipped the leather skirt and let it fall around her ankles. She
blinked a couple of times and peered at the camera. "Are you
getting all this? Is this what you freaks want?"

As though in response, the camera pulled further back to a
full-length shot of Underwood in bra, panties, garter belt, and
stockings. She attempted to strike a lingerie pin-up pose but
stumbled and momentarily went out of frame. When the camera picked her up again, Julia, dressed to kill in a black bodystocking, sunglasses, and cruelly exaggerated high heels, was
standing behind her, holding her steady. With her free hand,
Julia unhooked Underwood's bra and pulled it free. She
dropped it on the floor and used the same hand to cup the
human's breast. She gently caressed the nipple with two fingers.
"Does that feel nice?"

By way of response, Underwood's eyes closed and her face
went slack. She sighed and leaned back against Julia. The fa-
miliarity of sexual stimulation seemed to afford her a false sense

of much-needed security. Behind her back, an evil smile spread across Julia's face. "Of course, sweetie. Of course it feels nice."

The video was starting to make Renquist feel profoundly uncomfortable. He had known Chelsea Underwood and even liked her, in so far as a nosferatu could have a liking for a human. The young ones had no need to be treating her like this. Again, he turned and looked at Julia. "Are you proud of this endeavor?"

Julia continued to stare at the screen, avoiding his eyes. "No, I'm not proud of it. It was done mainly to amuse Carfax and Blasco. They're close enough to their human past to enjoy this kind of thing."

Cynara, who was sitting on the other side of the playroom, scowled. "You don't look as though you're finding the experience exactly unpleasant."

Julia's head snapped round, but before she could say anything, Renquist raised a commanding hand. "No more of that."

On the video monitor, Carfax, helped by Julia, was securing Underwood's wrists with a length of white rope that seemed to be attached to some unseen hook or beam above her head. The rope was then pulled tight, so she hung helplessly, arms dragged upwards, suspended by her wrists. Carfax momentarily went out of frame, and then reappeared holding a thin-bladed dagger. Underwood's eyes remained closed but her face twisted anxiously like a sleeper in the grip of bad dream. Carfax stroked her hair to calm her and her face took on a strangely serene expression. Quickly, Carfax reached around her body and skillfully cut a vertical slit about an inch and half long in the right side of Chelsea Underwood's throat. As the blood appeared, he put his mouth to the wound and drank.

Renquist hit the stop button, and the monitor dissolved into unfocused snow. "I think I've seen as much as I want to."

Julia stood up. She seemed to have regained some of her previous truculence. "What's the matter, Victor? Does the tape disturb you?"

Renquist, in his new authoritarian mood, wasn't willing to tolerate any further nonsense from Julia or anyone else. "Yes, Julia, the tape does disturb me. Its very existence disturbs me. On one level, it's a piece of arrant stupidity to make a permanent record of our so-called crimes. I want this tape, and any other copies that may be around, destroyed right now."

Julia immediately protested. "You can't destroy the tape. Blasco made it, and it belongs to him."

As far as Renquist was concerned, the subject was not open to negotiation. "You still don't understand what's happened tonight, do you? The tape will be destroyed. If Blasco has a problem with that, he can complain to me about it."

Cynara looked hard at Renquist. "And what's the other level on which the tape disturbs you, Victor?"

Julia immediately echoed the question. "Yes, Victor, what is this other level?"

Renquist turned and faced Julia. He didn't bother to keep the contempt out of either his face, his voice, or his obvious aura. The image of Julia, in bodystocking and high heels, pornographically preparing Chelsea Underwood for the slaughter, was still strong in his mind, as was the fact that he had all but bonded with Julia a little less than an hour earlier. "No excuse exists for that kind of behavior. The kill should be fast and painless. We are predators by nature, but that doesn't mean that we also have to become sadists by preference."

Renquist got to his feet and popped the cassette out of the VCR. With Julia, though, old habits died hard and she couldn't resist one final sarcastic barb. "So what are you saying to us, Victor? That we shouldn't play with our food?"

Three video cassettes went into the flames, and, when Renquist was satisfied that they had been completely consumed, he slammed the cast-iron firedoor of the big, old-fashioned furnace. The furnace had been used countless times to destroy the remains of a kill, but, as far as he could remember, it was the first time that it had ever been employed to eradicate the electronic record of one. Julia and Cynara stood on the other side of the cellar, watchful and silent, waiting to see what he was going to do next. Renquist knew that he had the two females well off balance, and for the time being he intended to keep them that way.

"Now I want to see Blasco and Carfax."

Julia spread her hands. "There's nothing I can do about that. They're both out in the city somewhere."

"No doubt looking for new ways to endanger the colony. Are they together?"

"I don't know. I had other plans for tonight."

Renquist nodded. "Yes, you did, didn't you?"

"Perhaps if they return before dawn . . ."

Renquist shook his head. "No, I will see them at sunset tomorrow. In the gallery. You will be responsible for making sure they receive the summons, and ensuring that they are there. I have plans of my own for what's left of this night."

Cynara looked at him questioningly. "Plans?"

"Is there any reason why I shouldn't have plans?"

Cynara quickly shook her head. She seemed to have decided that watchfully submissive was the way to go with Renquist in his current frame of mind. "No, Victor, no reason at all."

"I intend to spend the rest of the night hunting."

Renquist had dropped a bombshell. Both women's auras displayed their surprise and, just a moment later, the question that sprang simultaneously into their two minds. Renquist couldn't help laughing. Neither of them seemed totally capable of either reading or understanding him. "And now you want to know which of you I intend to take hunting with me?"

Julia voiced the response the pair of them. "It has to be one of us, doesn't it, after all that's happened?"

Renquist permitted his aura to show how amused he was. Cynara immediately grew angry. "You have to make a choice, Victor."

Julia grinned slyly. "Unless, of course, you're planning to hunt with both of us."

With a motion of his right hand, Renquist treated Julia to a small, exclusive vision that showed her how the remark about not playing with her food had effectively extinguished any spark that might have been kindled between them. Julia's smile faded and she gestured to Cynara. "Then you hunt with her?

Cynara's aura blazed in triumph, but the triumph was short-lived. Renquist firmly shook his head. "Tonight I hunt alone."

chapter Three

The cab driver was Haitian. According to his license, his name was Francis Charles Pastorelle. During the ride, Renquist had routinely scanned the man, and was fascinated to discover a mind so distorted by religious misconceptions and so filled with demons and zombies that it seemed to have trapped him in some place midway between perceived reality and a spirit world of his own creating. For the unfortunate Francis Charles Pastorelle, the streets of New York City were a labyrinth of dark and dangerous mysteries. He lived in fear, not only of tangible menaces like muggers, police officers, the Taxi and Limousine Commission, and the ethnic Haitian underworld that preyed on immigrants like himself, but also an extensive pantheon of evil supernatural entities.

Even random combinations of numbers on the taximeter, or coincidental occurrences like three black birds on a telephone wire, could break him out in a sweat of irrational dread. He was constantly on guard against devils who floated on the night air waiting to devour him. He couldn't walk more than a block without agonizing about the shapeless evil things that lurked beneath the ground, in the sewers and subways, intent on dragging him into their sinister realm. From the corner of his eye, he constantly imagined that he saw the shadowy forms of the walking dead who, according to his convoluted belief system, haunted the nighttime streets and alleys, waiting to steal his soul and drag him to eternal slavery in some nether hell of infinite agony. His ultimate worry was the sinister Baron Samedi, who commanded the whole malevolent army and seemed to like nothing better than to create torment and misery for hapless taxidrivers.

To protect himself against the more real, temporal dangers, Renquist observed that Pastorelle kept an unregistered .38-calibre revolver hidden under the driver's seat of the Chevy cab. For the metaphysical threats, he made frequent offerings, performed sacrifices, and attended ceremonies at a storefront voodoo temple way up on 177th Street. He also hung a rosary from the rearview mirror and carried a powerful monkey skull charm in the glove compartment.

Renquist couldn't help but find it amusing that, despite all of the driver's fears, phobias, and precautions, he didn't have an inkling as to the nature of the being he carried in the back of his cab. He had no clue that he was riding with a passenger who could, should he expend the effort, make Baron Samedi's mythic horrors look like pathetic child's play. Obviously Pastorelle wasn't among the ones Lupo feared, one who was possessed of the ancient ability to recognize nosferatu for what they really were. Renquist was once again reminded of how humans were so narrowly selective in what they chose to believe. Although maybe that was just as well. If humans ever came to suspect the truth—the real truth—either about themselves or the world that they inhabited, the shock would probably tip them over into lemming-like self-destruction. And then, as essential parasites, what would the nosferatu do for a host species? Would they have to farm the survivors the way the humans raised beef cattle?

As the cab headed across town on Houston Street, Renquist

toyed with the idea of making the driver his victim and sparing him the further horrors of his hag-ridden life, but decided against it. Pastorelle was the kind who could well die of shock long before Renquist ever tasted a drop of his blood. It was also possible that the *houn'gan* or a *mam'bo* woman up at the 177th Street temple might recognize the signs and know what had befallen this unfortunate member of their flock. How had Lupo put it: "those who remember the old ways"? By far the most persuasive reason to spare the driver, however, was also the most mundane. On his first lone hunt in so long, it was a little pathetic to settle for the first randomly encountered human. It lacked any vestige of class. Thus, instead of killing Francis Charles Pastorelle, Renquist had him stop at the corner of 26th Street and Park Avenue South.

For a few moments, after he'd paid off the cab, Renquist stood at the curb watching its taillights merge with those of the other northbound traffic. He savored being alone and away from the Residence with all its claustrophobic burdens. The weight of time hung less heavily upon him and he felt positively young again. Like the old TV show used to say: "There are eight million stories in the Naked City." He might as well find one that afforded him a little interest before he terminated it. A breath of warm wind gusted across the intersection, one of those wind spirals that twist between buildings, part of the city's unnatural ground-level weather patterns. The long black raincoat Renquist had thrown over his shoulders on the way out of the Residence momentarily billowed like a batwing cape. Renquist smiled to himself and started walking.

The density of humans on the sidewalks of the city in the early hours of the morning was exactly the way Renquist liked it. Enough still roamed the streets to make it interesting, but not so many of them that their thoughts became an oppressive intrusion. He was able to walk and browse, looking into minds and reading thoughts and auras, gauging the moods and feelings of these creatures on which he would ultimately feed, but who also shaped the milieu in which he lived and moved. After walking for a number of blocks, he found himself in the night marketplace of the streetwalkers just to the south of Grand Central Station. Even though it was well after midnight, the air was still heavy with heat and humidity. The women were both practically and professionally clad in the scantiest of costumes. They gathered, skittish and nervous, in the doorways of the closed and shuttered stores and the silent office buildings, keeping one eye on the sidewalk and the other on the moving traffic. Every so often, one, two, or even a small group would suddenly skitter out, showing themselves to what might be a prospective trick in a curb-crawling vehicle, ready to scatter and run if the cruiser proved to be a prowling vice cop. One girl, a pretty, dark-haired Puerto Rican, was all but causing traffic accidents by using nothing more than a white teddy, stockings, garters, and a G-string to show off a lithe body and long legs that deserved better than a doorway on Park Avenue and quickly bestowed thirty-dollar blowjobs in the passenger seats of passing automobiles.

A burly black girl, teetering in white thigh boots with four-inch heels, and with a face turned into a clown mask by garish blue eyeshadow and purple lip gloss, stepped into Renquist's path. "Hi, honey, looking for a date?"

A hooker was the last thing Renquist was seeking. They were too easy, too vulnerable. Hookers were only for nights when all else failed, when no other prey presented itself, or when dawn was closing in and time was too short for finesse. With a single fast pass of his hand, he temporarily blanked her perception and quickly sidestepped. The black woman wouldn't even remember he had existed.

Another spiral eddy of street wind swirled the pages of a discarded newspaper up into the air. The newspaper was a copy of the one with the picture of Chelsea Underwood's body on the front page. A second woman, who had remained half-hidden in the same doorway from which the black girl had made her foray for business, caught Renquist's attention by registering a sudden flash of dull alarm at the flutter of newsprint. She was a skinny little thing with tiny breasts, dirty blonde hair, and a figure like a boy, a runaway from some miserably dysfunctional home in the agricultural Midwest, the classic castoff of the hopeless heartland. Even from a distance, he could read how her thoughts were clouded from smoking speedball cocktails of rock cocaine and heroin from a sheet of heated tinfoil. When she saw Renquist, she appeared to recognize something about him that caused her aura to glow dirty emerald. She was hardly able to fake even a token allure, and her come-on was nothing more than a plaintive cry. "Hey, baby, what about me?"

Renquist paused for a moment and looked at her. Her mind was a place of sluggish terror where extremes of pain were only held back by an overpowering, although very transitory, numbness. It could only confirm for Renquist that, when a woman like her, who might have once lived a productive, blue-collar life, had no alternative but to sell herself into misery, mindlessness, and degradation, this phase of human society had to be well into its downward arc. Right at that moment, she wanted him to want her. She was telling herself that she had to get more money. Someone called Shake was back in a cheap hotel room, waiting on her to return with the cash so he could feed his multilateral drug habits. If he wasn't pleased, he would more than likely beat her. He used a doubled-over length of electrical cord when he inflicted these regular and protracted punishments. She was telling herself that her sudden flash of attraction to Renquist was all about money, but Renquist knew better. What she'd seen in him was an opportunity for merciful death.

Dietrich had once suggested that victims presented themselves because they were either fated shortly to die, or because they desperately sought death but lacked the courage to organize it for themselves. The skinny whore certainly had the aura of a victim, but this was not Renquist's night to dispense fatal charity. The likelihood also existed that the woman's narcotic-saturated blood would turn out to be toxic to his nosferatu metabolism. As he had with the first woman, Renquist blanked her with a single pass. She too would remember nothing about him, although a terrible sense of loss and disappointment would linger with her for some time.

Renquist had always been of the opinion that the relationship between the nosferatu and his or her victim was more complex than many of his people imagined. Some of his kind hardly recognized that any relationship existed at all. They slew indiscriminately, with little or no regard for the mood or welfare of the host species. A long time ago, in Africa, Renquist had watched a lioness moving through a herd of gazelle, stalking the one particular beast she had instinctively selected as a target. The designated victim had appeared sick and lame, and, as the big cat crept towards her prey, the other deer in the herd exhibited only a minimal nervousness. They sniffed the air and twitched their ears, but it wasn't until the lioness made her final killer rush that the herd broke and ran, leaving the sick one to its fate. Renquist had sensed what amounted to an instinctive trade-off between lioness and gazelle herd. As long as the cat selected her victims from those gazelle least equipped for survival, she was able to kill with ease and the herd benefitted from a continuous and ongoing strengthening of its collective gene pool by culling out the ailing and the weak.

While Renquist would never claim that any such symbiotic transaction was in effect between nosferatu and humans, he tried to conduct his hunting much in the manner of that lioness. When Renquist stalked the night, he looked for the outcasts, the ones who were in the process of slipping through the cracks, the members of the human herd who had limped and stumbled, and those who were so deeply unhappy that they actively courted death. The prostitute on Park Avenue had simply been too polluted, too close to carrion. Renquist was wampyr enough to have a need to take pride in his conquests, but, in general, the principle held good. When he killed, he chose those who would not be missed or contributed nothing to the general well-being of their kind. Some nosferatu, particularly the young and the recently transformed, scoffed at Renquist's theories and called him a hypocrite, claiming that his ideas were nothing more than guilt responses, the product of an over-weening morality.

Hypocrite or not, though, Renquist hunted the way he chose to hunt, and that was why, on this specific night, he prowled the dark streets, seeking exactly the right victim, the one he knew was somewhere in the city, already waiting for him.

He finally found her just a few minutes after three o'clock in the morning. She was seated on the last barstool at the end of the bar in an old-fashioned, late-night drinkers' saloon at Third Avenue and 21st Street, a place of nicotine-dark wood, ranked liquor bottles, and antique beer signs, with a jukebox that played records by Billie Holiday, Frank Sinatra, and Tony Bennett. She was in her late thirties, well-dressed and dark-haired, good-looking, except that her mouth had recently lost a pre-vious generosity, and defeat was clearly etched in the circles under her eyes. In front of her was a Dewar's on the rocks that was far from being the first of the evening, and an ashtray that contained the butts of a half-dozen Marlboros with lipstick traces. Renquist noted that she had positioned herself so she didn't have to look into the mirror behind the bar.

As was often the case with victims of this type, it was she who spotted Renquist even before he recognized her. As he came through the door, her eyes widened and her aura shimmered with a thrill of fear. She started to say something, as though Renquist was an acquaintance she recognized. Then she real-ized that, in actuality, he was a perfect stranger, and she was overtaken by a sudden confusion. In that first widening of the eyes, however, she revealed a story to him that, although by no means unusual in the night and the city, seemed to her to be the terminal edge of personal disaster and shattered dreams. Her name was Fay Latimer and, until four months ago, she had held a respectable job as an editor of romance novels at a major publishing house and enjoyed a seemingly stable relationship with a real-estate broker from Long Island.

Although vaguely dissatisfied, she had considered herself happy enough, but then a series of massive hammer blows had smashed her life into wrecked and dislocated ruin. Her job had been eliminated in a pogrom of corporate downsizing, and, with her age and narrow range of experience acting against her, she had so far been unable to find another. The Long Island boyfriend had also dumped her for a younger, more status-enhancing bimbo. Now her money was all but gone, and she was only consuming scotch because, by some miracle, her credit card still held up.

The only other customers in the place were a solitary man drinking himself into melancholy depression and an adulterous couple with no other place to go except to a cheap hot-sheet hotel room, the potential of which they had already exhausted. The bartender had cultivated a professionally jovial personality and an archaic waxed mustache, both of which were good for tips, but also served to disguise a deep dislike of humanity in general. He straightened up as Renquist approached. "So what will it be, my friend?"

Renquist positioned himself so he was sitting with three empty stools between himself and Fay Latimer. He laid out a gentle, tentative mental massage, soothing her into believing he was harmless, and planting the idea that she might like to speak to him. Then he turned his attention to the bartender. "An Absolut on the rocks, if I may."

The bartender set the drink in front of Renquist, and Renquist paid him. Using money after two years was still something of a novelty. As he took the first sip of the cold vodka, Latimer lit another cigarette and looked in his direction. "Do you remember David Niven, the actor?"

"Of course."

"You kinda look like him."

Renquist smiled, suavely amused. "You think so?"

Latimer nodded solemnly. "Oh, yes. Indeed."

In fact, the resemblance was largely illusionary and a creation of Renquist's. Not shape-shifting, just a suggestion planted in Latimer's mind, which was already sufficiently dulled by scotch that she would never know the difference. When he had first probed her, he had tangentially learned that the actor represented the ideal father she never had, and he decided to play on that as a means to overcome her natural New York reluctance to speak to strangers in bars in the middle of the night.

"I'm flattered you think so."

"Of course, you don't have the English accent."

"I also don't have a Hungarian accent."

Latimer frowned. "I don't understand."

Renquist smiled disarmingly. "Just a private joke."

Latimer was suspicious. "I don't like private jokes."

"Forgive me."

"Maybe."

"Perhaps I could buy you a drink?"

"That might help me forgive you."

Renquist signaled to the bartender. "A Dewar's for the lady."

Suspicion returned. "How did you know I drank Dewar's?"

Renquist had overreached himself, but he deftly covered his slip. "It just seemed right."

This appeared to satisfy Latimer. Again she was too drunk to think it through. As the bartender filled her glass, Renquist changed stools so he was sitting right next to her. The move produced a sad resignation in the woman, akin to a passive form of self-destruction. She didn't want a man, but she also didn't want to go home alone to an empty and depressing apartment where her only options were late-show TV or sitting and listening to the air conditioner. Her remaining self-respect left her unanxious to face the reality that she had become the kind of lonely alcoholic slut who could be picked up in a bar by any stranger with minimal charm. On the other hand, his attention was at least flattering to her on what she saw as her downward curve, and she hardly had the energy to reject him should he make the suggestion. So the son of a bitch turned out to be an axe murderer or refused to use a rubber. So fucking be it. That would be the culmination of her karma. She remembered how, back in the eighties, when she had been the perfect stereotype of the grasping, upwardly mobile bitch, red in tooth and nail polish and armored by Gucci, a freewheeling musician friend had warned her that the next decade was going to see a lot of disappointed yuppies. "You won't all get a gig as corporate vice presidents." And now she was one of the disappointed. After all of the dedicated scratching, gouging, and attempting to claw her way to the top of the heap, she had wound up penniless and loveless, totally screwed and seldom fucked. At best, this vodka drinker in the black raincoat might represent a temporary shelter in her continuous personal storm.

As Renquist followed this train of thought, he knew, if any confirmation had been needed, that she was the one. Her shredded self-esteem would demand that he buy her a couple more drinks and expend a little more charm and small talk, but at the end of the process she would leave with him. He also suspected that, when the final and terrible revelation came, she would accept it with the same fatalism that currently colored most of her daily existence. Accordingly, he talked, he charmed, he went inside her and caressed her ego, and sure enough, at quarter to four, just five minutes before the bartender would announce last call, he didn't even have to make the suggestion. She leaned close to him. "Why don't you take me to your place?"

"Why don't you take me to yours?"

Latimer sagged, as though the last straw of the night had finally dropped. "Oh shit, you're fucking married."

"I'm not married."

"So why do we have to go to my place?"

"Because I live in Jersey."

She laughed and shook her head. "There was a time when that would have been enough for me to drop you like a hot rock."

Renquist smiled and went along with the game. "There was a time when I never would have lived in Jersey."

Latimer slid from her stool. "Then I guess you better come to my bijou residence on Fifteenth Street."

The building in which Fay Latimer lived had originally been constructed as a single-occupancy home, back in the early part of the century when families were extended and employed numerous servants, and 14th Street had been the lateral axis of fashionable Manhattan. As the population grew and the smart addresses moved progressively further north, it and all the similar houses on the block had been remodeled and subdivided into small, one-bedroom apartments.

As soon as they left the bar and hit the air, the scotch Latimer had consumed hit back. Renquist found that he had to take her arm to support her as they walked south on Third Avenue. As he gripped her elbow, she leaned against him with a sigh. "You have strong hands."

"I like to keep a grip on reality."

"You say some strange things."

"Only at night."

As they climbed the front steps to her building, Latimer stumbled and almost fell. Renquist had to grab for her and pull her to her feet. The distraction was just enough for him to miss seeing the individual in the stained combat coat standing on the other side of the street between two parked cars, staring at him with an expression of shock and horror.

* * *

The apartment was neat and furnished in what had passed for urban professional taste in the eighties, although Renquist noted as Latimer removed her coat and went through into the small kitchen that there were a number of lighter rectangles on the walls where pictures had once hung but had since been removed. Apparently she had been selling her small collection of art to keep up the mortgage payments on the apartment.

"You drink vodka, right?"

Renquist nodded. "That's right."

"I'm afraid I've only got scotch."

"I don't really need a drink."

"Well, I do."

She came back into the living room with a tumbler of straight scotch. "This isn't something I normally do. You realize that, don't you?"

"I know."

She was suddenly looking for a reason to dislike him. He had forced her to admit her own needs and desires, and she hated that. "Why are you so damned understanding?"

"Because I'm not what I appear."

The glass stopped halfway to her lips. "What's that supposed to mean?"

Renquist removed all controls and suggestions. "I think, deep down, you know that already."

Latimer swallowed half the scotch in a single gulp. "I think I need to lie down."

Renquist followed her into the bedroom. The time for mere mortal words was now passed. In a single seamless vision, he showed her who he was, what he was, and what was about to happen to her. Her breath came out in a long sigh; she seemed almost relieved. "You're my nightmare, aren't you?"

Renquist nodded. His voice was very gentle. "Yes, I am."

"Will I become like you once I'm dead?"

Renquist shook his head. "No, you won't become like me."

She smiled sadly. "That's a pity. It might have been interesting."

"I'm sorry."

She suddenly frowned as though she'd just thought of something. "You won't hurt me, will you?"

"No, I won't hurt you."

"I mean, you can do it in a way that's quite painless, can't you?"

"It will be quite painless. In fact, I will make it extremely pleasurable."

She let her head fall back on the pillow and closed her eyes. "Then please do it. Do it now."

As Renquist left the building, he stood for a moment on the street and carefully looked around. The only possible witness was a figure in a combat coat leaning on a hydrant, but he was so obviously one of the great ragged army of the derelicts that threatened to choke the city, Renquist didn't bother either to block or read him. New York was getting worse than Constantinople during its decline, and a certain fastidiousness in Renquist's character made him avoid the minds of such human flotsam. They were too violent, too confused, and too filled with images that even he found offensive in their brutality. He had killed and fed and he felt better than he had in a very long time. He certainly didn't need this creature's bitter, psychotic hallucinations to spoil his sense of well-being. He walked quickly to the corner with a spring in his step, humming an Italian folk melody that had suddenly sprung into his mind from the fourteenth century. Without looking back, he hailed a cab. Had he turned, however, he would have seen that the wino was doggedly following him.

Evil. Gideon Kelly sensed evil as he had never sensed it before. A reeking stench of foulness that was as final as an epitaph, as persuasive as the plague. Gideon Kelly knew he was not mis-

taken. He had spent most of his life on intimate terms with evil.
Where evil was concerned, his instincts were sharp and precise.
When the evil passed so close by him, brushing him with its fetid
wing, right there on 15th Street, he knew there was no mistake. Neither nightmare nor illusion was deceiving him. His legs
became weak, his stomach churned, and for almost a full minute
he had to cling, doubled over, to a fire hydrant, only stopping
himself from vomiting with the greatest concentrated effort.
Gideon Kelly was in an extreme state of shock. He had encountered the Devil in the very heart of Manhattan.

In the first moment, he had thought it was the woman. She
was drunk and without shame or propriety, leaning against the
tall man in the dark coat, who held her to prevent her falling.
He had quickly realized, though, that such an all-consuming
wickedness was more than any squalid barfly tramp could hope
to achieve. This evil was very different from the wretched but
mundane depravity of the female. This evil was hellbright and
vibrant, radiating a power old and complex, finely honed, arrogant, and infinitely knowing. Furthermore, it had been well
hidden for a very long time, weaving its spells, casting the net
formed by the vectors of its iniquity, growing almost compla-
cent in its absolute sense of security and power. And yet Gideon
Kelly had sensed it and recognized it for what it was. Only for
a moment had he been confused by his long struggle against
the lures of womankind. When the confusion cleared, he saw
with a hideous clarity. The tall man in the black coat that
flapped like a cape, if not Lucifer himself, was at least one who
ranked high in Hell's hierarchy and stood very close to the Dark
Prince's throne.

The woman and the evil one entered a building together and
Gideon Kelly could do nothing but stand and watch. His mind
raced but his body refused to move. He no longer had to lean
on the fire hydrant for support, but neither could he walk away.
To encounter such a fiend while out on one of his solitary
night walks could hardly be dismissed as mere chance. Either

this Devil had been sent to him or he had been guided to it by the Infinite Cruelty of his God. He didn't know if it was a sign or a test or perhaps a snare, and to discover the answer was a prospect terrifying in the extreme. And yet he continued to wait. He prayed that his appointed task wasn't to bring down this Monster from the Pit, but he feared that he prayed in vain.

Gideon Kelly waited in the street for the Devil to emerge. If need be, he was prepared to wait all night. The more he thought about it, the more he realized that this encounter was almost certainly a test, or, to be more precise, the commencement of a test. To challenge the fiend, to destroy it, to return it to the frozen netherworld from whence it came, might well be the price of his own redemption. It could be the single act that would readmit him to Grace. How a weak, drunken, and abject sinner like himself could rise from his degeneracy to vanquish such a mighty source of evil was a question he was fearful to ask. He had questioned his God before, and that had consigned him to the slime in which he was currently drowning. For the moment, Gideon Kelly was content simply to wait and let the trials of the future reveal themselves at the appointed time.

The first revelation was only a matter of minutes in coming. To Kelly's surprise, the front door of the building quietly opened and the Devil came out. The Devil paused on the top step. He seemed to be checking the street before proceeding. Kelly could only assume it was a Devil who wanted no witnesses. It looked straight at him but registered no response. Clearly a Devil who didn't believe that a mere drunkard could pose any threat. The Devil walked quickly to the corner and Kelly followed at a distance. Somewhere in the city, the Devil might have its lair, maybe in the company of others like itself. Kelly knew that his first task was to track the Devil and locate this lair. He couldn't pretend otherwise. His path to redemption lay through the very heart of the blackest sin.

At the corner, the Devil stopped and hailed a cab. For a moment, Kelly was shaken in his resolve. It had been years since he had taken a cab. It had been years since he had possessed the money to take a cab. But, on that night, he actually had the money. Only that morning, he had cashed the cheque that had been sent to him by his brother Fillmore. Another sign. As he flagged down the very next passing hack and climbed inside, he could hardly believe what he said to the driver.

"Follow that cab."

A practical caution caused Renquist to stop his taxi some five blocks north and three blocks east of the Residence. Presumably the police would at least go through the motions of investigating the killing of Fay Latimer, and there was always the outside chance that the driver, despite the block Renquist had placed on him, could have his memory triggered in some way and come forward with the information that he had picked up a fare near the victim's building within the supposed timeframe of the crime. The police already had an interest in the Residence, and to go directly there would be unreasonable folly.

Although he was meticulous enough to take the precaution, Renquist's mood was such that the need for it rankled him. After a kill, caution was something to be thrown to the wind. How dare these inferior humans, with their telescoped lives and their isolated and befuddled senses, force him to skulk and deceive? The beast within him was awake and alive. It wanted to run and howl until the pearl glow in the eastern sky made the first announcement of impending dawn. His whole being surged with burning energy. For the first time in seven years, he was free of the dissatisfaction, the soul hunger, and the constant craving. He had feasted and now felt complete and real.

All around him, the nightcity breathed; its colors were intense, its pulse like a distant orchestra. Each prowling cat, each scurrying rat, and the thousands upon thousands of sleeping humans made their contribution to the background radiation of raw vitality. It tempted him to go on and on, consuming and luxuriating in the consumption. The beast-desire wanted to run mindless and unchecked, killing until it could kill no more, but high-spectrum light, beyond the range of human vision yet plain to Renquist, was diffusing through the high clouds over the ocean, a warning that the night had less than two hours to run. He would kill no more, no matter how seductive the prospect. Renquist hadn't survived for a thousand years by succumbing to the recklessness of post-kill euphoria, or abandoning basic caution to the insanity of the beast.

This second cab driver was at the end of a double shift and close to exhaustion. He thought in some obscure Arabic dialect that was virtually unintelligible to Renquist, despite all of the time, from the Crusades onwards, that he had spent in the Near and Middle East. He couldn't, however, miss the flicker of fear as the man touched the twenty that Renquist proffered to cover the fare. Clearly, life in the so-called civilized city hadn't totally buried the man's deep desert perceptions.

Renquist tweaked the man's fear by smiling his most saturnine smile and all but baring his fangs. "Keep the change."

Renquist derived a certain modest pleasure from overtipping. He took a lot from humanity, and it pleased him, now and again, to give the poor brutes something back in the form of unexpected alms. The driver's surprise at receiving a twenty for a five-dollar fare clashed with his moment of unreasoning fear and combined with it in an uneasy confusion. The man grunted, and accelerated away, happy to be free of his disquieting passenger. Renquist laughed and began walking. Humans were truly such fogbound creatures.

Renquist strolled slowly, taking his time, listening to his regular footfalls echo back to him from the silent downtown buildings, savoring the solitude of this time before dawn. One of the countless homeless and helpless lay sleeping in a doorway, half-concealed in a nest of cardboard packing material, gripped by a dull, hopeless nightmare. Renquist toyed for an instant with the idea of going to excess, of quickly taking the man and draining him. As Renquist's streetlamp shadow passed over the bum, he stirred uneasily in his drab dream-state. Suddenly his dream had become vivid and threatening, and from out of nowhere a vision came of a black horse with red, glowing eyes pawing at the soft, pungent earth of a freshly filled grave. The man let out a desolate groan, but Renquist smiled and shook his head. *Dream on, human. I will not harm you.* The drinking of this one's blood was altogether beneath a wampyr of his status. It would be shamefully declassé, not to mention that the bum's polluted blood would quite likely destroy his currently excellent mood. *Tonight the black horse has dug at some other's grave.*

A tangle of scarlet ribbons lay discarded in the gutter. Probably some fallout from one of the remaining garment shops that had yet to be priced out of the neighborhood by relentless gentrification. Renquist stooped down and picked up a single strand of ribbon about twelve inches long and slowly looped it around his index finger. Centuries ago, during the Thirty Years' War, Renquist had been the nominal warlord of a troop of mounted boyars, savage night-riding brigands who roamed the ravaged lands of northern Germany, fighting for any prince, Protestant or Catholic, who could feed them and pay their price in gold. Before going into battle, his men had tied lengths of blood-red ribbon, very like the one he was holding, around the unsheathed blades of their sabres. Should one of them return from combat with his ribbon still intact, he would be judged a coward and hacked to pieces on the spot by his comrades. No excuses were accepted, and Renquist's time with the boyars had rid him of any lingering pity he might have felt for the human species. He slipped the ribbon from his finger and let it flutter to the ground.

The Devil stooped and picked up something from the gutter. Gideon Kelly was maintaining a healthy distance between himself and the Evil One, too far to see what had taken his fancy.

Back when he had followed in the cab, a moment of panic had gripped him when he thought he had lost the taxi carrying the demon, but then he saw it halted at the curb. His heart had leapt, though at the same time his stomach had churned. Inside the cab, he felt secure and unobserved. Alone on the street, it would be a whole different matter. Nevertheless, spurred by the excitement of his newfound mission and equally newfound courage, he had leaned quickly forward and hissed at the driver, "Pull over and let me out! Pull over right here!"

The driver stamped on his brakes, and Kelly was pitched against the steel and plexiglass partition that separated passenger and driver. As he picked himself up, the driver had cursed Kelly in a language he didn't recognize. Kelly had ignored him. He was too taken up with watching the other cab. A dark figure had emerged from its interior. Kelly was gripped by a sudden surge of triumph. He was still in pursuit, and the Devil didn't seem to suspect a thing. He felt a power like he'd never known, except maybe while conducting mass in the days before his fall. The driver was looking at him expectantly. Kelly fumbled in his pockets and handed the driver the exact amount on the meter. The driver snarled at the lack of a tip, but Kelly was already climbing out of the cab. "Away with you, you Third World fornicator!"

Kelly moved quickly down the sidewalk, fearing he might again lose sight of his quarry in these unfamiliar downtown streets. The Devil appeared to be in no hurry, however. He strolled and sauntered. Every now and again, he even stopped to look at something along the way. He paused to stare down a bum sleeping in a doorway, and peered into the window of a closed café. At no point did he betray any awareness that Kelly was dogging his heels. Perhaps God was already protecting Kelly, wrapping him in a new Cloak of Righteousness.

For some minutes, the Devil seemed to be merely wandering aimlessly, and Kelly began to worry that he was being made the butt of some demonic ruse to walk him around the city until he was exhausted, leading him nowhere. Kelly certainly wasn't about to accept that the Devil was exclusively a thing of the streets, without a sanctuary or bolt-hole from where he could work unseen at his iniquities. And then the Devil turned onto a street with a row of elderly, four-storey townhouses on one side. Even before the Devil started up the steps of one of the buildings, Kelly knew that this was the place. This had to be the satanic lair. One could always count on Evil to have immaculate taste both in dress and in place of abode. The townhouse was no Gothic pile or dark, mysterious mansion. From the outside, it resembled nothing more than the home of perfectly normal, if rather affluent New Yorkers. It was certainly far finer than any place Kelly had ever been able to call his own.

The Devil stopped for a few moments outside the front door of the building, apparently working his way through a complicated set of locks, both electronic and mechanical. Seemingly the Devil didn't rely on magic alone as protection against temporal intruders. Using parked cars as cover, Kelly moved closer, hoping that he might catch a second glimpse of the face of Evil. He was all but close enough when the Devil completed the ritual of the locks, opened the front door, and went inside. Kelly straightened from where he'd been crouching behind a blue Toyota Celica. Now he was alone in the empty street, disappointed that he hadn't been able to get a clear look at his enemy, but still elated that his life now had a structure and a purpose. The night had been far from in vain. He took a pencil stub and a scrap of paper from the pocket of his combat coat and made a careful note of the address of the building that the Evil One had entered. He carefully folded the paper and, with a deep sigh, put it away in his breast pocket.

"Oh yes, my friend, I shall return. You can count on that. If Lucifer's a gambler, you can even bet on it."

The door closed behind Renquist and he leaned against it for a second before going on into the Residence. A sudden sense of fatigue had come over him. He wasn't sure if it was merely a natural result of the coming dawn, or whether his previous sense of elation had been dispelled by re-entering the building with its now tainted atmosphere of intrigue and in-fighting and nosferatu under stress snapping at everything that moved. And then, just to further complicate matters, as he stood with the euphoria draining out of him, he heard the sound of women chanting.

"Ph'nglui mglw'nafh fhatgn."

The phrase was sung in a weirdly discordant 14-note scale that hadn't been heard in the world of men for many thousands of years, but was still a singular part of the secret music of the undead. The call phrase was intoned by a single voice that he immediately recognized. Cynara was conducting the ritual and, most likely, consolidating her power in the process.

"Dia ad agaidh's ad Aodaun."

The responses, half spoken and half sung in the same pattern by massed voices, all of them female, produced eerie, uncomfortable harmonies that could set dogs howling and men sweating in their sleep. The language was as old as the nosferatu themselves. Older than either Latin or Greek, it went all the way back to the days when the Great Ones had ruled the earth and his kind had originally been born of their monstrous experiments.

"Ph'nglui mglw'nafh fhatgn."
"Dia ad agaidh's ad Aodaun."

The Aodaun ceremony was one of gender bonding, conducted exclusively by the females of a colony. The males had a similar ritual, although it was a great deal more violent and noisy, involving as it did the beating of drums and cymbals and a considerable volume of stylized aggression. Both ceremonies were equally ancient and both had largely fallen into disuse in the industrial world. That Cynara should have revived one of these at this time said a lot for her awareness of the perils that faced the colony, although he suspected that, in part, she had organized the ritual on such short notice to gain an advantage in the simmering conflict between herself and Julia. Whatever Cynara's root motives, a revival of the ancient ways could only be a positive move for the colony as a whole, although, at that exact moment in time, it was possibly the last thing Renquist needed. At the climax of the ceremony, in the very instant before the first sliver of sun appeared over the horizon, he, as Master, would be invited to enter the otherwise closed ritual and expected, in deeply symbolic display, to allow the women to partake of his energy.

"Ph'nglui mglw'nafh fhatgn."

"Dia ad agaidh's ad Aodaun."

"Damn it to hell."

After adding this muttered coda, Renquist squared his shoulders and walked on down the hall. The chanting was plainly coming from the library. Renquist might have expected Cynara to have staged the ceremony in the effectively soundproofed playroom, but, as he thought more about it, he realized that the library actually made a lot more sense. The women really had no need of soundproofing. Males might be excluded from the proceedings, but that didn't mean they should not be aware of what was taking place or hear the sung reminder of distaff power reverberating through the building. The library also had definite aesthetic advantages. The playroom was too functional and high-tech, and also tainted by Carfax and the other young ones staging their cruel and unusual games there. Better to use the library. The rows upon rows of bookshelves with their antique leather volumes, the deep gloss of the old dark mahogany and the carved gargoyles, provided a quasi-ecclesiastical background for what was, after all, one of the most solemn of the nosferatu rites.

As Renquist approached the library door, he saw that Segal was standing in the shadows, surrounded by a satisfied aura, deep burgundy in color, that wreathed him like expensive cigar smoke. Renquist halted a few feet from the door and raised a questioning eyebrow. Was Segal actually eavesdropping on the women? Perhaps even spying? It was hard to know how exactly the minds of grotesques functioned. So many of their thought processes seemed to be couched not in conventional language but in unfathomable patterns of images and symbols.

"I thought you were hunting with Lupo."

Segal slowly nodded his massive head. "The contract was completed and we returned some hours ago. Lupo does not waste time when he kills."

Renquist smiled. "I can imagine. I trust all went well."

"Lupo seemed pleased with his night's work."

"And you?"

Segal's blank white moon-face showed not the slightest trace of emotion. "It was a learning experience for me."

"So what are you doing here?"

"When I returned, the females made me the Watcher at the Door."

Renquist bowed slightly, acknowledging Segal's role in the ceremony. Apparently Cynara, and whomever else she might have conspired with to set up the Aodaun, were observing the esoteric details of tradition, right down to having a lone male stand guard at the approach to the area where the ceremony was taking place. In the ancient days, when the Aodaun was held on wind-blasted mountainsides, or in the nightchill of desert caves, the Watcher at the Door was posted with the highly practical purpose of guarding against humans and other intruders. Here in New York, the Watcher could only be a vestigial piece of history, perhaps with certain overtones of one gender proving a point to the other. Renquist also knew that before the Aodaun itself, a preliminary rite was enacted between the women and the Watcher. Although Renquist had never experienced it firsthand, he had heard that it was both highly tactile and highly pleasurable for the male. Perhaps this was a second reason, in addition to having hunted with Lupo, that Segal was exhibiting such a self-satisfied aura.

"And has being the Watcher at the Door also proved educational?"

"It has certainly put me in touch with the ancient ways."

Inside the library, the chanting continued.

"Ph'nglui mglw'nafh wgah'nagl fhatgn."

"Dia ad agaidh's ad Aodaun."

"Ph'nglui mglw'nafh wgah'nagl fhatgn."

"Fhatgn leat-sa ad Aodaun."

The sung response had changed. Renquist stiffened and half smiled at Segal. "I believe that's my cue."

Segal nodded. "Those were my instructions. The Master enters when the response makes the final change." The door of the library silently opened and the smell of musk-heavy incense wafted into the corridor.

The females came at him in a semicircle. The library carpeting had been removed from the floor, and their bare feet made soft whispers on the polished wood. Each woman wore the ceremonial *alluai,* a one-piece, tabard-like garment, black with red trim, belted at the waist with a gold chain and decorated with the symbol of the coiled *leat-sa.* The alluai extended to the wearer's ankles, but, having no sides, allowed her the freedom to perform the complex contortions that were demanded at certain key points in the Aodaun. It also revealed very plainly that the wearer was otherwise naked. Directed auras, purple and magenta, rose above each female, arching like threatening talons, down and towards Renquist. Thick perfumed smoke rolled from a glowing brazier, and tall iron candleholders were arranged at the points of the hexagon that was central to the ritual. The women's faces were set and predatory, mouths open, lips drawn back and teeth flashing, arms outstretched, clawed hands reaching towards him in a stylized ballet of slow-motion menace. Most terrifying of all was the sound that came from those hungry mouths, part snarl, part hiss, an intense and wordless expression of lethal intent. Even though Renquist was familiar with the sound and the choreography of this final phase of the ceremony, he had to exert a degree of control to hold his ground in the face of their coordinated advance.

"Dhonas s'dholas."

The women informed him that he was helpless against their combined power. Renquist widened his eyes, hunched his shoulders and ritualistically folded his hands in front of him, fingers interlaced.

"Ayaet ytrwne!"

His snarl was the reminder that he was their Master and he would resist any power they might bring against him. This climactic portion of the ceremony was, at one and the same time, symbolic play-acting and absolute reality. Masters who had faltered in that split second before the rising of the sun had been torn apart by their female followers and their remains thrown out to smoke and burn in the daylight. The Aodaun was not only a role-playing reinforcement of bonding and authority, but also a very practical test of the Master's fitness to survive.

"Dhonas s'dholas!"

The threat was louder this time. The purple light grew more intense. The air in the room was so thick with incense that it was scarcely breathable. A weakness in his legs and a hollowness in his stomach told Renquist that, outside in the world, the moment of dawn was very close. He looked from face to face, Cynara at the center, Julia and Sada directly to her right, Dahlia and Imogene, the strange sisters, on her left. Not one of the five gave any indication that they were playing the ritual in anything but deadly earnest, or that he could expect the slightest mercy if he weakened. As dictated by tradition, Renquist took a step forward, allowing his own crimson aura to rise like unfurling wings.

"Ayaet ytrwne!"

The women pressed forward.

"Dhonas s'dholas!"

Renquist knew it was the moment to use the voice. *"AYAET YTRWNE!"*

Like a pitched note shattering a fine wine glass, the mood in the room was blown apart by Renquist's violent response. The females halted and stood motionless, their eyes directed downward and their auras fading to a supposedly demure blue. Cynara stepped forward and formally knelt before him. *"Nal ayaet. Sil Ayaet-sil."*

Her voice was soft and submissive. Such was the final movement of the ceremony. First the challenge and then, if he could face that without flinching, the bowing to his superior power. Before the Feasting began in earnest, Lupo would almost certainly insist that the males conduct their own ritual, the Pualdis. Renquist wondered how Carfax would handle the moment of submission at the end of that ceremony.

As was expected, he graciously acknowledged Cynara's symbolic submission. *"Ytrwne."*

He brought out his steel spike in its silver sheath. In a single swift motion, he penetrated a vein in his wrist. Blood immediately started to flow. He extended his bleeding arm to Cynara. She gently took hold of his hand and covered the wound with her mouth, drinking deeply. After a few seconds, she withdrew and rose to her feet. *"Nal ayaet."*

Renquist repeated the response. *"Ytrwne."*

Now it was Julia's turn. Renquist suspected that she wouldn't be able to complete her act of submission without some token revolt against convention, and, sure enough, as she took his hand, she raised her eyes to his, letting the slightest flash of defiance pass between them. Then she too drank his blood. *"Nal ayaet."*

"Ytrwne."

Sada came next and, after her, Dahlia, the first of the sisters. Dahlia had been created nosferatu while still a child of nine or ten and she had elected to stay that way through all the passing years. Although she was dressed in the alluai for the Ao-daun, she normally affected a perverse Victorian image, Alice in Wonderland dresses with white lace and blue bows, white stockings, tiny gold shoes, and blond Shirley Temple ringlets. Only her white dollface with its bright rosebud mouth and dark-circled baby blue eyes told of her real nature. Despite its childishness, Dahlia's face had the remorselessness of the hunter. As she bent over Renquist's wrist, her eyes glittered at the sight of his freely flowing blood. In total contradiction to those eyes, her voice was a high, girlish lisp. *"Nal ayaet."*

"Ytrwne."

Her sister Imogene was something else entirely. She had been brought across in her early teens, some said by her own younger sister. Imogene was tall but painfully thin and oddly insubstantial, with skin that verged on pale blue and was all but transparent. She also totally lacked hair anywhere on her head or body, a loss that was reputed to have occurred during her transition from human. Normally her clothing was flowing and diaphanous, as wraithlike as she was. Apart from her lack of hair, she resembled a figure in a Maxfield Parrish painting, or maybe a pupil of Isadora Duncan, which apparently she had been at the time of her conversion. Renquist scarcely felt her lips on his wrist, just a faint cold breath chilling his blood. When she spoke her submission, her voice was nothing more than the sound of two ice cubes rubbing against each other. It struck Renquist that Imogene might actually be trying to become invisible.

"Nal ayaet."

"Ytrwne."

Colony rumor claimed that Imogene wrote epic and ex-tremely depressing poetry that she showed to no one but her sibling. Although the sisters were full members of the colony, and, as in the case of the Aodaun, they would perform any com-munity duty that was expected of them, they rarely mingled with the others, preferring to spend the greater part of their time in the rear basement rooms they claimed as their private domain, and which no one else was ever allowed to enter. They rarely left the Residence except to hunt, and their hunting habits were the subject of even more colony rumor. These claimed that Dahlia, using her child persona as a lure, made all of the kills, and even after some ninety or more years still fed her sister like one of the newly created. If even half the stories about Dahlia and Imogene were true, the sisters were weird to the point of major maladjustment, even by the highly permissive standards of the undead. As long as they followed the rules of the colony, though, which was something they did with scrupulous correctness, how they lived was of no concern to Renquist or any of the others.

As Imogene straightened from Renquist's wrist, the ritual was completed. Ever since Cynara had drunk of his blood, his legs had felt progressively weaker, to the point where he was now having difficulty staying on his feet. The rite of feeding the females had dangerously drained him, and as they filed past him on their way out of the library, he remained standing only with the greatest of effort. The effort was required by tradition, however, and to collapse after the bloodletting would have been extremely bad and very risky form.

Finally, when they all had left, Renquist sagged. Segal was immediately at his side, supporting him. "Are you harmed?"

Renquist shook his head and waved Segal away. "No, no, I'm fine. I just need to sleep. I need to sleep right now."

The ceremony must have drained Renquist even more than he had originally suspected. He found he had no control over his dreams. Even in his deepest of daysleeps, he always managed to maintain a thread of sentient consciousness that afforded him the power to steer the scenarios of his fantasies. On this day, they came at him unbidden and unchecked. He found himself once again riding to battle with his boyars, as he'd done all those centuries before. His dreamscape took the form of a roaring nighttime holocaust—towns and villages burned, bodies swung from mass gibbets, and rival armies staggered forward and back, locked in mortal combat. The air was filled with the stench of death and a society breaking down into barbarism. The thunder of cannon and musketry was deafening, combined as it was with the roar of flame, the clash of steel, the howl of shot and shell, and the death-screams of gored and mutilated men.

He rode at the head of his cavalry troop on a massive horse with eyes like glowing coals, the same dream-beast that had invaded the nightmare of the bum in the doorway. He had no time to ponder the significance of the horse. His boyars were close to suicidal in their driven need to gallop into the thickest and most deadly areas of the fray, with plumes tossing and red ribbons fluttering from the honed blades of their sabres. Renquist was fully occupied with staying in front of the headlong charge. Over on his right, a church collapsed in on itself, its spire toppling in an incandescent galaxy of sparks as fire ate through the roofbeams. A troop of Zouave lancers from a totally different era came at them, and the boyars hurled themselves at the enemy in full frontal assault. Renquist found himself surrounded by dark-skinned men in red tunics and round spiked helmets, so close that he could see their gold earrings and flashing eyes. Furiously he slashed and hacked with his sabre. Blood was everywhere. The black horse seemed to be wading in a crimson river. His arms were slick with the blood of Zouaves. It spattered his silver cuirass and soaked the white cloak that streamed from his shoulders. And yet, even though he was in the thick of the fighting and his sword arm ached from wielding the weapon, the red ribbon still remained attached to the blade.

Finally the surviving Zouaves scattered and ran. A roar of cheering went up from his boyars. They turned to him as their leader with grins of savage triumph on their faces. Then they saw the red ribbon still on his blade and those grins hardened. No words were possible. His ribbon was intact after the battle, and therefore he had to die. It made no difference that he was their captain and liege lord; in these circumstances, death alone held dominion. The boyars advanced on him with drawn swords, and he had no choice but to stand his ground and accept the inevitable.

And then the voice, followed by a violent alpha-jerk, shattered the dreamstate, and the fantasy was derailed in the nick of time. "Victor . . ."

"Victor . . ."

The voice belonged to Cynara. Renquist's eyes remained closed. Let her believe that he couldn't hear her.

"Victor, you must wake."

Renquist sighed and opened his eyes. It was impossible to deceive Cynara. Also she had saved him from the boyars. He had no idea what might have happened had the dream run its dangerously uncontrolled course. "We went already went through this."

"And it's happening again."

Renquist lay motionless. It was time that someone else took care of the colony's troubles instead of constantly running to him. "You know what Aodaun did to me? You know how long it takes to recover from something like that damned ceremony?"

"Victor, please . . ."

Renquist closed his eyes, determined to return to the dreamstate, whatever it might prove to be. "It isn't even sunset yet."

"The police are back and Carfax is threatening to make a complete fool of himself. His arrogance is making him stupid."

Renquist knew he couldn't duck the responsibility. "Kurt Carfax should burn in the sunlight."

Cynara looked grim. "We could all burn if you don't go down and throw a net over him."

Carfax waved a limp but dismissive hand. "What is the name of that Oscar Wilde play? *A Woman of No Importance*? I think that adequately sums up Chelsea Underwood as far as I'm concerned."

As before, the intruding detectives were McGuire and Williams. A muscle twitched in McGuire's cheek. Carfax's blasé attitude was obviously irritating him, or maybe worse. "The woman's dead, pal."

Carfax sighed as though the whole business was just too boring. "And how am I supposed to react to that, Detective McGuire? People die in this city every day. Isn't the average three murders a day?"

"This was a woman you knew."

"Barely."

This time the interview was being conducted in the library. As Renquist stood in the doorway, taking stock of the situation, he was surprised to note that someone had already cleaned up after the night's ritual. McGuire sat facing Carfax, while Williams remained on his feet, wandering the room inspecting various items, just as he'd done during the pair's previous visit. Right at that moment, the black detective was studying the bookshelves, head inclined to one side to read the titles on the spines of Renquist's collection of German philosophers. Then he turned and stared balefully at Carfax. "You could have been the last person to see her alive."

"I greatly doubt that."

McGuire leaned back in his chair. "And why's that?"

Carfax permitted himself a faint but superior smirk. He was dressed in a hastily pulled-on, dark-green robe, and his hair was tousled as though he'd just been roused from his bed. He looked every inch of his chosen human persona, the young, dissolute, and probably degenerate wastrel. "The killer would have been the last person to see her alive. And I'm certainly not the killer."

"That's your story."

Carfax's smirk broadened. "Yes, and I'm sticking to it."

McGuire and Williams exchanged a glance but said nothing.

Their silent ploy yielded immediate results. Carfax couldn't resist giving them a demonstration of his cleverness. "Just suppose I was the killer . . ."

Renquist decided it was time to intervene. He walked briskly into the room. "So you gentlemen are back already?"

Renquist was also wearing a robe and Williams took instant exception to this. "All of you people spend the whole day sleeping?"

Renquist smiled urbanely. "More moral judgments, Detective Williams?"

"Just an observation."

"There was something of a party here last night."

Carfax couldn't resist pushing matters one stage further. "The hours we keep are really our affair and no one else's."

McGuire shrugged. "I guess it's okay for some."

Williams refused to be faked out by Renquist's strategic entrance. He moved behind Carfax's chair and continued to press the point. "You were saying, if you were the killer . . ."

McGuire picked up the ball. "What would you do if you were the killer, Mr. Carfax?"

Renquist quickly interrupted. "These officers are busy men, Kurt. I really don't think they need to waste their time listening to your half-baked speculations."

Carfax looked sourly at Renquist. "I was merely going to say that if I was the killer . . ."

At that moment, a child's voice came from the doorway of the library. "Oh, I'm sorry. I only came to get a book."

Dahlia walked slowly into the room. She had taken the time to dress and do her makeup, and was wearing one of her seemingly infinite number of Alice in Wonderland costumes. "Who are these men, Uncle Victor?"

Renquist wasn't absolutely sure what tactic Dahlia had in mind, but he was quite prepared to play along. He spoke as though to a ten-year-old. "They're policemen, Dahlia dear. Like on television. They've been talking to your Uncle Kurt."

So far, Dahlia was exactly the right distraction. Williams turned to Renquist. "This is your niece?"

Renquist nodded. "That's right. Say hello to Detectives Williams and McGuire, Dahlia."

Dahlia curtsied to the cops. "Uncle Victor has been looking after me since my parents died."

In a way, this was true, except that Dahlia's parents had died well before World War I, and were reputed to have been killed by none other than her and her sister. Dahlia looked solemnly up at Williams. "Are you going to take Uncle Kurt to prison?"

Williams stooped down so his face was level with Dahlia's. "What makes you think we'd do a thing like that?"

"Isn't that what policemen do? Take people to prison?"

While Williams was occupied with Dahlia, Renquist took the opportunity to scan him and was instantly rewarded. Williams had a guilty desire for small girls. During the previous visit, Renquist had brushed against William's deeply repressed memory of the rape and murder of a young girl in Vietnam. Now more was apparently being revealed. The cop believed he was sexually attracted to Dahlia and loathed himself for the feelings he was desperately trying to wrestle into the safety of his subconscious. Renquist could also see the surface of Dahlia's mind. She was doing everything possible to bring out the worst in Williams, teasing every one of his guilt-ridden impulses, feeding him lewd and erotic images, and building a fever in his imagination that he was quite helpless to resist. What Renquist couldn't see were Dahlia's motives. Was she actively running interference for Carfax, or simply lighting a fire under Williams for her own amusement? Deliberately or not, she was effectively throwing a very large spanner into the efficient workings of the McGuire-and-Williams investigative technique.

McGuire, of course, had no idea what was being done to his partner, and was concentrating all his attention on Carfax. "There's something you ought to realize, kid."

Carfax's lip curled. "And what might that be?"

"This is a high-profile murder, and when there's a high-profile murder in this town, both the media and my bosses want to see results."

"Is that a fact?"

"It surely is, my friend. Everyone wants to see arrests. Suspects brought in for questioning. Penalty and due process. The whole bit. You know what I'm saying?"

"I'd strongly advise against trying to arrest me, McGuire."

"Would you, now?"

"In any case, you wouldn't hold me for five minutes. I'd have lawyers down on you so fast you'd be amazed. Alan Dershowitz is well within our price range."

Renquist was becoming angry. Either Carfax simply wasn't thinking or he was too stupid to realize that the Irish cop wasn't the kind that you threatened with expensive celebrity lawyers. To do so would only make McGuire dig in and become more determined to screw with him. If McGuire and Williams so much as walked Carfax to their car in handcuffs, something they were probably itching to do, he'd immediately burn up in the sun and the aftermath of that spectacle would be a disaster for the entire colony.

McGuire leaned closer to Carfax. "Let me tell you something, boy. We have ways of avoiding lawyers. We can run figure eights around lawyers. We can bounce you from precinct to precinct. We can lose you in the Tombs. You could shuffle your papers and have to vanish into Rikers for a week or more. How'd you like to get down with the psychos and mother-rapers, Kurt?"

Williams stood up, moving away from Dahlia. He gestured to McGuire. "Let's cut the crap and take the son of a bitch in for questioning."

For the very first time, fear dawned on Carfax's horizon. The deadly potential of what could happen had finally penetrated the barriers to reality thrown up by his inflated ego. "Listen . . ."

"We're listening."

"I didn't kill the woman. She glommed onto us for a while when we left Section Eight, but that was all."

"And then?"

"After a while she attached herself to some other people."

"What other people?"

If Carfax had been human, he would have been sweating at this point. "How should I know? Some Upper East Side Eurotrash. Not our kind of people at all. That was the way she operated. She kept moving. First she was with Victor, then she was with us, and then God knows what happened."

Williams' expression was grim. He was still trying to put the demons unleashed by Dahlia back in their boxes. "She died, that's what happened."

McGuire was more practical. "Why didn't you tell us all that in the first place? It would have saved a whole lot of time."

Williams answered for him. "Because the little snot was more interested in copping an attitude than helping us with our investigation. That's how it is with his kind of people."

Renquist took a deep breath. "I really don't think there's any need to sink to the level of insults."

Williams scowled. "I just call it as I see it."

"So it would seem."

"I don't like you people."

"You made that very clear on your last visit."

"And I've had no reason to change my mind."

"I hardly expected that you would."

Dahlia moved so she was standing beside Carfax. Her voice was as sweet as syrup. "Are they taking you to prison, Uncle Kurt?"

Carfax looked from McGuire to Williams. "I really don't know, pumpkin. That's up to the officers."

Renquist almost smiled as he observed Dahlia making a mental note. Sometime, when the crisis was passed, Carfax was going to pay for calling her pumpkin. Dahlia looked up at Williams with the same cloying sweetness. "Are you taking Uncle Kurt to prison?"

The demons were dancing in Williams brain again. He almost had difficulty forming words. "That depends on Uncle Kurt."

Renquist decided that it was time for him to assume control of this situation. When he spoke, he used just the faintest trace of the voice. "The child does have a point. Are you going to arrest Mr. Carfax? Because, if you are, I really don't think this should go any further without an attorney being present."

McGuire's eyes narrowed. "Now you're threatening us with lawyers?"

Renquist placed a calming mental overlay on the entire room, hoping that Carfax and Dahlia would pick up on what he was doing and refrain from making any further waves. "I'm not threatening anyone with anything, I'd just like to see this situation resolved, one way or another."

McGuire slowly stood up. "No, we're not going to arrest Carfax at this time. Not because we're afraid of any high-priced lawyer, just because we'd rather have a bit more hard physical evidence."

Not even a human could miss Carfax's obvious relief and McGuire regarded him with open contempt. "Before you start celebrating, though, be assured that you haven't seen the last of me and my partner. I still believe you know more than you're telling us about this business."

Renquist drew himself up to his full height and used a greater measure of his power. "Does that mean we can expect you to be invading our privacy on something like a daily basis?"

Renquist had to give McGuire full marks for courage and determination. Where a lesser individual might have withered, the detective neither flinched or faltered. "It means I'll do whatever I need to do until I have the killer of Chelsea Underwood behind bars. You know what I'm saying, Mr. Renquist?"

* * *

"And you are nothing less than a goddamned fool!"

Dahlia had started into Carfax with a vengeance from the moment that Williams and McGuire were safely out of the Residence, and her attack, coming so hard on the heels of Carfax's brush with the law, left the young one with nothing to do but to retreat in the face of the onslaught, mumbling excuses. "I knew what I was doing. I was just being cool with them."

Fury blazed around Dahlia as though her small body was on fire. "Cool? You were being cool? You really don't have a clue, do you? You don't have the slightest inkling of what constitutes cool and what constitutes fucking pig witlessness. You're nothing more than an arrogant little prick, Kurt Carfax, and even that's being fucking charitable. And if you don't wise up pretty damn fast, some asshole human is going to drive a big ugly stake through your hairless lily-white chest and into your sorry ignorant heart. And I for one won't shed a single fucking tear."

"That's if the rest of us don't toss you out into the sun to save them the trouble." Imogene had been standing silently just inside the door of the library ever since the two detectives had made their exit. Although her voice was little more than the softest whisper, the message was loud and clear. Carfax was now on very thin ice with the rest of the colony.

All Renquist could do was to stand back and watch the confrontation, relieved that, for once, he wasn't expected to lead the charge. Dahlia took a perverse delight in her foul mouth and could curse like a teamster when she felt the need. Obscenities had a disturbing force when they were screamed in a melodically lisping, little-girl voice.

Carfax apparently wasn't bright enough to realize that his only workable option was to shut up, stand still, and mutely accept Dahlia's wrath until it had run its course. Partway through the tirade, he made a second attempt to justify himself. "You seriously expect me to grovel at the feet of two stupid policemen?"

"Those two stupid policemen were quite ready to drag you downtown and book you—"

Imogene's whisper suddenly interrupted her sister. "Dahlia dear, I really don't think that they take people downtown and book them anymore. I believe that's only in old black-and-white movies."

Dahlia halted in mid-assault. "What?"

"I don't think they take people downtown and book them anymore."

Dahlia turned and looked at her sister. Renquist totally expected her to explode at the interruption, but her voice was suddenly soft and gentle. "Imogene dear, I'm trying to make a point to this young idiot here. I wasn't striving for detailed accuracy."

Imogene nodded, and Dahlia returned her attention to Carfax. "Wherever they would have taken you—"

Now Carfax interrupted. "They weren't going to take me anywhere. I knew that."

Now Dahlia reacted as Renquist had anticipated. Her rage rose to near critical level and she looked as though she was more than ready to do Carfax actual harm. "Did I ask you to speak?"

Carfax gestured to Imogene. "She . . ."

It didn't help anything. "My sister may interrupt me any time she likes. Such is the nature of our relationship. A little shit like you, on the other hand, keeps fucking quiet until I've done with him."

Carfax's aura turned a sullen puce, but he said nothing.

"I'll have you know that if the black one hadn't been a closet child molester, and I hadn't worked on that weakness for all I was worth, they'd have busted you without a second thought. And wherever they intended taking you . . ." She glanced at Imogene. ". . . even if it was only to lunch, you'd have been fried to a crisp before you made it across the fucking sidewalk. And that would have taken some explaining away."

"But it didn't happen. They didn't arrest me."

"No thanks to you."

Carfax was starting to regain some of his previous attitude. "Why do we have to be so damned afraid of two humans? If it had come to it, I could have crushed both of them."

Renquist's mouth became a thin uncompromising line. "Two trained and armed police officers are not quite the same as a bound and helpless woman. I think even you might have found them something of a challenge. It's broad daylight outside, remember? You're not that strong when the sun's up."

Carfax's face hardened. "I could have handled them."

Dahlia's anger came back to the boil. "And that's why I say you're a fucking cretin. Can you imagine the repercussions for the rest of us if two cops had walked in here and vanished without trace?"

Carfax squared his shoulders. "I really don't have to listen to anymore of this. Nothing happened and that's what ultimately counts. So if you'll all excuse me, I'm going to go back to sleep."

He turned on his heel and stalked quickly towards where Imogene was still standing by the door. Dahlia shouted after him. "You can run but you can't hide. You're an idiot and the sooner you recognize it the better."

Carfax walked straight past Imogene and out of the door as Dahlia got in one last shot. "And if you ever dare call me 'pumpkin' again, I'll drive a stake through you myself."

Renquist sighed and looked at Imogene. He also wanted to go back to sleep. "Do you think he learned anything?"

Imogene moved away from the door and came to stand by her sister. "Personally, I doubt it. Right now, he's probably imagining ways to be revenged on the whole pack of us."

By the time Renquist finally rose from his interrupted sleep, it was late evening, and the Residence was strangely silent. Perhaps they were all out hunting. Despite what fresh complications a night of mass hunting might produce, Renquist was relieved to have the place free of what he was rapidly coming to think of as an unwholesome collection of snapping, biting, quarreling carnivores. Something he had so far avoided thinking about was that, along with the Feasting, there frequently came a form of madness. The bloodlust could run so high that all rationality was driven before it. He had hoped that, living in an urban center as they did, the huge numbers of humans they encountered on every side would not only feed the lust, but also ground the worst of the insanity. Now he wasn't so sure. He had appealed to the collective reason of the colony, but that appeared to be unravelling like a cheap sweater. Dahlia and Imogene had emerged from seclusion. Carfax seemed to take a lunatic delight in flouting every dictate of common sense. Julia and Cynara were at each other's throats. Only Lupo, Segal, and Sada had so far shown no symptoms of this uniquely wampyr stress. And, of course, he wasn't affected. Or was he? Was his preoccupation with concealment and control the accepted responsibility of a Master, or was that his growing mania? And how did you recognize whether seeds of madness were indeed germinating and flourishing inside you? How did you find that kind of detachment and objectivity?

"If I had half a brain, I'd leave them. I'd find myself a high mountain and live as a hermit. Like Dietrich. Away from all these bickering animals."

But he knew that he wouldn't. He was welded inexorably to the group. He had functioned as part of a pack for too long suddenly to divorce himself from its obvious protection. Sometime in the future, he might go back to being a loner, but this was hardly the time to be making a sudden and precipitous break with a way of life which he had enjoyed for so long.

Renquist sighed, grudgingly bowing to the inevitable. He walked to his closet and selected a fresh black silk shirt. Renquist felt light-headed and weak, presumably a continuing aftereffect of the Aodaun. He wondered if that, combined with too many interruptions of his sleep, might be coloring his perception and causing him to view everything in such a dark and desolate manner. He was aware that, before the night was through, he would have to feed again or resort to the packaged blood. Neither prospect inspired any enthusiasm. He ought to have been excited by the anticipation of the hunt, but he found the idea strangely unappealing.

"That damned ceremony has thrown my entire metabolism out of whack."

He finished dressing and left the bedroom. The Residence was still as quiet as the communal grave. Apparently the entire colony was out there, slipping through the Manhattan shadows. The next morning should prove interesting when the humans rose from their beds and totalled the dead. Renquist started gloomily down the stairs, refusing to dwell on that eventuality until he absolutely had to. On the second floor landing, he paused beside the door of the formal dining room. It had been used quite regularly back in the days when Renquist had been strengthening the colony's financial base, when entertaining and interaction with humans had been both regular and necessary. He pushed open the door. For two long years, the room had been allowed to fall into neglect, until it actually looked like the Hollywood conception of the vampire's lair. The heavy antique furniture was thick with dust and festooned with cobwebs. A family of armadillos scuttled for their nests in the wainscoting. The way that armadillos inhabited the residences of nosferatu might be worthy of study, should Renquist ever have the time. The creatures had been doing it for so long that it now amounted to a tradition and even a sign of good luck.

Renquist walked down the length of the long dining table. He paused for a moment and wrote his name in the dust with his index finger. He wrote the old name, in the old script. Looked at it for a moment, and then wiped it away. It was possible that no living being even knew that name. Perhaps Dietrich, but what Dietrich now knew was a matter beyond conjecture. Renquist's mind went back to all the human guests who had graced that table, Henry Kissinger, Joan Collins, Edward Kennedy, the financier Ivan Boesky, even the entertainer Mick Jagger, who had been so totally unaware of how close he been to true satanic majesty. Julia had wanted to get Jagger drunk and bring him across to be one of them. Renquist had seen the humor of her plan, but he had reluctantly vetoed it. No individual so fully in the public spotlight could hope to conceal his new nature, and what Mick Jagger might get up to in nosferatu mode hardly bore thinking about.

In theory, the idea of the colony entertaining prominent humans at the Residence was both strange and should have been fraught with potential danger. Oddly, though, it had all been extremely simple. An outside catering firm had been brought in to prepare the food because clearly nosferatu, with no conventional sense of taste, could hardly do it themselves. The dinner parties were obviously held after sunset, so that was no problem. All that really remained, apart from a general securing of the house, was to cover the fact the nosferatu who were present at dinner never actually ate anything. This again turned out to be laughably easy. When the food arrived, the colony members just picked up their knives and forks and moved it around their plates, but never actually put it in their mouths, chewed, or swallowed it. Renquist had quickly discovered that the wealthy, influential, and celebrity guests were so self-absorbed that they failed to notice the lack of appetite on the part of their host and his companions. Also, it had been the greedy eighties. So much cocaine had been in circulation that someone toying with their food was completely unremarkable.

In fact, Renquist had kept the number of nosferatu present at dinner down to a manageable minimum. Cynara was always there, filling the role of the lady of the house—his wife, so to speak. Julia and Sada were included when the need arose for "young" vivacious single women, or when Julia absolutely insisted, as she had on the evening when Jagger had come to dinner. On one occasion, Blasco had been trotted out to charm Joan Collins.

Renquist idly opened the liquor cabinet. A few months earlier, Blasco had asked Renquist if he could take over the disused dining room to conduct his experiments. Renquist had said no. He wasn't quite ready to believe that the days of elegant dinners would never come again. The bottles in the cabinet were untouched since the last dinner party. He picked up a bottle of very fine Napoleon cognac, pulled the cork, and inhaled the bouquet.

"Am I interrupting you, Don Victor?"

Renquist turned at the sound of the familiar gravel voice. "No, Lupo, I was just remembering how things used to be."

Lupo looked round the room. "A lot used to happen in here."

"That's exactly what I was thinking."

Renquist showed him the bottle of cognac. "Would you care to join me in remembering those days?"

Lupo looked uncomfortable. "I have something to tell you that may displease you. Perhaps when you hear it you may want to reconsider the invitation."

Renquist blew the dust off two brandy snifters. "Share the alcohol with me anyway. If nothing else, it will make the telling of this thing easier."

Although outwardly Renquist was formal and correct with Lupo, he inwardly groaned as he carefully poured the cognac. He really didn't need any more bad news. Lupo sat down and dust billowed up around him. He seemed unconcerned whether he messed up his old-fashioned, double-breasted suit. Renquist was a great deal more fastidious about his clothing. He dusted off the chair at the head of the table before he seated himself.

Lupo picked up the proffered glass, swirled the golden liquor, and sniffed it appreciatively. "Isn't this the cognac we served when Senator D'Amato came to dinner?"

Renquist nodded. "You have an amazing memory."

Lupo shrugged. "Some things stick in one's mind for no reason. I recall thinking at the time that it was probably better than he deserved."

Lupo placed his glass on the table. "I'm afraid I have failed in a task that you set me, Don Victor."

"What do you mean?"

"You charged me to conceal the young ones' leavings. I'm afraid that I missed one. A drug seller by the name of Hector Vargas is in the city morgue. His body was found in a dumpster behind a pizza joint on One hundred thirty-ninth Street. The body was drained of blood, and I believe that Julia was responsible. Fortunately the police seem to think that it's connected to some kind of cult ritual. Voodoo or Santería, or something of that kind."

Renquist shook his head and smiled sadly. "I really didn't expect you personally to dispose of every body left behind by this round of Feasting."

"I did what I could."

"That's all that I ever expect of you."

Lupo picked up his glass again. "Thank you, Don Victor."

"How did you hear about this new corpse?"

Lupo tapped the side of massive nose with a stubby finger. "I have people in the morgue who tell me things."

"Do you also have people in the police department who tell you things?"

"Indirectly."

"Has any connection been made between this corpse and the Underwood woman?"

Lupo shook his head. "Not so far. The difference in gender will confuse them, but there's always the desanguination, the total loss of blood."

"Another body is waiting to be found in an apartment on Fifteenth Street. I also hunted last night."

"That was probably just as well. You might not have survived the Aodaun on a blood bag. Do I need to do anything about this body?"

"No. I arranged things so the body didn't immediately resemble one of our kills."

"I would expect no less of you, Don Victor. Was it a woman?"

Renquist nodded. "She seemed to welcome death."

"Those are the best kind, the ones who desire death and the ones who deserve it."

For a while, Lupo and Renquist sipped their cognac in silence. "It's strange to have the Residence so empty."

"It isn't entirely empty."

Renquist looked up sharply. "I didn't notice anyone."

"Carfax has shut himself in the playroom. When I looked in there, he had headphones clamped to his head, listening to that noise he pretends is music." Lupo, a lover of grand opera, had no time for modern music, with the possible exception of Frank Sinatra. "He's been like that ever since Dahlia bawled him out."

"At least he's quiet. How is it that he's not out littering the city with fresh corpses?"

"None of the women would hunt with him. The aftermath of the Aodaun bonding."

Renquist frowned. "The women are hunting together as a pack?"

Lupo shook his head. "No, the Aodaun didn't take them quite that far in their bonding, but they made it clear that they wanted no men with them."

Renquist chuckled. "I imagine Carfax took that personally. What are Blasco and Segal doing?"

"They too are hunting."

"Together?"

Lupo nodded, and Renquist thought about it. "Is that a good idea?"

Lupo didn't seem particularly concerned. "They're harmless

when they're away from Carfax. They went to the west side, prowling the old piers looking for derelicts. I persuaded them to resist the urge for females for a few nights."

"Do you think they will?"

"They'll try for a while; that's all that can be expected."

"I'm surprised Carfax took his encounter with Dahlia so hard."

Lupo looked at Renquist as though he had missed the obvious. "He was castigated by one whom he still essentially thinks of as a small child. His sense of invincibility is bruised and he's taking a little time to nurse the hurt. He'll be back causing trouble soon enough. Now he has resentment to drive him."

Renquist sipped his cognac. "What would I do without you, Lupo?"

"He's an evil one, that Carfax."

Renquist laughed. "Evil? Aren't we all evil? Aren't we supposed to be the personification of evil? By our very nature?"

Lupo shook his head. "Nature is nature, Don Victor. We are what we are and we do what we do. There's no evil in that. Evil comes by choice and by the exercise of will."

"So what makes Carfax evil? He exercises his will?"

Lupo nodded. "He's like a human. He thinks like a human. His body and soul may have been brought across, but emotionally he's obsessed with what he's become. He still can't believe his newfound power, and he sees nothing beyond it. Perhaps, deep down, he fears that one day it will all be taken away and he will wake to find himself weak and mortal again. He's cruel to prove to himself that he's really able to do it, and the more proof he receives, the more proof he requires. It pushes him to extremes. He inflicts pain for its own sake and kills for the sake of killing. He kills and does not bother to feed. That is not only cruelty, Don Victor, it is also wasteful, and waste is evil, as evil as self-indulgence and stupidity."

Lupo never ceased to amaze Renquist. His level of insight

was completely at odds with his seemingly brutal exterior. "You may have a point there, old friend."

"Hunting with Segal revealed a lot to me."

Lupo hesitated and Renquist looked at him curiously. "What is it? There's something else that you have to tell me?"

Lupo looked uncomfortable. "I'm not sure if I should say this."

"We're alone. You can speak freely."

Lupo took a deep breath. "I think it would be better for the whole colony if Carfax was killed."

"Killed?"

"That's what I said."

Renquist scanned Lupo's face. Neither his thoughts nor his features revealed a thing. Renquist spoke very carefully. "So far he's done nothing that would give me reason to expel him from the colony."

Lupo's gaze fixed on Renquist's. "I said nothing about expelling him from the colony."

"You mean simply . . ."

"I mean kill him."

"That would be against the most basic code."

"He's determined either to take over this colony or destroy it."

"But we don't kill our own kind. It's one of the most ancient traditions."

"He's attempting to learn the techniques of creation. He's dreaming of converting humans to provide himself with a following of slaves."

"You got all this from Segal?"

"Carfax makes no secret of it when he's around the other young ones."

Renquist sighed. "He'll learn it isn't as easy as he imagines."

Lupo's expression was grim. "By that time, the damage would be done. I have given this a good deal of thought, Don Victor. Carfax, with a gang of slaves behind him, could create havoc in this city, a reign of terror. We both know how mind-lessly savage the newly created can be. As you've said yourself many times, our surest protection against the humans is the hu-mans' own disbelief. If ever they come to accept the reality of our existence, we could all be destroyed. It would be like the Slaughter of 1919 all over again."

"You've certainly thought this through."

"And I've come to the conclusion that he should be killed."

Renquist slowly set down his glass. "Killing him would in-deed circumvent a great many problems. But if we just killed him . . ."

Lupo answered for him. "We'd be outcasts, damned in the eyes of nosferatu the world over."

"We kill in anger, and we kill in combat, and we also kill by formal expulsion. What we do not do is to plot to murder our own in cold blood. That is human behavior."

Lupo looked hard at Renquist. "I'm not saying that you and I kill him together. I would do the deed alone and I alone would take the responsibility."

Renquist could detect no Feasting madness in Lupo's flinty stare, but he imagined he could feel it in the air. "I can't allow that."

"As you said, it would circumvent a great many problems."

"I'd be forced to expel you from the colony."

"I would survive."

For a moment, Renquist was tempted. To have Carfax gone would make his life a great deal easier. On the other hand, he knew this would have to be played by the code. Lupo would expect nothing less, and the colony without Lupo was un-thinkable. With great finality, Renquist shook his head. "No."

"No?"

"I cannot allow you to take such a weight upon yourself. We will find some other way to deal with Carfax."

"That's your last word on the subject, Don Victor?"

"That's my decision."

"The offer will remain open should you change your mind."

Renquist reached out and placed his hand on Lupo's. "I know that."

The two men sat for a long time without speaking. In the end, it was Lupo who broke the silence. "You should hunt, Don Victor. If you don't you will grow weak."

Renquist nodded. "I know."

"Perhaps you would like me to accompany you?"

"To look for derelicts along the waterfront like Blasco and Segal?"

Lupo's eyes glittered for an instant with a flash of unholy knowing. "Let the young have the dregs of the city. I think I can take us to a place where we might find prey more fitting to our venerable tastes."

As Renquist and Lupo let themselves out of the front door of the Residence, the subject of their discussion suddenly appeared at the other end of the entrance hall. Carfax's aura momentarily registered surprise and the faintest trace of guilt. Whomever he'd expected it to be, it clearly wasn't them. "I thought it was some of the females returning."

Renquist looked at Carfax in amusement. "I'm afraid it's just us. I hope you're not too disappointed." He couldn't resist a momentary temptation to bait the young one. "You're a very lucky young man, Brother Carfax. Just a few minutes ago, I made a decision not to have you killed." Renquist grinned wolfishly before he turned away. "Please lock up behind us."

Before Carfax could respond, Renquist let the door swing closed behind Lupo and himself.

chapter FOUR

Three full days passed before the body of Fay Latimer was discovered, and then it was only because her neighbors in the building on 15th Street noticed a strange smell coming from her apartment. Such could be the isolation of a single human female in the city of New York in the final decade of the twentieth century. Renquist had spent the latter part of these 72 hours in a state of sated semi-somnolence, only rising from his bed to drink copious quantities of water, then quickly returning to it again. Few nosferatu consumed water in the way that Renquist did, but he felt under no obligation to anyone to explain or offer excuses for the phenomenon. It was something that had come to him in the last hundred years and, if the truth were told, he was also at a loss to explain it to himself.

If anyone but Renquist himself was to blame for his torpid satiation, it had to be Lupo. When they'd left the Residence to hunt together, Lupo had been as good as his word that he could "find prey fitting to our venerable tastes." He had led Renquist to a place where human degeneracy had advanced to such unbelievable extremes that the only response was one of jaded delight when the two of them had offered blood and death as the final mind-bending confection in an evening of ingeniously creative depravity.

The elaborately twisted entertainment had taken place in a huge mirrored room with red lights, dark leather banquettes, a wide polished performance floor, and a mezzanine spectators gallery. Renquist could only assume that, once upon a time, the aging structure had been a commercial ballroom along the lines of Roseland, now disused or abandoned. He was hardly shocked by its denizens, the performers in their masks and costumes and pornographic prosthetics, and the watchers in their street clothes, robes, or jewel-adorned nudity. With his centuries of experience, little remained that could shock him, but the scene certainly ranked among the strangest and most debased examples of what humans might do to amuse themselves when possessed of both unlimited resources and the necessary levels of extreme boredom.

The bizarre party had started innocently enough, if the word innocent could be applied strictly in the context of what would transpire later in the night. While waiters and waitresses in the trappings of sado-masochistic servitude had circulated, bearing trays of innovatively presented food and drink plus a wide variety of cutely packaged stimulants and narcotics, public sexual displays had started to be acted out on the main performance floor by hired prostitutes of both genders and also a number of inspired and exhibitionistic amateurs. These were staged and lit with all the panache and style of a Las Vegas review, although with a considerably more explicit content. To ensure that the voyeurs on the mezzanine missed nothing, a number of large projection TV screens had been set up at various points around the room that showed almost gynecological details of the most intimate action.

By the time Lupo and Renquist arrived, matters had progressed from relatively normal (if gymnastically complex) copulation, to a menu of increasingly pain-related perversion. Some of the set pieces had so pushed the envelope of physical tolerance that one fairly well known socialite/fashion model, who had initially thrown herself into the games on the floor with willing abandon, had become noisily hysterical and only been calmed by powerful injections of liquid Valium. Even these convoluted displays receded to the near mundane when the two nosferatu decided that the moment had come to provide their finale to the entertainment. Both spectators and performers had watched, open mouthed and transfixed, as live, on-camera death topped everything that had gone before.

If Renquist accepted Lupo's definition that evil was a matter of inclination, choice, and capricious waste, the spectacle that had confronted him certainly conformed to it in the maximum degree, and Renquist had wondered if Lupo had brought him to the place not only as a highly esoteric feeding, but also to give a firsthand, practical reinforcement to his philosophy. Certainly when Renquist had finally returned to the Residence, it had not only been with a heavy feeling of overindulgence but also an enlarged appreciation of both his physical and moral superiority. If human beings could do so much calculatedly vicious damage to the minds and bodies of members of their own species in the name of recreation or entertainment, they could hardly expect compassion or sympathy from nosferatu who were merely doing what came naturally.

Much later, as he and Lupo had ridden back to the Residence in a yellow cab, just ahead of the dawn, Lupo had turned to Renquist with a smug smile. "So how does it feel to be the Prince of Darkness?"

Renquist had laughed. "I can't say that I'm too impressed with the quality of my followers."

"You'd prefer to be God?"

Renquist had quickly shaken his head. "Hell, no. That would be far too much effort."

The final advantage of the excursion with Lupo had been that the humans had actually disposed of the corpses that had been among the debris of the frenzied and insane climax of their stage-managed orgy. Instead of blaming Renquist and Lupo for the deaths, they viewed them as the logical outcome of their own terminally extreme excesses, assuming that the killing was the product of some kind of self-induced satanic intervention. They took the guilt fully upon themselves. The videotapes had been destroyed and the victims were hustled away for immediate incineration. By way of an extra precaution, Renquist and Lupo had administered a massive psychic shock to the remaining humans to cloud their memories regarding the details of what had occurred and reinforce the idea that something diabolic and supernatural had taken place.

At the same time, though, Renquist had carefully filed away his own memories. Among those present in the strange and secret ballroom were well-known faces from the fields of politics, entertainment, big business, and the professionally beautiful. Many were so powerful, public, and instantly recognizable that, should the slightest whisper of their participation in the outlandish proceedings ever have leaked out, it would not only have triggered a media frenzy to eclipse all previous media frenzies, but also brought about major upheavals in both the Democratic and Republican parties as well as some huge multinational corporations, and given rise to multiple TV movies-of-the-week.

When the news broke that Fay Latimer's body had been discovered, Renquist was actually one of the last to hear about it. The story had blazed across the afternoon editions of the tabloids and then been quickly picked up by the early evening TV news. The window dressing that Renquist had left behind, the mutilated body and the blood writing scrawled on the walls, had elevated the story to the front page of the *New York Post* and to the lead on all TV channels—including CNN, which had briefly managed to get a camera inside the crime scene. Renquist had slept soundly while words like "horror," "carnage," "butcher," and "maniac" were being bandied around in the press. He had left unshakable instructions that he should not be wakened again during the hours of daylight unless armed police and National Guard were actually laying siege to the Residence.

When he finally rose and scanned the papers and TV coverage Blasco had taped for him, he felt reasonably pleased with himself. The colony would now have a body disposal mode that it could follow without his even having to tell them about it. All he needed to provide were those small but essential details the police liked to withhold from the media and the public to guard against copycat killers and those crazies with a pathological need to confess to crimes that they had never committed. By way of a bonus, the murder of Fay Latimer seemed to be the only one making headlines. When the women had gone hunting en masse, they had managed it with great tidiness and attention to post-mortem detail. The females of the colony had created no fuss, no muss, and no threats of exposure. If matters could just stay that way, if the entire colony could manage to adhere to his serial killer deception, they might possibly come through this Feasting intact.

Gideon Kelly fumbled for pocket change. His endeavor was made more difficult by the fact that he felt obliged to keep his eyes averted from the ranks of painted sluts on the covers of the rows of racked magazines, the blue, black, and green-shaded eyes attempting to make contact with his and lure him into their maws of scented impurity with their pouting lips and moist tongues, their scandalous hair, their long legs and contorted coital poses, the lace and the leather, the heels, garters, dark stockings, and scantily revealing undergarments, their exposed breasts and buttocks.

The newsvendor was gesturing impatiently to him. "C'mon, c'mon, I gotta business to run here."

Panic began to close in on Kelly. Demons in the night he could face, but a Sixth Avenue newsstand in the rush of the afternoon was almost more than he was able to handle. Without counting them, he tossed a handful of coins down on the pile of the latest edition of the *Post*, seized the top copy, and hurried away.

He had spotted a bar just a short way down the block, a long-standing Irish pub called McShane's, marked by a neon shamrock and signs advertising Guinness and Harp Lager. Kelly knew that this place would be his next natural refuge. Kelly's God might have saddled him with this testing mission, but he couldn't see that even God could seriously expect him to go through the next part without at least one drink inside him. Thus, with his still unopened copy of the *Post* securely under his arm, he hurried in the direction of McShane's. He had already heard about the murder on 15th Street, back at the hotel, on the desk clerk's radio. He had then walked there, past the building from which the Devil had emerged, and observed the police cars, the TV trucks, the waiting reporters, and the yellow crime scene tape for himself. He knew there was no mistake, but to see it in black and white, right there in the newspaper, was the final confirmation.

Aside from the church from which he had been so long excluded, Kelly knew no place as comforting as a barroom in daytime. Dusty sunlight filtered through the windows, the place smelled of beer, French fries, and hot water, and a baseball game was playing on ESPN. The bartender was talking to a middle-aged woman in a lavender jogging suit who was nursing what appeared to be a gin and tonic. Three elderly Italian men wearing leisure suits and golf caps who looked like elderly *mafiosi* sat side by side, so absorbed in the contemplation of their own silence that they hardly bothered to glance up as Kelly walked in. Kelly took a stool at the opposite end of the bar from the old Italians. The bartender broke off his conversation with the woman in lavender and moved toward where Kelly was sitting. He didn't say anything, just stared at Kelly inquiringly. Kelly knew that he didn't look so good, still wearing his stained army coat when the temperature outside must have been in the eighties, so he took out a ten-dollar bill and placed it on the counter to prove beyond doubt that he had the money for a drink. "A shot of Paddy and a beer back."

"You want the Paddy straight up?"

"Of course."

Kelly swallowed hard as the bartender carefully poured the shot and then filled a small glass with draught beer. The first drink of the day was always invested with such a desperate significance. The man scooped up Kelly's ten to complete the ritual. The register was the old-fashioned kind on which one had to hit three keys in sequence for the amount and then the larger bar at the side to get a total and open the cash drawer. Clack-clack-clack-crash. The bartender had placed the ten on the ledge above the drawer, leaving it there as he made change so Kelly couldn't claim that he'd given him a twenty. No one trusted anyone anymore in this God-cursed world.

With his drink poured and paid for, Kelly slowly raised the shot to his lips. The communion was hardly holy, but Kelly could console himself that it was deadly serious. And, if he couldn't, the whiskey would console him instead. He allowed his upper lip to touch the surface of the liquor and, using it as a guide, he threw back half of the shot. In the old days, when his drinking had been a self-administered punishment, he would have drunk it all in one. Now he had his mission from the Almighty, he had to be more circumspect. He let the whiskey burn until the pain was too good and too much and he couldn't stand it any more, and then he chased it away with a mouthful of beer.

"Sweet Saint Michael and all the angels."

The warmth was spreading through his belly. Kelly had intended to make the one shot last through the entire time it took to read the newspaper report of the 15th Street murder, but he should have known better than that. One was never enough. He quickly downed the remainder of the shot and looked to the bartender. The bartender reached for the bottle of Paddy, but Kelly examined his change and shook his head. "No, make it the cheap stuff, the real cheap stuff."

The bartender's face hardened. When a customer switches to well whiskey after just one drink, a barkeep can be reasonably certain that any potential tip is going to be drunk away. Kelly ignored his displeasure. Worst things happened in this world than unhappy bartenders. He spread out the *Post* and started to read.

In less than a minute, he confirmed what he had heard on the radio and seen with his own eyes. The murder building was definitely the one that had been visited by the Devil. He had half hoped it would be a different building. Now he had no choice but to go ahead with what he must do. The *Post* had printed a picture of the woman as she had been when she was still alive. Kelly could only imagine that she was probably a slut. One could hope for little else in a city like New York, but the eyes that stared from the page looked as though they had seen their fair share of sadness. He drank down his second shot, finished the beer, picked up what was left of his ten, folded the newspaper, and stood up. He nodded to the bartender and began to walk out. The bartender called after him in a voice that was little more than an overt sneer. "Yeah, come again real soon."

The nearest police precinct was just two stops away on the subway, but Kelly didn't think that he could face being under the ground with all those strangers, so he decided to walk. Outside the precinct house, his resolve all but failed. He wanted to run away. He wanted one more drink. Most of all, he wanted not to go inside. Once he crossed the threshold of the police station, turning back would be impossible. He'd be locked into the course of action by his cruel and personal God. To falter would assure damnation, but to continue was a weight almost too heavy to bear.

"Please, Lord of Hosts, give me strength." But no strength came and Kelly knew he was on his own. The testing continued. He took a deep breath and walked inside.

He had to wait for almost an hour in an area that smelled of sweat, panic, and Lysol before he finally got to see a detective assigned to the Fay Latimer case. The detective took Kelly to a small interview room screened off by panels of dirty frosted glass and scuffed wood painted washed-out municipal green. Kelly didn't know quite what he had expected, certainly not Clint Eastwood playing Dirty Harry Callahan, but whatever it might have been, it certainly wasn't Detective Jesus Escobar. The Puerto Rican detective was small, harried, and clearly impatient to get done with Kelly and his story, and on to something else much more important. All the while he was dealing with Kelly, he juggled a maple glazed donut and a blue and white cardboard cup of coffeeshop coffee.

"They don't give us time around here to fucking feed ourselves. You know what I'm talking about?"

As if this casualness of attitude wasn't bad enough, Kelly had a long-running problem with never being comfortable around men named Jesus. Even though the pronunciation might be different, it seemed a little too close to blasphemy to give a child the name of the Savior. When Escobar closed the door to the interview room behind them, he indicated that Kelly should sit and then came straight to the point.

"So let me get this straight, Mr. . . . . Kelly. You're telling me that, three nights ago, you were tripping around on Fifteenth Street and you saw a man coming out of a building that you think was the same one where the woman Latimer was murdered."

Kelly knew, just by the way he looked, he was going to provoke this kind of reaction in any policeman, but being forewarned didn't make it any more comfortable. "I don't think it's the building, I know it's the building. I even doublechecked with the picture in today's *Post*."

"And you somehow sensed that the man was evil?"

"That's right."

"Did he have blood on him?"

"No."

"Did he act strange, furtive, freaked out, anything like that?"

"No, but . . ."

"You just felt the vibes, right? You divined his chakra? What are we talking about here?"

"I don't know exactly. I just felt it. The man was evil."

"Are you an expert on evil, Mr. Kelly?"

Kelly looked away. He was starting to regret ever thinking that God intended him to go to the police. "I was once a priest."

Escobar was in the act of biting into his donut but Kelly's words stopped him dead. He slowly lowered it from his mouth. "You want to run that past me one more time?"

Kelly sighed. Now he was really regretting having come to the police. "I used to be a priest."

Escobar looked Kelly up and down. "So what happened?"

"I had some problems."

Escobar looked sideways at Kelly. "Not altar boys, I hope?"

"No, Detective Escobar, not altar boys or anything like that."

Kelly thought that he'd said enough, but Escobar continued to stare at him as though he expected some kind of longer and more detailed explanation. Kelly pushed his hair back out of his eyes. "Drink. Drinking was the cause of my problems."

Escobar looked surprised. "Irish whiskey priest? I thought that was a tradition. James Cagney could play you in the movie."

"A woman was also involved. She made accusations. After I tried to end it. I somehow don't think James Cagney would play me in the movie. Even if he was alive."

"You still drink?"

It was pointless to pretend. The cop could probably still smell the Paddy on his breath. "Yes, I still drink."

Escobar sipped his coffee as though digesting what Kelly had told him. "So let's move onto the next phase, Father Kelly."

"You shouldn't call me that."

"Not even for old times' sake?"

"I'd rather you didn't."

"Whatever you say."

"I followed him."

Escobar frowned. He seemed confused. "You followed who?"

"The man who came out of the building."

"Aaah."

"In a cab."

Escobar nodded and finally took a bite out of his donut. He spoke with his mouth full and sprayed crumbs. "In a cab?"

"Yes."

"You don't look like you got too much money Fa . . . Mr. Kelly, and yet you sprang for a cab to follow some guy on a hunch . . . on a feeling?"

"Yes."

"So what was it? A mission from God?"

"You wouldn't believe me if I told you."

"Try me."

"I followed him to his house."

"Why didn't you come to us three days ago, Mr. Kelly?"

"I didn't know there'd been a murder."

"But you followed the guy. Even though you had no idea that a crime had been committed."

Kelly wished that he could simply leave and forget the whole thing. He was plainly getting nowhere in this policeman's world. "Yes, I followed him."

"On a feeling?"

It was pointless. "On a feeling."

"To his house?"

"To his house."

"So evil has an address?"

Kelly suddenly felt a chill. He'd never though of the lair of the Devil as something so commonplace as an address. "I know where he lives."

Escobar raised an eyebrow. "You want to tell me the address?"

The chill increased. "I'd rather not say it out loud."

Escobar shrugged and pushed a pad and pencil at Kelly. "So write it down."

After a moment's hesitation, Kelly wrote down the address, and returned the pad to Escobar. Immediately he felt better. The chill receded. The good feeling didn't last, though. It quickly faded as the detective pushed the pad back at him again. "Write down your own address as well."

"My address?" It wasn't right. The chill returned with a vengeance. The very last thing that Kelly wanted to do was to have his own name and address on the same sheet of paper as that of the demon.

Escobar tapped the pad with his index finger. "That's what I said."

"Why do you want my address?"

"For the record, Mr. Kelly."

Kelly felt sick and afraid, but he did as he was instructed. To do otherwise would be to further invite Escobar to dismiss him as a lunatic. Escobar took the pad back and looked at it. "So you live at the Dupont?"

"Is there something wrong with that?"

"I don't know. You tell me."

"It suits me."

Escobar finished his donut. "Each to his own. I doubt there are many residents of the Dupont who follow strangers around in cabs, but like I said, each to his own."

"So what happens now?"

Escobar stood up, in a way that unmistakably indicated the interview was at an end. "We'll look into it."

Kelly was amazed and not a little angry. "That's it? You'll look into it?"

"What did you expect, Mr. Kelly? That we'd race around there with sirens blasting and guns blazing?"

"I don't know. I . . ."

Escobar opened the door to the interview room, making it clear that Kelly should be moving on. "If we need you, we know where to find you." He suddenly grinned. "You weren't planning on leaving town, were you?"

Julia's tone was accusatory. "Kurt tells me that you decided to spare his life?"

Renquist remained as still as the silent paintings that lined the walls of the gallery. "I believe my exact words were that I'd decided not to kill him."

Carfax's voice was brittle and edgy. "So you were contemplating killing me?" The young one was nervous and his aura billowed around him like smoke.

Renquist smiled in the darkness. "The thought had briefly crossed my mind."

His first reaction as Julia and Carfax entered the gallery was that they intended to assassinate him. One to hold him and one to wield the stake. Renquist had been standing, deep in thought, with his back to the door, not expecting an intrusion of any kind. The two of them had appeared like wraiths, auras so tightly reined in that Renquist perceived them as nothing more than wisps of fragile and tenuous light like drifting gauze, floating above their own faint reflections in the polished floor. It was only when they started speaking that Renquist realized they had no intention of killing him. Assassins, even neophyte nosferatu assassins, simply did the deed. They didn't discuss it first with the intended victim.

Julia's aura slowly began to assume her physical shape, as though the gauze of light was being molded to her face and body. "Why would you want to kill Kurt, Victor? Wouldn't that be going directly against the code you put so much store by?"

Carfax echoed the question. "That's right, Victor, why would you want to kill me?"

Renquist allowed his own aura to expand. "It was just idle conversation."

"Suppose I started talking about killing you?"

"I think you'd find that a lot harder to accomplish than you might imagine."

Carfax remained an indistinct shape. "Were you entertaining the possibility of killing me?"

"Perhaps I was merely in a facetious mood." As he spoke, Renquist extended a slender tendril of his own aura in the direction of Carfax. Although he now doubted that the pair meant to do him any bodily harm, it didn't hurt to take a precaution.

Julia's form suddenly solidified, bringing her fully into the material world. "I know what you're doing, Victor."

"Do you, now?"

"There's really no need for it."

"So why all the spectral effects and drama? You wanted to ensure you had my attention?"

"You could say that."

Carfax also attempted to solidify, but he lacked the skill to accomplish the transition as smoothly as Julia had. His voice came out high and strained. "Julia and I . . ."

Renquist gave him no time to recover. "Yes?"

Carfax faltered and lost the transition entirely. For a moment, Renquist's darkvision perceived him as a distorted thing, top heavy and ape-like. Then the young one had himself under control and was able to take on his normal shape and normal voice register. "Julia and I have something very important to discuss with you."

"Indeed?" Renquist reminded himself not to treat Carfax as too much of joke. He might fumble some of the more difficult changes, but he was also possessed of a great raw power. "And what might that be?"

Julia answered. "I want to teach Kurt the Art of Changing.

I want to teach him how to make a human into one of our own kind."

Renquist slowly nodded. It was just as Lupo had warned him. Carfax's craving for what he thought of as power was off in a new direction. The Art of Changing was the final secret that he had to penetrate. From his point of view, it had to be a frustratingly closed door, the last obstacle that prevented him from being fully equal to any other member of the colony. Doubtless the boy was conjuring dreams of conquering the world with an army of nosferatu slaves behind him. He wouldn't be the first to entertain such a fantasy and most probably wouldn't be the last. The unfortunate truth was that these kind of megalomaniacal schemes invariably came to nothing except disaster. If any proof was required, one only had to look around. The world was dominated by humankind, not some wampyr dictatorship or elite.

Renquist faced Carfax. "You want to learn the art of changing?"

"I believe it's time."

Renquist shook his head. "I don't think so."

Carfax stiffened. "What do you mean, you don't think so?"

"Exactly what I said. I don't think so."

Carfax's aura was starting to throb. His anger was building. "Don't I have a right?"

"A right?"

"Isn't this knowledge my basic birthright?"

Renquist saw that a confrontation was coming, but this time he wasn't willing to back down or play the diplomat. Carfax had pulled this kind of thing once too often, and Renquist let his irritation plainly show. "And where did you get that idea? You believe that there's some nosferatu charter that guarantees us life, liberty, and the pursuit of hemoglobin?"

"Of course not, but . . ."

"We have no rights, Brother Carfax. We simply desire and then take what we can to fulfill that desire."

"And I desire to create more of my own kind."

"And while you're a part of this colony, I will be the one to decide when you are ready to fulfill that particular whim."

"It's more than a whim."

"Whatever it is, you're not ready."

Carfax's aura was throbbing harder now. "I'm ready."

"You'll be ready when you grasp the significance of creating more of our kind, when you have the experience to handle the responsibilities involved."

"I'm telling you, I'm ready."

"And I'm telling you, I don't think so."

Carfax was moving closer to the point of losing control. "How can you stop me?"

Renquist countered the young one's emotion by becoming coldly formal. "While you remain a member of this colony, and I continue to be Master, no one will instruct you in the Art. It's as simple as that. If you care to resign from the colony and leave the Residence, and then locate a loner or a ronin tutor who will take the time to initiate you, you may do exactly what you want. While you remain here, I will stop you, and I will continue to stop you until I decide that you can be trusted with the secret. Do I make myself clear?"

Carfax all but spat at Renquist. "Abundantly clear. You want me out of the colony, don't you?"

Renquist almost smiled. "Nothing would please me more than to see the back of you, but sadly that is not a decision I can make on my own. Your expulsion would have to be ratified by two-thirds of the colony. Thus I accept your presence whether I like it or not."

"But privately you hate me?"

Renquist did nothing to conceal the disdain with which he viewed the question. "I'm a thousand years old, boy. I am long past feeling hate for one like you. You are very young, very wild, and seemingly rather stupid. As an individual, you mean very little to me. I do, however, believe that your gauche power posturings are a potential danger to all of us, and that's why I have no intention of allowing you to be initiated in the Art of Creation at this time." Renquist glanced at Julia. "Do either of you have any more questions? I came to this gallery to be alone and meditate, and it's a tradition in this colony that I am not disturbed while I'm doing it."

Carfax's face twisted venomously. "That's all you have left to cling to, isn't it, Victor? The single fact that you've managed to live so damned long. I'm telling you, I'm not going to wait a thousand years before I realize my potential."

Renquist's aura blossomed blue with sudden amusement. "I very much doubt that you will survive for anything like a thousand years."

The aura of Carfax turned black as a thundercloud. "Are you threatening me?"

"Merely making an informed prediction."

Carfax took a step towards Renquist. "Why don't you keep your predictions to yourself, old man?"

"If that's what you want."

"You know what I want."

"And for that, you have no alternative but to wait."

"Julia will initiate me in the Act. I don't need to come crawling to you for permission."

Renquist slowly turned to face Julia fully. His aura contracted to a hard steel grey. "Is that true, Julia? Are you going to initiate this boy?"

Julia said nothing and Carfax rounded on her angrily. "So tell him! Tell him, Julia."

Renquist didn't even breath. He knew that the breaking point had come. "Why don't you tell us both, Julia?"

Julia looked uncomfortably at Carfax and shook her head. "I can't do it."

Carfax could not have been more stunned if she had slapped him. "What?"

"It would mean my immediate expulsion from the colony."

"So?"

"So I can't do it."

"We don't need them."

"But I do need this colony, Kurt. I'm not going out there on my own again, not even for you."

Carfax's voice became an angry snarl. "This is betrayal, Julia."

Julia's own anger began climbing as though attempting to match his. "Don't be so goddamned melodramatic! I'm not betraying you. I'm being practical. If you weren't so wrapped up in yourself and your delusions of grandeur, you'd realize that."

Renquist watched Carfax carefully through Julia's outburst. He was starting to resemble a volcano on the threshold of eruption. When it began to seem as though he might actually strike Julia, Renquist moved quickly. "Don't you dare touch her, boy!"

Carfax's rage-shriek must have been audible for blocks around. The force of it alone sent Renquist reeling back a number of paces.

"Stop calling me boy!"

In the same instant, Carfax was springing at him, pressing his attack while Renquist was still off balance. His fangs were bared and his taloned hands reached for Renquist's throat. And then, inexplicably, Carfax was suddenly flying sideways. He crashed into the wall just a few inches to the left of the Rembrandt portrait of Bent Van Leyden, and dropped to the floor like an unstrung puppet. Twitches of purple and yellow light shimmered down the length of his body as though he was either stunned or in great pain. As Carfax had come at him, Renquist had instinctively dropped into a defensive crouch. When he straightened up, he saw a dark bulky figure standing protectively beside Julia.

"Lupo?"

"I was worried he was going to hit the Rembrandt. I didn't have a lot of time to calculate where the young fool might land."

"I'm grateful, Lupo, but I think I could have handled him."

Lupo spread his massive hands as though Renquist was stating the obvious. "Of course, Don Victor, but why bother yourself when I am here to take care of such things?"

Julia, who had stood rigid from the moment that Carfax hurled himself at Renquist, finally spoke. "Why are you here, Lupo?"

Lupo looked at her with hooded eyes. "I am wherever my don needs me."

Julia dismissed this impatiently. "Yes, yes, but what brought you here right at this crucial moment. Had you been following us?"

"I saw the two of you come into the gallery. I knew the Master was alone."

"And you didn't trust us?"

"Should I have trusted you?"

On the floor, Carfax was now slowly curling into a fetal ball beneath the Rembrandt. Julia sighed. "I suppose not. I take it you heard the conversation that just went down."

Lupo nodded. "I heard it."

"So I suppose we're finished in this colony?"

Lupo glanced at Renquist. "What happens to you is not my decision."

Carfax seemed to be recovering some of his strength. His aura was now a uniform algae green and his breath came with short angry rasps that were partway between grunts and snarls. Julia looked at Renquist. "What happens now?"

Renquist didn't respond. Carfax was struggling to get to his feet. "You're . . . lucky . . . your gorilla . . . was here . . . to save you . . . Victor."

Lupo advanced on Carfax until he was standing over him. "You don't talk to your Master like that . . . boy."

Using the wall for support, Carfax managed to rise to his feet. Renquist read his aura. Two ribs and his right collarbone had been broken, but they were already knitting and reforming at the typical nosferatu speed of recovery. His pain must have been considerable, but he was still able to hiss defiantly, "You'll both regret this. You too, Julia."

Still with one hand on the wall to steady himself, he turned and started to limp slowly towards the door. Before he had gone more than a couple of painful steps, Lupo's voice graveled after him. "And where do you think you're going?"

Renquist had little respect for Carfax's intelligence, but he had to give him a certain recognition for idiot courage. Injured as he was, he slowly turned and looked Lupo directly in the eye. "It's none of your fucking business, you antiquated dinosaur."

Renquist actually winced in sympathy as Lupo seized the back of Carfax's neck, just like he was an erring puppy, and lifted him clean off the ground. "You don't talk to me like that. You hear me, boy? You don't talk to me like that."

Carfax at least had the minimal sense to say nothing. Lupo, on the other hand, pressed his point. "I think, before you leave here, you should kneel before your Master and beg forgiveness."

Renquist decided that perhaps Lupo was possibly going a little far. Carfax should be left some measure of dignity. "I don't think there's any need for that . . ."

Lupo cut him off. "Please let me do this my way, Don Victor. The young have to learn."

He placed Carfax on his feet in front of Renquist and then stepped away. "Kneel to your Master, boy."

Carfax stiffened his shoulders. The bones were knitting and he was quickly recovering his strength. "I kneel to no one."

Lupo moved closer again. "I said kneel, boy."

"And I told you I don't kneel."

A huge crushing hand clamped itself on Carfax's shoulder. "You will kneel."

Renquist could see the arcs of pain spasming from Carfax's freshly healed collarbone, but the young one continued to resist. His face was ashen and his teeth clenched. "I will not."

"Kneel!"

"No!"

Julia took a step towards Carfax and Lupo. "Give in, Kurt. He can break you in half."

"Let him try."

She looked quickly to Renquist. "Victor?"

Renquist said nothing. His face was like stone. He knew that he could stop what was happening in an instant, but Lupo was right. The young had to learn. Also a part of him was quite enjoying watching his rival being taught this painful and humiliating lesson.

"Kneel!"

"No!"

But Carfax's left leg was already starting to tremble and the sound of more bones cracking in his shoulder was clearly audible. His knees buckled and, irrevocably, he was forced down. When he was finally kneeling, Lupo released him and took a step back. "Now apologize to your Master, boy. Beg for his forgiveness."

Carfax said nothing and Lupo stepped forward again. He placed a stubby finger on a pressure point close to Carfax's spine. "Beg, boy!"

Lupo pressed down and Carfax's pain all but lit up the gallery. This time there was no possibility of resistance. His words came out in a single agonized breath. "Master, I beg your forgiveness."

Renquist would have stopped there, but Lupo had been raised in an old and cruel school. The dungeon torturers of the fifteenth century, masters of the rack and the branding iron, had educated him in the basics of persuasion.

"Louder and more slowly, boy. I not sure the Master heard you clearly."

With Lupo's finger hovering over the pressure point in his back, Carfax's enunciation was instantly clear and distinct. "Master, I beg your forgiveness."

Renquist could hardly keep himself from smiling, but he suspected that Carfax would most likely go critical if he actually laughed in his face. "Forgiveness is granted. You are forgiven."

Carfax turned his head and looked up at Lupo. "Can I get up now? Can I get out of here?"

Renquist had assumed that, with Carfax so thoroughly humiliated, Lupo would step back and allow him to crawl off to lick his wounds and further nurture his resentment. Lupo, however, didn't move. "You just stay where you are, boy. I haven't done with you."

Renquist had serious misgivings about the lengths to which Lupo seemed to be taking the situation, but respect dictated that he not intervene. Lupo moved so he was standing beside the still kneeling Carfax.

"I've been hearing a lot of excrement from you since you decided to start flexing your muscles around this colony. I've heard a lot of ranting about freedom and the power of the wild nosferatu. Up until now, I've made no comment, but as in all things, enough is enough. Now I have to say my piece."

His voice was low and hoarse, and at times he paused as though searching for exactly the right word to make his point. No one, not even Renquist would have dared to interrupt him. "Your problem, Brother Carfax, is that you're ignorant. You know nothing of the history of our kind. You don't learn and, in consequence, you don't understand. I remember a time when our people were wild and free, but I also remember the time when we came close to being destroyed because, in our wildness, we abused that freedom. Both Don Victor and I lived through the destruction that came to us in 1919, and we will never forget it."

He looked to Renquist for confirmation. "Is that not correct, Don Victor?"

Renquist nodded. "It's absolutely correct."

Carfax used this break in Lupo's monologue to gather some fragments of his shattered pride. "Is this going to be another of your old one stories?"

"Yes it is boy, and you are going shut your mouth and listen to the old one. You understand what I'm saying?"

"Do I have to remain kneeling like this?"

"Yes, you do. I think what I'm going to tell you will make more of an impression if you remain as you are. It's been my experience that submission sharpens concentration."

A wave of hate swept across Carfax, but he neither moved nor spoke. Apparently Lupo was correct. Submission did aid learning. "This is the story, boy. I suggest you pay careful attention. The year 1919 saw almost the whole of Europe devastated by war, a shambles that stretched from Poland to the Pyrenees. And as that war had raged, the nosferatu had been able to run wild. With so much death on every side, we were able to feed to our hearts' content. Also we brought over humans with no thought to the future. Rapidly, our numbers doubled, tripled, quadrupled. Soon there were so many of us that we were rapidly becoming visible. When the hostilities ceased, some of the humans observed what was happening. At first, it was just peasant talk and nightfear, the hanging of crosses and garlic. Some of us were destroyed, but it was mainly the careless, the stupid, and the isolated. In the end, though, men of command and influence began to be aware of what we were doing, and of what, potentially, we might be capable. They saw that we were more than just folktales or the imaginings of Bram Stoker and others. They began not only to react to our existence, but also to think what might happen if beings like us began to infiltrate their political structures and haunt their palaces and their corridors of power. The first one actually to make a move against us was a German, a Catholic bishop. His name was Rauch, an accursed name, a name that will live in infamy until our kind pass from the Earth. Go to the colony's library, boy, and look up the records. Believe me, it makes chilling reading."

Lupo paused to let this preamble sink in before he continued. "Even for Rauch, it wasn't easy to bring others to the point of belief. It took him some time to convince the Vatican that we actually existed, but in our thoughtless wildness, we all but handed him the evidence he needed to demonstrate to the Pope and the College of Cardinals that nosferatu truly walked the earth and that we posed a deadly threat to both humanity and the Church. Rauch was fortunate in that, through the Dominican Order and his contacts with secret groups like the Carbonari, the Society of Ultima Thule, and other Christian *fascisti* mystics, he was able to bring considerable influence to bear. These organizations and individuals who backed him were not only powerful but sinister and vicious, even by human standards. The Pope had little alternative but to approve the plans of Rauch and his backers. And once the Pope had given his blessing, our extermination was a foregone conclusion."

While he talked, Lupo was, at the same time, filling Carfax's mind with subtle visual images. He showed him the raped and shattered moonscapes that were the abandoned battlefields of the Western Front, dead men and dead horses, torn and bloated, lining the sides of the roads, while dirty and defeated armies grimly straggled home. All the while, dark figures of nosferatu shadow-prowled the darkness of ruined cities, and streams of blood flowed like rivers. A ghostly print-through montage of this psychic input was visible to both Renquist and Julia, filling the electric space between the two men. Lupo had Carfax completely under his control. The young one's eyes had glazed over and he knelt motionless and transfixed. Although Lupo liked to present a blunt and brutal exterior, his mind was far more complex and devious than he cared to admit.

"To do the actual killing for him, Rauch used the ones that called themselves the *Freikorps*, armed gangs of disaffected German soldiers, just back from the trenches. They were the same ones who would later flock to the red and black banners of the Nazis. The Order of the Knights of St. Michael and St. John, such as they were in those days, used their millionaire vassals and their fat munitions profits to coordinate the finance and the logistic support. The whole deadly business was conducted under the code name Fifth Seal, and it was one of the darkest secrets ever harbored by humanity and their black celibate clerics. The Freikorps soldiers, amply provided with women and alcohol, travelled in convoys of military trucks. They would fall upon a specific area and begin seeking out our resting places while we slept. We were staked and beheaded and burned with fire and with the sun. At night they would build huge bonfires, to guard against a counterattack on our part, but would otherwise pass the hours of darkness drinking and whoring. The killing started in Germany, but rapidly spread west into France, east into Poland, Hungary, and Rumania, and even south to the warmth of Italy. The only countries that didn't play host to this holocaust were revolution-torn Russia and England, where there was only a tiny nosferatu population because of our innate, if illogical, fear of crossing water."

The images that flowed between Lupo and Carfax became more graphic and detailed. Humans in ragged military uniforms, gripped by a mass killing frenzy, hacked their way into the lairs of nosferatu, sunlight streaming in behind them as they broke down doors and smashed through walls. Hammers and axes swung and now the blood streamed from the bodies of the nosferatu themselves, bodies that contorted, fangs bared and snapping at the air, in gnashing death spasms.

"Hundreds and more hundreds of us were destroyed in that long, terrible summer. Some who survived the first onslaught were forced to hide in the very earthworks and fortifications that still remained from the humans' war. I myself crawled through the stinking mud of the deserted trenches, while humans, howling and carrying burning torches, pursued us across their former killing fields. We went to ground in bunkers and foxholes. Some of us even buried ourselves in that bloodsoaked ground that still stank of gunpowder and corpses. One group of nosferatu were blown to bits when they blundered into a minefield, and there weren't enough pieces left of them for the rest of us to put back together so they could mend themselves."

Lupo stared down at Carfax. "Can you imagine that, boy? They could have lived, but we couldn't find enough parts to put them back together."

Carfax nodded like a zombie. "I can imagine."

Just in case he couldn't, Lupo fed him a quick string of grossly explicit images before he went on with the story. "When the worst of the destruction was over, some of us fled to Africa, while others came here to the New World. We all realized that the time had come to change the way we conducted ourselves. The first colonies were formed, our hunting became a great deal more circumspect, and we carefully regulated the numbers of new nosferatu that were created. Do you understand now, boy? Do you understand why elders like Don Victor and myself are very concerned when you want to go around and bring over humans like there was no tomorrow? To create too many of us in one place is the surest way to guarantee that there actually will be no tomorrow."

Again Carfax nodded. "I understand."

Lupo waved a dismissive hand. The spell was broken. "I'm finished, so now you can get up. Just never turn on your Master again, or it will be more than a matter of a simple apology."

Carfax got slowly to his feet. He seemed dazed. He looked from Lupo to Renquist and back again. Lupo waved him away. "Go, get out of here. Don't let me see you for the next few days."

Carfax turned and walked slowly away. As he passed Julia, he hissed under his breath. "I didn't think you would betray me."

Lupo tensed to go after Carfax, but Renquist placed a lightly restraining hand on his arm. "Let him have one last snap. You've given him plenty to think about."

"Let's hope he does think about it."

Renquist thoughtfully stroked his chin. "You did what you could, but I don't think this game is by any means played out."

Lupo shook his head. "He knows he's beaten. He isn't so

foolish that he'd try another move on you."

Renquist wasn't convinced. "I think you underestimate that one's capacity for foolishness."

"Kurt may be full of himself, but you're nothing more than a damned hypocrite, Victor."

Renquist looked at Julia in surprise. "How so?"

"You and Lupo and all your pompous talk about not irresponsibly creating new nosferatu."

"Lupo meant everything he said."

"And you?"

"I can't have Carfax out there creating his own private army of the night. It's absurd. The whole city would fall on us."

"You weren't being particularly responsible when you created me."

"That's different."

"How?"

"I knew what I was doing."

Julia's lip curled. "Bullshit."

"I knew you'd come through alright."

"Bullshit."

"You did, though, didn't you?"

"You can't take any credit for that."

Renquist knew that Julia was right, but he wasn't about to admit it to her. "As I said, I knew what I was doing. You were the right material."

"I was nothing more than a little whore-actress and you thought it would be a fine joke to bring me across and then set me loose among the Nazi hierarchy. I was your parting shot at Goebbels."

"That's not true."

"Of course it's true. You didn't give a thought to what happened to me, or how much damage it did. You just left me there to sink or swim on my own."

When Lupo had finally left the gallery, Julia had indicated

that she wanted to talk privately to Renquist. He hadn't expected, however, that she would take him to task for being a bad quasi-father.

"That was a long time ago."

"It was well after the legendary Slaughter of 1919, when you all started supposedly being so fucking careful."

"It was also Nazi Germany." He knew his excuses were getting lame, but they were the best that he could come up with on the spur of the moment.

"So all deals were off?"

"I wanted to do some harm to those swine."

Julia wasn't buying his high moral tone. "You just wanted to piss them off."

"Believe what you like."

"And what about me?"

"What was I supposed to do? Throw you a coming-out party?"

"You could have taught me to hunt. You could have helped me get past the rage and disorientation."

Renquist gave up in a final outburst of bluster. "Okay, okay, I admit it. I was irresponsible. None of us is perfect."

Having conceded her the victory, Renquist expected Julia to take her leave. Instead, she stood looking at him, standing in front of the psychedelic portrait of Cynara with a glass of red wine in her hand. "I think that's the first time I ever heard you admit that you might be wrong."

Renquist looked for a way out of this less-than-comfortable conversation. "What do you expect Carfax to do now?"

"Don't change the subject."

"I'm not. It's Carfax who started all this, and while we're on the subject, you didn't do such a good aftercare job on him, did you? His rage is really quite exceptional. It's a long time since I saw anyone stand up to Lupo like that."

"Perhaps I raised him to get back at you."

"I don't doubt it."

"You may end up killing him, you know that?"

"And how would you feel about that?"

Julia sipped her wine thoughtfully. "I really don't know."

"The ties of creation can go deeper than you think."

Julia smiled. "Is that a fact?"

"It's no laughing matter."

She treated Renquist to a long sultry look. "Then perhaps you'd better protect yourself against one set of ties by forming another."

"We're back on that are we?"

Julia's eyes twinkled. "If you were firmly bonded with me before you finished him, I might not miss my baby boy quite so much."

Gideon Kelly began to feel as though any self-will on his part was being rapidly withdrawn. Kelly had largely stopped sleeping, and the few hours that he managed were now uniformly plagued by teeth-grinding nightmares that largely featured the Devil he had seen on 15th Street and subsequently followed to his lair. The Devil pursued him through a city thronged with fleshy, unclean, and scantily clad women who laughed at him as he ran and tried to fondle him intimately and rip the clothing from his body. The women of his dreams were quite familiar to him, so much so that he even recognized recurrent faces. They had been with him for almost as long as he could remember, certainly ever since he had been expelled from the Church. The Devil, however, was a new recruit to the ranks of the tormentors of his unconscious, and Kelly was becoming increasingly convinced that some kind of psychic connection was being formed. What he didn't know was if this possible link might be the work of God, and, as unpleasant as it proved to be at the moment, would ultimately aid him in his task, or if it was an affliction of Satan, designed to thwart him in his mission.

With sleep proving to be more of an ordeal than a blessing, Kelly had taken to rising early, shortly after dawn, leaving the

Dupont Hotel and walking the early morning streets of Manhattan. At that time, the city was somewhat more manageable. Cool white sunlight streamed down the cross streets, and everyone moved with a sense of purpose, walking their dogs, opening their stores for business, heading for the subway and the early shift. The smells of the city, the coffeeshops, bakeries, freshly printed newspapers, had yet to be tainted and finally obscured by the rush hour auto exhaust. He still felt like an alien amid all the urgency and bustle, but the hustle on the sidewalks also gave him a subjective invisibility. People had more to do than to bother with just one more deadbeat in a dirty combat coat.

On this morning a new factor and new diminishment of his control seemed to have been added to the overall picture. Kelly found himself irrevocably drawn to walk south, down through the village and beyond. At first, he didn't realize the full significance of what was happening, but then to his growing horror he saw that his steps were taking him slowly but surely in the direction of the house of the Devil. He was unable to turn back, but to delay the inevitable, he stopped at a diner close to where Canal Street came to a stop at the West Side Highway. Sadly, not even the warm normality of hamburgers on a griddle, hot coffee, frying bacon, and the radio tuned to a classic rock station could offer anything but a temporary refuge. He sat at the counter, part of a crowd of delivery drivers and print workers on a break, making a cup of very sweet black coffee and a greasy grilled cheese sandwich last as long as he could. The ploy was of little avail, though. He couldn't bury the knowledge of where he was being drawn. Although he was about as reluctant as a man could be, he knew he had no power to stop himself. He could linger over five cups of coffee, but in the end he would have to leave the noise and humanity and resume his preordained course to the sinister house on the strange block.

The house of the Devil somehow came upon him before he was ready for it. Kelly had been quite convinced that he remembered it being four or five blocks to the south, but suddenly there it was. Without warning, in the middle of what was otherwise industrial and loft territory, he had turned onto the short street with the four tall houses on its north side. An eerie quiet seemed to hang over the block, as though the normal sounds of the city had somehow been suppressed. Trees grew on the street, but no birds, not even the ubiquitous New York pigeons and sparrows, flew from branch to branch or pecked for crumbs or perched on phone wires. No cats sunned themselves on ledges or prowled the alleys between buildings. No winos lolled in any of the doorways, and cabs didn't appear to use the street as a shortcut.

For a full five minutes, Kelly stood diagonally across from the house, just watching and waiting. Such he had learned was the true nature of obsession. One might feel compelled to seek out a particular person or location, but once one was there, once the initial object had been achieved, once the quest had been completed, no more instructions were forthcoming. The obsessive dangled in an incomplete limbo with little idea as to what to do next. Now that he'd reached his appointed destination, Kelly could only stand and wonder, hoping some sign or indication would present itself. To maybe hasten the coming of the sign, he slowly and carefully approached the house, walking as casually as he could down the opposite sidewalk, trying not to show undue interest in any specific building.

In daylight, the house of the Devil revealed no secrets. The exterior had not been painted or otherwise maintained in what looked to be quite a long time. The only exception to this lack of exterior care was an almost new security system, complete with surveillance cameras mounted high on the wall, out of the reach of thieves, vandals, or junkies. It looked as though it must have been installed as recently as in the last three or four months. That the Devil should need state-of-the-art electronic protection came as something of a surprise to Kelly. He could only assume that the Devil's use of temporal devices to defend his domain against temporal intruders was some inverted version of rendering unto Caesar that which was Caesar's. The windows of the house stared down like blind eyes, and no light or movement was apparent. The more Kelly looked, the more it seemed to him that all of the windows had been boarded over or otherwise sealed on the inside. Obviously the Devil wanted no oversight of the iniquities that came to pass inside his infernal sanctuary.

Lacking a sign and unable to think of anything better to do, Kelly settled himself on a doorstep on the opposite side of the street from the house. To stand around simply staring was to invite suspicion that he might be casing one of the houses on the block with the object of burglary. He assumed that the police still now and then patrolled this street, unless, of course, they too shunned it like the cats, birds, and winos. As he seated himself, he realized that he might, in a small way, be breaking the Devil's power over the block. To all outward appearances, he was himself a drunk or derelict sitting in a doorway where no drunk or derelict had sat before, at least since the Devil had taken up residence. He wished that he'd had the foresight to bring a bottle with him. A bottle in a brown bag would have afforded him not only a considerable measure of plausible cover but also an equal measure of actual comfort. Maybe later he would break his compulsive vigil and look for a liquor store.

Later, however, came and went, and Kelly made no move. Morning dragged to lunchtime and advanced into afternoon, Kelly remained motionless, watching the house in a semi-dream. At around three, as far as he could figure the time, having no wristwatch, a mailman made a delivery, but beyond that nothing happened. No one came, no one went. No sound or disturbance emanated from the building. As the mailman continued on his appointed route, rounding the corner and vanishing from sight, Kelly, numb with boredom, slowly shook his head. It would seem that the Devil conducted his business exclusively at night. Was it that Devils feared the sun?

Two, possibly three minutes passed before Kelly realized the significance of his thought. His spine straightened, his sagging head snapped upright, and a look of bemused awe slowly spread across his face. "It would seem that the Devil conducted his business exclusively at night."

Kelly was suddenly scrambling to his feet. "It would seem that the Devil conducted his business exclusively at night!"

He had his sign. God had not abandoned him. God had merely forced him to wait until his own internal puzzle came together and the pieces were in place. With God Almighty, the first thing you learned was that you always had to wait. "It would seem that the Devil conducts his business exclusively at night!"

He repeated the phrase over and over like a newfound mantra. "It would seem that the Devil conducts his business exclusively at night."

He had much to do, but he knew in his heart that his instincts were correct. He had found the truth and it had set him free. He no longer had to sit staring at the grim enigmatic house across the street. Indeed, even if he sat there through the rest of the afternoon, he was confident that he would see nothing. "Do Devils fear the sun? Of course they do."

He was on his feet and walking now. Back the way he had come. Down the block with no birds or cats or cabs. He knew where he was going and exactly what he was going to do. When he reached the end of the block, he didn't even bother to look back at the house. It all made such perfect sense.

"Do Devils fear the sun? Of course they do!"

The sun had set, and inside the Residence, the colony was rising, one by one, from their respective beds and coffins. In some cases, they were bleary eyed, but all were up and moving into the night mode. Almost in parody of a human household, those who didn't plan to spend the night in either meditative, secretive, or just plain antisocial isolation tended to converge on the kitchen of the Residence to check the mail, read the newspapers, or watch videotapes of previously recorded daytime TV before going about their business of the evening. Unlike the dining room, the big Residence kitchen was maintained in a clean and functional condition, even though it was now rarely used for food preparation. The range, sinks, cabinets, counter surfaces, and spice racks all gleamed, and of course, the freezer and the large Maytag refrigerator were in constant use for the packs of whole blood stolen from St. Vincent's, plus any other organic material that one or another of the inhabitants might feel the need to preserve by chilling or deep freezing.

The bizarre echoes of a human family breakfast were accentuated by the rich smell of Italian coffee. One of Lupo's idiosyncrasies was a taste for espresso when he first crawled from his coffin. Sada was usually the first to rise, and she set the coffee-making process in action before retiring to the far end of the long kitchen table to watch the previous afternoon's "Oprah" on a Sony Watchman that was plugged into a small VCR. She did this early viewing in private since no one else in the colony shared her perverse enthusiasm for human TV talk shows.

Renquist was second to arrive in the kitchen, wrapped in a black silk robe with a high, upturned Elvis Presley collar and looking haggard and ill tempered. He nodded curtly to Sada, went to the refrigerator, removed a large jug of ice water, and began to drink copiously. Even after a full day's sleep, Renquist was able to cope with very little until he felt himself fully rehydrated.

Dahlia and Imogene came next, carrying the day's newspapers. Even by their own strange standards, the sisters looked decidedly odd as they walked into the kitchen. The newspapers were about the only normal touch in the picture they had taken such pains to create. Dahlia was wearing a Shirley Temple toy soldier's uniform, childish and cute, apart from a symbolically threatening lightning flash insignia emblazoned on the chest of her outfit. For some inexplicable reason, she was leading Imogene by a leather leash that was looped around her wrist. For her part in this odd masquerade, Imogene was naked apart from an orange chiffon scarf draped about her emaciated hips, a leather collar around her neck to which the leash was attached, and an elaborate owlhead mask constructed from exotic feathers. Insubstantial in her nudity, she seemed little more than the sum total of the adornments that she wore.

The spectacle was sufficiently bizarre that it caused Sada to look up from "Oprah" and frown, and Renquist carefully placed his jug of water on the table to avoid spilling it down the front of his robe. It had taken the Feasting to draw the weird sisters out of their previous, tightly cloistered seclusion, but now they seemed to be going into a radical character realignment. Renquist had long ago ceased trying to chart any logical course in Dahlia and Imogene's complex and ongoing internal drama, but he did wonder what behavioral changes this new and perverse exhibitionism might herald.

As though nothing was even slightly untoward about their entrance, Dahlia placed the stack of newspapers on the table and tapped them authoritatively. "There's something on the front page that may constitute a message from Carfax."

On top of the pile was an early edition of the *Daily News*. The headline read: NEW YORK RIPPER? Renquist picked it up and looked questioningly at Dahlia. "Ripper?"

"I assume as in 'Jack the.' "

Renquist opened the *News* and quickly scanned the story on pages two and three. A dismembered body had been found in a studio apartment on East 34th Street after an anonymous tip. The room had been such a bloody shambles that the *News*, in the endless quest for a banner headline, had dredged up obvious surface parallels with the final Jack the Ripper murder in nineteenth-century London, the stylistically similar mutilation killing of the prostitute Mary Kelly. It was a major leap of cross-cultural reference, but Renquist supposed it made for an eye-catching headline. More significant connections had been made further into the story. Although the police had issued no official statement linking this killing to that of either Fay Latimer or Chelsea Underwood, the *News* didn't fail to recognize the obvious inference. A madman could well be loose in the city, killing and now mutilating women with progressive savagery.

Renquist finished reading, put down the paper, and looked up at Dahlia. "What makes you think it's Carfax?"

Dahlia regarded Renquist as though he was an idiot. "What makes you think it isn't?"

Sada paused the "Oprah" tape and reached for the *Daily News* to see for herself. The scene was starting to remind Renquist of the cast of a newly opened play reading their own reviews. "We could be jumping to conclusions."

Dahlia shook her head. "I think it's safe to assume it's him. Obeying your instructions but going that little bit further to let us know he's still out there."

"Has he been back to the Residence?"

"Not since you and Lupo beat up on him."

"We didn't exactly beat up on him."

Sada glanced up from the *Daily News*. "I understood some of his bones were broken."

Renquist nodded. "That's possible."

Dahlia indicated that it was hardly worth discussing. "You don't have to defend yourself to me, Victor. I'm sure he deserved whatever the two of you did to him."

Renquist looked down at the first paper in the stack, a later edition of the *Post*. This headline had picked up on the idea in the *News* and taken it through a few more leaps of speculation. It read: COPS FEAR RIPPER CULT. Renquist put this one aside without even bothering to scan the report. "I think we're witnessing the start of a media feeding frenzy. I'll be interested to see how the TV stations treat this."

"Isn't this exactly what you wanted?"

Renquist sighed. "I suppose so, but now it's started, it feels a lot like we've commenced to ride the tiger."

Sada nodded. "We probably have." She reached over and took the *Post*, beginning to read the story that Renquist had discarded. "The *Post* seems to think that there are killer satanists on the rampage in the city. Something like the Manson family, only worse."

At that moment, Cynara came into the kitchen. She was smartly dressed for the outside world in a black tailored jacket and leather miniskirt. "Who's like the Manson family?"

This time Dahlia answered. "The killer satanists."

Imogene added the details. "The killer satanists who are supposed to be murdering all our victims."

Dahlia seated herself at the table and indicated that Imogene should kneel on the floor at her feet. Cynara glanced at Dahlia and Imogene, briefly raised an eyebrow but said nothing. She checked the contents of her purse, apparently preparing to go out. "You don't look too happy, Victor. I thought this was your essential master plan."

Renquist shrugged. "I just got up. I'm never too happy when I've just got up."

Sada sniffed. "We all know that."

"I'm also concerned that the police don't start wondering if we're the killer satanists. Thanks to Carfax, we've already attracted official attention."

Sada turned a page. "That would be unfortunate."

"But unfortunately just the way police thinking works."

Cynara snapped her purse closed. "Well, we can all talk about that later. I have to go out."

Renquist looked round. "Go where?"

Cynara's mouth was a bad-tempered, downturned curve. "Out."

"Out?"

"I have a date."

"A date?"

"A date with a human. A mathematician if you're interested." And, with that, she swept out of the kitchen.

Dahlia glanced up at Renquist. "What's her problem?"

"There's a certain competitiveness between her and Julia at the moment. I seem to be caught in the middle."

Imogene was idly stroking her sister's leg. "You shouldn't play them off against each other."

"I don't."

Dahlia clearly didn't believe him. "We heard the fight the other night."

Renquist didn't quite understand why he felt the need to defend himself. "I stopped that."

"That's not to say that you didn't also instigate it."

Sada yawned like a cat and, having finished with the *Post*, pushed it away and turned on "Oprah" again. "Anna Scarlatti has a column about the murders, by the way."

Dahlia frowned. "Who's Anna Scarlatti?"

Imogene answered. "She's the *Post*'s pseudo-angry, quasi-feminist columnist. She's also dark-haired, pretty, and Italian."

"And what does she have to say for herself?"

Sada sighed and once again put "Oprah" on pause. "In a nutshell and between the convolutions of style, she says that these murders are just another example of institutionalized sexism on the part of Mayor Racine and Police Commissioner Washington that leaves women in New York totally unprotected against psycho-killers. She also hints obliquely that the women in this town who have to venture out after dark maybe ought to arm themselves and unhesitatingly blow away any male who so much as looks sideways at them. She seems to think that's what it will take to get any action out of the elected officials. She's also talked to the friends and acquaintances of the two dead women and she paints a picture of them and their lives that's sentimental to the point of being sickening." Sada smiled archly. "Is that what you wanted to know?"

Dahlia grinned nastily at Renquist. "Is that how you remember them, Victor? Sentimental to the point of being sickening?"

Renquist eyed her bleakly. He didn't like to talk about his victims. If nothing else, it made luck turn bad. "As I recall, they both had something of a deathwish."

Imogene fingered the collar around her neck. "Still going after the marginal, Victor?"

Dahlia shook her head. "Humans do have such serious problems with gender. Unlike us, of course." She paused. "Although it might be nice to see a female leading a colony once in a while."

Sada came into the library with a portable phone in her hand. "Carfax wants to speak to you."

"On the telephone?"

Sada eyed Renquist wearily from beneath her dark Betty Page bangs. "That's why I brought the damned thing with me."

Renquist marked his place and closed the large leatherbound book that he had been studying. It was one of the many volumes of Dietrich's journal, and he been going through it looking for insights. He held out his hand. "Then you'd better give it to me."

As Renquist took the phone from her, he realized that it was months since he had conversed by telephone. It was simply something that he didn't do. Lately, Sada and Cynara tended to conduct the bulk of the colony's day-to-day business with the human tradespeople, corporations, and the City. Renquist found that if he needed to communicate with a human, psychic compulsion and thought imposition was faster, easier, and a great deal more satisfying than cumbersome electronics. If he had met a human, even fleetingly, it was simplicity itself either to implant an idea or instruction in the man or woman's mind or to summon them to his presence. For two nosferatu to be talking on the telephone was unthinkably ludicrous, and he had to assume that Carfax was merely trying to irritate him. Carfax's first words immediately confirmed this. "Did you read the newspapers today, Victor?"

Renquist tried not to allow his annoyance to come through too obviously. "Of course, I always read the papers."

"So you've seen what a good boy I've been?"

"I take it the woman on Thirty-fourth Street was one of yours."

"And I did just as you suggested. I made it look like some human maniac."

"Do you think maybe you overdid it just a little?"

"You're never satisfied, are you, Victor?"

"My idea was to cover our tracks. You, on the other hand, seem to be in the process of starting a total media circus."

"I'll try and do better tonight. They do say that practice makes perfect."

"I'd rather you didn't."

A sneer came into Carfax's voice. "Are you telling me that you don't want me to hunt at all?"

"I'm just advising you use a little discretion. Dispose of the remains so things don't get completely out of hand."

The sneer advanced to full-blown nastiness, with maybe even a trace of madness. Another reason Renquist didn't like to talk on the phone was that it gave him a very imprecise picture of the other person. "Are you telling me not to hunt tonight, Victor?"

Renquist's patience was wearing thin. "Of course I'm not telling you that. I'm just advising you to clear up your leavings. You can surely do that, can't you?"

"I don't know, Victor. Can I? I mean, I'm very young and stupid. I don't know what went down in 1919 unless someone forces me to my knees and tells me about it at length and in detail. In fact, I'm so young and stupid, I can't be trusted with the Art of Changing."

Now Renquist could clearly hear the madness. "Why don't

you come back here so we can talk about this face to face?"

"And Lupo can break my bones again if I don't do what you want?"

"This phone conversation is ridiculous."

"Isn't it just, Victor?"

"Where are you?"

"That's for me to know."

"Don't be childish."

"But I am childish, I'm just a wild child."

"You're playing with disaster."

Carfax laughed. He seemed to be either developing or deliberately affecting a high-pitched, psychopathic laugh, not unlike the young Richard Widmark, that gave Renquist the distinct impression that the young one was gorged to the point of craziness. "Maybe we should just see what happens tonight, Victor. Blasco is with me. Between the two of us, we ought to be able to rack up quite a body count."

"I'd recommend that you stop this."

"We haven't even started yet, Victor. Can you imagine what would happen if Blasco and I ran loose in a big luxury hotel, the Plaza or the Hilton or the St. Regis? All those sleeping humans? All those tourists? Think about it, Victor. That would be really causing trouble, a whole lot more radical than some penny-ante body in the lake."

"Are you threatening me?"

"Just fantasizing, Victor. Just fantasizing."

"Is Julia with you?"

Carfax laughed again. "Is Julia with me? I don't think so. I really don't think so."

The line went dead. Renquist put the phone down on the table. He did it slowly and with great care, arranging it so it was exactly parallel to the edge of Dietrich's journal. It was a test of how well he could hold his anger under control. Carfax had brought him to the point where, should he have vented how he felt, he probably could have leveled buildings. He wanted to bring his fist down on the colonial oak table, smashing it to splinters and matchwood. The most he allowed himself, however, was a single furious hiss. "Is Julia with you, you son of a bitch?"

"Of course I'm not with him."

Renquist turned. His face showed no emotion. "I do wish you'd stop sneaking up on me. I'm getting bored with people appearing in doorways."

"I learned it from the movies. At least I don't flap in like a bat."

Despite himself, Renquist smiled and shook his head. "Oh, please."

Julia pouted. "So what am I supposed to do? I'm nosferatu. We take a deathless delight in dramatic entrances. Have you seen the Weird Sisters today?"

Renquist rolled his eyes. "Yes, I saw them first thing."

"That must have improved your day."

"And then Carfax called me on the phone."

"So I gathered."

"Listening at the door?"

"It goes with the dramatic entrance."

"So where is he?"

"What are you going to do to him?"

"Just tell me where he is."

"Not until you tell me what you to intend to do to him."

"I think, this time, I may have to kill him."

"It's just along here. Stop beside that red Toyota."

It had taken almost a half-hour before Julia had finally agreed to lead Lupo and Renquist to Carfax's secondary lair. As she had told them when she finally gave in, "I felt I owed him that much. I did create him, after all. It's a lot like turning in your child."

The limousine came to a smooth halt outside a loft building on Prince Street, just like any one of a hundred other SoHo loft buildings. The limo driver lowered the partition. "Do you want me to wait?"

Renquist shook his head. "No, we won't need you again tonight."

As he spoke, he quickly planted an illusion in the driver's mind. The man would ever after be convinced that, at the time in question, he had dropped three black rap artists at a nightclub on Seventh Avenue and would, in all good faith, swear on a stack of Bibles that it was so. As the limo pulled away into the night Renquist grinned at Lupo and Julia. "There is a lot to be said for being possessed of the ability to cloud men's minds. What human assassin could get away with something like that?"

The first problem was to gain access to the building. The street door bristled with as formidable an array of security devices, locks, and alarms as those that protected the Residence. The common vampires of folklore and bad movies were supposed to be able to transform themselves into diaphanous mist and effortlessly flow under doors and similar obstacles. The true nosferatu, on the other hand, were no more able to alter their molecular structure that any human. Lupo examined the locks and other hardware, loudly sucked on his teeth, and produced a leather folder of picklocks and skeleton keys. "This is complicated. It may take a few minutes."

Julia smiled with a smug superiority. "Don't bother, I have keys."

Lupo's eyes narrowed and he scowled at Renquist. "Are you sure she's not setting us up?"

Julia keyed in a five-digit code on the alarm pad and started to unlock the door. "If you still don't trust me, forget the whole thing."

She opened the door and went inside. Renquist and Lupo followed. Lupo went in, cautious as a pro, moving from one piece of cover to the next as though he expected to come under attack at any given moment. Julia watched him smiling. "You've been running with wiseguys for too long, Brother Lupo."

Lupo scowled and said nothing.

Carfax's lair-away-from-home occupied the fourth floor of the building, and as the old-fashioned, freight-style elevator rose, the lights from each floor cast weirdly angled shadows across the black-clad, pale-faced trio. Stepping out of the elevator, they were confronted by another security door, a fresh set of locks, and another alarm. Lupo treated Julia to a sour look. "I suppose you have the keys to this door as well?"

"It'd be stupidly pointless if I didn't, wouldn't it?"

Again Julia facilitated their entry. Lupo seemed almost disappointed that he wasn't going to have a chance to demonstrate his expertise at breaking and entering. All this was immediately forgotten, though, once they were inside the loft. Lupo and Renquist stopped and looked around in surprise and amazement. "Carfax did all this?"

The large space that they had entered was an unorthodox recreation room decorated in orange and gold velvet and polished black wood. The room contained no furniture, as such, although it was dotted with various devices and strange contraptions specifically designed and purpose-built to control and immobilize the human body in ways that, in a number of cases, looked to verge on the impossible. The benches and frames, the vertical post that could accommodate a tall human male with his arms stretched above his head, the tall X-shaped cross that was the focal point of one end of the room, were all arranged in a manner reminiscent not so much of a torture chamber but of some extraordinary gymnasium, except that where the commercial fitness centers and workout clubs that had become so popular in the last decade or so favored polished chrome, vibrant colors, clean plastic surfaces, and space and light, the prevailing motif here was expensive, hand-tooled leather and decorative patterns of chromium studs. Even though the room was actually very spacious, the design, lighting, and overall ambiance managed to produce an effect of womblike claustrophobia.

Julia regarded Lupo and Renquist's reaction with amusement. "Of course Carfax didn't put all this together. Kurt has neither the expertise, the taste, or even the patience. This place used to be a very exclusive domination parlor. He was able to buy the lease and fittings dirt cheap after a highly placed Brazilian diplomat died of a heart attack in harness, so to speak. The Austrian woman who was the owner-operator decided she'd be well advised to leave the country for a while and was anxious for a quick sale and no questions. Kurt liked the set-up, and he was also attracted by the fact that the place had been professionally soundproofed."

The three nosferatu moved slowly through the room, examining its mechanisms and accoutrements like visitors at a some outlandish museum. Renquist viewed it as the logical extension of what Carfax had done with the playroom. Julia stopped by the central whipping post and ran her hand over the smooth surface of the wood as though feeling for the ingrained echoes of ecstatic suffering and unholy excitement. "When mortals can do this to themselves, it makes you wonder why they need us."

Lupo was far less impressed. "The Inquisition was a great deal more innovative."

Renquist had long since given up on trying to figure the convolutions of human behavior. "The Inquisition also took itself more seriously. This is merely a place of fun."

Julia took a long bullwhip of plaited red and black leather from a wall rack of various implements and cracked it experimentally. The expertise with which she handled it showed that she was no novice when it came to whips. She coiled it and slipped it over her shoulder. "Humanity is a deeply weird species. Do you really think they can survive much longer?"

"Unfortunately, we have to hope they do. We would have a problem being undead without them."

The trio moved through an archway into a smaller space beyond the main room. Here the walls, floor, and ceiling had been painted a uniform black. In total contrast, three gleaming white coffins stood on a raised dais—deluxe funeral parlor models, with gilt hardware and lined with purple satin. Renquist looked questioningly at Julia. "I presume this is Carfax's handiwork?"

Julia avoided Renquist's glance. "That's right."

"One for him, one for Blasco . . ."

Julia shifted uncomfortably. "The one on the right is mine."

Renquist's voice chilled. "If you'd all gone to such pains to create this place, why did you still bother to belong to the colony?"

"I still thought of the colony as home."

"Home?"

Lupo diplomatically interrupted, "Since Carfax obviously isn't here, shouldn't our most important consideration be what to do next?"

Almost in answer, a faint mewing sound came from somewhere else in the loft. The three froze, quickly exchanging glances. They were instantly a hunting pack, a troika unit, ready to act as one. Renquist moved, taking the point, lupine and silent, towards a second archway beyond which seemed to lay the source of the sound. The other two spread out, flanking Renquist and extending their radians of power, ready for anything. Renquist stepped through the arch into a third space that was decorated entirely in red. The source of the sound was immediately apparent. Two aluminum cages, the kind used by zoos and circuses to confine wild animals in transit, were suspended from a steel ceiling beam by chains from each of their four top corners. In each cage was a naked human, a young male and a young female. They were either heavily drugged or hypnotised to the point of mindlessness. The male was curled up as though seeking fetal self-protection, apparently comatose except that his glazed eyes were wide open. The female was kneeling, face pressed to the bars. She was the one making the mewing sounds.

Renquist gestured to Lupo and Julia. "You can come ahead.

In fact, there's something you ought to see."

Lupo and Julia came through the arch and looked up at the two humans. Renquist confronted Julia. "More of Carfax's handiwork?"

She nodded. At least she had the good grace to look a little shamefaced. "He likes to torment them before he kills them."

Victor grimaced. "Children like to pull the wings off flies."

"We don't all share your fine-tuned principles, Victor."

Lupo moved closer to the female's cage. "The question is, what do we do with them?"

Renquist listened to the male's shallow breathing. "I don't feel inclined to leave them as they are, and we clearly can't set them free."

Julia's eyes took on a feral gleam. "None of us have fed tonight."

Renquist hesitated. The idea had a definite appeal, although feeding in such a way seemed distastefully easy after Fay Latimer and the extraordinary orgy in the clandestine ballroom. Julia's breath, however, was already taking on the rich musk of the hunter. "Principles again, Victor?"

Without waiting for an answer, she grasped the padlock that secured the door of the male's cage and snapped it off with one easy twist. She tossed the lock aside and, picking the youth up like a small child, swung him down from the cage. As his feet hit the floor, the boy staggered, but he seemed to recover at least some of his senses. As he blearily looked round for a way out, Renquist quickly read the surface of his mind, but all he found was a vortex of absolute, unfocused terror. The kid seemed unable to distinguish between the present and the immediate past. The faces of Carfax, Blasco, and Julia, laughing and fiendishly distorted, were the front focus of his horror.

Renquist looked swiftly at Julia and Lupo. "Kill them quickly and let's be done with it!"

The boy darted first one way and then the other. His only possible escape route was through the room where the coffins stood on their dais, and he seemed equally as terrified of going in there as he was of the three nosferatu who surrounded him. Julia uncoiled the whip and snapped it at the boy. He let out a gasp as a short angry welt blossomed on his left shoulder. The pain caused the boy to bolt blindly, and he collided with the red wall. The whip cracked again. This time he didn't try to run. He merely sank to his knees whimpering piteously. Pity for humans, though, was alien to Julia. Laughing like a delighted child, she flicked the whip again and advanced on the cringing boy. "Don't make such a fuss. The people who used to come here paid a great deal of money for treatment like this."

The boy seemed to be trying to say something. His mouth moved, but no words came, just an unintelligible animal gibber. Two small puncture marks showed red on his throat. He had been used previously for partial, nonlethal feeding. Julia gestured to Lupo. "Loose the female."

Lupo needed no second urging. The lust to feed also had him in its grip. Lupo didn't bother with the lock. He used his massive strength to rip the door clear off the second cage, and then jerked the girl to the floor. The female was much more focused on survival than the male had been. She darted past Lupo, going straight to the coffin room. Seemingly she could distinguish between a symbolic fear and a clear and present danger. Lupo lunged for her, but terror made her agile. She ducked under his arm and was away through the arch. Lupo went after her and Renquist was about to follow when Julia's voice halted him. "Stay with me, Victor."

Renquist turned. With one hand, she had a paralyzing grip on the back of the boy's neck. Her other hand held a long narrow switchblade, and she was about to open a vein in his throat. The boy made one desperate lunge to get away, but Julia smashed him down with her forearm. The knife flashed and blood spurted. It was not going to be tidy. Screams came from the other part of the loft. Lupo had evidently caught up with the girl.

Julia's mouth was at the boy's neck. She drank deeply and, at the same time beckoned to Renquist. "Quickly, Victor! He won't last long."

Instantly Renquist was at her side and his own mouth was pressed to the same bleeding wound that Julia's lips had vacated a moment before. The blood flowed into him and with it came the terrible serenity and the infusion of strength that was the consummation of the kill. He paused for breath and Julia pushed him to one side. Her voice was hoarse with excitement and wampyr greed. "I want the final moment."

Renquist wanted to hurl her away and take it for himself, but decorum won out and he moved to one side. As the boy died, his back arched in one last reflex spasm, then he shuddered and became limp. Julia lowered the lifeless body to the ground and slowly rose from the corpse. Blood smeared her mouth and chin. She smiled crookedly at Renquist. "You see, Victor, we've fed together. I knew we would. It never happens in the way that you expect."

The boy's body and the long black-and-red plaited whip lay on the floor behind them. Renquist wiped his own mouth. "That's right, we've fed together."

"That rather alters things, doesn't it?"

"I suppose it does."

Julia moved towards him. Suddenly Cynara's face was superimposed over hers. Renquist quickly turned and walked back to where the three coffins stood on their dais. Without a word, and with great silent concentration, starting with the one in which Julia had slept, he began smashing them to pieces. He continued until nothing remained but fragments of white paint, raw wood, and tatters of purple satin.

chapter Five

"So you hunted with Julia?"

Cynara was an accusatory sheet of ice—no warmth, no aura, expressing nothing but a bitter and angry disappointment. Renquist, just back inside the Residence after racing through the streets with Lupo and Julia to beat the coming dawn, was taken completely off guard and instantly placed on the defensive. The hour was late. The sun would be up in a matter of minutes. He was tired and certainly in no mood for further conflict. "We went looking for Carfax—Lupo, Julia, and myself. He had called me by telephone, threatening to go on an uncontrolled rampage."

"And did you find him?"

"We found his lair, but neither he nor Blasco were there."

"And, failing to find him, you and Julia decided to indulge in a little hunting trip of your own?"

Renquist emphatically shook his head. Why the hell was he defending himself? He'd done nothing for which he felt the need to feel any guilt. "It wasn't like that at all. The prey was already there. Two young humans, locked in cages. Carfax and Blasco had been taking them by the slow path."

"That must have been extremely convenient. You didn't even have to go out to eat."

"All we did was put them out of their misery."

Cynara's sarcasm was of such intensity that it might easily have shattered glass. "Well, Victor, what can I say? If you were human, you'd probably qualify for sainthood."

"I don't need this, Cynara. It's entirely the wrong time, and you have entirely the wrong idea."

"The wrong idea, Victor? Are you telling me you weren't bonding with Julia?"

"I'm warning you, Cynara . . ."

"Were they males or females?"

Renquist was confused. Cynara still had him off balance. "Were who males or females?"

"The young humans."

"One of each, why?"

"And which one did you and Julia feed from?"

"The boy. What does that have to do with anything?"

"So you and Julia fed from the same male human. How cozy."

Renquist experienced a brief recall flash of Julia's bloody lips rising from the wound in the boy's neck. In the next instant, he hoped that Cynara hadn't also seen it in his mind. At that point, all he could do was bluster. "This has nothing to do with you, Cynara."

"So it would seem."

Renquist suddenly flashed with anger. "Damn it, I wasn't deliberately bonding with Julia."

Cynara's frozen cool was the perfect foil for Renquist's anger. "As you say, it has nothing to do with me. I suppose I'm making too much of the fact that you and I have run and hunted together for more than a century. I know that your little protégé has been throwing herself at you lately, but I must confess that I imagined you were somehow above her youthfully obvious blandishments. It seems I was wrong, though, doesn't it?"

"It was merely the heat of feeding."

Cynara's emotional temperature dropped to somewhere near the level of liquid nitrogen. "The heat of feeding?"

"That's right. Believe me, I am not having any liaison with Julia."

"You created her. I suppose you can do what you like with her."

The dawn was just minutes away and all Renquist wanted was for the conversation to cease. Wasn't Cynara tired? "Listen, I have a great deal to contend with at the moment. I am trying to hold this colony together and ensure that we all survive. You have no reason to be jealous of a relationship forming between myself and Julia because there is no relationship."

Cynara clearly was not interested in being convinced. "I wonder if she sees it that way."

"Cynara, please . . ."

Cynara cut him off. "Oh, don't worry, Victor. I'm not about to do anything that would in any way jeopardize the colony. As Master, you can still count on my absolute loyalty. We can wait until the crisis has passed before we re-evaluate our personal relationship."

Renquist was at a loss to know what to say. He wished that he could enter Cynara's mind and prove to her that the furthest thing from his thoughts was to be running around with someone like Julia. The barrier, however, was impenetrable. "There's really no need for any of this, Cynara. After all we've been through together, after all we've meant to each other . . ."

Cynara radiated contempt. "After all we've meant to each other?"

"That's what I said."

"Could the word you're grasping for be 'love,' Victor?"

* * *

The pay phone in the lobby of the Dupont Hotel was hardly the place to be making a call to the Library of the Archdiocese, but Kelly could only tell himself that it had to be better than calling from either a tavern or from the street. Even though it was only ten in the morning, the old men had already gathered around the big old TV with the cigarette-scarred fake colonial cabinet, watching Jenny Jones refereeing some gender-based family conflict.

Kelly dropped a quarter into the slot and dialed the number scrawled on the piece of paper. He was answered on the third ring.

"Hello, can I help you?"

"Could I please speak with Father Rattigan?"

The voice at the other end was cautious. "This is he."

"My name is Gideon Kelly and I need to consult a collection of papers, copies of which I believe are kept in the library."

Father Rattigan was still cautious. "What papers would those be, Mr. Kelly?"

"The records and journals of a Bishop Rauch. From 1919. They refer to something called the Fifth Seal."

"One moment, Mr. Kelly."

Kelly could hear the sound of a computer being keyed, followed by a lengthy pause. Finally Father Rattigan came back on the line. Now he was more than cautious, he was overtly guarded. "Mr. Kelly . . ."

"Yes?"

"Mr. Kelly, I've checked on the material you're asking about and we do have copies of the Bishop Rauch papers. The originals are, of course, at the Vatican."

"So can I come by and inspect what you have?"

"I have to check on that with my immediate superior."

Kelly smelled trouble. Old Catholic trouble. "Why do you have to do that?"

"There was a note in the computer file that a check should

be run on any lay person inquiring about the Bishop Rauch or Fifth Seal papers."

Even though he knew what was coming, Kelly went along with the game. "So check me out. My name is Gideon Aaron Kelly. Do you want me to spell that?"

"I already checked, Mr. Kelly. That's why I have to talk with the head librarian."

"That's okay. Go talk with him. I'll hold."

"It could take a few minutes."

Kelly had come prepared for exactly this eventuality. He had a further nine quarters ready in his hand. "I'll wait."

Rattigan was only gone for three quarters' worth of time. "Mr. Kelly . . ."

"Yes?"

"I talked with Father Muncie and he says that you may come and look at the papers. He did add, though, that, should there be a repetition of the business of the exorcism, he will personally punch your lights out and enjoy doing it. He'd said that you'd understand. Do you understand, Mr. Kelly?"

Kelly was amazed. Muncie had to be mellowing in his old age. "Yes, I understand. I understand completely. Thank Father Muncie for me. Tell him I'll be along in about an hour."

Kelly hung up the phone. He looked slowly around at the old men watching Jenny Jones. They had no idea what was happening right under their noses. He, Gideon Kelly, was on the move again!

As sleep came, Renquist discovered that he once again had no control over the progression of his dream state, and this time around, the body in which he found himself was not even his own. He recognized this fact immediately, even before the horror of being out in the sun under a brilliant blue sky had began to subside. The body in which he found himself was larger and heavier than his. It was also stronger and faster, but it seemed to boast little in the way of logic or memory, and compensated for the lack by being possessed of an unrefined savagery. The body in which he found himself also wasn't at all happy. Its emotions seemed to fluctuate between a violent, hate-filled fury and a desperation so absolute that it made him cringe to be even close to such a feeling. The body in which he found himself wanted to die. The only thing it now truly craved was death, but death was among the many things that were currently being denied to it. The sun beat down on its leathery armored skin, but it was too dehydrated to sweat. It was weak with hunger and exhaustion, but it could neither feed nor stop to rest. With each step, it sank almost to its knees in the soft white sand of the featureless desert that stretched clear to the horizon. The discs were still hunting it and each time it sensed that one was approaching, it would furiously dig downwards with its powerful, clawed hands and feet to conceal itself in the sand until the glowing machine had passed overhead.

Even in the dream state, Renquist knew that this wasn't any conventional random looping of the neurons, a synaptic butterfly dance to evaluate and download the input of wakefulness. Renquist knew that he had entered a pod of memory, not his own, but something much more ancient and venerable, a memory common to all of his kind, vividly preserved in the helix of the complex and recombinant nosferatu DNA. He could only assume that he had entered the memory of one of the Original Beings, that he was in the time of the Great Experiment, the Great Failure, and the Flight.

For the first time, he looked around and saw that the body in which he found himself was not alone. Maybe a dozen other creatures struggled through the sand as he did. They were humanoid, but nothing close to human, tall bipeds with bodies covered in black plate-like scales, small reptilian heads, and red slanted eyes. As they stumbled across the seemingly endless desert, they continually scanned the skies for the pursuing discs. A faint drumming from the ground beneath his feet gave early warning of a disc beyond the horizon and once again the body hurled itself into the sand, scrabbling for cover. One of the others wasn't fast enough. The glowing disc cleared the horizon and a deathray shot from the underside of the disc, incinerating the unfortunate victim in the flash of a nanosecond. The body considered ending its entire ordeal by simply standing motionless, but its remorseless, built-in survival instinct wouldn't allow it the relief of suicide. The Creators had designed them too well. Such had been the nature of the Great Mistake.

The Creators had sought to make a weapon, but then They had discovered that the weapon They had made posed a threat even to Their existence. In Their horror, They had attempted to destroy the things to which They had given such ruthless and violent life. For the most part They had succeeded. First with the sunbomb and then with the discs and the deathrays, the Creators had annihilated all but a handful of the Original Beings. The body in which Renquist found himself had to be one of the survivors, one of his own ancient ancestors actually taking part in the Flight.

Renquist was awed. To experience such a moment in nosferatu history could hardly be pure happenstance. Something wickedly synchronous had to be at work. He would have liked to wonder why, but he was rapidly merging with the body in which he had found himself and his previous objectivity was fading fast as he sank into the psyche of the Being. His last independent hope was that he would have some recall of this when waking came, if waking came.

The young priest behind the desk had the headphones of a Walkman clamped over his head. Gideon Kelly wondered what he was listening to. Vivaldi? U2? A teach-yourself Swahili tape? Whatever it was, it prevented him from hearing Kelly's approach. When he finally looked up and saw Kelly's disheveled figure standing over him, he was unable to keep his face from registering a combination of shock and alarm. Kelly had to give him secondary points for a fast recovery, though. As quickly as he could, the young priest put on a watery smile of inquiry. "Can I help you?"

"I came here to do some research."

The young priest's face hardened and he removed the light-weight headphones. "I'm sorry sir, this library isn't normally open to the general public. The public library is over on Sixth Avenue, by Forty-second Street."

He put particular emphasis on his second use of the word "public." Kelly's eyes narrowed. The young man was one of a breed Kelly loathed, what he categorized as corporate priests. They thought in terms of their career, and they always seemed to manage to wind up in some big city, close to the centers of power. They were natural aides, staff officers, bureaucrats, and protectors of their superiors' space and time. The same ones had probably conspired and plotted in the rear echelons of the Inquisition. This one looked as though he only just started shaving, and Kelly decided he needed to learn that, in the House of the Lord, it didn't always pay to judge by appearances. "The public library? That's the one with the stone lions outside, right?"

The young priest nodded. "That's the one." He was suddenly wary. He believed he was dealing with a nut and he was moving his defenses into place. Kelly caught his glance at the phone. He was already considering calling for backup. "I don't think they'd have what I need in the public library."

"Well, I'm sorry, but the material we have in this library is only available by specific appointment."

Kelly smiled. "Yes, well, as it happens, I have a specific appointment."

The priest swivelled in his chair so he was facing that computer that stood to the right of the reception desk. "Your name?"

"Are you Rattigan?"

The priest looked as though he'd suddenly bitten into a lemon. "Father Rattigan isn't here right now. He's taking an early lunch. If you'd just tell me your name."

"It'll probably be quicker if, instead of looking in your computer, you just call Father Muncie."

The priest swallowed. "Father Muncie?"

Kelly laughed. Obviously Muncie was still laying the fear on his boy assistants. "Just call Father Muncie and tell him that Gideon Kelly is here to look at the Rauch file."

"The Rauch file?"

"That's what I said."

The young priest reluctantly picked up the phone and keyed in three digits. "Father Muncie? Yes, this is Father Schnabel at the front desk. There's a person here who says his name is Gideon Kelly and he wants . . ." He stopped and listened, with his expression becoming increasingly confused. "Yes. Very well. I'll tell him that." He looked up at Kelly. "Father Muncie will be right down."

Kelly was actually starting to enjoy himself. He had just realized that he'd been borrowing his attitude from an old private eye novel, a Mickey Spillane book, the one in which Mike Hammer is dragging himself back from the seven-year drunk he went on when his secretary Velda was kidnapped by the communists. He wished that he could remember the title. Perhaps he should ask the young librarian priest, but he suspected that he wouldn't know either. "You don't know what I am, do you, boy?"

The young priest looked thoroughly bewildered. "I'm sorry . . ."

"I'm the Hammer of God, boy. I'm the Lost Lamb working his way back to the State of Grace. You've probably never met anything like me."

The priest glanced nervously at the door behind him that led to the library's inner sanctum. To his relief, Father Muncie, the head librarian, almost immediately came through the door. Father Dwayne Muncie was something completely different. He was a massive man, once muscular but now running to middle-aged fat. The claim was that he had once played tight end for Notre Dame but Kelly had never actually confirmed this. Sports had never really interested him. Muncie advanced on Kelly as though it was no pleasure seeing him again. "What hole did you crawl out of, Kelly?"

"My own private sink of iniquity."

"I don't doubt it. And now you want to look at the Rauch file?"

"That's right. I—"

Muncie cut him off. "Don't tell me. It's these murders, isn't it? You've got it into your sick and demented head that there are vampires on the loose in New York City. Am I right?"

"I just want to look through the file. That's all."

"Don't bullshit me, Kelly. This is Dwayne Muncie you're talking to. One minute after you called, I guessed what was on your mind."

The young priest was looking from one man to the other with an expression of total amazement. Kelly knew that the only way to handle Muncie was to hold his ground and not back down. "Just suppose there was an outbreak of vampirism in the city? Wouldn't that be the concern of the Church?"

"This is a rerun of the exorcism business, isn't it? Didn't I already warn you about pulling something like this? Why don't you get it into your head that, for all practical purposes, there are no such things as vampires in this day and age?"

"You've read Rauch's journals, haven't you?"

Muncie scowled. "The current position is that Rauch was crazy."

"You know better than that."

"I also know better than to make waves. I like this job and I intend to hang on to it until I'm good and ready to retire. I certainly don't need a lunatic like you coming round here and causing trouble."

"Suppose I could furnish proof, actual hard evidence."

Muncie wearily leaned on the desk. "You really don't get it, do you? The very last thing that the Holy Church needs at the end of the twentieth century are ghouls, goblins, flying saucers, or the walking dead. You could bring Count Dracula himself into the Cathedral and drive a stake through him on the high altar and the Cardinal would deny that it ever happened. How can you expect someone like the Cardinal to preach a return to family values or condemn the sins of the flesh, and at the same time countenance the existence of vampires in New York City?"

Kelly had heard speeches like this before, but he doggedly continued to go for his goal. "Do I get to see the Rauch file or not?"

Muncie sighed. "You're a stubborn little bastard, aren't you?"

Kelly knew that the game might have to go through a few more twists and passes, but Muncie wasn't going deny him the file. Muncie was too much of an independent thinker and too much of a scholar of the bizarre. He would never admit it, but he was probably fascinated as to what Kelly might be up to now. "So?"

Muncie wasn't ready to give anything away quite yet. "So I think you should get out of here and stop bothering me."

"It'd be easier to shut me up by giving me the file."

"It'd be easier if I gave you a sound thrashing for your damned impudence."

"Just give me a few hours with the Rauch papers and I'll never bother you again."

"Is that a promise?"

"I swear."

"And if you get yourself into trouble you won't come running to the Church for protection?"

"I swear."

"And if anyone asks you, you were never here and I never gave you the file."

"I swear."

Muncie turned to the young priest. "Get this miserable

wretch the files on Bishop Rauch, but if he does anything else but read them in total silence, throw him out of here on his ass. Or if you don't think you can manage that, call me, and I'll throw him out myself."

Renquist had done nothing to change the scenario, but nevertheless the scenario had changed. It felt as though some entity, some external force, had taken control of his dreams. He didn't like it one bit, but he realized that he had absolutely no choice in the matter. Resist as he might, the force or entity was going to take him exactly where it wanted him to go and he couldn't do a single thing about it. In all of his considerable lifespan, he had experienced nothing to match it, and he would have liked to have had a moment to pause, to consider the nature of whatever it was that had him in its power. He would also have liked a moment to pause and to be just plain scared. Anything that could bend his sleeping will in this way had to be able to wield a force that defied even his imaginings. The change from the white, hot desert and the remorseless blue sky had come like a cinematic dissolve. With only the most fractional moment of transition, he found himself in a new body and new place. At least the place was cool and dark, and the body was contented and actually seemed rather pleased with itself. He was in a rock cavern with what appeared to be sandstone walls daubed with crude prehistoric paintings of men and animals. It was lit by guttering torches of plaited, oil-soaked straw that burned with smoky red flames.

This new body was much more like his own than that of the Original Being that he had just left. It was still taller and more muscular, some seven-and-a-half feet in height, but its DNA had obviously been combining with that of humanity for some time. Gone was the plate-like armored hide. The head was larger and more human in shape, although the mouth was filled with long, nonretractable, and dangerously pointed fangs, making it impossible to close. Renquist recalled from his reading that a similar condition had contributed to the extinction of the saber-toothed tiger. The red eyes had been replaced by ones almost identical to those of the contemporary nosferatu, but it was hard in the smoky gloom to judge exactly what their capacity might be. The mind was no longer driven by programmed rage. It wasn't particularly brilliant, but it at least had memory and the capacity to reason. The body had also developed gender; he was inside the mind and personality of something that was definitely male.

At the moment that Renquist entered him, however, the creature was neither reasoning nor remembering, and no effort on his part could force it to do otherwise. He was totally absorbed in savoring the dread, the fearful worship of the humans who were also in the cave, and the anticipation that, very shortly, he would feed upon one or more of them. The humans were small brown people, with the look of Indo-Europeans, but their minds were so paralyzed by terror that he could read nothing else about them. The being he inhabited also had no interest in reading these people. He was aware that they worshipped him as their resident God of Death and that was all that seemed to matter.

Renquist found that, in this new environment, he didn't slip so quickly into the subjectivity of the host body. The Original Being had been under intense stress, fleeing as it had been from the flying discs and their deathrays. This new being felt strangely passive. He apparently didn't have to hunt, and in his role as a God, he also had nothing to fear. Having made a cursory inspection of the body, Renquist began to look round at the larger environment. He discovered that he actually had a small measure of control over the creature. He could focus his eyes and even turn his head a little. As far as he could tell, the host was aware of Renquist's intrusion, but it didn't worry him in the slightest. The creature was smugly contented in its apathy.

The cave was large, maybe 20 or 30 yards long and ten yards

wide. It looked as though it had started out as a natural, probably water-created formation that had then been worked on by many humans with crude hand tools both to enlarge it and to make it more symmetrical. His host sat at one end of the cave on a large chair or throne, hewn out of the living rock. The throne in turn stood on a rock shelf or platform, akin to a stage, that plainly was supposed to emphasize its superiority. What could only have been massive quantities of human blood had stained the area at the foot of the throne a dull rust color. The group of humans, some 25 or 30 strong, remained at the other end of the cave, kneeling prostrate, arms stretched out in front of them and with faces pressed to the rock floor.

Renquist seemed to have come into the picture somewhere in the middle of some crude ceremony. From the creature's brutish sense of anticipation, he judged that the ritual would culminate in the sacrifice of one or more of the humans. In this new world, everything seemed to move incredibly slowly. Obviously the humans were in no hurry to bring the proceedings to their logical finale, but neither, it appeared, was the thing that he now inhabited. He was coming to the conclusion that his first impression had tended to overestimate the thing's intellect, and, in fact, it was extremely stupid.

Finally, the creature, which Renquist was starting to think of as maybe the nosferatu equivalent of a neanderthal, raised a heavy hand, signalling to the humans. It uttered three words in a deep, booming voice, which Renquist suspected the humans found quite god-like as it reverberated around the ceiling of the cavern.

"Ygnaiih dunach ort!"

Renquist recognized the language as a crude and degraded version of the old speech that the nosferatu of his time still used in ceremonies like the Aodaun or the Pualdis. Whoever or whatever was controlling this dream had taken him not only thousands of years into the past, but also to some strange backwater of nosferatu evolution.

THE TIME OF FEASTING 213

The words and gesture had an instant and electrifying effect on the humans. A half-dozen of them immediately scrambled to their feet, seized two more of their number from out of the group, a young male and a young female, and dragged them in the direction of the throne. The ones doing the dragging were clad in loincloths of some rough woven material and had necklaces of what looked to be turquoise around their necks. The dragees were naked. Their bodies were painted with circles and triangles in red and indigo and they appeared to be heavily drugged, since they put up little resistance to the fate that so clearly awaited them. It occurred to Renquist that maybe his host was so dumb, dull, and sluggish because he survived on a diet of blood that was heavy with some ancient and probably highly crude narcotic. Perhaps this was the way the humans exercised some measure of control over their god. They kept him sedated and brought his food to him rather than risk him running amok, hunting through their villages or whatever passed for habitations in this primitive time.

The two human sacrifices were deposited at the foot of the platform that supported the creature's throne, and then the ones who had brought them there beat a hasty retreat back to their still prostrate companions. Renquist's host rose creakingly from his seat, leaned forward, and seized each of the offerings by the back of their necks, one in each massive hand, and lifted them clean off their feet. With the first move that approached anything like swift, he twisted his head, one way and then the other, and bit out each of their throats, that of the male first and the female second. The crudeness of the action was a severe shock to Renquist's twentieth-century sensibilities. He had to have been transported to a time well before the discovery of wampyr finesse. This ancient feeding was going to be a bloody and disgusting business.

The Rauch File could not have been examined by anyone for at least a couple of decades. The three storage boxes that Schnabel brought him were old and dusty, and Kelly had to handle their contents, both the translations and the photocopies of the original German text, with almost archaeological care. Most of the individual pages were brown around the edges, damaged by the chemicals used in the copying process that speeded up the natural oxidization and breakdown of the paper. A great deal of the material in the manila folders Kelly found crammed into the boxes was also irrelevant to his purpose. He might have learned something from the letters that had passed between Bishop Rauch and his assistants and the office of the Pope and other Vatican officials. Unfortunately around 80 percent of the information contained in them had been obliterated by some heavy-handed censor wielding a black marking pen, arbitrarily deciding what was and what was not appropriate for inclusion in the semi-public record. Kelly also discovered that almost one entire box was filled with fundamentally useless day-by-day accounts of the great Fifth Seal vampire hunt that Rauch had organized in 1919, couched in almost balance-sheet terms of actions taken, results obtained, expenses incurred, and assets seized.

Kelly had worked his way through close to two of the three boxes before he came across anything that had any bearing on his own mission. The good news was that, almost as soon as he opened the manila file containing the unusually lengthy record of an action at an old and isolated house outside of Munich, he knew he had struck the pay dirt he was seeking. It must have been realized at the time that, in the course of this extermination, the vampire hunters had struck something both exceptional and extraordinary. Bishop Rauch himself had felt moved to pen a personal introduction to the file. The exact location of the house had been obliterated by the censor, but otherwise the file was virtually intact, and Kelly could hardly believe his luck when he discovered the section on the finding of the Munich vampire's library. He quickly leafed through the pages in question to confirm his first impression and then settled down to detailed reading.

The first party to gain entrance to the house was surprised to discover that one of the cursed night-crawlers had taken such pride in its debased and repulsive condition that it had actually maintained an extensive and carefully catalogued library of books appertaining to all aspects of the vampire and its behavior. Some of these hellish volumes were printed while others were hand written, and taken as a whole, they provided a gruesome compendium of the legends, mores, and beliefs of the creature and its kind. Also included was what purported to be a wholly blasphemous history of the vampires' origins and development. Some of those who first inspected the books had much difficulty in believing that such a thing could come to pass. They initially assumed that the library had belonged to some unfortunate previous occupant of the house who had been done away with by the nightcrawler, but whose library had remained intact.

It was only when the books themselves were examined by a specially commissioned group of clerics and bibliophiles that the truth became apparent. A vampire had been discovered and dispatched that somehow, in its infinite vanity, had indulged in some perverted parody of human scholarship. In addition to the volumes relating to the vampire and the cult of vampirism, the collection also included rare and obscure works on the black arts and other abominations and obscenities. This fact caused some of the learned group to entertain the idea that the library had in fact belonged to some human necromancer and diabolist who had perhaps actually conjured this particular nightcrawler into being by use of the Satanic arts. The evidence that, at the very last moment, when it clearly knew that its end was inevitable, the vampire had set a fire with the aim of destroying the library and its contents, appeared to prove, however, that the collection had been amassed, at least in the greater part, by the vampire itself.

Kelly moved on through the papers to the various summaries of the books from the vampire library that had survived the final attempt at destruction. The summary of the vampire history began with a stern warning from Bishop Rauch.

The following is clearly a fiendishly deceitful ploy on the part of the foul fiend to disguise its unholy and satanic origins and invest itself with a spurious historical context. It is simply presented as both a point of interest and a guide to the limitless capacity for deception that is practiced by these creatures. The reader should view what follows with the most rigorous skepticism and not allow himself to be lured into any sympathy for or belief of its author.

Having digested the disclaimer, Kelly moved on to the meat of the matter.

The supposed history of the vampire as a species, as recounted in documents discovered at [deleted] in Bavaria, commences in approximately 14,000 B.C. According to the work's hellish author, this time was an era of visitation by beings from outer space who are generally referred to in the vampire texts as The Creators, but are also, with a devilish perversion of Holy Writ, identified as "The Nephilim," blatantly defined as the same Nephilim that are mentioned as malign spirits in the Book of Enoch. The Creators/Nephilim are alleged to have come from a star system called Zeta Reticuli. It is also alleged that they not only visited the Earth regularly throughout ancient history, but continue to do so right up to the present day. This statement is patently absurd, but, appearing as it does in a patently absurd document, it constitutes no paradox.

During the time in question, some sixteen thousand years ago, before the dawn of human civilization, these supposed alien beings had, according to the vampire author, actually established what amounted to a colonial settlement in the area between the rivers Tigris and Euphrates, near the site that would later be occupied by the city of Babylon.

Again according to the author, The Creators, among other bizarre practices, conducted genetic experiments on human beings, and the vampire, along with other forms of demonic being, were the products of these experiments. In the case of the vampire, The Creators had sought to breed the perfect warrior being. These beings were allegedly bipedal and some nine feet tall, an apparent combination of human and reptile with thick armored hide and incredible physical strength. The things were also deathless, indestructible, and possessed of a sustained and savage fighting rage. To be free of the need for constant supplies, these genetically tailored warriors were designed with the capability of feeding on the blood of the native population.

Unfortunately for The Creators, they discovered that their new creations, referred to in the text as the "Original Beings," turned out to be far from perfect. Their fighting rage was so intense that they were impossible to discipline or organize into any coherent military unit. Their strength and rapacious instincts made them almost impossible to confine, but if they were permitted to run free, they ceaselessly hunted and killed the human population and even posed a threat to The Creators themselves. A further complication arose when it was discovered that their blood, when commingled with that of humans, reorganized the genetic structure of the human victims, who returned to life in a new and altered state, stronger, taller, and with the same insatiable thirst for blood. These hybrid creatures did, however, exhibit a single weakness. They had a marked sensitivity to direct sunlight.

The Creators decided that the only course of action they could take in the matter of their failed experiment, called in the text "The Great Mistake," was to admit their error and utterly destroy the fruits of their failed experiment. Accordingly, they attempted to gather all of the Original Beings in one place and something called the "sunbomb" was dropped on them from a Nephilim flying machine. The sunbomb is one of the least plausible of the vampire author's inventions, claiming as he does that it is the product of some manner of atomic fission, a device that would be beyond the capabilities of even our most advanced scientists here in the 1920s.

The story goes on to declare that a small number of the Original Beings managed to escape the destruction of the sunbomb, and were hunted across the deserts of Asia Minor by flying discs, controlled by The Creators and armed with death rays. A small number of the Original Beings were able to escape even this fate and they travelled east to the Indus valley where, it is claimed, either they or their transformed human victims established themselves as counterfeit Gods of Death, demanding sacrificial tribute from the haplessly ignorant prehistoric inhabitants of the region.

At this point, an editorial note of warning had been inserted into the summary:

> Such concepts as invaders from another world, the sunbomb, the flying discs, and deathrays should be a clear indication to the reader that this Bavarian text is entirely fabricated. It is not even a deluded attempt to record something that the vampire author actually believed, no matter how erroneously, to be a true and faithful account of the history of creatures like himself. Even the most cursory examination can only reveal that it is nothing more than a transparent hoax, undoubtedly inspired, in the large part, by the fictional writings of the English fantasist and agnostic, Herbert George Wells.

Kelly looked up from the 70-year-old papers. Although the Rauch file was proving fascinating reading, the day was now well into midafternoon. He was hungry and, more than that, he could have used a drink in the worst possible way. He saw that the young librarian, Father Schnabel, was covertly watching him from behind his computer. Neither Schnabel nor even Muncie wanted him there, pawing through papers that were probably something of an embarrassment to the contemporary Church. He could imagine the bureaucracy that he'd run into if he tried to leave the library for a half-hour and then come back and resume his research. He returned to the page in front of him.

> The author of the vampire text has been quite cunning in the way in which he makes use of history

and ancient literature to add a dubious credence to his imaginings. The creature not only cites the Book of Enoch but uses other pre-Christian texts to add some support to his sinister deception. He claims that the ancient Sumerian "Epic of Gilgamesh" is a distorted account of a rebellion against Nephilim by their human vassals, and their abandonment of their colony and departure from Earth. The vampire further claims that the mother and son deities of the Sumerians, Innin and Tammuz, were, in fact, two of the most advanced forms of the hybrid that had developed from the Original Beings, and that the death of the god-son Tammuz was one of the first recorded vampire deaths from being burned in the sun. He states that by 3,000 B.C. vampires had infiltrated Danubian culture, and even points to the Minotaur legend of Minoan Crete as being a garbled version of one of the last surviving Original Beings dwelling in the subterranean labyrinth under the city of Minos. He even claims that cult of Isis and Osiris in Egypt in the twenty-fifth century B.C. was founded by yet another pair of the disgusting creatures. As the devout reader should have thoroughly realized by now, the so-called vampire historian not only seeks to deceive, but also seems to be attempting to elevate the degraded condition of it and its kind by making any number of preposterous and overweening claims to a place and a role in the history of God and man.

After the next shift of dreamstate, Renquist knew exactly where he was. The cool limestone walls with their colored, stylized paintings, the small pottery lamp, the furniture with its scrollwork, enamel, and gold leaf were all highly familiar from his years of study. Even the rectilinear architecture and the high flat ceiling would have been enough to tell him that he was in ancient Egypt, some 2,000 years prior to the Christian era. Renquist had dreamed of places like this before and he had often wished that he possessed the power to direct his dreams to such a place more often. It had been a time when the nosferatu had enjoyed a coexistent role in the society of men. Their place had been separate and feared, but still respected. The priests of Isis had realized that cooperation and a liberal if formalized response to the intelligence, memory, and power of the nosferatu was well worth the compromise bargain that had been struck between his kind and humanity. It had, of course, taken a totally death-obsessed culture to strike and consummate such a deal. In an epoch when even the crude popular songs of the slave and laboring classes lamented the brevity and pointlessness of human life, the hope of the priests and philosophers had been that, eventually, the nosferatu would teach them what lay beyond the veil of mortality. What the priests in the temple of Isis refused to understand was that the nosferatu knew no more about the void on the other side of death than even the most humble human, and, if anything, having something close to immortality within their grasp, feared it all the more. Some nosferatu historians made the exaggerated claim that Isis and Osiris had been wampyr themselves, but Renquist knew that wasn't the truth. The two deities had been something else entirely, something that he had never cared to investigate.

The body that Renquist had entered was, in most respects, very similar to his own (albeit female) and he felt fairly comfortable inside it. He was visiting what he judged to be a true nosferatu. Unlike the two previous beings he had encountered in the strange dream progression, this one was also aware of Renquist's presence. She appeared to have no objection to a stranger quietly inhabiting a part of her mind, and oddly, she showed no curiosity as to what Renquist might be or where he might have come from. Although the individual showed no inclination to communicate with Renquist, he did receive the impression that an intrusion of this kind was not a unique experience and that it had happened before.

In this phase of the bizarre and uncontrolled dream, and in contrast to the two other encounters, Renquist found himself completely excluded from the entity's subjective thoughts and feelings. He could see through the host eyes, but he was being allowed no contact with her reactions. Sufficient leak-through existed, however, for Renquist to receive a fairly comprehensive impression of his host's situation and mental state. He even received a name. The humans with whom his host interacted knew her as Amu-Sinsobe. Renquist made a mental note that, if he woke with a recall of any of this, he would attempt to find out if reference to a nosferatu called Amu-Sinsobe could be found in the Residence's extensive library.

The strongest impression that Renquist received was that Amu-Sinsobe was in the grip of such boredom and isolation that she was close to being incapacitated. She had been confined in this place for close to half a century, and although she was provided with every material need to such a lavish degree that her life was one of undeniable luxury, she saw himself as being little different from one of the exotic animals that were caged in the royal zoo, or the tiny pygmy people from the scarcely explored lands in the distant south who were exhibited at court for the amusement of the Pharaoh and his entourage. Relays of scribes watched Amu-Sinsobe constantly, recording her every utterance or observation. Every two days a terrified slave was brought to her on whom she could feed, and at regular intervals she was even allowed out of the city to feed freely, although she would always be escorted at a distance by a squadron of the Pharaoh's bodyguard to prevent her from effecting a permanent escape.

The reason for all this intensive and concentrated human focus on even the smallest and most trivial details of her life was that both the current Pharaoh and his immediate successor firmly believed that Amu-Sinsobe was possessed of the secret of immortality. In the early days of her confinement, Amu-Sinsobe had been tortured, starved, and even threatened with death by sunlight in an effort to wrest the imagined secret from her. When that approach proved to be of no avail, she had been placed in her current state of benign imprisonment in the hope that eventually she would reveal her supposed knowledge.

It wasn't even that Amu-Sinsobe had attempted to be un-cooperative. She had gone so far as to allow the previous Pharaoh and his priests to be present as she brought a slave across, letting them watch as she had taken the unfortunate creature through the entire process of transformation to the wampyr state. That last Pharaoh had toyed with the idea of staving off his death by going through the transformation and becoming nosferatu himself, but had decided against it at the last moment. Fear of the unknown condition had seemed to outweigh the fear of death itself. Out of pure curiosity, Renquist made an effort to discover the names of either of these two Pharaohs, or the city in which he found himself, but for some reason he couldn't figure, Amu-Sinsobe blocked him in that endeavor. While she didn't seem to resent his intrusion, she certainly didn't show any inclination to supply him with any information that he couldn't easily obtain for himself by other means.

As Renquist became more familiar with both his physical and emotional surroundings, he began to understand more about Amu-Sinsobe's state of mind. She nursed a cold core of anger and resentment, sustained by her captor's policy of denying her of all contact with others of her kind. Although the Pharaoh and the high priest of Isis were prepared to allow her a limited and protected existence as they studied her, they were afraid to let her have contact with others of her nightbreed, even though no less than three other nosferatu, two males and another female, were confined in much the same manner in different parts of the city. She could feel their presence but was unable to contact them directly. The very knowledge that they were so close and yet their companionship was so totally closed to her made her isolation all the more painful. She had begged the Pharaoh to allow her to keep the slave who had been used for the demonstration of transformation. On the advice of his priests, the Pharaoh had refused even this request, and the newly wampyr slave, before she'd had the time to so much as grasp what had happened to her, was thrust out into the sunlight to burn and die.

In the early days of her incarceration, Amu-Sinsobe had raged against the attitude of her jailers and spent long hours imagining what agonies she would inflict on them if she ever regained her freedom. As the years passed, though, she had let go of the surface anger and allowed her fury to lapse into an infinitely patient waiting game. Sooner or later, lifespan would make her the winner. Those who held her prisoner would die out. Perhaps their very civilization would have to die out along with them, but ultimately she would be free. Renquist had attempted to communicate to her the fact that he was also nosferatu. He had hoped that knowing the uninvited visitation in her mind was by one of her own might provide some minimal measure of comfort or, at least, a little relief from her isolation, but either she didn't understand the contact that he was trying to make or she simply blocked his overture just as she blocked his probes for more information.

Renquist was somewhat surprised at the relationship between Amu-Sinsobe and her captors. His studies of the role of nosferatu in ancient Egypt had led him to believe that his kind, those whom he liked to think of as his ancestors, had enjoyed a privileged position during the era of Isis-worship, and that some had even been valued nocturnal advisors to both princes and priests. Either the recorded history was in error or he had been precipitated into a situation that was unique to the reigns of the two anonymous monarchs. It was also possible that he had arrived at a point in the timeline of upper Egypt that was either later or earlier than he had imagined. He wished he could somehow get outside and look around, but, from what little he had gleaned from the brain of Amu-Sinsobe, that was all but impossible.

Egyptology had always held a deep fascination for Renquist. He knew that somewhere outside the room in which Amu-Sinsobe was confined, the Great Pyramid stood in all its original splendor, the last and crowning glory of The Creators before they had withdrawn from the Earth. Renquist had first seen the Great Pyramid in the time of the Crusades, but even then its white marble facing had already been stripped away by vandals and scavengers, cannibalizing the precious material for other less worthy building projects. The construction of the Great Pyramid had been one of the final acts of The Creators. The primary settlement in Mesopotamia had already gone, destroyed when the human insurgents had accidentally set off the sunbombs and the other devices in the arsenal. The enclave on the upper Nile and the spaceport at Nazca were the last two facilities operational when The Creators had decided to make their magnificent, architectural parting gesture before they quit the unlucky Monkey Planet. The Great Pyramid would remain for a hundred thousand years as clear proof to both the ungrateful natives and to other travelers in the void between stars that the Nephilim had been there in all their might and grandeur. If only he could see it as it had been, its marble sides and the gold triangle at its apex still brilliant in the moonlight.

As he yearned for the experience, he felt a stirring in the mind of Amu-Sinsobe, an ironic whisper of ill will. No one had asked him to come blundering into her mind, and, since he had, he might as well share at least a tiny fraction of her own deprivation and isolated misery.

Kelly's shoulders started to ache and he leaned back in the hard wooden library chair. His eyes were tired and, yet again, he was starting to regret that he had ever embarked on this fool's errand. Unfortunately, though, he had. God had insisted on it and there wasn't a single thing that he could do about it. He sighed wearily, fought down his need for a large scotch and looked back down at the papers spread out before him. He could kick against the demands of the Almighty, but the Almighty was relentless. Sooner or later, he would have to confront the Devil that he now knew was a vampire, and his greatest weapon had to be information about his adversary. In his situation, ignorance could be his downfall. Ignorance and weakness could be the death of him when it came to the ultimate battle. Supporting his head on his clenched fist, Kelly resumed his reading.

By the start of the Christian era, the Original Beings would appear to have vanished from the earth, along with many of the intermediate creatures descended from them. According to the admittedly unreliable vampire history, the vampire had fully become the same nocturnal humanoid that we encounter today. The vampire historian also bemoans the fact that, by the first century of Our Lord, the creatures' bloodlines had strayed so far from those of the Original Beings that the original sensitivity to sunlight had deteriorated to an incapacitating vulnerability. This we know from firsthand experience, and the statement is possibly the only true part of the entire blasphemous document. Those of us who have hunted them are well aware that the vampire exposed to sunlight, even momentarily, quite literally explodes in flame.

During the pagan period of the Roman Empire, the vampire appears to have continued with its nocturnal depredations on humanity. The conceit of the writer once again, however, seems to compel him to insist upon attempting to insinuate the nightcrawler into a far more influential role in the political affairs of the time than could in any way be given plausible credit. Liaisons between the creeping undead and such depraved figures as the Emperors Caligula, Nero, and even Caesar Augustus, Hadrian, and Tiberius, plus the ladies Livia and Messalina, are recounted at considerable length. The lies being propagated, in this instance, are that the vampires of ancient Rome were not only employed as assassins by members of the imperial family and other prominent senators and noblemen, but also as advisors in the darker levels of political intrigue. The former might, at a stretch of the imagination, have some small kernel of veracity, but obviously the latter can have no foundation in fact. We can hardly imagine that even the most decadent inhabitant of those Godless times could freely seek the council of such repulsive beings.

After the fall of Rome and the coming of the Dark Ages, the vampire, or, to be more precise, the European vampire, is said to have sought refuge and subsequently flourished in the forests of North Germany, and, in parts, was even worshiped as some kind of minor pagan symbol of the Power of Evil. Fortunately not all of the inhabitants of the area fell under the creatures' demonic sway. Some recognized them for the pariahs that they were, and rooted them out wherever they could be found. Indeed, the vampire chronicler goes into some lengthy detail regarding the destruction of some hundred or more of the abominations in an elaborate death ritual. This community of nightcrawlers was seized by a righteously vengeful party of Saxon tribesmen in those moments before dawn when their strength is at its lowest ebb. They were dragged from their lairs in underground tunnels, taken to a clearing in the forest where they were herded into huge, specially prepared wood and wicker effigies of a man and a woman, which served as massive cages. The author states that these effigies were more than fifty feet tall, although that must be judged as an extreme exaggeration, if, in fact, the incident occurred at all. They were set in a standing position facing the rising sun, and, as the first rays touched the vampires so imprisoned, they immediately burst into flames. Perhaps, at this point, it is possibly worth quoting the original text. It will be noted that the author recounts the story as though he was actually present. A fact that would make him more than fifteen hundred years old.

"As the grey of dawn tinged the eastern sky above the trees beyond the clearing, those of us who had escaped the hunters crouched in the shadowed safety of the disguised excavation that had become our refuge and watched in horror as the final act of the hideous drama was played out. A strange silence fell over those imprisoned in the monstrous cages. When the first rays of the rising sun touched the treetops, those at the very top of the cages, realizing that they would be the first to be consumed by the coming sunlight, attempted to climb down to a lower level, but were prevented from descending very far by others who were cowering below. Many, in a last desperate attempt to escape their fate, tore at the very structure of the cages, attempting, with their bare hands, to break through the withies and green branches that enclosed them. All the while, the soldiers and villagers stood in a circle, laughing, shouting crude remarks and cruel jokes as they watched these hopeless struggles.

"The sunlight touched the very top branches of

the trees in the surrounding forest and then began to move relentlessly downwards. As the deadly rays lit up the tops of the two huge structures, a terrible cry went up from the victims as though, with its utterance, they were giving up the last vestige of hope. The first to be touched by the light was Urich, a swarthy, bearded nosferatu clad in a leather jerkin, who immediately bust into flames. At the moment that he started to burn, he was clinging to the high woodwork that represented the face of the man-shaped construction. Straightaway, he lost his grip and his flaming body plunged down amid those below him. It was impossible, however, to distinguish him from the others as more and more of the unfortunate nosferatu began to burst into flames and the 'heads' of both the male and female cages became nothing more than a roaring mass of fire.

"With the sun now clear of the horizon, we who had survived retreated deeper into the excavations to avoid sharing the fate of our unfortunate kin. Although we could no longer watch, we could still hear the awful sound of the destruction, the death-screams of our burning former companions, the cheers and jeers of the humans, the crackling of the wood as it was consumed by the fire and the terrible roaring of the flames."

Kelly put down the file and let out a long sigh. Up to this moment, he had only thought in terms of the destruction of the vampire as his ordained mission. Now he imagined himself standing over the evil creature as it writhed in its death agony and the sense of power that filled him gave him an entire new perspective on the task at hand. This vision of the moment of triumph and conquest when the evil one died brought him a sense of holy excitement that more than offset the fear that had previously dogged him. He knew that both the vision and the excitement came directly from God.

His first impression was that he had woken and that the dream was over. Renquist seemed to be back in his own body, but he had certainly not returned either to his own room or his own bed. He appeared to be lying on the ground on some mountain promontory high above a vast expanse of seemingly endless white sand desert of rolling dunes like a paralyzed sea, punctuated here and there by outcrops of dark rock. This new environment was as silent as the grave, no night birds cried and no desert creatures called to the empty darkness. In many respects, these surroundings greatly resembled the wasteland where he had found himself precipitated into the body of the Original Being, but despite the similarities, he somehow didn't think he had returned to the same time or the same location. After the Egyptian interlude, he had totally given up trying to theorize about what might be happening to him, or to resist the plainly irresistible. His dreams were beyond control and, to employ a very tired cliché, he could only go with the flow.

A bright and almost full moon hung overhead against a background of a million stars. In the clear desert air, the moon looked enormous and every one of its surface markings was clearly visible. He wondered if the moon was in the same phase as it had been in his New York reality. In the city, the night sky was so unimportant, obscured as it was by pollution and reflected light from the streets and buildings. Not that he could have expected to be able to gain much in the way of orientation from the phase of the moon when his consciousness had just been bounced around through a dozen or more millennia.

It was only when he attempted to move that he discovered he wasn't back in his physical body at all. This came as both a relief and a puzzlement. To find himself inexplicably dumped in some unspecified desert would have been, at the very best, inconvenient, and in the worst case scenario, would have proved fatal with the coming of the dawn. On the other hand, he had no idea at all what was now happening to him. He felt both weightless, and at the same time immobile. He could shift his perception in an approximation of turning his head and looking around, but to stand up or otherwise propel himself in any direction proved quite beyond his capability in this state of being. For a moment he wondered if he had died, but how was it possible for him to have failed to notice his own death? Experimentally, he spoke out loud, wondering how his voice might sound, or even if it would sound or function at all. "Am I dead?"

To his amazement, he immediately received a reply. "Of course you're not dead, Victor. You're undead. You know that." The voice sounded as though it was right inside his head, at the same time both grating and soft, the whisper of the sand in a dune repositioning itself, flowing and sinking to a new level. Renquist immediately recognized the voice, although he could hardly believe that he was hearing it. "Master Dietrich?"

"Who else?"

"Why can't I see you?"

"I don't choose to show myself."

"I don't understand."

"The physical clay is now all but set hard, Brother Victor. You will come to the same condition in two or three thousand years."

"If I survive."

"Yes, if you survive."

"I would be more comfortable if I could look upon you."

"Do you insist on that?"

"I don't insist but I am curious as to what you have become."

The voice of Dietrich made an odd scraping, abrasive sound. Renquist wasn't sure if it was a laugh or something that he had never encountered before. "You are curious?"

If Renquist had been possessed of a body he would have

smiled. "You know me, Master Dietrich. I have always been curious."

Deitrich made a sound like a sigh. "Wait where you are."

"Do I have any choice?"

"No."

Renquist waited. At first there was nothing except the all-pervading, oppressive silence, but, after perhaps a minute, he heard a noise like the rustling of dry leaves. This time the sound had a spacial dimension rather than materializing inside his head. It seemed to come from some distance away, but moved progressively closer. Finally a figure rounded a rock formation to what Renquist thought of as his left. This figure moved with a ponderous, robot-like tread that resembled a statue in motion. As it came closer, Renquist could see that it was unmistakably Dietrich, although it was Dietrich as he had never seen him before. He was uniformly grey in color, as though coated in pale ash, and what Renquist could only think of a winding sheet, a shroud of the same color, hung loosely from his shoulders. He also lacked an aura of any kind. When he spoke, Dietrich's face remained immobile and the voice was once again inside Renquist's head. "So now you see me, Brother Renquist. What do you think of what you may eventually become?"

"I've always been aware that the physical externals weren't everything."

"I'm glad you can accept that."

"Perhaps you can tell me what has become of my own external physicality?"

Dietrich slowly seated himself on a rock and stared for a long time across the desert. Renquist had begun to think that the elderly nosferatu had actually forgotten him before he finally spoke. "You don't know what's been happening to you while you dreamed?"

Renquist would have shaken his head had he been able. "I have lived a long time, but I have never felt like this before."

"That is because you are travelling as your *ka*."

"The Egyptian *ka?*"

"The core entity of being that remains after discorporation."

"Then I am dead?"

"I've already said that you aren't. You are merely out of your body. European mystics call it astral travelling. The Native Americans use the term 'wind walking.' It is only a directed mobility of the dream-state. Are you saying that it has never happened to you before, Victor?"

"Only of my own volition."

"Ah, Victor, you are so intent on commanding your own destiny. Your need for control was always one of your least endearing features."

"I only do what I have to."

Dietrich said nothing. Again he stared out to the horizon as though he had somehow drifted away from the conversation. Renquist wondered if Dietrich had actually reached a point that was the nosferatu equivalent of senility.

"Quite the reverse, my boy."

Renquist stared. He hadn't realized that Dietrich was hearing his thoughts. "I didn't know you were reading me."

"With you so close, I have no choice. Your thoughts are as clear and as present as if you voiced them out loud."

Despite himself, Renquist was beginning to resent his former master's superior attitude. It was infinitely possible that Dietrich was now his absolute superior, but it didn't make it any easier to swallow. "And you had no choice but to manipulate the movements of my *ka?*"

Dietrich sighed. The sound was not unlike a dry, soft wind blowing across the surface of the desert. "Do not become angered, Victor. I do not mean to be patronizing, but you are not even able to approach the place that I now occupy, let alone understand it. At times, I hardly understand it myself. The number and complexity of levels is so immense . . ."

His voice trailed off, but Renquist wasn't about to wait out another lengthy silence. "But you were the one conducting me through this guided tour of the nosferatu past?"

Dietrich's body creaked and sand drifted down from his winding-sheet as he moved his hand in a mildly apologetic gesture. "You resent the imposition?"

"No, not any longer, but I wonder about the reason."

Dietrich sighed again. "So many pawns stand on the squares of so many chessboards. It is hard to resist taking it upon oneself to make a crucial move when it presents itself."

"Altering my dreams was a crucial move?"

"That was but preparation for what is to come, a strengthening process, if you like. A positioning of the pieces."

"Strength through dreams?"

Dietrich again made the strange grating sound. "Isn't that what dreams are for?"

"For what, exactly, are you preparing me?"

"The eventualities that you will shortly face."

Renquist was surprised. "You can see future events in this place that you occupy?"

"No, of course not. No one can see what has yet to happen. The cat's-cradle of patterns and projections does, however, become abundantly clear."

"And what are the patterns and projections for the colony?"

"For the colony, or for you personally?"

"Aren't they approximately the same thing?"

"At the moment, yes, but you should not always operate on that assumption."

Renquist was coming to realize that it was impossible to hurry Dietrich, but he tried anyway. "I'll remember that. Now, if you'll excuse my haste and presumption, will you tell me about the patterns?"

Dietrich took almost a full minute to answer. "You are almost upon a convergence. The internal and external threats seem set to intersect almost simultaneously."

Renquist found that, in the *ka* state, he couldn't feel anxiety, but he came as close to it as he could. "Are you talking about the general external threat, or are you aware of something specific?"

"The threat is specific."

"You know this threat?"

Dietrich's voice was like the toll of doom. "One Who Knows."

Renquist's non-anxiety turned to non-alarm. "A human, One Who Knows, is in New York City?"

"Hundreds in that city possess the Potential, but this one has made the Connection. He knows you and he knows of the Residence. I discovered him delving into the records of our past. Right now he is at the Cathedral studying the files of the accursed Rauch. His thoughts of Rauch were enough to alert me, even in this place."

"So you still keep an eye on us all."

"I still watch over my wild children of the night."

"How serious is this threat?"

"He is just one man, but he is learning more and more as each day passes. He will have trouble convincing others because he has a history of mental dysfunction. On the other hand, he has grown strong enough to come to my attention. Also, he believes that he has the support of God."

"We don't acknowledge God."

"We cover all bets."

Renquist found it hard not to be able to react except by vocal inflection. "Are you serious?"

The grating sound came again, only this time it seemed more irritable than amused. "Of course not, but his very belief gives him strength and a sense that he is invulnerable. He is driven and he will not turn back. Over and above all the other things with which you have to contend at the moment, this one is by far the most dangerous."

"If he's just one lone human, how dangerous can he be?"

"The worst thing you could do would be to underestimate this man. He's already learning about the weaknesses of our kind, and he may well gain both power and allies."

"So you're saying that I should fear this human?"

"You know better than that."

"But I should do everything to arm myself against him?"

"Just as you arm yourself against the young one, Carfax . . ."

"Are you able to identify him? Do you know his name or where he dwells?"

This time, it took Dietrich a full two minutes to respond. "For some reason, I fail to see a name. My only advice is to beware of any human you may observe keeping watch on the Residence."

"That's all you can tell me?"

"That's all I can tell you."

"Does that mean this encounter is at an end?"

The ensuing silence seemed to go on for ever. When Dietrich finally spoke again, it seemed to Renquist that his voice was tinged with the sadness of isolation. "It would seem that it is."

"So what happens now? Do I return to my own body?"

Dietrich's voice quickly hardened. "You think we should perhaps sit and make small talk?"

Renquist sighed. The meeting seemed somehow incomplete. "I will return to my own body?"

"Don't grieve for me, Brother Victor. I am old. I have made my choice. On occasion I mourn for the vigor of youth, but I also have endless possibilities to explore in this new universe."

"I would like to spend more time with you, Brother Dietrich."

Dietrich sounded weary. "That is not possible. It is already sunset in New York City and you have much to do."

"What do I need to do to return?"

"Nothing, I will do it for you."

"Will I remember all of this when I wake?"

"I think you will be able to handle that."

"Will I see you again?"

Dietrich stared across the desert for a long time. "That's

something that neither of us can know. It is possible, however, that you may feel my presence. As I said, I watch over my wild children of the night."

"Are you saying that you might assist me in this conflict to come?"

Dietrich grated one last time. "Perhaps. Although perhaps not in any way that you might imagine, or even recognize."

Kelly placed the last folder of the Rauch file into the last of the boxes and signaled to Father Rattigan that he was finished. At some point, as late afternoon had merged into evening, Father Rattigan had taken over again from Father Schnabel. The difference was hardly noticeable. Both of the young priests took the same quietly hostile attitude to Kelly's presence in the library. As Kelly waved him over, Rattigan reluctantly rose from his desk and came to collect the first box and take it back to the subterranean vault in which it would probably languish until some other marginally connected Catholic madman believed that there was an outbreak of vampirism in the city. Rattigan looked at Kelly and the other two boxes with undisguised distaste, presumably unhappy that he would have to make two trips to the basement because of someone who looked like little more than a wino. "Is that everything for today?"

Kelly nodded and tapped the spiral-bound pad in which he'd been making notes. "Yes, I think I have everything that I need."

"Will you be needing this stuff tomorrow?"

Kelly shook his head. He didn't have to tolerate attitude from a goddamned novice, but he was too tired to make an issue of it. "No, my young friend. I think I have it all covered. I'm sure you and Father Schnabel will be relieved to hear that I won't be back. You want me to put this box on top of the other one, so you only have to make two trips?"

Kelly walked out of the library and into the corridor that led to the street door. He was thinking how, now that the rush hour was over, he could take the subway back downtown with-

out being subjected to too much undue stress, and he was star-
tled when a voice called after him. "Hey, Kelly. Wait up a
minute."

Kelly turned and saw Father Muncie walking down the hall
towards him. He was immediately on the defensive. "What's
the matter? Rattigan and Schnabel been complaining about
me?"

Muncie shook his head. "No, no, nothing like that."

"So what?"

"I was just wondering about this vampire thing of yours."

"What about it?"

"You're serious about this?"

"I spent most of the day reading up on it, didn't I?"

Muncie scratched his chin. "You want to talk about it?"

Kelly stiffened. "I don't think so." He was aware that Muncie
was probably just trying to show that he was concerned, but it
had been so long since anyone had shown any kind of concern
about him that Kelly was out of practice when it came to responding to kindness.

Muncie shrugged. "If you do, you know where I am."

Kelly took a deep breath. "Listen, I appreciate your offer, but
I have to see this thing through on my own."

"You really believe that there's something supernatural going
on right here in New York?"

"I thought the Church didn't want to hear about it."

"You're not talking to the Church, just Dwayne Muncie."

For a moment, Kelly felt like breaking down and telling
Muncie everything that he knew, but then he steeled himself.
"I figure this is something I have to do on my own. Then, if it
goes wrong, I'm the only one to take the shit . . . and everyone knows that I'm crazy."

Muncie frowned. "You don't have to play it that way."

Kelly was adamant. "Yes, I'm afraid I do."

"Is it something to do with these murders?"

"That's what I'm trying to find out."

Muncie paused awkwardly. "You're not involved in the murders, are you?"

Kelly laughed. So that was what Muncie was worried about. He thought that Kelly had turned homicidal on top of being a sinner and a drunk. "No, Dwayne. I'm not involved in the murders. In fact, I'm trying to prevent any more of them happening."

"Don't you think you ought to leave that to the cops?"

"The cops don't have the same perspective that I have."

Muncie seemed at a loss for words so Kelly smiled and then turned and started walking away. "I'll be seeing you, Dwayne."

"Kelly . . ."

Kelly looked back. "Don't worry about me, Dwayne."

"Be careful, okay?"

"There ain't no such thing as a vampire, is there, Dwayne? So what can possibly hurt me, huh?"

"Just be careful, Kelly."

Calloused as his feelings might be, Kelly almost felt touched. "Sure, Dwayne. I'll be careful."

"What happened?"

Renquist took a long draught of water before answering. "What do you mean, what happened?"

"Both Sada and Julia have been trying to wake you since sunset. You couldn't be roused. It was as though you were dead."

Renquist had no shame about repeating the pun Dietrich had used on him. "Haven't you heard? I'm undead."

"Don't be funny, Victor. We were starting to worry."

"I was on a trip."

Dahlia made no attempt to conceal the fact that she was rapidly becoming angry. "I asked you not to be funny."

"I'm not being funny."

Dahlia looked grim. "Well, Victor, while you were tripping or whatever you want to call it, I don't think it would be an exaggeration to say that all hell has been breaking loose."

Renquist took another long drink of water, partly because he needed it and partly to give him time to ready himself for what was clearly going to be a new catalogue of bad news. It seemed that, whether asleep or awake, the problems refused to stop. "Would you like to define 'all hell breaking loose'?"

Dahlia counted off the items in her fingers. "Two new bodies were discovered in Central Park this morning."

Renquist's eyes turned cold. "Carfax?"

"We don't know for sure but it sure as shit looks like his handy work. One of the victims was dismembered and bits of him were draped all over the Alice in Wonderland sculpture. Fortunately a cop was the first one to spot the mess so the media didn't get pictures."

"What about the other?"

"That was a bit more modest. Just a blood-drained corpse left at the edge of the Sheep Meadow."

"Does anyone know where Carfax is?"

"No one has a clue."

"What about the loft building on Prince Street?"

"Lupo went there as soon as the sun set, but he found no sign of Carfax."

Renquist began to pace. He was definitely going to kill Carfax as soon as he could get his hands on him. "Is there anything else?"

Dahlia and Imogene glanced at each other. Suddenly they seemed reluctant to speak. Renquist wondered how bad this final piece of information could be after the ones that had preceded it. "Don't leave me hanging, I've had a hard day in the void."

Dahlia avoided looking directly into his eyes. "Cynara has gone."

Renquist couldn't believe what he was hearing. "What?"

"Cynara's gone. She left with a travelling bag, right after sunset, at the same time as Lupo went to Prince Street. She left a note for you."

Imogene silently handed him a folded sheet of ivory note-paper. He unfolded it and started to read. It was penned in her unmistakable Gothic script.

Dear Victor,

This business between you and Julia has so greatly upset me that I feel I have to leave the Residence for a while. The feasting is not the time for any kind of rational thought, so I have decided that it would be better for all concerned if I went away on my own until the crisis has passed. Perhaps, when I return, we can talk about what kind of future we may or may not have together.

Knowing you, you'll probably assume that this is some kind of betrayal or desertion. In fact it isn't, and I hope you can understand that.

Take care of yourself and the others,
Cynara

Renquist slowly refolded the note and faced Dahlia and Imo-gene. At least the two of them were dressed in a fairly conser-vative manner. He didn't think that he could have quite han-dled the previous day's theatre of de Sade. "Is that the full complement of disasters?"

At that moment, Julia came into the kitchen. "I'm afraid it may not be. Three humans are standing in the street outside and they seem incredibly interested in this house."

chapter Six

The Mayor is coming on TV. His press conference is going to start at any minute."

Dahlia was monitoring the multiple TV screens. Renquist acknowledged this piece of information with a nod and turned to Imogene. "Anything new from Lupo?"

Imogene shook her head. Lupo was out in the city, attempting to find Blasco and Carfax before they could add further damage to their mounting record of killer insanity. The skeletal sister was maintaining a mental link with Lupo but the news from him was far from good. "Still nothing. He's working his way through the list of places that Julia gave him, but he feels that Carfax and Blasco are unlikely be waiting around in any of their bolt-holes. They're almost certainly running loose, hunting again. Also, they must be aware by now that we're looking for them."

Renquist switched his attention to Segal. "What about those people in the street?"

Segal was staring at the two black and white images from the outside security cameras. Some fifteen minutes earlier, three people, an elderly black man and two women, had arrived outside the house, and since that time they had remained there looking up at the building. With Dietrich's warning regarding the One Who Knows still fresh in his mind, Renquist had immediately ordered Segal to watch them like a hawk through the Residence's closed-circuit surveillance system. Segal answered without looking away from the screens. "They're just standing there."

"How do they look?"

"It's hard to say. I can't see an aura through this system, but it looks to me as though they were kind of frightened, like they were afraid to make their next move, to do whatever they came here for."

"They're definitely looking at this building?"

"Absolutely. And they seem real scared of it."

Again Renquist nodded. "The longer they stay scared of it the better."

Renquist had been awake for less than an hour, but it seemed like an eternity. In that time, he had moved the entire Residence into what amounted to crisis mode. Overcoming his dislike of the playroom and its mental echoes of the young ones' party games, he had turned the place into what amounted to an emergency command center. The video monitor screens were all tuned to the local TV stations, giving them a finger on the pulse of a city that appeared to have moved dangerously close to the edge of panic during the hours that he had slept his way through Dietrich's strange dreamtour. Following the two most recent killings, all but NBC had pre-empted their local programming for saturation coverage. As Julia had remarked when he first moved them into action, "Los Angeles had its riots and O.J. Simpson, and now New York has its kill-crazy Satan slaughter cult."

Renquist's success at welding a group of assorted nosferatu so quickly into a coherent team had surprised even him. The weird sisters had been his greatest asset. Without any prompting, Dahlia had positioned herself in front of the TV screens tuned to the broadcast channels to keep abreast of developments in and around the city, while Imogene had established the running link with Lupo. They had gone about their self-appointed tasks with such alacrity that one might have thought they were taking on the entire city of New York. Of course in some respects they were, only at that moment they were the only ones who knew it. Segal simply did what Renquist told him, and when he had asked him to watch the monitors hooked up to the building's outside security cameras, the grotesque had immediately hunkered his bulk down next to the diminutive Dahlia, without even asking why Renquist was so concerned about what might be going on in the street in front of the Residence. Segal and Dahlia, sitting side by side staring with rapt concentration at their respective screens, like two radar operators on alert for incoming enemy aircraft, were one of the stranger sights that Renquist had recently witnessed inside the Residence.

Renquist had no specific task for Sada, but she seemed more than willing to remain on standby, waiting for the moment that she might be needed. Only Julia insisted on treating the whole business as little more than an amusing sideshow. Looking sinister and sexy in a tight, second-skin leather jumpsuit, she had curled up on one of the oversized cushions, punctuating the general sense of serious concern with a series of glib jokes and smart remarks. After a whole comedy bit on the theme of the Satan slaughter cult, Renquist had lost his temper and snarled angrily at her. "Why don't you shut the fuck up, Julia? All you're managing to do is to irritate the rest of us. We all know that the Satan slaughter cult is actually two of our own."

Even Renquist's anger, however, hadn't done much to dampen Julia's amused detachment from the immediate reality. She seemed too buoyed up by her obvious delight that Cynara had walked out on both Renquist and the colony to take at all seriously the fact that their very lives might be hanging by the slenderest of threads.

Julia aside, Renquist was having a good deal of difficulty keeping his anger under control. He couldn't understand why Dietrich should have taken it into his strange and apparently senile head to run him through a historical show-and-tell excursion while, in the present, matters seemed to be dissolving into full-scale chaos. As the TV screens continued to attest, New York looked to be on the verge of coming unglued. Every channel consistently reran footage of the police raids that were going on all over town. The truth was that the cops had little idea who might be doing the murders, but with ingrained and institutionalized racism, they seemed to have taken it into their heads that they were somehow connected with one or another of the fringe cults and religions that flourished in the black and Latino immigrant enclaves.

Over and over, the TV screens showed earlier news crew tapes of heavily armed NYPD tactical squads, fully loaded with automatic weapons, riot guns, dark blue combat suits, flak jackets, and Nazi-looking kevlar helmets, smashing their way into storefront churches and backroom Santería and Voodoo temples. Men and women were being hauled out and loaded into buses and paddy wagons while ominous crowds started to gather on street corners, in front of bodegas and on the stoops of tenements.

The motivations of the mayor and the police commissioner were transparently clear. Even with no tangible leads, they still wanted to stage a show of force, a patently political demonstration that something, no matter how pointless and misdirected, was being done. Since all of the obviously identifiable victims were both relatively affluent and white, the official line of thought seemed to be that some obscure religious cult had tipped over into psychosis and was ritually murdering those they saw as the class and race enemy. From Renquist's point of view, it was a short-term and highly short-sighted strategy. He could only think that mass arrests in minority communities could all too easily backfire into full-scale race riots, but of course Renquist had the advantage of knowing the real truth. His feelings were, however, already being confirmed by the protestations already being made by the most vocal black and Hispanic leaders that scarcely veiled fascism was running loose in the streets.

Dahlia looked away from the TV screens. "Here comes the mayor."

The scenes of police action vanished from the screen and were replaced by one of scrambling confusion at Gracie Mansion. TV crews, print journalists, and still photographers jostled for position so violently that they seemed on the verge of throwing punches. Mayor Racine and Police Commissioner Washington stood on a podium at the focus of the whole disorderly scrimmage, surrounded by a protective phalanx of aides, plainclothes security men, and uniformed cops, waiting for the hubbub to come under some kind of control so they could start the hastily convened press conference. The idea presumably had been to project an image of calm and control, but this had obviously gone drastically awry, and was only bolstering the impression that city was teetering on the brink. While the mayor waited for the media to come to a semblance of order, Renquist looked quickly at Segal. "Are those humans still out there?"

"Just like they were before."

"Keep watching them."

Segal shifted uneasily. He wasn't about to question his Master's orders, but he was clearly uncomfortable with his so far passive role in the defense of the colony. "Might it not be better if I went out and joined Lupo in his search for Carfax?"

Renquist hadn't told any of the others about the One Who Knows. In fact, he hadn't told them anything about the bizarre sequence of dreams. He might have confided in Lupo. Lupo had the age and experience to understand the strange contact with Dietrich, but Lupo was out scouring the city for the renegades. As far as the others were concerned, Renquist knew that stresses would start running high soon enough, and he wasn't about to add to the pressure or possibly insinuate the idea that the supernormal was maybe against them or that the Master was heading for a crackup. He shook his head. "Just keep watching those humans for now. Maybe later you can join Lupo, but right now, I want to know that this place is secure before anyone else goes out there."

On TV, the mayor's press conference was finally about to start. An aide leaned into the battery of microphones. "The mayor will read a prepared statement and then he'll take questions, so if you could all hold it down until that time, it would be appreciated."

The media fell temporarily silent and Mayor Racine stepped forward. Renquist had known Racine as far back as the Koch administration, when he been a lawyer/bagman in the grey area between politics and the mob. He was a short, dapper man with slicked-back hair and a public attitude of rudeness and abrasive malice that the electorate had somehow mistaken for no-nonsense toughness. In Renquist's estimation, Racine was probably one of the most unsuitable individuals who had ever been elected to the office of mayor, and his handling of the current situation had done nothing to revise that opinion.

On camera, Racine cleared his throat. He was probably doing his best to present an image of what he fondly hoped to be statesmanship and calmness under duress. Unfortunately, with all the cameras at the hastily arranged media melee, he seemed uncertain as to where he should address his remarks. To Renquist, he only managed to come across as shifty and furtive.

"This city has faced all kinds of crises in its time. From the bombing of the World Trade Center to the current fiscal crisis, New Yorkers have been called upon to pull together and display courage and fortitude in the face of sometimes shocking adversity. Today, a killer or killers are loose in the streets of our city, slaughtering without conscience and, as far as we can tell, without reason. It would be easy to refer to the perpetrators of these hideous crimes as terrorists, but even terrorists work according to their own standards of twisted idealism. What is happening now is something entirely new and different. We have even seen serial killers in New York City before, but never a slaughter on this unprecedented and mindless scale. Today, we are dealing with something far more formidable and far more fundamentally twisted and evil that any mere Son of Sam."

Julia giggled. "He's talking about us."

Dahlia turned away from the screen with a look of disgust on her face. "The man's a fucking weasel. If anything's twisted, it's him."

"I have therefore instructed Commissioner Washington and the entire police department to spare no effort or expense and to leave no stone unturned as they endeavor to bring these monsters to justice and halt this unspeakable horror."

Racine paused to let the microphones and cameras digest this flourish of rhetoric before he started up again. "I have also talked with the governor about the possibility of bringing the National Guard into the city, but for the time being, we have come to the decision that so far the problem is one of law enforcement rather than public order, although the Guard will be held on readiness in case the situation should further deteriorate."

Sada glanced at Renquist. "Is that a warning to anyone who might be thinking of rioting?"

Renquist nodded. "Racine was never noted for his subtlety."

"Acting on information received, special police units have conducted raids in Brooklyn, the Bronx, and Manhattan and arrests have been made. Commissioner Washington will later go into more detail, but I believe he is confident that charges may shortly be brought in relation to a number of the recent murders."

Dahlia's lip curled. "He's not only a weasel but also a lying scumbag."

Imogene peered at the screen from over her sister's shoulder. "How could he be anything else? He's a politician."

Almost in confirmation of Imogene's remark, Racine adjusted his face into the standard political expression of concern. "Some criticism has been leveled at the police that possibly their actions of the last few hours may have been inappropriately heavy-handed. All I can say to these critics is that drastic circumstances necessitate drastic measures. A perceived overzealousness comes not as a result of any prejudice but from a united and common desire on the part of our law enforcement officials and the officers on the streets to put a stop, once and for all, to this wave of hideous crimes."

Julia pushed herself up on one elbow and looked around at the others in the room. "There's talk that this moron thinks he might be president one day."

Sada nodded. "I heard that too. It scarcely bears thinking about."

Renquist pursed his lips. "The humans have entered a time of miserably small men."

No sooner had he spoken than the mayor suddenly vanished from the one screen and then another. Only NBC went steadfastly on with its baseball game from Los Angeles; all else was a confusion of dead air. The first explanation came from the audio on Channel Eleven. "We interrupt the mayoral press conference to bring you pictures that are right now coming in from East One hundred thirteenth Street in Manhattan. We now go live to Theda Valdez on One hundred thirteenth Street."

The Channel Eleven picture showed a decidedly frightened reporter crouched beside a Channel Eleven news van, clutching her stick mike for dear life and looking as though she would be happier to be anywhere but where she was. Police in riot gear constantly ran past her carrying nightsticks, shotguns, and Plexiglas shields. Somewhere beyond the camera's focal range, what looked like a convenience store was burning. "Tensions have been building in this primarily Latino neighborhood through a long day of raids and arrests connected to what the Mayor and the police have been calling the Central Park cult murders. Many in this and other minority and immigrant communities have questioned that these murders have anything to do with the local fringe religions that seem to have become the primary targets of police murder investigations. Through most of the evening, angry verbal confrontations have taken place between police and local residents, and, at times, tempers have run high . . ."

The camera wavered and momentarily lost Theda Valdez as a burly cop pushed the operator to one side. As the reporter came back into frame, a thrown bottle smashed on the roof of the truck and she instinctively ducked away from the resulting shower of glass. "As you can all . . . clearly see, verbal protest has now given way to violent direct action . . ."

As Renquist watched what looked to be the start of a full-scale riot, a sudden stabbing pain lanced through his head, centered somewhere in the region of his inner ear. He noticed that Dahlia had also winced, so seemingly he wasn't the only one to experience it. Before he could do or say anything, the pain was followed by noise inside his head, a crackling racketing hum like a badly tuned radio producing between-stations static, overamplified to an intolerable level that obliterated everything else in the room. Renquist cringed away from the pain and cacophony. It was almost as though he was under some kind of psychic attack. "What the hell is this?"

The answer to his question was suddenly there, right there in his head along with the noise. "Are you watching your television, Victor? Are you seeing what we have achieved so far? How much further do you think we would have to go to actually take over the city itself?"

The voice was muffled and distorted, fading in and out of the deafening static. Renquist's initial reaction was that Dietrich was attempting to contact him. That didn't last, though. Despite the interference, he recognized the words as those of Carfax.

Fury erupted inside him. "What do you think you're doing, you damned idiot?"

"Doing, Victor? What do you think I'm doing? I'm doing what we should all be doing. I'm doing exactly what I feel like doing. I'm living free and following my impulses. I kill when I want to kill and I feed when I want to feed and I fear nothing but the sun itself. And you know what, Victor? The humans aren't hunting me. Look at your TV, Victor. They're not hunting me. They're attacking each other."

Most of the TV screens were now showing helicopter shots. A building in the middle of a block was burning and, at the end of the block, a confusion of police vehicles was setting up complex strobe patterns with their flashing and rotating lights.

"Look at it, Victor. How long do think it would take us to bring down this human civilization if we confronted them instead of cowering and hiding?"

Carfax's voice was so painfully loud and mad in Renquist's head that he was unable to focus on anything else. When nosferatu used the linkage óf minds, a directed extension of their other mental powers, it was supposed to be a delicately tuned exercise. Carfax was doing with it all the subtlety of a ball-peen hammer. He had clearly just learned the technique and he hadn't bothered to learn his lesson particularly well. Renquist even had trouble focusing his own thoughts. Carfax had him totally off balance. All his concentration had been on the physical defense of the Residence and he had left himself wide open to this mental invasion by someone who shouldn't have been able to cause him a moment of even slight discomfort. "Who . . . taught you this trick?"

"Who taught me, Victor? Who showed me how to slip into your mind while you were looking the other way? Now wouldn't you like to know that?"

Cynara? Renquist couldn't stop the thought from leaping straight to the center of his mind. Cynara? Would she have gone to Carfax as an act of revenge for his supposed infidelity with

Julia? It scarcely seemed possible except, in the madness of Feasting, perhaps anything was possible. Carfax had obviously lost his mind; could it be that Cynara had lost hers too?

Carfax laughed and the crazy Richard Widmark laughter doubled the pain in Renquist's head. "Cynara, Victor? You think Cynara has come to me? Maybe she has, Victor. That's another secret that you'll have to work out for yourself. Has she taught me everything that she knows? Cynara knows a lot, doesn't she, Victor? She's been your bonded companion for a very long time. Or maybe I worked all this out for myself. How will you know, Victor? How will you ever find out? You should never have come into the playroom, Victor. The playroom is mine. My imprint is all over it. My toys are there. In the playroom, Victor, it's me that has the power. I have killed so many in there that my very being has permeated the walls. You made a big mistake coming in there, Victor. You have Lupo out hunting for me, and here I am inside your head. You exposed yourself, Victor, and now I'm going to punish you. I give shriekback, Victor. In front of all your followers. Powerful, painful shriekback."

The white static that surrounded Carfax's voice suddenly formed itself into a closed butterfly loop and started to oscillate in a critical and destructive rhythm. It rapidly expanded outward to the very volumetric limits of Renquist's brain. The pain was unendurable. It felt as though the solid bone of his skull was picking up sympathetic vibrations and, if they continued for any length of time, it would fly apart in a cloud of tiny razor-sharp fragments. Renquist staggered backwards with his eyes tightly closed. He put out a hand to steady himself by holding onto the wall, and found to his disgust that he was touching one of the chains that Carfax had used to secure his victims.

"Stop this, damn you!"

"Beg, Victor. Beg me to stop. Look on it as payback for what you and Lupo did to me."

"I'm telling you to stop this."

"And I'm telling you to beg. I want the others to see this. All of them. Let them wonder if they would be better off with a Master who has some ambition beyond the hiding place and the bloodbag. Sada and Segal, Imogene and little pumpkin Dahlia, and of course Julia. Although, maybe I should also punish Julia for her disloyalty while I have everyone's attention."

Up to that moment, Renquist had assumed that what was taking place was solely between Carfax and himself. He hadn't stopped to think that everyone in the room was a party to the conflict. It only made sense, though. Carfax would obviously prefer a public humiliation of his former Master. Renquist looked around the room, trying to force himself to see through the pain. He found that every eye was fixed upon him. Then Julia suddenly jerked on her cushion, her spine arched as though it was threatening to snap. She gasped and then the gasp turned to a growl of pain. "Oh, you little bastard!"

"You made me what I am Julia, dear."

"Stop it, Kurt. I'm telling you to stop it."

"Beg, Julia. You and Victor together. Both of you will beg me to stop the pain."

Renquist noticed that Dahlia was on her feet. She looked at him regretfully. "This may hurt for a moment, Victor." Then she closed her eyes and clenched her tiny fists as though summoning every ounce of her strength.

"Go away, you miserable little bloodsucker!"

Dahlia had been right. It had hurt, For an instant, it had hurt more than what Carfax had been doing to him. But then all pain was gone. His head was clear. Only faint echoes remained, remainders and reminders of what might have happened if Carfax hadn't been stopped. He looked down at Dahlia and smiled weakly. "I owe you a lot. He could have done me serious and lasting damage."

Julia got shakily to her feet. "I owe you too."

Dahlia assumed her sweetest and most innocent of little girl smiles. "I didn't do it for you. I warned him that he should never call me 'pumpkin.' He's going to hurt for a long time and I doubt he'll ever try that trick again."

Segal turned from the security monitor that he had apparently been watching all through Carfax's mental intrusion. "This is probably something you don't want to hear, Don Victor, but those three people on the street outside . . ."

"What about them?"

"They're coming to the front door."

The man must have been in his late seventies at the very least, with a face like well-worn leather and eyes that had clearly seen suffering of the world. As Renquist, with Segal behind him like a shadow, swung open the front door of the Residence, he stood between the two women, frail and proud, clearly very afraid, but with the courage to face whatever might await him. White-haired and bareheaded, he was dressed with careful neatness in a dark pinstriped suit with wide lapels and a slight air of forties zoot suit bebop, a plain white shirt, and a floral patterned tie. He also carried a cane with a lion's head handle. The woman on his right was heavily built, in her early to mid-fifties, wearing a red satin dress that was stretched dangerously across her ample hips. A matching hat of red straw was perched on top of her head. The other woman was slightly older, tall and thin, with large, dark-flecked eyes that seemed to expect the worst of any given situation. She was dressed in funereal black and clutched a large and formidable pocketbook that could have been used as a weapon if the need arose. All three looked as though they could have easily come straight from a revival meeting or a Baptist service.

As he faced Renquist, the elderly man visibly squared his thin shoulders before he spoke. *"S'agus bach, agus leat-sa."*

The sound of the ancient tongue coming from such an incongruous figure stopped Renquist dead in his tracks and he stood stock-still with one hand on the doorframe. The words were strangely mispronounced and the old man spoke in a manner which indicated that he had learned them phonetically and was reciting them from memory without any true conception of their literal meaning. The fact that he, a human, was speaking them at all, however, was quite enough to leave Renquist stunned. Also, they were absolutely appropriate. The literal translation was complex and hard to render into English, or any other modern language, but the general meaning was the verbal equivalent of a flag of truce. The speaker essentially demanded that all hostile actions be put on hold while a negotiation took place.

The nosferatu had a saying to the effect that, like the fangs of a hunter, unpleasant shocks frequently came in pairs. Renquist received his second shock when he attempted to scan the trio for advance warning of why they might be knocking on his door. Normally he could read the thoughts and emotions of humans like an open book. These three, on the other hand, were closed, locked and sealed. Their auras glowed around them but they were a serene and uniform blue and yielded absolutely nothing in the way of hard information or even background feelings. Renquist was so mystified that he found he had no alternative but to step back, hold the door open, and invite the three to enter with the English version of the time-honored formula greeting. "I am Renquist. Welcome to my house. Enter freely and of your own will."

The old man and the two women didn't move. The old man looked worriedly past Renquist and into the dark hallway of the Residence. "Do we have your solemn word that we will not be harmed?" When the elderly black man spoke in English, Renquist could detect a smoothly sweet Louisiana Creole inflection.

Renquist continued to hold the door open. "Why should you expect me to harm you?"

"We know what you are."

"Then you should know that we are not indiscriminate killers."

"Do we have your word?"

Renquist made a slight bow. "You have my word that you will not be harmed in any way while you are under my roof."

"And we may leave whenever we want?"

"And you may leave whenever you want."

The old man nodded and stepped forward, crossing the threshold. The man kept his face straight, but the eyes of the heavier of the two women were wide with controlled anxiety. Renquist could understand her apprehension. If they truly knew his real nature and that of the others in the house, they probably felt as though they had just passed through the portals of Hell. On the other hand, it was also becoming clear to Renquist that these were no normal humans and they were possessed of their own extraordinary powers.

"The best place to talk would be in my library."

The old man nodded and he and the two women followed Renquist down the hall, not, however, without first looking askance at the looming figure of Segal who continued to stand in the shadows just inside the door, next to the grandfather clock with its carved demons.

When the three had first knocked, Renquist had instructed the others, with the exception of Segal, to remain in the playroom unless a real crisis erupted. Now, as he passed Segal on the way to the library, he flashed him a swift signal that he should return to the playroom and only rejoin Renquist if he called him.

Renquist entered the library, and indicated that the three humans should be seated and make themselves comfortable. The trio looked around the room, apparently impressed by their surroundings in a way that seemed reassuringly natural. When they were settled, Renquist also sat and looked at the trio inquiringly. "So how can I help you?"

The old man gestured to the thin woman. "This is Madame Sophie Mennesson . . ."

Renquist nodded courteously. "Madame."

The old man indicated the other woman. "And this is Madame Marie Clochette."

Again Renquist nodded. Observing the social niceties seemed to set the humans more at their ease, as though they still needed some reassurance he wasn't immediately going to spring upon them, red in tooth and claw.

"And I am Doctor Maurice d'Asson."

Renquist smiled. "And what can I do for you, Doctor d'Asson?"

The Doctor's ancient hands, with veins like ropes and long spatulate fingers, rested on the head of his cane, betraying no sign of fear or tension. Renquist had rarely seen a human maintain such a level of control in his presence. "As I said on the doorstep, we know what you are. We have known for a long time that a colony of—"

Renquist cut him off before d'Asson could use the word. "We prefer the term 'nosferatu.' "

The Doctor's eyes hardened. "You have the right to call yourself what you like. The end result is the same."

"Perhaps you'd like to tell me how you came by this information, Doctor d'Asson. I'd been under the impression that we had been a well-kept secret."

"I am the houn'gan, the shaman if you like, of a small oum'phar, a temple, in another part of the city. These two ladies are mam'bo, mistresses of the temple. We have a certain contact with the spirit world and, by that means, we were informed a very long time ago that a group of beings such as yourselves existed here downtown."

Renquist chose his words carefully. "This surprises me. My people have little or no contact with the spirit world. Some view us as supernatural beings, but our relationship with the spiritual is, in reality, little more than that of the average human.

Now and then, one of our number will adopt the path of the mystic, but, for the most part our lives, although sometimes infinitely extended, are mundanely temporal."

"And yet you must admit that you occupy a place that is midway between this world and the next."

Renquist slowly nodded. "That is one way of looking at it. I do wonder though, why, if you knew so much about us, you didn't reveal us to the world? Our habits and mode of survival have never been viewed by humanity with any degree of sympathy, and you must be aware that we have some very serious vulnerabilities."

Doctor d'Asson shrugged. It was a particularly Creole-Gallic gesture that signified it took all sorts to make a world. "We had no reason to reveal you to anyone. Our own beliefs have some extremely negative mythology attached to them. In our faith, we make few judgements and attempt, whenever possible, to maintain a policy of live and let live. You and your people seemed to have organized your lives and controlled your impulses according to a principle of minimum harm. Why should we have bothered you when you did nothing to bother us?"

"Until just recently?"

"Exactly."

"This recent period has been unfortunate."

D'Asson's mouth tightened. "It is become rather more than merely unfortunate. This current wave of indiscriminate killing directly threatens those of our faith and others like us. Worse than that, we have riots threatening to break out on our streets. How could you let things get so disastrously out of control?"

Renquist took a deep breath. It had been a very, very long time since a human being had put him on the spot in this way. He was very aware of three pairs of hawklike human eyes watching his every gesture and every flicker of expression. Very carefully he began to explain the pressures of Feasting and how it

THE TIME OF FEASTING 259

affected Carfax and ultimately triggered the killing spree that was now causing so much trouble. D'Asson listened in silence and, even when Renquist was finished, he didn't immediately speak. Finally, he leaned back in his chair. "I guess the question has to be what do you intend to do now? I realize that you have done your best to prevent the current situation, but you have to admit that your efforts so far have totally failed."

Madame Marie spoke for the first time. As she spoke, her right hand stroked an ivory charm, a hand with an eye engraved on the palm. "What we're here for is to find out what you gonna do about clearing up this mess, Mr. Renquist."

Now Madame Sophie joined in. It seemed the gloves were coming off and the elaborate and guarded courtesy was giving way to plain talking. "You say you got one of your men out on the streets looking for these young ones, but what's gonna happen when he catches up with them? Is he gonna be able to get them under control? Is he gonna be able to throw a net over them?"

"If need be, he's going to kill them."

"He's gonna kill them?"

"That may well be the only answer."

"Can we trust you do that? To kill two of your own kind?"

"I can only give you my word."

Madame Sophie didn't seem quite ready to accept Renquist's simple promise. "That's right, how do we know we can trust you?"

"Would the fact that these youths seem quite prepared to kill me help to convince you?"

"We gonna need a mighty lot of convincing. We got cops and who knows what running all over the place treating us like we were something out of a horror movie, and we got homeboys breaking out their AKs and talking uprising. Like I say, we gonna need a mighty lot of convincing, Mr. Renquist."

While the women had been talking, Doctor d'Asson seemed

to have been thinking. "Even if the killing stops, Mr. Renquist, that's not quite the end of it."

"The authorities are going to need a scapegoat."

"That's what I was thinking."

Gideon Kelly woke with a start and sat bolt upright with sweat pouring down his face. The late summer night heat was oppressive and the air in his room at the Dupont Hotel was scarcely breathable. His head hurt and his stomach was sour with scarcely digested whiskey. Outside, he could hear the weird urban hum of massed air conditioners, but of course the guests at the Dupont were permitted no such luxuries. The electricity cost too much and the wiring couldn't handle it. He looked quickly at the old alarm clock beside the bed. It was a half-hour after midnight and he had slept for far too long. On his return from the library, he had killed most of the pint of Queen Anne scotch he had purchased on the way home and then lay down on the bed, intending to nap for no more than a couple of hours. His plan had been to return to the downtown vampires' lair, shortly after the sun set, and observe their nocturnal habits, looking for some weakness that he might exploit to his advantage. Unlike Bishop Rauch, Kelly had no squads of out-of-work soldiers to do his, and God's bidding. He had to rely on his own resources and cunning. Now half the night had gone and he had done nothing but sprawl on his bed in a stupor. Why in the name of all that was holy had the Almighty chosen someone like him to do his dirty work for him?

He dragged himself from the bed and hurried to the sink in the corner of the small, cramped room. He splashed cold water on his face and under his armpits. He gathered up the clothing that he'd been wearing all day from where he'd dropped it on the floor. His intention was maybe to put on a clean T-shirt, but otherwise to go out dressed as he always did. Then a thought occurred to him. It was an outrageous thought, but he realized that it was also an idea that was close to brilliant.

He went to small closet and quickly sorted through his minuscule wardrobe. With a mixture of guilt and excitement, he took out the dark suit that he had worn when he was an ordained priest.

He removed the pants from their hanger, but hesitated before pulling them on over his torn underwear. What he was about to do was, as far as he knew, illegal, definitely immoral, almost certainly a sin, but eminently practical. A priest on the street might not be exactly invisible, but he had the next best advantage. No one ever invested a man of the cloth with any ulterior material motive. Even though he had hung on to this suit of clothes through all of his alcoholic trials, he had never worn it since the right to do so had been taken away from him. Somehow, though, he felt that the Lord would not hold him to account for the masquerade. He was doing the Lord's work, he was fighting the Good Fight and was sure a dispensation would be forthcoming if he went to battle in armor to which, technically, he had no right.

"Forgive me, Lord, but I know exactly what I'm doing." He pulled on the pants, shirt, clerical collar and finally slipped on the jacket. He looked quickly at himself in the cracked and fly-blown mirror over the sink. His haggard face and red-rimmed eyes were hardly theological, but he'd pass in the dark of night. Something else that he'd learned during his days in the church was that no one ever looked too closely at a priest.

Kelly carefully locked the door of his room behind him and walked down the stairs to the Dupont's lobby. It was empty apart from Jose, the immensely fat desk clerk, who was nodding out over a pornographic magazine. Kelly caught a fleeting glimpse of a photograph of a doubled-over woman in a black garterbelt, and quickly looked away. In this costume, it was even more crucial to keep his thoughts pure. The only other person in the lobby was one of the long-term residents, a long-haired, washed up, speedfreak rock & roller who went by the name of Hundred Hour Lem. He sat slumped in one of the beat-up chairs in front of the big TV watching an episode of Star Trek, chain-smoking Marlboros, and drinking Southern Comfort from a bottle in a brown paper bag. Hundred Hour Lem looked up as he came down the stairs and did a speed-rictus doubletake when he realized that it was Kelly in the charcoal suit and cleric collar. "Fuck, Kelly, what are you trying to pull?"

Kelly had hoped that he'd be able to slip out of the hotel without being noticed. He looked sullenly at Hundred Hour Lem. "Just a minor deception. Nothing for you to worry about." A though suddenly struck him. He moved to where Hundred Hour Lem was sitting and lowered his voice. "Could you sell me a small quantity of amphetamine?"

Hundred Hour Lem twitched and looked around furtively. "Will you keep your fucking voice down?"

Kelly glanced at Jose who was still dozing over his disgusting magazine. "I do have my voice down."

"How much do you want?"

"I don't know. I've never done this before. What would I get for twenty?"

"Enough to keep you going for a while."

Kelly pulled out a twenty and Hundred Hour Lem produced a small fold of paper out of the lining of his decrepit motorcycle jacket with the sleight of hand of a tired magician. "I didn't think this was your scene. I always had you pegged as a lush."

Kelly kept his face absolutely straight. "I'm forced to work nights at the moment."

The library was very quiet as Renquist pondered the ultimatum presented to him by d'Asson. The room seemed so civilized and secure, insulated as it was against the constant drone of the New York traffic. The single floor lamp cast a warm yellow light on the rich deep gleam of the woodwork and the leather spines of the long ranks of books. It seemed scarcely possible that the meeting taking place there was between a vampire and the shaman and priestesses of a voodoo temple. Even more impossible was the suggestion that a crew of zombies would be sent against the vampires if somehow Renquist couldn't come up with a solution to the current crisis.

"Not zombies, Mr. Renquist. We are not the kind who deal in the creation of zombies. They would, however, be very determined people. And they would come against you in the hours of daylight."

"You have a lot of courage to threaten me in my own home, Doctor. Especially when you know who and what I am."

"Please, Mr. Renquist. Do not take what I said as a threat. It was not meant as such."

"How else should I take it?"

"I was merely outlining the very worst-case scenario. I sincerely hope it would never come to such a confrontation."

Renquist half smiled. "You have to admit that it does have all the makings of a very bad horror movie from the nineteen-fifties."

D'Asson also allowed himself a dry smile. "Worthy of Edward D. Wood, Jr., himself."

Renquist looked serious again. "You're insisting that we leave the city? That point is not negotiable?"

Madame Sophie folded her arms, apparently indicating there could be no compromise. "You think you could stay here after all that's gone down?"

"I imagine not."

"You could perhaps move your colony to New Orleans?"

Renquist sighed. "That could be a little predictable."

"We would obviously leave the choice of where you'd relocate to you."

"You just want us gone?"

"I wouldn't presume to put it so crudely."

Madame Marie apparently wasn't so bothered by diplomacy. She clutched her pocket book belligerently in her lap. "We just want you gone."

"And how soon do you want us gone?"

"As soon as possible."

Renquist thought about this. "We don't travel easily. There's always the problem of sunlight. We also have to run down Carfax and put a stop to his games."

Madame Sophie didn't mince words. "Have the young ones dead in forty-eight hours, and then, in a further two days, be out of here."

"It may not be that easy."

"Then we begin to move towards the worst-case scenario."

Once again, Kelly was on the vampire street. Getting there had not been easy. Even though it was now after one in the morning, the streets of the city were still in an uneasy state of semi-turmoil. Police vehicles screamed up and down the avenues with lights flashing and sirens blaring, making their intimidating presence felt. On his way downtown, Kelly had passed no less than three NYPD tactical patrols in full riot gear rousting gangs of wandering black youths. From what he'd heard on the radio and seen of the newspapers since leaving the library at St. Patrick's, it appeared that everyone else in the city was assuming the killings that were causing all the trouble and unrest had a racial or cult motivation. No one but him, and perhaps Father Muncie, even suspected that they were the work of the monsters who lived in the tall dark house on the block on which he now stood. How well the demons preserved their anonymity in this city of the damned. No wonder they called New York "Babylon on the Hudson."

On his journey south, though, Kelly had received confirmation of one thing. He'd been right in his thinking that he would be able to move around a great deal easier while dressed as a priest. At one point, as he'd been walking, looking for a cab that had proved exceedingly hard to find, a patrol car had slowed to a crawl, pacing him, while the officers inside had subjected him to hard suspicious stares. Then they had spotted the clerical collar and immediately accelerated on about their business. If he'd been dressed in his normal wino attire, he would undoubtedly have been stopped and questioned. For once, he seemed to have made exactly the right move.

At first, both the block and the house looked as closed-down and quiet as they had during his daytime vigil, and he was starting to resign himself to a long and unproductive wait through the stifling night. Then, after about fifteen minutes, a large black Cadillac Fleetwood pulled up outside the house. The car's nearside rear door opened and a huge man in a bulky double-breasted suit stepped out. Kelly immediately got the demon vibration from him, but he was hardly what Kelly had expected. This demon looked like some old-time Little Italy, bent-nose mobster, and Kelly was gripped by a momentary panic that the task in front of him was even more complex than he had ever imagined. Fortunately the amphetamine buoyed him up and the urge to cut and run quickly left him.

The big man hurried quickly up the steps of the house, paused for a minute to work his way through the system of locks, and vanished inside. The Cadillac pulled away, and as it passed Kelly, he tried to get a look at the driver, but the reflection of a streetlamp totally obscured him.

"A scapegoat would not be too hard to set up, providing the authorities and the media were prepared not to look too hard at the evidence and, at the same time, the killings also stopped. Just as long as it's plausible and we don't create a Lee Oswald situation, or trigger a wave of conspiracy theories."

Directly Lupo had come into the mansion, Renquist had summoned him to the library. As he walked through the door, he had been forced to go through a number of very rapid changes. His prevailing mood had initially been one of considerable guilt and chagrin that he hadn't as yet been able to pin down Carfax. "I can only assume that he and Blasco are on the move around the city. I have borrowed a number of reliable human operatives from my friend Mr. Taglia, and they are watching all of Carfax's known bolt-holes. They will call by telephone the moment that he's spotted."

This fresh piece of information left Renquist more than a little bemused. In the past few hours, he had seen the police department running wild and the mayor making fatuous speeches, he had been offered an ultimatum by voodoo priests, and now Lupo was telling him that he had enlisted the aid of organized crime to track down Carfax. The reverberations of this current time of Feasting were spreading beyond all reason.

Lupo's worried expression had changed to one of total amazement when he found himself confronted by his don in conference with Doctor d'Asson, Madame Sophie, and Madame Marie. At first he had been unwilling to talk in front of the houn'gan and the two mam'bos, but as soon as Renquist had explained the situation, he had reluctantly delivered his negative report on the hunt for Carfax in front of the three strangers. Lupo clearly didn't like the necessity of doing this, but he was enough of a pragmatist to realize that it definitely wasn't the time for counterproductive face-saving.

Lupo became even less happy when d'Asson treated his failure to bring in Carfax, either dead or alive, as a further advantage to be pressed. "The scapegoat would obviously have to be a white man."

Lupo growled in his throat. "I can think of plenty of white men who hardly deserve to continue living. Any one of them could be made to serve the purpose, and play the part of a mass murderer and suicide."

Renquist glanced at Lupo and immediately conceded the point to d'Asson. "I had never thought our scapegoat would be anything but white. We clearly can't have any more trouble in the black and Latino communities."

Madame Sophie picked up on the same thread and stretched it a little further. "Maybe two white men. There's been an awful lot of killing. We gotta make this look convincing. Like you said, we don't want no Lee Oswald business here."

Madame Marie ran it one stage further. "It's gotta be done properly. You know what I'm saying? We gotta have a confession, maybe a suicide note left where it can be found. This thing has got to be watertight. Real watertight. You know what I mean?"

Renquist nodded. "We will make it look as convincing as possible."

Renquist was getting tired. Also a hunger was stirring inside him. The sleep that had been filled with Dietrich's weird imposed dreams had provided him with no rest or recuperation. The assault by Carfax had come hard on the heels of the dreams, and then this voodoo intrusion. Taken as a whole, the sequence of events had left him close to burned out. He wanted to get out of the Residence to kill and feed, but he doubted that he would be given the chance. He was also aware that the rest of the colony was still cooped up in the playroom observing whatever was going on in the city, and probably experiencing the same cravings. At least the meeting with the houn'gan and the mam'bos was all but over, bar the formalities of leave-taking.

Renquist stood up. "I think we've covered all the ground we can for the moment. I presume that we will remain in close touch over all the matters we've discussed?"

D'Asson also stood, with the creaking stiffness of a very old man. As Renquist watched him, he consoled himself that at least he was spared the human affliction of bodily deterioration. D'Asson faced Renquist. "I must confess that I didn't think this thing could be handled in such a civilized manner."

Renquist smiled. "We nosferatu are full of surprises."

After the three humans had left and Renquist had returned to the library from seeing them to the door, he looked exhaustedly at Lupo. "So it seems like we have to get out of town."

Lupo shrugged. "In the end, it would have been inevitable. The curse of the nosferatu is that, eventually, we always wear out any hunting ground we occupy for too long. In this urban world, we forget that the hunter is, by definition, a nomad."

"So where do we go?"

"That's hardly the immediate problem. I still haven't found Carfax, and he's probably out right now creating more havoc. There could well be fresh bodies turning up in the morning."

Renquist paced the length of the library. "I'm going to go down in history of one of the worst Masters who ever controlled this colony."

"You know that's not true, Don Victor."

"Isn't it?"

"It was I who failed to stop Carfax."

Renquist let his bitterness show. "This is a mess."

Lupo came up behind Renquist. "I do have one piece of information that might please you."

"What's that?"

"I know where Cynara is. And she's not with Carfax."

Renquist swung round so he was looking Lupo full in the face. "Where is she?"

"At a hotel, the Melmoth, up on Central Park West. You know the one, up above the Dakota, the one with all the turrets and gargoyles?"

Renquist laughed out loud, letting go of a lot of the accumulated tension. "I should have known she'd go there. She always liked the Gothic architecture."

Lupo turned away and walked to the door. "Despite everything else, you should go to her. You and she have been together for a long time. Her place is here with you and with the rest of us."

Renquist shook his head. "I can't leave now. Not with all that's going on."

"You should go to her. The rest of us can deal with things until dawn."

"I really don't think so."

"Go to her, Don Victor. She's important."

Renquist thought for a long time. Finally he nodded. "Ask Sada if she could order me a limo. I'll talk to Cynara and see if she'll come back. If we're going to move out of New York, I can't leave her here."

Kelly was quickly coming to realize that night in the vampire's house was a great deal more active than the day. The problem was that the activity he now observed was completely at odds with what he'd expected and it made no sense to him. He realized that he must have been basing his preconceptions on Gothic novels and late-night horror movies. He hadn't exactly expected to see black-caped figures flapping from the roof or crawling headfirst down the wall, but he hadn't been ready for the gangster demon and certainly wasn't prepared for the trio of elderly black people that now emerged from the house, walked to an equally elderly Chevy Impala, and drove away. He also didn't expect, some fifteen minutes later, a midnight blue stretch limousine to pull up outside the house. The chauffeur got out and stood waiting, alternately looking up at the house and glancing at his wristwatch. As far as Kelly could tell, he was a perfectly normal driver for hire. Presumably one of the denizens of the lair was going somewhere.

Kelly decided that it might well help him to know what demon was going where, and he began walking towards the waiting driver. Normally he wouldn't have been so bold as to simply stroll up to a total stranger and engage him in casual conversation, but both the speed pumping through his veins and the sense of protection that he derived from his Father Kelly outfit gave him an unaccustomed confidence. The driver of the car was a skinny sallow Italian, a happy accident that seemed totally to his advantage. The man even had a gold religious medal on a chain around his neck. Kelly strolled slowly towards the limo. At first the chauffeur didn't notice him, but then he turned and spotted Kelly and, for an instant, his expression took on that shadow of ingrained guilt that invariably passed over the faces of lapsed and semi-lapsed Catholics when suddenly confronted by one of the priesthood. He straightened up and half smiled. "Good evening, Father."

"You're working late, my son."

The driver shrugged. "A man's gotta work all hours, the way things are these days."

Kelly nodded. "Isn't that the truth."

The man's face took on that other look that people tended to assume around priests. What the hell would a priest know about supporting a family and paying the bills. Kelly was now level with the man, and he paused as though he was simply out for a nighttime stroll and had nothing better to do with his time. "You're not heading uptown, I hope. I hear there's still trouble brewing up there."

The man frowned. "As a matter of fact, I am." He gestured to the vampire house. "I'm taking this guy here up to the Melmoth Hotel up on Central Park West."

A plan sprang fully formed into Kelly's mind. He was so unaccustomed to that kind of thing happening that he had trouble keeping his excitement from showing in his face. He smiled at the man as though the exchange was over. "Well, you take care, my son."

The chauffeur nodded. "You too, Father."

Kelly strolled on to the end of the block, but once he was out of sight of the chauffeur, he raced as fast as he could to the nearest main street. Let there be a cab. Please let there be a cab. If one of the demons was going uptown to some hotel in the dead of night, it was probably with evil intent. Perhaps he had a victim there. If Kelly could get there before the demon and wait until he arrived, perhaps he could follow him to whatever room was his destination, perhaps he could even catch him in the act, maybe even destroy the foul fiend. If only he could find a cab. So few of them were plying for hire on this disturbed and uneasy night. At least, if he saw one, it wouldn't hesitate to stop for a priest. But that was if he saw one.

In answer to his silent prayer a yellow cab almost immediately came into sight with its "For Hire" sign shining like a beacon. He raised his arm. "Taxi!"

"The limo is waiting."

Renquist hesitated. "I ought to speak to the others. They should know about the shaman's ultimatum."

"Just go, I will explain it all to them."

"They should hear it from me."

Lupo put a hand on Renquist's shoulder. "It's more important that you see Cynara. She is strong. We all need her back with us. It's more than just a personal matter."

Renquist worriedly shook his head. "I don't know."

Lupo was insistent "Just go, Don Victor. Julia is there in the playroom. If she hears what you are about to do, she will only try to cause trouble or delay you. This is not the time to court any further delays."

"Perhaps you're right."

"You know I'm right, Don Victor. Just go. Like I said, the limo is waiting."

The cab carrying Gideon Kelly made good time uptown. He'd expected to encounter traffic problems caused by the troubles on the streets and the police efforts to contain them. In fact, in the small hours of the morning, the reverse seemed to be in effect. The streets were unusually clear, and Kelly found that he was enjoying a free run all the way up the west side of Manhattan. He would certainly arrive at the Melmoth Hotel well before the vampire in his limousine. As he rode in the back of the yellow cab he stared out of the window, leaning his forehead against the glass and letting the breeze of the slipstream disturb his hair. The city seemed to be covered in a glistening slick of oily sweat left from the heat of the day, as though the actual buildings were fevered and sick. The few people still walking on the sidewalks moved with a sluggish apathy as though beaten down by the long remorseless New York summer. The last whores who remained at work on Tenth Avenue plied their trade all but naked save for garters and stocking and some triviality covering crotch and nipples, but they also seemed beset by the same listless lack of purpose. Kelly looked upon them with more openness than he would have previously. Anything to take his mind away from what might be the next move in his blind and frightening mission. Although he knew he had no right to the cloth and collar that he wore, it still seemed to offer a certain protection against the stirrings of the flesh. Or maybe it was the mission itself that protected him.

The truth was that Kelly knew he couldn't distract himself from thoughts of his purpose for very long. He couldn't escape the fact that he was now operating on pure instinct. He had no formalized plan, or even the haziest idea of what he intended to do when he reached this Melmoth Hotel. His only consolation was that he also knew that no plan was possible. At least he could not be accused of dereliction in his thinking when the options open to him were only those of watching, waiting, and then recognizing and seizing an opportunity the moment it presented itself. As he crossed Columbus Circle, he realized that he had no idea even why the vampire should be leaving his lair and going to a strange hotel in the middle of the night. Was it a rendezvous with a victim, a meeting with another of his own kind?

If nothing else, the Melmoth Hotel seemed the ideal setting for the melodrama that was unfolding in front of Kelly. Its architecture was unique; it totally stood out from the other structures on the block. The facade was a towering, if grimy, twelve-storey confectioner's cake decoration of turrets and curlicues, gargoyles and gingerbread, false pillars and idealized bas-reliefs symbolic of abstract Victorian concepts like Health, Harvest, and Industry. As the cab pulled up at curbside by the Melmoth's main entrance, a uniformed commissionaire with the face of a Bolivian assassin and wearing a dirty but still gold-braided jacket opened the door of the cab for Kelly. Kelly quickly paid off the driver, realizing as he did so that his money was rapidly running out and, if his mission wasn't resolved fairly quickly, he would soon be too poor to pursue the calling of Vampire Finder to the Lord.

The commissionaire looked as though he expected a tip, but Kelly had no intention of wasting his meager funds on that kind of thing. He simply and quickly blessed the scowling flunky and hurried on into the hotel.

The interior of the Melmoth was absolutely in keeping with its outside facade. The ornate brass embellishments started right at the revolving doors and continued on throughout the entire lobby, highlighting the dark wood and deep burgundy walls that had been contrived in a style that Kelly presumed was either Austrian or South German in concept, if not in origin. A somnolent nightclerk was sitting behind the reception desk. Seemingly the Melmoth had a good deal more self-respect than the Dupont. The nightclerk was quite as shifty and untrustworthy as José at the Dupont, but at least he wore a tie, wasn't grossly obese, and wasn't openly ogling pornographic pictures. He looked up as Kelly entered the lobby and did an even more surprised version of the usual doubletake that greeted the arrival of a priest in unexpected circumstances.

"Can I help you, Father?"

Kelly was suddenly at a loss for words. He couldn't think of anything to say. He didn't even have the information to frame a plausible question. When he did speak, the words came out unbelievably lame. "Is there a telephone I might use?"

Apparently the surprise at seeing a priest in the middle of the night was more than enough for a normally watchful night clerk not to question that there might be anything suspect about the request. The fact that a priest wanted a telephone was quite enough for him. "Over there, to the left of the elevators."

"Thank you."

"You're welcome, Father."

Kelly walked to the line of three phone booths and stepped into the center one. He picked up the handset and began to go through a pantomime of making a call, wondering how long he could keep that up. Then he saw that his acting abilities wouldn't be needed any longer. A dark blue limousine had drawn up outside, and he was sure that it was the one hired to transport the vampire.

As the limo pulled up outside the Melmoth, a commissionaire approached the vehicle, hand already extended to open the rear door. Then suddenly he seemed to sense something about the limo or its occupants and stopped dead in his tracks. Renquist didn't move until the driver had climbed out and opened the door for him. Only then did he leave the car. On the sidewalk, he spoke quickly to the driver, totally ignoring the commissionaire who was still standing with an expression of puzzled apprehension. "Please wait. I may be back very quickly or I may have to stay a while."

The driver nodded impassively. He had already been warned by the dispatcher at the limousine company that Renquist and his associates were extremely good customers and he should not react to any request that might seem strange or unusual. With his return transportation settled, Renquist turned on his heel and walked quickly up the steps of the hotel, with the commissionaire staring after him. He already knew that Cynara was somewhere in the building, probably on one of the upper floors. He could clearly feel the vibrations of her presence. What he didn't know was if she would create any obstacles to his seeing her. He pushed his way through the revolving doors and walked directly to the reception desk. "I wish to see Ms. Cynara de Ville."

Renquist found the name highly ridiculous, but it was the one that Cynara always used when she stayed at a place like the Melmoth. The nightclerk consulted his computer. "Is Ms. de Ville expecting you, sir? It is rather late."

Renquist nodded. "She'll be expecting me by now. I'll guarantee that she won't be asleep."

The nightclerk picked up his phone. As he dialed Cynara's room, Renquist looked around the lobby. It was empty except for himself, the nightclerk, and a priest making a phone call. The priest had such a negative presence that Renquist didn't bother with even the most cursory glance inside his mind.

"Who should I tell Ms. de Ville is calling?"

"Victor Renquist."

The nightclerk spoke briefly into the phone and then looked at Renquist. "If you'd like to go up . . ."

"Which room?"

"1009."

"Thank you."

As Renquist turned away from the desk he had the fleeting impression that the priest had been listening to his conversation, but the dawn was well on its way and he was in too much of a hurry to see Cynara to bother to investigate some lurking cleric.

The moment the vampire stepped into the elevator, Kelly moved out of the phone booth. The Melmoth boasted three elevators which stood side by side. The night clerk had told the vampire that the woman he wanted was in room 1009. Kelly slipped into one of the other elevators, punched the button for the tenth floor, and waited anxiously as the elderly Otis cranked upwards. As the doors opened and Kelly peered cautiously out, the vampire was already walking swiftly down the tenth floor corridor. Kelly drew back slightly as it halted at the room or suite in question and tapped softly on the door. After a moment's delay, he heard the door of the room being opened and a soft female voice that didn't sound particularly pleased to be disturbed in the middle of the night, but also sounded as though the speaker was very familiar with the vampire. "What are you doing here, Victor?"

"Things have been happening. I absolutely have to talk to you."

The woman hesitated reluctantly before she spoke again. "You better come in."

It was in that brief time of hearing the other voice that Kelly became certain he was now dealing with two of the undead. The impact of the voice had left Kelly with the same desperate trembling that he had experienced when he had first encountered the male demon on 15th Street. He was obviously what Bishop Rauch had referred to in his notes as a "diviner," one who could sense the creatures long before they had revealed any outward signs of their true nature.

Although Kelly was now aware of exactly what he had to do, he leaned against the wall of the elevator for almost a minute before he pushed the button that would take him back down to the ground floor. The knowledge that he now had two of the monsters in his power left him breathless and shaking. They had, however, played right into his hands. The dawn was less than two hours away and he knew the vampires wouldn't risk moving to some fresh location. All he had to do was to return to his room at the Dupont, assemble the necessary implements for their destruction, and come back when the two of them were sleeping through the day. Aside from that, the only thing he needed was the courage to go through with the final act of termination. He pushed the button to take him back down again and let out a long sigh.

As he came out of the hotel, the commissionaire hurried up to him with a look of fear and desperation on his face. "Father, this man, he went into the hotel and . . ."

In his role of priest, Kelly patted the commissionaire on the arm. "Yes, yes, my son. I know all about that man. I intend to return and take care of him."

The first discovery that Renquist made on entering room 1009 in the Melmoth Hotel was that Cynara wasn't alone. A human female was sprawled on the bed, one knee raised and arms behind her head in a close approximation of a classic pinup pose. She was slim and attractive, maybe in her mid- to late twenties, with long legs and short cropped black hair, definitely one of Cynara's preferred types. She was dressed, if one could call it dressed, in a lace teddy and matching stockings. Renquist wondered if perhaps a better term would have been gift-wrapped. The small red puncture marks at her throat told him that Cynara had already partaken of the gift, and his arrival had presumably interrupted her further enjoyment. The woman pushed herself up on one elbow, and blinked at Renquist, looking vague and puzzled. "A man?"

Renquist nodded. "Yes, I suppose you could say that."

The woman's head swivelled and her eyes moved to Cynara. Her expression changed to a confused cocktail of adoration and resentment. Her voice was slurred, and her eyelids were heavy. Cynara either had her drugged or under some serious mental blockers. "Cynara . . ."

"What, baby?"

"A . . . man?"

"That's right."

"You didn't say . . . you were going to introduce . . . a man . . . to the equation."

Cynara smiled down at her. "The man invited himself to the equation." She turned to Renquist and her face hardened. "What is it that you want, Victor? As you can see, I'm rather involved right now."

"As I said, I have to talk to you. We have a serious situation."

"What are you talking about?"

"Have you seen a newspaper today?"

Cynara frowned and shook her head. "No."

"Or turned on the TV?"

Cynara gestured to the woman on the bed. "Elaine and I haven't been out of this room, and we certainly haven't been watching TV."

Renquist looked around the room. Empty wine bottles and a flotsam of room-service trays provided silent confirmation that Cynara and the woman had not only been in the room for quite some time, but they also hadn't allowed a maid in to clean up. Apparently Cynara hadn't merely been debauching the woman but feeding her and plying her with booze, too. After she'd closed the door behind him, Cynara had let her silk robe fall open, revealing that she was also arrayed for what appeared on the surface to be a celebration of trashy lesbian ecstasy. The sheer black stockings, high-heeled mules with red ostrich feathers, and the black basque decorated with tiny blood red bows were an ensemble hardly typical of Cynara, and Renquist briefly wondered what piece of through-the-looking-glass illusion was being conducted there. More serious matters were pressing, however, and he didn't have the time for psychosexual speculation. "If you haven't seen the news, then you probably don't know that New York could well be on the verge of a full-scale meltdown and the colony has to move on."

"I don't understand. I thought the very last thing you wanted to do was to move the colony."

"Carfax has made it impossible for us to remain here."

"What do you mean?"

Renquist nodded to the Elaine female. "Not in front of her."

Cynara's eyes narrowed and she regarded him archly. "Her name is Elaine and she's a mathematician."

"I still can't talk in front of her, whoever she is."

"She's in such a state of bliss she won't understand a word."

Elaine nodded solemnly. "I'm in . . . a state of bliss. Cynara has put me . . . in . . . a state of bliss. I love Cynara."

Renquist shook his head. "I can't take that risk."

"She's also drunk a great deal of red wine and had some of the last quaaludes known to man."

Renquist insisted. "She can't hear this."

Cynara moved to the bed. "I can put her in a little deeper."

"Please do that."

"Yes, Cynara, please do that." Elaine stretched back on the dark blue sheets, spreading and stretching herself luxuriously. "Please, baby, put me in deeper. Please Cynara, I love it when you put me in deeper."

Cynara sat down on the bed beside her and passed a hand in front of her eyes. "I'm going to park you in the dreamplace like I did when I went out. You like it there, don't you?"

"I love it when you put me in the dreamplace."

Cynara placed her fingertips on Elaine's forehead, producing a visible energy flow. Elaine let out a long deep-throated sigh as she made her entry to the world of erotic shadows and tactile foxfire visions that Cynara had created for her. Almost as a reflex, her right hand began idly to caress the inside of her thigh. "Oh, Cynara, I love you so much. No one has ever made me feel this way."

When Cynara was assured that Elaine was completely under, she turned her attention back to Renquist and became instantly businesslike. "So talk to me."

Renquist glanced at the bed. Elaine's eyes were closed, but in the tight grip of imposed fantasy, she was slowly and sensually rolling her hips, her breathing came in long heartfelt gasps, and her breasts undulated. Renquist turned from the spectacle and scowled at Cynara. "She's still a little distracting."

"There's nothing I can do about that. I'm not about to just shut her down. I have too much time and effort invested in her."

"What are you doing with her?"

"I don't think that's any concern of yours."

"But you've already blissed her out."

"So?"

"Are you planning to bring her across?"

"I haven't decided yet. I don't think that's really any of your concern either."

"You may think differently when you hear what I have to tell you."

"So tell me and stop complaining about Elaine."

Renquist moved discarded clothing from a hotel armchair and sat down so he was facing Cynara. He then proceeded to recount the events that had led to him being there in the Mel-moth Hotel. He spoke carefully and calmly, leaving nothing out, and doing his best to draw no conclusions or apply any pressure. As he talked, much of Cynara's icy hostility dropped away. Her face became serious, but she neither questioned or interrupted him. Finally, after he had finished up the grim monologue with the details of the agreement he had made with Dr. d'Asson, she stared at him thoughtfully. "So, essentially, we have no choice. We have to kill Carfax and Blasco and then get the entire colony out of town. Otherwise the zombies come down on us."

Renquist noticed she had used the word "us" and found it an encouraging sign. "D'Asson explained that they weren't ac-tually zombies."

" 'The Zombies Battle the Vampires' does sound rather like a creature feature on the late movie."

Renquist nodded. "I made much the same remark to d'As-son."

Cynara avoided Renquist's eyes. "So you want me to come back?"

Renquist got up from the chair. "I need you to come back."

Cynara said nothing. Renquist stood waiting, but still she was silent. He walked slowly to the room's French windows. He opened one of them and stepped out onto the balcony. The dark mass of Central Park was spread in front of him, the same Central Park that had played its own passive role in the drama by providing the location for so many of the incidents that had led to their current predicament. On the far side, he could see the lights of buildings on Fifth Avenue. Cynara came and stood in the doorway behind him. "The matter of you and Julia would remain, wherever the colony might go."

Renquist stood with his back to her. "How many times do

I have to tell you that I am not bonding with Julia?"

"If I didn't come back, would you bond with her then?"

"I don't know. I might say, if you didn't return, it wouldn't be any of your concern."

"Touché."

Renquist very deliberately turned. "Exactly."

Cynara slowly extended a hand until the tips of her fingers just brushed his cheek. Without any conscious effort, the easy energy of long-term bonding immediately began to flow between them. It started as nothing more than a single dancing spasm of light, but after all that had passed between them over all the years they had been together, it was impossible for it to remain just that. Their auras grew around them and began to merge and pulse, gathering a terrible strength and luminosity. Raw power crackled and swirled into tiny quasar vortices of Kirlian plasma as though proving to anyone who could see that, together, Cynara and Renquist were a thousand times more formidable than either one could be on his or her own. They stood close, scarcely touching, but surrounded by a column of ancient and magical fire that all but threatened to illuminate the park itself.

Elaine was now on her hands and knees at the foot of the bed. She seemed to have somehow emerged from the dreamplace and was starring at the two of them in wide-eyed, almost childish wonder. "My God, you two look beautiful together. Beautiful and . . . so . . . very dangerous. Please take me . . . to wherever you're going."

Cynara put her face close to Renquist's and smiled a lupine smile that was pure, wicked nosferatu. "Shall we go back inside? I've gone to a lot of trouble to prepare her, and there's still an hour or more until dawn."

Kelly had intended to sleep between the time, shortly after dawn, that he had arrived back at the Dupont and the hour when the hardware store opened for business. He had quickly realized that sleep would be impossible. He was too keyed up and still tweaking from what remained of the amphetamine he had obtained from Hundred Hour Lem. In the end, he had simply sat in the lobby, listening to Jose's snoring and watching the flickering images on the TV screen. At six in the morning, the choice afforded by the TV was strictly limited to kids' cartoon shows, evangelical and fundamentalist preachers, or market reports. Mercifully, the hardware store, just three blocks away, opened at eight, so the wait, even though it seemed like an eternity, was objectively humane. Quarter to eight saw Kelly hurrying away from the hotel and eight-fifteen saw him coming back again with a long length of stout, broom-handle dowel and two brown bags that contained a number of other items.

Once up in his room, Kelly removed a small cheap handsaw and a sharp clasp knife from the larger of the two bags and set to work, performing an exercise in minimal carpentry. He sawed the dowelling into 18-inch sections and then used the knife to sharpen one end of each of the three of the sections into an uneven but serviceable point. While he worked, he nipped repeatedly at a pint of Queen Anne scotch. In addition to the hardware store, he had also gone to the liquor store and picked up the pint. Kelly had few illusions where his weaknesses and limitations were concerned. After each drink, he would pause, gasp, screw up his face, and then go back to work. He had decided that three stakes had to be enough for two vampires. He doubted that, if he screwed up, he'd live long enough to have need of more than one spare.

He had intended to carry the tools of his newfound calling—the stakes, the freshly purchased club hammer with which to drive them home, the crucifix with the silver figure of Christ, his old and dogeared Bible, plus the scotch—in a small but serviceable leather bag. When he pulled the bag from the back of his closet, however, he discovered that the stakes were too long to fit inside. According to Bishop Rauch, an 18-inch stake was the ideal length for the destruction of the undead, although somewhat shorter ones might still be serviceable. Rauch hadn't specified an exact minimum length, but Kelly figured that 14 inches wasn't taking too much of a chance in the interests of portability. It did mean, though, that he had to take up the handsaw once more and cut four inches from each stake, a task that he found irksome in his current impatient frame of mind.

When he was finally done and the bag was packed, he looked quickly round the room. The floor was covered with sawdust and wood shavings, but he would deal with that later. The moment of ultimate testing was at hand and Kelly had no time or inclination for housekeeping.

"I have to return to the Residence."

Cynara lifted her face from Elaine's breast. A tatter of white lace had somehow attached itself to her hair. "Don't be ridiculous. It's almost dawn. You'll never make it. You must sleep here."

Renquist wouldn't listen. "I can't do that. There's too much at risk. I have to get back. This has been an interesting interlude but I must go. I should never really have stayed in the first place. I am still the Master, remember."

"That's suicidal, Victor. You don't have time to get downtown. It's an insane idea. You'll be caught by the dawn."

"I have a limousine waiting downstairs. It's been there ever since I got here. I'll make it."

"Are you sure?"

Renquist eased himself from the bed. "Yes, I'm sure. It will be no problem."

Cynara lay back and took a deep breath. "You don't expect me to come with you do you?"

Renquist was already making himself presentable for the street and the limousine. "No, of course not, stay here. We'll be in touch after sunset."

Cynara smiled a heavy lidded, sultry smile. "That sounds good."

Renquist gestured to Elaine, who, once again, appeared to be riding her own private fantasy. "What are you going to do about her?"

"I'll either bring her across or cut her loose."

"You won't finish her?"

Cynara shook her head. "That would be a waste. You have to admit that she has the right potential."

Renquist rubbed his chin. "If you do bring her across, it would mean that females would hold the majority in the colony."

"And what would be so wrong with that? The males of the colony seem far more prone to fuck up."

Renquist's instructions to the limo driver were simple and curt. "Back downtown, and absolutely as fast as you can."

As soon as he had emerged from the Melmoth Hotel, Renquist had realized that it was even later than he had thought. The east was grey and sunrise was dangerously close. Even the diffused light on the sidewalk caused his eyes to feel sandblasted and his skin to tingle unpleasantly. For a moment, he was tempted to retreat back inside, and back to the arms of Cynara and Elaine, but he knew that he wasn't able do that. Anything could happen at the Residence during these coming and crucial hours of daylight, and he absolutely had to be there to take charge.

The limousine sped downtown, encountering little traffic, but he could already see direct sunlight pinking the tops of Manhattan's tallest towers. A sinking feeling in his chest told him that he had actually cut it too fine. Already he might be in trouble. He leaned forward in the backseat of the limo and concentrated as hard as he could on the dark interior of the Residence and attempted to make contact. Surely one of them would be listening out for his projected thoughts. "Lupo? Dahlia? Segal? Do you hear me?"

Almost immediately, he was rewarded with a hum of receptive awareness. From the tone of the hum, he knew that he was in contact with Lupo. "Lupo, my friend, I am racing with the sun and I fear that the sun has the edge. Can you please open the front door of the Residence and be prepared to get me inside if need be?"

He instantly received a hum of ascent. Along with the worded instructions, he had also sent a clear visual image of both his predicament and his current situation. Since it was Lupo that he had contacted first, he knew that there would be no misunderstanding or foul-up. Just so long as the sun wasn't actually clear of the horizon, he'd survive. He might suffer some pain and discomfort, but he would make it safely into the building. On the other hand, he wasn't in the least certain that, by the time he arrived at the house, the sun would still be partially down.

Temporarily safe behind the smoked glass of the limousine, he again leaned forward in his seat. This time, he also opened the partition that separated him from the driver. When he gave his instructions, he used as much of the voice of authority as he could without paralyzing the human and causing him to lose control of the vehicle. He spoke slowly and enunciated with great care.

"When you reach the block where I live, I want you to bring this vehicle to a halt as close as you can to the main door of my building. I don't care if you have to take it up on the sidewalk. I want to be as close to the doorway as I can be. I just need enough space between the car and the wall so I can partially open the rear door and slide out. When we reach the building, you will not attempt to get out of the car to assist me in any way. You will remain in the driver's seat and pull away directly I am clear of the car. Only when you are at the other end of the block, may you get out of the vehicle and securely close the rear door. Do you understand what I have just told you?"

The driver nodded without looking round. "Yes, sir. I believe I do."

"And you will do exactly what I told you and nothing else?"

"Yes, sir, I will."

"And afterwards you will have no clear memory of what happened."

"Afterwards I will have no clear memory of what happened."

Renquist checked that he'd covered all contingencies. It was never a good idea to leave anything to chance when giving explicit instructions to humans. "Oh, yes, one more thing."

"What's that, sir?"

"You have no concern about scratching the vehicle's paintwork while any of this is going on."

"Right, sir."

"Repeat it, please."

"I have no concern about scratching the vehicle's paintwork while any of this is going on."

"Very good."

They were now only a handful of blocks from the Residence. Renquist quickly prepared himself. He took a bottle of vodka from the limo's bar and splashed the liquor liberally on his face and hands. In a pinch, the alcohol might serve as a coolant. Next, he slid his jacket up and off his shoulders, without removing his arms from the sleeves so he could pull it over his head in a manner resembling a cowl. Then he folded his elbows so he could tug the jacket's cuffs down over the exposed skin of his hands.

As the limo rounded the corner onto his block, he crouched on its floor, already grasping the nearside door handle. Even through the black glass windows, Renquist could see that the sun was well over the horizon and he was in a great deal of trouble. Everything had to go exactly right or he would find himself cooked to oblivion. His only consolation was that no direct sunlight was hitting the sidewalk in front of the Residence itself. Even so, he was sufficiently at risk that he needed to suppress any temptation to think about what he intended to do.

He simply had to act with the precision of an automaton and come through alive.

The limo bumped up onto the sidewalk and Renquist tensed. The car lurched to a halt and, without the slightest hesitation, he threw the door open and sprung forward. The light hit him as both a physical force and an assault of excruciating pain. His eyeballs felt as though they were exploding in slow motion, and he stumbled as he hit the steps. Mercifully, the limo driver had put the car in exactly the right place. He had a brief glimpse of the open door and Lupo's worried face, back in the shadows, before his vision was obliterated by a wash of all-encompassing flame.

He forced himself to make one more spring and, as he crashed to the ground, he knew he was away from the deadly light. Cold hands were pulling him in and trying to soothe his agony. He knew he was still alive, but all he could see was the searingly bright fire. He looked around helplessly scarcely believing the horror of what had happened to him.

"I am blind."

His voice cracked when he said it a second time. A sightless nosferatu was a pitiful helpless thing and ultimately doomed. He had diced with the sun and won an empty victory. He might just as well have burned up there right on the sidewalk.

"I am blind!"

Kelly hurried along Central Park West, coming from the subway and heading with tight-lipped determination towards the Melmoth Hotel. Now he was so close to what he was increasingly thinking of as his baptism of fire, he found himself moving on such a singular and preordained path that he hardly noticed the woman until he was right on top of her. The first thing about her to break his total concentration on his mission was her slurred, uncomprehending voice and the strange words that she was saying.

"I loved Cynara. Why did she have to send me away?"

Kelly started with surprise. "What?"

"Why do my eyes hurt?"

"What the hell are you talking about?"

She didn't look like the usual New York street madwoman. She was young, attractive, and clean. Her short black hair was neatly and professionally cropped and her clothes had never been slept in. She had nice legs and the high heels, which at that moment were causing her to stumble and stagger, were all but brand new. The expensive Burberry trenchcoat that was wrapped around her, unbuttoned but tightly belted, was also fairly new. Beneath the coat, as far as Kelly could tell, she was clad only in a slip. Her behavior, on the other hand, was pure street madness. Despite the fact that she was wearing a pair of heavy black Ray-Ban sunglasses, she kept trying to shield her eyes from the sun as though it caused her pain.

"Help me, Father. My eyes hurt and Cynara doesn't want me. She won't take me to the other side where she is. She won't let me live forever."

Kelly could only presume that the woman was some normally affluent bitch who had somehow been dosed with acid, Ecstasy, or some other psychedelic, and then abandoned to wander the Upper West Side with her mind blown. He was about to snarl at her to get the fuck away from him, when he spotted the key she was clutching in her hand. He could read the name Melmoth Hotel on the red plastic tag and also a room number. The number was 1009. The self-same room that the vampire had entered earlier in the night. Kelly had no time to try and figure out the connection between this lunatic and the room containing the vampire. All he knew was that God was once again moving mysteriously and that key was for him.

"Please help me, Father."

Kelly could hardly restrain himself from snatching the key out of her hand, but he knew if he did that, she would almost certainly cause a scene on the street and he wanted to avoid attracting attention at all cost.

"What is that key, my child?"

The woman looked at the key as though she was seeing it for the first time. "I took it while Cynara wasn't looking."

"Give me the key and I will go and speak to Cynara."

The woman shook her head. "I can't give you the key. My eyes hurt."

"Give me the key, child. It's the only way that I can make it right."

Kelly was rethinking the idea of snatching the key. People had already paused to stare at the confrontation between the supposed priest and the obvious lunatic, and he was starting to feel profoundly uncomfortable. "Give me the key. Now. And I will make it better."

The woman was uncertain. "You will?"

"I will."

"You promise?"

"I promise."

Very reluctantly she handed Kelly the key. He took it with the best grace he could muster and then he walked quickly on to the Melmoth Hotel with the woman gaping after him.

"You're not permanently blind, Victor."

Lupo and Sada were helping him up the stairs, guiding him carefully as he stumbled weakly in the direction of what he supposed must be his bedroom. He felt burned, desperate, blind, and incapable. He wondered if Sada was telling him the truth or simply attempting to calm him. The observation of auras was such a major part of the penetration of other minds that he found he was as shut off as any human. When Lupo joined in the reassurance, Renquist started to take it a little more seriously. "Your power of recovery will put it right, Don Victor. You must know that."

But Renquist was not yet daring to hope. He was too consumed by his fear of the darkness and the flame-red unknown.

Kelly quietly slid the key into the lock without removing the DO NOT DISTURB card that hung from the doorknob. He turned it and the lock clacked back. He paused for a moment before actually pushing open the door. In this culminating moment, he had reached the point where it was no longer possible to pretend that his terror hadn't risen to the level of the absolute. Every rational part of him screamed that he should give this up. He should get away from that hellish door and whatever was behind its seemingly innocuous cream paint. The fact that despite every howling instinct he still leaned on the door until it swung open said a lot about how he was more afraid of the Wrath of his God than all the monsters that might lurk in room 1009.

He took his first step inside and was almost surprised to discover that it was essentially a regular hotel room, although it looked as though it hadn't seen maid service for a number of days. The room was littered with the trays and dirty dishes from at least a half-dozen meals, plus a clutter of dropped towels, clothing, and empty wine bottles. Some kind of opaque material seemed to have been taped over the windows, and Kelly had some initial difficulty adjusting his eyes to the gloom. In the light that came from behind him from the lights in the tenth floor corridor, he could, however, make out a figure lying prone on the bed.

He knew that he had to close the door behind him. He could not have some passing guest or member of the hotel staff looking in and seeing what he was doing. Bishop Rauch had insisted that the undead were very hard to wake during their daytime sleep, but Kelly was a little reluctant to trust his entire life to the words of the long-dead Bishop. All he could do was compromise. He left the door sufficiently ajar so he could see to move, and quickly crossed the room to where a lamp stood on a side table. His hand shook as he turned on the lamp. He quickly glanced at the figure, but it didn't move. He darted back to the door, closed it, and shot the lock back into place. He also hooked up the thoughtfully provided chain. Kelly again looked at the figure. It wasn't moving, but he also saw that it wasn't the male demon that he had followed to the room from the building downtown. The figure was that of a woman, presumably the woman who in the night had opened the door to the vampire while he, Kelly, had waited and listened in the elevator.

For a moment, he thought the woman was dead. She lay stiffly on the bed, flat on her back, legs slightly apart and arms formally at her sides, hands arranged palms upward, in a way reminiscent of some hindu goddess of the Kali ilk. Her makeup was immaculate as though she had freshly redone it, or had it redone for her, before she had retired to this unnatural sleep. She was dressed in a sheer black peignoir that, even if the front of it hadn't been gaping open, would have done absolutely nothing to cover her nudity and only enhanced its erotic impact. Kelly noted that she was somewhat on the skinny side, with small breasts and long slender legs. The hair on her head was almost albino white and elaborately arranged. He pubic hair on the other hand was dyed dark blue and had been shaved into a geometric dagger pattern, unless, of course, her kind had some demonic method of controlling the growth and color of their hair. A small red dragon was tattooed on her lower stomach. It was similar, although not identical to the *dracul* of Magyar mythology, woodcuts of which Kelly had seen among the illustrations appended to the Rauch papers.

To Kelly's mindset, this female creature looked like nothing more than a prostitute laid out for burial, or perhaps performing for a client with deviate necrophilic fantasies. These two ideas started some very unwelcome stirrings at a deep subconscious level and had to be immediately suppressed. He knew, however, that she wasn't dead or even faking, at least in any conventional sense. She had no pulse, no movement of breathing, not even a heartbeat, but she was possessed of what witnesses in Bishop Rauch's records described as "the warmth of life." Her eyes were wide open, and although apparently seeing nothing, they had none of blank glaze of those of a corpse. The male vampire had somehow eluded him, but this female was another of the same blasphemous tribe and, with poetic irony, she would be his maiden kill.

Kelly crossed the room and placed the leather bag on the table under the light. First he took out the pint of scotch and treated himself to a long pull of potable courage. Next came the hammer and the stakes. He also took out the cross for safety. He left the Bible where it was, though. He intended to read no words over this debased and satanic thing. When all was ready, he began to strip off his clothes. In Rauch, he had found a recommendation that the deed should be performed naked, or while wearing some kind of oilskin or protective clothing. The same footnote had warned that, when the stake entered the doomed creature, a considerable spray of disgusting mess and sometimes even blue flame could erupt from the body, gushing for some feet into the air. Although Kelly suspected that this might be a lurid and germanically bloodthirsty exaggeration, he had no desire to ruin the suit he was wearing.

He took his clothes to the protection of the bathroom, and then returned naked to the table. His body was unhealthily white, bony, and angular. He took one more hit of scotch and then picked up the hammer and two of the stakes. He deliberately fixed his eyes on a point on the wall above the bed. He knew he should not look upon the woman until he was in place to actually do the act. He feared that any further sexual stirring might deflect him in his purpose, or that a carnal tension might somehow alert her to his presence. Without looking down and with the Implements of Retribution in his hands, he advanced upon the bed and upon the woman.

chapter Seven

Cynara!"

Renquist sat bolt upright, and his shout was a wolfhowl of rage and pain.

"Cynara!"

Something new and terrible had happened. Cynara had gone and her passing had jolted him out of a sleep so deep that he had been sunk well below the level of dreams. Without any other thought or memory, his mind searched desperately for any possible trace of her. Bonded pairs could always sense each other within the kind of area encompassed by the boundaries of New York City. When he found nothing, he knew that Cynara had left the entire reality. Cynara had been destroyed, and it was that instant of destruction, her dying scream of fear and anger, that had kicked him awake. He wanted it all to be a mistake, but he knew it wasn't. Through his long lifetime, he had heard the same kind of scream many times, and known the small, slowly closing voids that remained behind for a few transitory minutes after the nosferatu parting. In 1919, he had heard the same screaming countless times. He had even experienced the destruction of one with whom he had bonded. He had never expected such a thing to happen to Cynara, however, especially at a moment when they had resolved the momentary problems in their relationship and renewed their bonds both physically and emotionally.

"Oh no, Cynara! Not you!"

Lupo was the first to arrive in the Master's bedroom and he came at a run. "I heard . . ."

Renquist covered his face with his hands. "I know, Lupo. I know."

"You can see?"

Renquist suddenly looked up. "You're right. I can see."

He had been so much in shock over the destruction of Cynara that he hadn't bothered to think about the other, and lesser, of their recent disasters. His vision was a little blurred and two-dimensional in the broad central ranges but he was definitely on the way to recovery. The fact that Cynara should be gone while he appeared to be surviving had to be some bitter joke, a vicious reminder that what might be given with one hand could be taken away with the other. He dazedly looked at his own hands and arms. The skin was darker, more alive than his usual deathly pallor, and, here and there, it was peeling, but the burns were almost healed. He imagined that his face would be the same, although he'd never know that.

Moving more slowly than his first alarmed sprint, Lupo approached the bed. "Are you sure it was Cynara?"

Renquist barred his teeth with a hiss. "It was Cynara. Someone or something has just wantonly snuffed out her life." He climbed quickly from the bed. "And I am going to find it and kill it, whatever it was!"

He looked around for his clothes. Black, he could only wear black, nothing else would be proper. Rage was building inside him, displacing the shock and grief. Also his energy levels were rising. A violent fury was even better than sleep for hastening recovery. Lupo quickly put a hand on his arm. "Don Victor, be sensible. You cannot go . . ."

"I can go, and I am going to go."

Still fastening his pants and carrying a black shirt with him, Renquist strode stiffly from the Master bedroom. Lupo hurried after him. "You cannot go anywhere, Don Victor. It is broad daylight outside."

Kelly stood in the shower for more than twenty minutes, bowed under the cascade, shocked and motionless, just letting the scalding hot water stream down his body and doing nothing else. He was even doing his best not to think. He wanted to remove every disgusting trace of what had just come to pass. He wanted it all gone—the sight, the smell, the entire terrible memory. He knew that the water would, given time, remove the stain and stench of the vampire, but he knew that the horror of the spectacle that he had just witnessed would be etched on his soul forever. Little wonder that Bishop Rauch had used men who had spent brutal years in the trenches of World War I to do his dirty work for him. They were the only ones calloused and desensitized enough to do repeatedly what he had just done. Even some of them, if the records were to be believed, had gone mad in the course of their hideous duties. The fact that he seemed to have been selected to repeat the obscene process over and over until no vampires remained on the island of Manhattan had to be another of the Almighty's horrible, unconscionable jokes.

A short time earlier, standing naked beside that awful bed in the other room, he had looked down at the vampire female, right into those sightlessly staring eyes. With the club hammer grasped firmly in his right hand, he had used his left to position the pointed end of the stake above the creature's chest, on a level with her breasts and slightly right of center. He kept the point of the stake raised so it wasn't touching the thing's inhuman flesh. When he finally lowered it, it made the slightest indentation in the skin. In that instant, the creature's eyes moved, locking with his. Kelly had been all but paralyzed by the first flash of shock and horror and then almost undone in his mission by the explosion of perverted and sensual possibilities and scenarios with which she engulfed him in a last-ditch attempt to save her miserable life. Her voice and even her polluted touch had been right inside his head. Any vice known to man, woman, and beyond, it could all be his if he just turned away from his appointed task and joined her.

The vampire female had, however, picked the wrong man on whom to work her blasphemous wiles. A lifelong rage against the deceptions of whores and wantons was what had swung the hammer, a rage that allowed Kelly no time to reflect or consider or weigh the possibilities. The hammer had come down hard on the flat upper end of the stake with a solid and wholesome crack, driving the wood deep into that dangerous and provocative body. The erotic visions had been cut off as though by a pulled plug, and were replaced by a screaming fearful rage. He had expected the vampire simply to die when the stake had entered her, but she had fought him every inch of the way down the plunge to final oblivion. As the stake had gone in, her face had twisted and her legs had pumped, heels pounding on the bed. Her arms reached for him, long talon-like nails trying to rip at his face and body. His instinct was to flee, but the job had to be finished. Ducking the slashing claws, he swung the hammer a second time and this was when the real horror had started.

It began in the smallest way: A fine purple mist sprayed out from around where the stake had penetrated the body and, along with it, the room was permeated by a smell of blood and burning. The vampire was still thrashing, so Kelly had hammered the stake a third time. The fine spray had immediately turned into a gusher. Thick purple fluid and other more unspeakable materials squirted as high as the ceiling, spattering walls, floor, and drapes, and drenching Kelly's head, arms, and shoulders and plastering his hair. The smell turned into a stench of such intensity that it seemed to have replaced all of the air in the room, and Kelly staggered back, gagging. The hammer dropped from his hand and fell on a pile rug already soaked through with the purple vampire blood. On the bed, the stinking cascade had all but abated, but the female was still jerking, snarling, and thrashing, splashing in the pool of fluid that surrounded her. She repeatedly tried to pull the stake loose from her chest, but seemed somehow unable to do that. Gradually her movements grew weaker and he knew that she was dying. Her contortions dwindled to nothing more than a spasmodic twitching. Kelly leaned against the wall trying to hold on to his stomach, while sweat and purple goo ran down his naked body. Believing it was all over, he reached for the bottle of scotch. He had no way of knowing that the worst had yet to come.

The blue flame exploded with a flash like a lightning discharge, and Kelly cowered away from it, expecting to be fried to a crisp, but still awed by its intensity and beauty. He couldn't understand how something as loathsome as the vampire could produce something so beautiful as the color of the flame at the moment of her passing. The flame turned out to have no physical heat and it rose, passed through the ceiling, and vanished. On the bed, the body began to change. Before his very eyes, its skin was drying and hardening until it took on the look of an ancient and long-mummified corpse. What had once been liquid turned to paste and finally a dry, crumbling powder. The very substance of the corpse started to collapse in on itself with crackling reports like tiny explosions that threw up small puffs of dust. As the now dried and brittle flesh started to fall away from the skeleton, Kelly had taken a fast pull on the whiskey bottle and staggered to the bathroom, a hand pressed to his mouth to stop the liquor coming back up his throat.

Renquist was going for the front door. He stalked through the daytime gloom of the Residence, ignoring the elevator, going down one flight of stairs after another. His footfalls on each tread rang like ghosts of gunfire through the silence of the house, and his eyes blazed red with a mad fury that excluded all reason. Lupo and Segal followed after him, saying nothing but exchanging worried and significant glances that clearly indicated they were both well aware that the Master had, temporarily at least, taken leave of his senses. They stopped short, though, of physically restraining him. Segal could never have done it without an instruction from someone else, and the idea of actually laying hands on his don was something so totally alien to Lupo's code of behavior that it could only have occurred in the most outlandish of circumstances. Unfortunately, the circumstances were becoming more and more outlandish by the moment. Renquist was walking with furious determination, not only to the front door, but also the blazing sunlight and certain death. Segal looked helplessly at Lupo. "What do we do?"

Lupo shrugged unhappily. "I suppose we have to stop him by force."

"He'll fight."

"Of course he'll fight. He's crazy. I've seen others of our kind go into shock at the loss of a bond mate but never as badly as this."

"Coming on top of the burning he received this morning . . ."

Lupo nodded. "Exactly."

Renquist had started down the final flight of stairs that led directly down to the front hallway and the main door. Lupo leaned close to Segal. "We'll have to take him when he gets to the bottom of the stairs. That minimizes the chance of any of us getting too badly hurt."

Segal frowned. "You think we can stop him without any of us getting hurt?"

Lupo tersely shook his head. "No. I think we're all going to get hurt. I'm not even sure that we can stop him at all. We do have to try, though. He's still our Master and we have to save him if we can."

Renquist reached the bottom of the stairs; as one, Segal and

Lupo tensed to rush him. Lupo signalled that he would go left and Segal should go right. Together, and with supernatural vampire speed, they charged. At the bottom of the stairs, each seized Renquist by one of his arms and attempted to carry him on and down with their sheer momentum. They were partially successful. Renquist staggered forward for a couple of paces, but then he braced his legs, lunged backwards, and using their momentum against them, threw both off. Lupo went sprawling, crashing into the grandfather clock and setting the chimes clamoring, but Segal managed to stay on his feet. Despite his misshapen bulk, he spun like a dancer and came back at Renquist. Renquist quickly stepped back. His hand flashed up glowing with a white warning light. "Don't touch me again, boy. I will injure you badly if you touch me again. I'm going to avenge Cynara and no one's going to stop me. Do you hear me?"

Lupo was back on his feet. In all the years of their association, he had never seen Renquist like this: savage, self-destructive, and consumed by the need to hurt, to damage, to inflict suffering. "Victor, after a thousand years, this would seem like a terrible waste. Incinerating yourself in the sunlight won't bring Cynara back."

Renquist ignored him. He continued to stare at Segal, his hand still blazing with lethal energy. Segal seemed lost as to what to do. His Master was attempting to kill himself but if he tried to stop him it could result in a fight that could well destroy all of them, and the Residence along with them. He glanced to Lupo for some suggestion, but Renquist angrily shook his head. "Don't be looking to him, boy. Look at me. I asked you if you heard me."

This was all getting to be a little too much for Segal. He had little experience in dealing with the insane and the raving. "I don't know what to say."

"Just tell me if you heard me?"

"Of course he heard you, Victor. I imagine they've been

hearing you for blocks around." Dahlia had suddenly appeared in back of Renquist. The other women stood in the shadows behind her, almost invisible save for their eyes. "If you boys can't sleep, it would be nice if you could at least play quietly."

Renquist slowly turned. "Cynara is gone."

Now Sada spoke. "We know that, Victor, but you won't turn back time or achieve anything by walking out into the sun and going after her."

Renquist was petulant. "I want to destroy something."

"We know that Victor, but this irrational rage is hardly becoming to a nosferatu of your vintage."

"I can destroy all of us."

"We know that too."

With a motion of his fingers, not unlike that of a human conjurer, he produced a sphere of energy, bright white, but tinged with pink and blue like an opal. He turned his hand so the palm was upward and the energy sphere floated just above it, crackling and quietly spitting power. "I can destroy us all so easily."

Now Imogene whispered. "Yes, Victor, we know that. But it would be stupid."

"I want to be stupid. I've tried being responsible and look where it got me. In fact, watch this for a piece of stupidity."

He tilted his hand and the sphere moved slowly through the air, moving directly towards the assembled women.

As Kelly, carrying his leather bag and trying hard not to look as though he had just been to Hell and back, once again walked into the lobby of the Dupont Hotel, two men were waiting for him. When he first entered, the men were leaning on the check-in desk, in conversation with Ishmael, the day man, but as he pushed through the dirty glass door, Ishmael gestured to Kelly and the two men straightened and turned. Kelly knew instantly that they were police officers. Their attitude and bearing was quite unmistakable. Kelly had expected, somewhere down the line, before his mission was over, he would run into some kind of confrontation with the authorities. He hadn't expected, though, that it would have come quite this soon. One cop was burly, black, and running to fat. The other was slighter, with a definite Irish cast to his features, but Kelly didn't think he was the kind who would be about to cut him any ethnic slack. The white man flashed a gold detective's shield. "Gideon Kelly?"

Kelly nodded. "Yes."

"I'm Detective McGuire and this is Detective Williams. We'd like to ask you a few questions."

The old men gathered around the television set had all turned away from the afternoon talk show to watch what was going on. It certainly wasn't the first time an arrest had been made in the lobby of the Dupont, but they didn't occur on such a regular basis that this incident didn't constitute something of a gratuitous sideshow. Kelly glared at the old men and they reluctantly went back to the TV. Then he faced the cops. "What is this about?"

"We believe you filed a police report about a week ago. You talked to a Detective Escobar."

Kelly nodded. "That's right. At the time, Detective Escobar didn't seem very interested in what I had to tell him."

Detective Williams spoke for the first time. "You'll find that we're a whole lot more interested than Escobar."

McGuire quickly moved to the specific. "Does the name Kurt Carfax mean anything to you?"

Kelly shook his head. He almost grinned with relief. The two cops were totally on the wrong track. "Not a thing."

"How about Victor Renquist?"

Had Kelly grinned, the grin would have immediately faded. Victor Renquist was the name that male vampire had used when he'd talked to the night clerk at the Melmoth. Kelly decided that it was no time to be keeping secrets. "Yes. I now know that Victor Renquist was the name of the individual I talked to Escobar about, but as I already said, Detective Escobar didn't seem terribly interested."

"You want to talk to us about Victor Renquist?"

"I'd rather have done that days ago."

"Better late than never?"

"Possibly."

McGuire looked around the Dupont's lobby. The old men had once again become an audience for their conversation. "Perhaps we could talk somewhere a little more private? You have a room here?"

Kelly nodded. "Yes, I have a room, but it's a bit of a mess. You have a car?"

Williams and McGuire exchanged glances. "Yes, we've got a car."

"Can we talk there?"

McGuire looked at Williams. "I don't have a problem with that. Do you?"

Williams shrugged. "We can talk in the car, if he wants." He faced Kelly. "You got something in your room you don't want us to see?"

This remark confirmed what Kelly had already suspected. Williams was the heavy of the partnership. He wasn't, however, going to allow himself to be intimidated at this stage of the game. "No, there's nothing I want to hide in my room. It's just as I said. I've been very busy over the last few days and my room is a mess. Shall we go to your car?"

The three of them walked out of the hotel, McGuire leading the way, Kelly next, and Williams bringing up the rear. As they descended the front steps of the Dupont, McGuire looked back over his shoulder. "I thought you told Detective Escobar that you were no longer a priest."

"That's correct.'

"So what's with the clerical collar and the whole bit?"

"I'll explain it all when we get to the car."

* * *

Dahlia deftly caught the energy sphere with her left hand and folded it in on itself as easily as crumpling a paper bag. "You see, Victor. You aren't the only one who can do magic tricks. We all have our hidden resources. Don't you think that it's time you drew on some of yours and brought yourself out of this craziness?"

The other women were now grouped protectively around Dahlia. Segal and Lupo stood worriedly at the other end of the hallway. Behind them was the front door of the Residence, and beyond that, the deadly New York noonday sun. If Renquist decided to make a determined break for the outside and his own destruction, they would be hard-pressed to stop him. Dahlia's collapse of the energy sphere seemed to have collapsed some of Renquist's mad rage along with it. Renquist's shoulders sagged and he slowly shook his head. "Cynara is gone."

Julia moved to the front of the group of women. Her voice was acid and she was clearly angry that Renquist should be taking Cynara's death so hard. "Haven't you lost someone close to you before, Victor? Did Cynara mean so much to you that you have to fall totally to pieces at her death? I really thought you were made of sterner stuff."

Dahlia flashed Julia a warning look, but Julia took no notice of her. "You're pathetic, Victor. I can understand grief, but that you should come apart like this, at a time like this, is nothing short of disgusting."

Renquist slowly raised his head. He looked totally drained. "I'm sorry. The madness has passed." He turned to Lupo and Segal. "I'm sorry, gentlemen. I hope I didn't hurt either of you when we struggled."

Both Lupo and Segal shook their heads. "It could have been a great deal worse."

This change in Renquist didn't seem to be enough for Julia. "You could have severely damaged all of us with that energy sphere if Dahlia hadn't stopped it."

Renquist closed his eyes. "I'm sorry."

"You're sorry? Is that all you've got to say? You're sorry? You make me ashamed to have been created by you."

Dahlia flashed a warning at Julia. "I think that's enough."

"You do? I'm not sure I do. He needs to hear some plain speaking for a change."

Sada stood beside Dahlia. "That's quite enough, Julia. Victor needs to sleep now. Unless he recovers quickly, we all have a problem."

Julia mimicked Sada. "Victor needs to sleep. Poor Victor. Let's all feel sorry for Victor."

Sada's eyes flashed. "That's enough, Julia."

Julia faced her angrily. "Well, I don't think so. It's about time Victor heard a few things about himself. He has it too easy with everyone here kissing his ass all the time."

Dahlia took a step towards Julia. Her voice had an edge that would brook no argument. "That's more than enough, Julia. I think we all agree on that."

Julia seemed about to launch into a further tirade, but then she looked at the faces and auras of the other three women and changed her mind. Dahlia moved towards Renquist and extended a hand. "Come with me, Victor. You have to sleep. There will much to do when the sun goes down."

Renquist took Dahlia's hand, and while Lupo, Segal, and the women looked on, she led him towards the stairs. The sight of the tiny childlike figure leading the tall and apparently so much more powerful one by the hand was both strange and unique.

"You just killed one of the vampires?"

"How many times do I have to tell you? I'll take you to the Melmoth and show you the body. When you see it, you'll possibly be more willing to believe what I'm saying."

McGuire and Williams seemed at a loss to know how to deal with Kelly. When the three of them had seated themselves in the detectives' unmarked Chevy, he had told them, with almost no prompting, the entire story, from that first moment when he had spotted Renquist outside Fay Latimer's apartment building all the way through to the killing of the female vampire in room 1009 at the Melmoth that same morning. The only slight editing that he'd allowed himself was in not placing too much emphasis on his belief that his mission against the vampires had been instigated and placed on him personally by God. He could see from their faces that they were having enough trouble coming to terms with the basic narrative without burying them in the metaphysical subplot. McGuire and Williams had let him talk without too much interruption, but when he'd finished, McGuire had closed his eyes with the expression of man who had suddenly developed a blinding headache.

"You seriously expect us to believe that a colony of vampires exists right in the middle of New York City?"

"You can't believe in vampires?"

"Frankly, I can't."

"Can you think of a better explanation for all the killings? All the blood-drained corpses?"

Williams and McGuire were sitting in the front of the car and Kelly in the back. Williams leaned across the seat so his face was close to Kelly's. "Are you sure it wasn't you doing those killings?"

"I've never killed a human being in my life."

"You're certain that the woman you murdered at the Melmoth Hotel wasn't human?"

"If you'd seen her die, you wouldn't ask that."

Kelly could feel the tension that was building inside the two officers. On one hand, they could hardly contain their excitement that they might have actually, and almost by accident, picked up the New York serial killer who had sparked so much chaos in the city. If that was the case, their careers were made. On the other hand, this story of vampires and night stalking that he was telling was so insanely complicated that it might take them a goodly part of those careers to sort out the truth from the fantasy.

"I think we'd better continue this conversation at the precinct."

"You don't believe me, do you?"

"You have to admit that your story is a little hard to follow."

"So come to the Melmoth and look at the evidence. Then go to the library and read up on Bishop Rauch."

"I think we'd be better off taking you to the precinct and then getting a crime scene team to the Melmoth."

"If I can't convince you that I'm telling the truth, how do you expect to be able to convince a lot of other cops when the time comes?"

"That's not really our problem is it?"

"Isn't it? I'm not your supposed serial killer, and if you go on working on that assumption, you'll start running into the most terrible contradictions. Believe me, I've already been there."

McGuire looked at Williams. "What do you think?"

"What do I think about what?"

"What do you think about going to this Melmoth Hotel and taking a look. Just taking a look. There might be nothing there at all, but if it's like he said . . ."

"If it's like he said, we've got something on our hands that I, for one, absolutely do not want to know about."

Kelly smiled. It was probably a mistake, but he couldn't resist the urge to take the superior position. "Perhaps you're afraid that you'll discover I'm telling the truth?"

For a moment, Kelly thought that Williams was going to punch him. Then McGuire shot Williams a warning look and the other cop backed off. Kelly pushed his luck just one fraction further. "So what's it going to be, gentlemen? The precinct or the Melmoth? If I'm crazy, the Melmoth will confirm that soon enough."

Kelly knew he was getting to McGuire. The Irish cop wanted to take a look at the Melmoth before he went any further. Williams was different. He didn't want to face the idea that there might be even a grain of truth in Kelly's story. A total disbelief in the paranormal and everything connected with it was apparently crucial to something in the man's psyche. Kelly's eyes flicked from McGuire to Williams and back again. "What's it to be?"

McGuire was also studying Williams. "Perhaps we ought to take a look. At least whatever we find there will give us a handle on what we're dealing with. I for one could use that handle before we go charging around yelling that we've cracked the case."

Williams had the face of an unhappy man. "With all the heat on this case, we ought to be doing everything by the book."

"What does the book say about some nut who claims he's a vampire hunter?"

Williams now looked profoundly unhappy. "We could get ourselves in deep shit."

McGuire leaned on the steering wheel. "And we could look like complete fucking idiots if we take him in on the strength of what he's told us, and it turns out to be an entire fairy story from start to finish."

Williams cursed under his breath. "Jesus Christ. I don't fucking need this."

McGuire had the keys to the car in his hand. "It's up to you, bro."

Williams slumped back in his seat. "Okay, okay. Let's go uptown and chase fucking vampires."

Renquist lay back on his bed in the formal position, but sleep refused to come. A disorganized dance of thoughts moved through his mind, unbidden and quite beyond his control. He had succumbed to the madness in front of the whole colony, and for that he was quite unable to forgive himself. Cynara was

gone, the New York colony was all but a thing of the past, and
Carfax and Blasco would have to die before the night was out.
Taken as a whole, and even divorced from any emotional coloring on his part, it constituted nothing more than a catalogue
of the most abject failure. The only way that he could possibly
redeem even a fraction of his self-respect, and the respect of the
others, was to bring this disastrous sequence of events to the
swiftest possible termination. Carfax and Blasco had to die.
The killer of Cynara, who or whatever it might be, also had to
be hunted down and destroyed. This was no longer a matter
of rage or personal revenge. It was as Dietrich had warned him.
Someone or something out there knew all about them and was
acting on the knowledge. A vampire killer was on the loose and
had to be stopped. If it could destroy Cynara while she slept
helplessly in that cursed hotel room, it was quite capable of destroying the rest of them while they slept in the Residence.

Renquist did his best to fight down his frustration. The sun
was still bright outside, and until it went down he was helpless,
as much a prisoner as any of the others, as much a prisoner as
Cynara had been when the murderer had come upon her. The
ever-present vulnerability to sunlight was the worst weakness
of the nosferatu, the weakness that had cost them so dearly
down the centuries, the true curse of the vampire.

It was then that a thought crossed Renquist's mind. What
had happened to the woman Elaine? Had she too died at the
hands of the mysterious hunter? She might possibly be the
hunter herself—although, after such close contact with her,
Renquist thoroughly doubted that. Cynara had seemed halfway
determined to transform her into nosferatu, and Elaine had certainly seemed more than willing. Yet he had only felt that single termination. If Elaine had somehow escaped or eluded the
killer, she might be able to identify him or it. She might well
be the key to the next phase of the whole grim charade. He realized that he had yet another task in front of him. If it was in

any way possible, and if she was still living, he also had to find Elaine.

Again the frustration mounted inside him. He could ill afford to waste the hours before sunset laying prone and inert, but as he knew only too well, he had absolutely no other choice.

McGuire let out a groan. "Oh God."

Williams couldn't stop shaking his head. "I seen some shit in my time, but . . ."

"That was shit to beat all."

"What the fuck are we going to do now? Who the hell is going to believe us?"

"The evidence is there."

"The brass is going to bury that shit with a backhoe and us along with it. You see the mayor and the commissioner going on TV to announce that New York got vampires?"

"That thing in there might not have been a vampire."

"It sure was something. I never saw a corpse like that before. It looked like it was a hundred years old."

"And the fucking stench."

"Jesus."

Kelly, McGuire, and Williams leaned against the wall on the tenth-floor corridor of the Melmoth Hotel. Kelly let the two cops do all the talking. They needed to ventilate. They needed to curse away some of the surface horror. He had seen the process that had made that hellish and unspeakable room the way it was. McGuire and Williams had only viewed the aftermath, and that had been more than enough for them. It was no exaggeration to say that the two of them were in shock. As homicide detectives, they had repeatedly seen the worst that one man could do to another, but the sight and smell of room 1009 had stopped them in their tracks.

Finally, when Kelly decided that the cops had taken enough time to recover their wits, he made a quietly tentative suggestion. "I don't know about you, but I could use a drink."

McGuire blinked. "A drink?"

Kelly nodded. "Unless you want to go back in there."

McGuire let out a long breath. "I could use a drink."

Williams looked as though the whole situation was getting away from him. "We can't just go to a bar. Not after what we've seen."

McGuire turned on his partner. "You've got a better idea?"

"We have to do something about that."

"You want to call this in? Or go back downtown and make out a report?"

"I don't know. We've gotta do something."

"And how exactly would you call this in? What would you put in the report? That we have a hundred-year-old body that was alive yesterday and appears to have spewed purple crud all over an entire hotel room after a stake was driven into its heart by a phoney priest. We need to talk about this, partner. We have to talk this through before we do anything."

Kelly pushed himself away from the wall. "It rather looks as though we're all in the same club now." He started to walk away, but Williams grabbed him by the arm. "Where the hell do you think you're going?"

Kelly turned. He suddenly realized that he wasn't afraid of Williams any longer. He might be big and he might be holding down a lot of repressed violence, but after looking in that room, he was as lost as Kelly was. Maybe more so. Despite all his muscle and bluster, Williams could no more call his superiors and report that a dead vampire was laying in an Upper West Side hotel room than Kelly could call the Cardinal and tell him the same thing. What had Father Muncie said? "You could drag Count Dracula himself into the Cathedral and drive a stake through him on the high altar and the Cardinal would deny it had ever happened."

Kelly shook himself free of Williams. "I'm going for a drink in the nearest bar and I suggest you two come with me because

I think we have a whole lot of talking to do before we go anywhere. You can stay up here as long as you like, circling from anger to denial, but I've been up all night and I need a drink. I don't know about you, but there are limits to how much of this I can take. In case it hasn't occurred to you, there are more of those things where that one came from, only they're still alive and at sunset they'll probably be hungry."

For a moment, he though Williams was going to hit him. He spoke fast. "Just think about this, pal. If we can finish off the rest of the nest, the killings will stop, and we'll at least have that going for us."

This seemed to penetrate and deflect Williams' need to punch Kelly's face. He turned away and snarled at McGuire. "Okay, so what do we do about the room while we're sitting in some bar somewhere trying to find enlightenment in a bottle of Jameson?"

McGuire snarled back. "Flash a badge on the manager and intimidate the fuck out of him. Tell him to seal the room and seal his mouth at the same time. Tell him, if he plays ball, we keep his miserable hotel out of the papers."

"Let me talk to Anthony Ferrari. Tell him it's Victor Renquist and I'm calling in one of his markers."

Renquist waited until a flustered Anthony Ferrari came on the line. Even through the phone, Renquist could sense the human's fear. Renquist laughed. "Listen carefully, Anthony. I'm going to give you a chance to erase some of the information I have on you, so don't talk. Just listen. I need two things from you. The first concerns Kurt Carfax. You know Carfax? Of course you do. I want you to put the word out on him. If he shows up in public tonight, I want to hear about it immediately. The second is that I need the services of an extremely discreet air freight company. I will have seven large flight cases to go out of New York tomorrow night. Probably to Los Angeles. How large? About the size of coffins, Anthony. Someone will call you later with the details. Now, if you accomplish these things, you will find yourself basking in my extreme gratitude. That's something you haven't experienced for a long time. That's right. I think we understand each other. Goodbye, Anthony. Don't let me down in these things."

Twenty minutes before Renquist hung up on the financier, he had lain in bed with his mind sufficiently recovered to curse himself aloud for a fool. If he was unable to sleep, he could still be doing a number of productive things before the sun went down. It was only his prejudice against telephones and his sun-seared near-breakdown that had blinded him to the obvious. Even though he couldn't leave the Residence for some hours yet, he could set up a number of things in advance that would make matters a good deal easier when he was finally free to move around the city.

He took out the card that Dr. d'Asson had left for him. As well as the shaman's phone number and address, the card also bore the symbol of a downturned hand with an eye in the palm, the same design as the charm that Madame Marie, the mam'bo woman, had carried. Okay, voodoo man, let's see if your eye can find Carfax. Renquist was sure of what it signified. He dialed the number. A woman's voice answered. Renquist asked for d'Asson and then, again, he waited. Finally the elderly shaman came on the line.

"Mr. Renquist?"

"I could use a little help, Doctor."

The shaman sounded cautious. "What kind of help, Mr. Renquist?"

"Tonight, during the hours of darkness, we will be conducting a hunt for the two who have caused all the trouble. I wondered if there might be anything your people could do to assist us. Something that could be brought down, perhaps from the spirit world, something that, at the very least, might disorient them and make them unwilling to go into your neighborhoods."

"I think I understand what you have in mind."

"And is it possible?"

"I believe it is."

"I'm very grateful, Dr. d'Asson."

"I wish you luck, Mr. Renquist."

Renquist started dialing again. This number was in Beverly Hills. "Robert Evans, please. Tell him it's Victor Renquist calling about the house."

Bob Moore's was an old-fashioned shot-and-beer joint that had somehow escaped the decade and a half of creeping gentrification on the Upper West Side. It was owned and run in the traditional manner by an ex-Marine, and it had appeared as if by magic, only a four-block drive from the Melmoth in the cops' Chevy. Once inside, Kelly, McGuire, and Williams sat in silence through the first round of drinks, although Kelly noted with some satisfaction that McGuire didn't hesitate before paying for them. Kelly felt that he was getting closer to McGuire. It was probably an Irish Catholic thing, maybe coupled with a lifetime of police work and police discipline. Even though McGuire knew that Kelly had no right to be dressed a priest, he seemed to treat him, or at least the clothing—the uniform, so to speak—with a degree of respect that Kelly certainly wouldn't have received had he been wearing his old, stained wino army coat.

Williams proved to be quite another matter. Something in room 1009 had knocked some serious psychological props out from under him. Each time either of the other two tried to initiate any sort of practical discussion as to their possible options, the black cop would hunch harder over the bar and glare into his drink. Kelly's most charitable interpretation of his behavior was that throughout his career in the police department, Williams had always been a team player. Now he was confronted with a situation that would almost certainly be disbelieved by 99 percent of his colleagues. He felt isolated from the team, lost and cut adrift. Or maybe, as a black man who had rejected much of his heritage, he might also have a problem with anything that hinted at the supernatural or a loss of the rational and civilized. Whatever the reason, Williams made conversation so difficult that it was quite a while before Kelly discovered the two detectives had actually been inside the vampires' lair. When this fact emerged, however, Kelly pounced on it and began asking a string of detailed questions.

"How many of the creatures do you estimate are living there?"

McGuire shrugged. "It's really hard to say. I got the distinct impression we were only being allowed to see what they wanted us to see."

"I mean, were there five? A dozen? You must have some idea."

McGuire frowned. "I saw Renquist and Carfax, a couple of women, the little kid. Beyond that I really don't know. From the size of the place, I'd have said there could have been a few more living there, maybe nine or ten of them in total. But what do I know about these things? I mean, according to the movies, aren't vampires supposed to create a new one each time they claim a victim? If that was the case, wouldn't we be up to our ass in the things by now?"

Kelly shook his head. "I don't think it quite works like that. It isn't like the movies. From what I can gather from the stuff I read, it takes quite an elaborate process to create a new vampire."

Each time Kelly or McGuire used the word "vampire," Williams looked round uneasily as though he was afraid of being overheard. Fortunately, the bartender was down at the other end of the bar checking invoices, and the only other customers were a couple of middle-aged out-of-towners sitting together in a booth.

"How hard do you think it'd be to get inside that place?"

"Hard, going on impossible. Unless you had a full-scale tactical squad." This time, Williams answered. About the only time he seemed willing to contribute anything verbally was when a negative response was called for.

McGuire nodded in confirmation. "The whole place looked to be wired. A full state-of-the-art security system, plus who knows what other gimmicks on the side. If you were thinking of breaking in and staking a few more of the things, you can forget it. You'd never make it on your own. A real skilled burglar would have trouble cracking that place."

That seemed to cancel what Kelly had been considering as a possible next move, an all-out assault on the vampires' lair. He continued to worry at the problem, though, like a dog with a well-gnawed bone. "You say there was a little girl in the house?"

Williams grunted. "That's what she looked like, but there was something not at all right with that kid."

"What do mean 'not right?' "

"She had these eyes, eyes like no kid ought to have. She had old eyes, eyes that had seen more than any little kid ought to have seen. You know what I'm talking about?"

Renquist had read in the Rauch papers how some vampires, who were made that way while still children, perversely chose to retain their childlike form. He wanted to question Williams further about this "little girl," but the cop seemed to have been somewhat disturbed by the encounter, and Kelly had enough sense not to push the point right there and then.

As things turned out, Kelly would never have the chance to question Williams any further regarding the childlike vampire. At that moment, the woman from the street outside the Melmoth, the one who had given him the key to the vampire's room, stumbled into the bar. For a moment, she stood blinking, trying to see in the gloom of the interior. The bartender saw her first and began strategically positioning himself. Presumably, from the unsteady way she was walking and the uncertainty with which she entered the bar, he figured she was already drunk and was preparing himself to order her out of the place. Even though she was having difficulty seeing, there were so few customers in Bob Moore's that she had no difficulty spotting Kelly, and even before the bartender could speak, she homed in on him. "Father, did you find Cynara?"

She was the last person that Kelly had expected, and the only response he think of on the spur of the moment was to go on with the charade by which he had obtained the room key in the first place. "No, my child, Cynara had gone."

"But she promised she was going to take me with her."

"I'm afraid she won't be doing that."

McGuire looked sharply at Kelly. "Who's this?"

Kelly spoke rapidly in a low voice. "She's the woman on the street that gave me the key to the room."

Williams almost choked on his drink and his face paled. "You mean she's one of them?"

Kelly quickly shook his head. "No, she isn't one of them, although I think she might have been well on her way to being one."

"She spent time with the vampire?"

"That's how it seems."

The bartender was shaking his head at the woman. "Not in here, lady. I think you've had enough already."

McGuire gestured to the bartender. "Let the lady stay, pal. She'll be okay."

The bartender shot McGuire a bleak look. "Not in here, buddy. I don't need it."

Without the woman being able to see what he was doing, McGuire slid his badge out and let the bartender see it. "I'd appreciate it if you'd let the lady stay for a while."

The bartender looked doubtful. "You'll be responsible?"

McGuire put the badge away. "Sure, I'll be responsible."

Williams looked at him as if he was crazy. "What the fuck do you think you're doing?"

"You heard what he said. She spent time with the vampire. She may know something."

THE TIME OF FEASTING   317

"This is getting out of control, pal."

"Yeah, and all we can do is go with it."

Kelly was also looking a little unhappy. The last thing he wanted was to have this woman sitting down with them. McGuire, however, seemed to know what he was doing. He pulled out a stool for the woman. "Come and sit here, kid."

The woman looked at Kelly. He seemed to be her only acceptable reference point in the room. "Who are these men, Father?"

"They're policemen, my child. They're helping me find Cynara."

"Do you think you'll find her?"

McGuire gestured to the stool. "Sit down here and tell us all about it."

She looked to Kelly for approval. "Should I sit down?"

Kelly nodded, but said nothing. He wanted to see how McGuire handled this. The detective's first move in the game was to assume a persona of gruff charm. "What's your name, kid?"

"Elaine."

"Elaine what?"

Again she looked uncertain. "I think just Elaine will be enough for now."

"And you were friends with Cynara?"

"I loved Cynara."

"You were her girlfriend?"

"I guess you could say that. Certainly at first."

"And after that?"

"I don't know what you'd call it. Perhaps I was her pupil."

"But you stayed with her at the Melmoth?"

Elaine suddenly became tense and wary. "Yes, we were there together." She had obviously regained some of her wits since Kelly had first encountered her on the street. At that time, she had been completely scattered. "Is something wrong?"

McGuire smiled disarmingly. "No, there's nothing wrong."

Kelly started to slump over his third whiskey. Lack of sleep, the booze, and the fact that he was coming down from amphetamine were combination punches, doing nothing to improve his frame of mind. Since the two cops had picked him up at the Dupont, he had been the center of attention. Although Kelly would never have admitted it, even to himself, he had been thoroughly enjoying the experience, coming as it did after years of isolation and only the most tenuous of human contacts. Now he seemed to have been supplanted by some damn lesbian who was infatuated with a vampire. It scarcely seemed fair, and his mood was deteriorating with increasing rapidity. He turned and looked sourly at Elaine. "You wanted to be the same as her, didn't you?"

Elaine twitched nervously. "You know about that?"

McGuire was making signs from behind Elaine that Kelly should butt out and leave the questions to him, but Kelly could not resist getting in one more shot. "Nothing is hidden from us."

Elaine was half off the bar stool. "I really don't think I should be talking to you people."

McGuire glared at Kelly and then did his best to try and calm her. "Listen, Elaine. We're only asking you these questions so we can help you find Cynara."

"Why should you want to help me find Cynara?"

McGuire dodged the question, Instead, he practically radiated sympathy. "Elaine, you look like you've been under a great deal of stress. Would you like me to buy you a drink?"

Kelly was amazed that the simple ploy actually worked. Maybe McGuire really did know what he was doing. Elaine let out a long heartfelt sigh. "Please, buy me a drink."

McGuire waited until a vodka and orange juice had been placed in front of Elaine and she had taken a couple of tentative sips. "When you were staying at the hotel with Cynara, did any others come by or were the two of you alone for the entire time?"

Kelly immediately wanted to chime in with the information about Renquist's visit, but another covert glare from McGuire stopped him. McGuire seemed to be trying to convey the message that he would probably kill him if he opened his mouth again.

Elaine frowned. "Why do you want to know that?"

"Just casting around for a direction. Every little detail may be of help."

"Victor came by last night. Cynara and Victor were very beautiful together."

"Any others?"

"The two boys came by. I think it was the first night we were there."

"The boys?"

"Kurt and the other one."

"Would that be Kurt Carfax?"

Elaine actually smiled. "You know Kurt? You know where he is? He may know what's happened to Cynara."

Very slowly, McGuire sipped his drink, trying to look as innocuous as possible. "I thought Kurt lived with Victor."

Elaine shook her head. "Oh, no, that's why he came to see Cynara. He'd broken with Victor and moved to another place. I think he was in some kind of trouble."

"I'd like to find Kurt and talk to him. Did he say where this other place might be?"

Elaine's brow furrowed as she tried to bring a memory up through the fog that still clouded her mind. "It was someplace way downtown."

McGuire did his best to appear casual, but his excitement at being onto something tangible was certainly plain to Kelly. "Did he happen to mention where downtown?"

Elaine suddenly beamed. "He said he'd gone to the old loft on Ludlow Street, the old loft above the rehearsal studio."

McGuire all but let out a sigh. "That's very good, Elaine. Do you want another drink?"

Kelly was tired of the way that he seemed to have been written out of the action. As McGuire signaled for another drink for Elaine. Kelly turned to her with an unpleasant smile. "Cynara promised to make you just like her, didn't she?"

Elaine started like a deer who suddenly sees the hunter. "I . . ."

"She promised you that you'd live forever, didn't she?"

"I don't like you. I don't think you're trying to find Cynara at all."

Kelly hit out in the dark. "She took your blood, didn't she?"

Kelly had struck the mark. Elaine looked round the bar in panic. "I think I should go back to the hotel and see if Cynara has come back."

Kelly's expression was one of pure meanness and he made his voice very quiet so no one except him, Elaine, and the two cops could hear. "Cynara won't be coming back. A few hours ago, I drove a stake through her heart and finished her. If she'd done what you wanted, I'd be doing the same to you. So you see, my dear, you wouldn't have lived forever at all. Cynara really did you a favor by cutting you loose."

Elaine clapped a hand to her mouth, knocking over her drink in the process. She looked as though she was about to throw up. Before McGuire or Williams could do anything, she was on her feet and running from the bar. Williams was about to go after her, but McGuire motioned him to stay where he was, then turned and stared balefully at Kelly. "You really fucked that up, didn't you?"

Kelly returned his stare truculently. "Does it matter? We know where two more vampires are sleeping."

At the moment, the bartender entered the picture. He mopped up the spilled drink and glowered at the three men. He seemed disturbed by the incident that had sent Elaine running out of the bar. "I think maybe you guys should drink up and leave, okay?"

McGuire nodded. Williams looked at him. "So where do we go now?"

McGuire sighed. "Let's go down to Ludlow Street and get Carfax. I never did like that little snot."

Williams drowned his drink. "If she hasn't already warned him."

Kelly smiled triumphantly. "She can't warn him. If he lived with Renquist, he's one of them. And it's daylight, so he'll still be sleeping."

Renquist's last call was to the limousine company, ordering a car for himself for the entire night. The dispatcher fortunately said nothing about the damage to the car that he'd rented the night before. He leaned back in his chair with a certain grim satisfaction. He had done everything that he could possibly do to ready things for the coming night, and in so doing had, at least in his own mind, marginally restored a little of his authority and self-respect. Now nothing was left but to wait for the coming sunset, and as far as he was concerned, it couldn't come fast enough.

McGuire looked at Williams. "Carfax used to be a musician, right?"

Williams grunted. "If you could call it that."

McGuire looked up and down the narrow downtown street in one of the oldest parts of Manhattan. "So we're searching for some kind of rock & roll rehearsal studio on ground floor level?"

"Something like that."

"So let's start searching."

Kelly looked up at the sky. "We'd better hurry. It'll be sunset pretty damn soon."

After a drive downtown and liberal use of the car's removable light and siren to bully their way through the traffic jams in midtown, the three of them had parked on Ludlow Street. Ludlow was pretty much the same as any other side street on the Lower East Side. Once the home of newly arrived Ellis Island immigrants, it now sported a collection of bodegas, small stores, industrial premises, and a few struggling restaurants and bars that had started up during the yuppie real estate boom of the eighties. Any number of buildings on the street could have housed a rehearsal studio and the loft that was supposedly occupied by Carfax and his companion.

Williams started in grumbling almost immediately. "The damned place may not even have a sign."

McGuire seemed to have the knack of not letting his partner's complaining get to him. "All we can do is look."

Williams now turned on Kelly. "It's a pity we didn't get the street number out of that girl."

Kelly scowled. "She probably didn't even know the number."

"It might have helped if we'd found that out before she bolted." Since Kelly's outburst in the bar, the two cops' attitude towards him had been noticeably cool.

McGuire took one side of the street and Williams the other. Kelly was left to tag along as best he could. They covered three blocks without finding anything. Then Williams halted, pointed, and gestured to McGuire. "I think we got something here."

McGuire crossed the street and Kelly followed. Williams was pointing to a small sign that read: WILD CHILD STUDIOS. "You think this is it?"

McGuire looked up at the building. It was a three-storey industrial unit of fairly recent construction. According to the tags on the entry system, Wild Child Studios was on the ground floor. The top floor was a screen printing shop. The buzzer for the second floor carried no name or any other kind of sign or identification. "This is looking better and better."

"So how do we get inside?"

Williams grinned. "Buzz the rehearsal studio and pressure

them to let us in. There's probably some asshole in there smoking a joint, so they'll be paranoid."

McGuire laughed. "Intimidate the fuck out of them?"

Williams nodded. "You got it. Intimidate the fuck out of them."

The words seemed to be some kind of catch phrase between the two partners. Kelly assumed that such pairings were based on that kind of bonding. It turned out that no intimidation was needed. As they were speaking, a beat-up van pulled up at the curb and three young men in black jeans and dirty record company T-shirts, who obviously belonged to a rock & roll band, got out and started unloading equipment. They looked a little askance at the trio as they pushed past them and into the building, but they raised no objection. Kelly, McGuire, and Williams hurried up to the second floor and found themselves confronted by a heavy steel door with an impressive array of locks. Kelly inspected the door and then faced the two cops. "So how do we get past this?"

McGuire appeared to find it no problem. "We've got a few toys in the car that will deal with it."

Williams looked sideways at McGuire. "I suppose you're not considering that maybe we ought to have a warrant before we start crashing in on private property?"

McGuire avoided the look. "I think we moved beyond legal niceties some hours ago."

Williams made a rumbling sound in his throat. "I guess we did."

McGuire was businesslike. "You go get the car. Kelly and I will wait here and see that no one goes in or out."

Williams nodded and clattered away down the stairs to the ground floor. McGuire and Kelly waited in silence. Williams was back inside of seven minutes, and he yelled up the stairs to McGuire. "Get down here and help me with the stuff."

McGuire gestured curtly to Kelly. "Wait here."

He too vanished down the stairs, only to appear a minute or so later carry a pump action shotgun and a small tool kit. Williams followed with a sledgehammer and a small plastic carrying case. As they started up the stairs, a rock & roller stuck his head out of the door of the rehearsal studio, then saw the hammer and the shotgun and swiftly withdrew.

When the cops were back at the door to the anonymous second floor, they put down the tools of their trade and took stock of its strength of construction. Williams ran his hands around the door frame, then straightened up with an expression of satisfaction. "This won't be any trouble. People spend all this money on doors like a fucking safe and all these fancy-ass locks, but they never realize that a door is only as good as the frame they hang it on." He nodded to the sledgehammer. "Two good whacks and we'll be in. Unless, of course, you want to knock first?"

McGuire grinned. "I think I hear a woman in there being murdered, don't you?"

Williams nodded. "I surely do."

McGuire's grin broadened. "I think that qualifies as just cause, don't you?"

"I surely do."

McGuire pumped a round into the breech of the shotgun. "So let's get to it."

Williams held up a hand. "One moment."

He knelt down on the floor and opened the plastic carrying case. Inside was a huge pistol, a Magnum like something out of a Clint Eastwood movie. "I've always wanted an excuse to use this sucker."

Kelly looked doubtful. "I wouldn't get too overconfident. It's close enough to sunset, and if there are vampires awake inside, they'll be dangerous. They can't be killed by a bullet."

Williams looked as though he was all the way to the end of his rope with Kelly. "Listen, pal, firstly this is the most powerful handgun in the world and it could take your fucking head clean off, and secondly, I've got this motherfucker loaded with Black Talons. You know what Black Talons are, punk?"

Kelly shook his head. "No, I don't."

"The Black Talon is a round that bursts open on impact releasing these razor-sharp hooks. It makes a hole as big as a fist in a human body, and if it won't stop your vampire, it'll sure slow it down some."

He stuck the huge pistol in the back of his pants and picked up the sledgehammer. "Ready?"

McGuire stepped away from the door and leveled the shotgun. "Ready."

Williams raised the hammer. "I just hope we don't break in on a bunch of innocent bystanders." He swung the hammer hard into the doorframe.

chapter EIGHT

McGuire was through the door almost before the crash of its falling in had finished echoing round the dark room. Williams dropped the sledgehammer, pulled out the Magnum and a flashlight, and went through after him. McGuire went left. Williams went right. The flashlight showed little of the interior of the loft, except that it seemed to be some kind of cross between a slum and a construction site. It also reeked with an overpowering smell of dirt and decay that would probably have been worse except the air conditioning was set so high that the air was almost frigid.

McGuire shouted back to Kelly, who was still standing on the outside landing, having felt neither the need nor the urge to be in on the first assault. "Lights! Let's get some lights in here."

Kelly stepped through the shattered doorway and fumbled around on the wall, searching by touch, looking for a switch. His fingers found a loop of unsecured electrical wire and he followed it down until he found what seemed to be a switch. He turned it and a geometric arrangement of blue fluorescent tubes blossomed into life on the other side of the room. The scene that these lights revealed was more than enough to stop the three in their tracks. The first impression was hardly incorrect. The single big room did have many aspects of both slum and construction site, but also a great deal more besides. The floor was littered with all manner of debris, bottles, food wrappers, empty packing cases, discarded lumber, and broken cinder blocks. The walls were either raw brick or half-finished sheet rock, and electrical cables hung in festoons like jungle vines from overhead framing that would presumably support a ceiling at some time in the future.

Carfax and Blasco had, however, already put their own stamp on the place. An elaborate array of video equipment had been set up on one side of the room along with a couple of rudimentary bondage devices. Seemingly Blasco was continuing to indulge his taste for blood, death, and videotape. More important, two fiberglass coffins, decorated like hot rods with a deep-gloss, hand-rubbed, black-metalflake-and-silver finish stood on makeshift platforms built with planks and two-by-fours. McGuire and Williams approached the coffins with their weapons raised, and Kelly followed with his black bag clutched in his hand, wondering where, even in New York City, it was possible to have such flashy, unreal custom coffins made to order. The airbrush work alone must have taken at least a week in each case. Something in the almost mocking flamboyance of the things angered Kelly in the extreme. It was as if these creatures rested so securely in their degeneracy that they felt free to indulge their most offensive fantasies. Finishing these two might even afford him some measure of grim enjoyment. He shook the leather bag reassuringly and listened to the rattle of wood on the head of the club hammer. At least he had two stakes left. As he had expected, two young men lay in the coffins, identically dressed in black pants and black rollneck sweaters, obviously the ones the crazy lesbian had referred to as "the boys." Kelly had never seen either of them before, but McGuire and Williams instantly recognized the one in the right-hand coffin.

"That's Carfax."

"It looks like Kelly was right."

Kelly placed the bag on the floor and took out the stakes and the hammer. He started to strip off his jacket. "We have to do this quickly."

Williams and McGuire stared at him in amazement. "What the fuck do you think you're doing?"

"We're going to destroy these two. And quickly. The sun's almost down and we can't afford any delay."

Williams eyeballed him as though he was crazy. "You're going to drive stakes through these two?"

"That's what we came here for, isn't it?"

"We're police officers, goddamn it. We can't just stand here and watch while you murder two people."

"I rather thought you were going to assist me. Besides, they aren't people, they're damned vampires."

The only part of the room that wasn't immediately visible was a screened-off corner beyond the video setup. When the noise of someone or something moving came from that area, McGuire and Williams spun round with their guns leveled, the conversation with Kelly totally forgotten. They exchanged glances and advanced on the source of the noise. It came again. It sounded like a combination of a moving body, a whimper, and the dragging of a chain. In a half-crouch, and with the shotgun held in his right hand, McGuire dragged away the makeshift wood-and-fabric screen while Williams covered him with the Magnum. "Sweet Jesus Christ, will you look at this."

The removal of the screen revealed two dirty mattresses laid side by side. Two young women lay on the filthy pallets; one was moving, the other was either dead or unconscious. Both had leather collars fastened around their necks which in turn were attached to lengths of chain padlocked to a section of waterpipe. Their bodies were unnaturally white, and small wounds high on their throats seemed to indicate that they had been used by the vampires for repeated feeding. A plastic container of water had been placed beside the mattresses, but otherwise the two women had nothing. The one who was still moving was also shivering with cold. She looked up piteously at McGuire. "Please. No more. I think Tiffany died already."

Williams looked quickly at McGuire. "We gotta get an ambulance for these two."

McGuire nodded. "Right, I'm on my way."

Kelly immediately began to protest. "We have to deal with the two vampires first."

McGuire attempted to brush past him. "First things first. This is police business."

Kelly stood his ground. "This is way beyond police business. If we don't stake those two, it will all be too late."

McGuire started to grow angry. "And what about the damned victims?"

"We could be victims ourselves if we leave it any longer."

McGuire rounded furiously on Kelly. "You don't get it, do you? We can't let you hammer stakes into those two. We've given you all the slack we can, but it stops here."

"And what are you going to do about these vampires? Arrest them?"

A cold, powerful voice came from the other side of the room. "That's right, McGuire, what are you going to do? Arrest us?"

Carfax was sitting bolt upright in his coffin. Blasco was slowly rising beside him. Carfax's smile was demonic. "You should have listened to the priest, McGuire. You should have let him finish us while there was still the time. Now it's too late."

Kelly took a step back. He knew that they had all entered the most hellish of worst-case scenarios. McGuire had momentarily frozen, and Williams stood open-mouthed and paralyzed. Carfax stood up with a debonair flourish and stepped out of the coffin. The move brought McGuire to his senses and he leveled the shotgun so it was pointing directly at Carfax's chest. "Stay right where you are. I'm warning you."

Carfax started walking slowly towards McGuire. "Don't be

ridiculous. Your pathetic weapon means nothing to me."

McGuire gave Carfax one more warning. "Stay where you are."

Carfax merely laughed and continued to advance on McGuire. The shotgun roared and Kelly was shocked at how loud it was in the enclosed space. The blast took Carfax squarely in the chest. The vampire staggered back a couple of paces. His sweater was shredded and blood ran down his chest, but once he had recovered his balance, he laughed again. "You humans are such idiots."

McGuire pumped up another round and raised the shotgun to fire again, but before he could pull the trigger, Carfax had sprung. With speed quite beyond human perception, he leapt on McGuire, tore the gun from his hands, and hurled him across the room. As his partner crashed into the mess on the floor, Williams suddenly came alive, swung the Magnum to fire at Carfax, but Blasco was on him, apparently out of nowhere. Williams was also flung to one side, but somehow he managed to hold onto the pistol. He rolled and fired at Blasco, two shots in quick succession. The two Black Talons struck the vampire; it was as though Blasco's chest had actually exploded. He staggered backwards and fell, letting out a hideous, inhuman scream. If Kelly hadn't read some of the chilling accounts in the Rauch papers of the hideous wounds from which vampires had subsequently recovered, Kelly wouldn't have believed that Blasco could be anything but stone dead or dying. He lay on filthy floor, leaking purple blood from a hole in his chest the size of a grapefruit. One leg made a violent, involuntary pedalling motion as though trying to kick away from the pain.

Carfax howled and sprang at Williams. Williams must have been so full of rage, fear, and adrenaline that his actions also seemed close to the superhuman. Without time to aim, he loosed a third shot. It only nicked Carfax, though, tearing a lump out of his arm. This again caused the vampire to stagger, but only momentarily. Carfax leapt on Williams, cursing in some ancient and obscene language. He seized his head, twisting it as if the big man was nothing more than a child's doll. Kelly heard the snap as Williams' neck broke from clear across the room. As Carfax hurled the body away from himself, he let out another bloodcurdling cry, this time of triumph rather than pain and fury.

As Carfax looked round for his next victim, Kelly dived for McGuire's shotgun. His only thought was that, if he pumped enough deershot into the vampire, he might be able keep the monster at bay, at least until the clip ran out. Beyond that, he didn't care to project. He picked up the gun and jerked the slide. At first it seemed to be jammed, but then it freed itself. Carfax was poised to spring at him, and Kelly fired. The vampire was again knocked off balance. Kelly pumped another round, and the vampire snarled and retreated. His shots might not be killing the thing, but Kelly did seem to be hurting it. Over on the other side of the room, he saw that McGuire was up on his knees and pulling his regulation 9mm automatic from a shoulder holster. He too fired at Carfax. The bullet took the vampire in its shoulder and set it staggering in the other direction.

Carfax clapped a hand to his injured shoulder and let out a snarl. "You haven't seen the last of me by any means." And with that, he spun on his heel and leapt headfirst for the painted-over glass of the nearest window. Both frame and glass burst into an explosion of fragments, wreathing Carfax like a smoke-cloud billow of tiny, glittering shards as he sailed through. McGuire ran to the window and looked down to see where Carfax had landed. He apparently had dropped down into the street, because McGuire immediately turned and raced for the door by which they'd entered. "I'm going after him!"

Kelly's first instinct was to follow, but he quickly thought better of it. Let McGuire chase after Carfax. The vampire had almost certainly made good his escape. It had to be dark outside now, and the vampire had his speed, his strength, and was in his natural habitat of the night. Kelly grabbed his bag and pulled out the claw hammer and one of the stakes. Blasco was already rapidly recovering from his terrible wound. He was still curled fetally around the chest injury, but his legs had stopped twitching and his growls of pain were become stronger and more controlled. Even the wound itself was now only half the size it had been right after the impact.

Kelly ran at Blasco. No time for the trouble and care that he had taken with his previous kill. He stabbed the stake as hard as he could into the vampire's chest and then followed through with a flurry of hammer blows. The death of Blasco was very different from that of the female. The spurt of goop was mercifully brief and the blue flame, which seemed to signal the creatures' ultimate demise, came almost immediately in a single flash like an electrical discharge. When it was all over, this male didn't fall apart as radically as the woman had. The remains that were left behind were more like an almost normal corpse, with only the faintest trace of mummification. Kelly could only think that this was a very young vampire, comparatively new to the condition of the undead, and that the young died more easily than the old.

As he rose from the body of the young vampire, McGuire came back into the room. His eyes were staring and he was breathing heavily. The full horror of what had just happened seemed to be in the process of hitting him. "He got away."

"I thought he would. They are incredibly fast."

"He got into a car. A black Firebird with black windows. The damn thing had a car." McGuire seemed outraged that a vampire should have anything as contemporary as an automobile.

Kelly put the hammer back in the leather bag. "It's the modern world."

McGuire looked down at Williams' body. "Jesus Christ."

"He's dead."

"This is a mess."

"I managed to finish the other one."

"I suppose we should have listened to you in the first place."

Kelly made his face impassive. "I believe you should have."

"I thought I understood."

"That seems to be the great mistake. With the undead, we understand little and know less."

"My partner's dead. Dead for real."

"There's not time to dwell on that now."

McGuire looked slowly round the room. It was a bloody shambles. A dead vampire with stake protruding from its chest lay on one side of the room, and a dead police officer, with his head screwed around so it appeared to be on backwards, lay on the other. Huddled in a corner were two dead or dying women. McGuire stared at Kelly with an expression of blank incredulity. His voice was probably the closest McGuire had come to a sob in many years. "What the fuck do we do now?"

"We get out of here."

"We can't leave all this."

"We have to. Regular uniformed police will be here at any moment. Someone must have reported gunfire, even in New York."

McGuire pointed to Williams. "I can't leave him like this. And those women, they need medical attention."

"Other officers are on their way. We must go. If we tried to explain any of this, they'd have us both in straitjackets."

Sunset was almost immediately followed by the shock of a second nosferatu gone. The colony, or what was left of it, had been in the process of gearing up for a night of intense activity, but the psychic jolt of pain and destruction brought things instantly to a halt. Once everyone had gathered in the library to review this new development, Sada voiced the question that had come first and foremost into every one of their minds. "Who is it now? It has to be either Carfax or Blasco, unless there's another of us out there that we don't even know about."

Julia quickly ruled out Carfax as the victim. "If it had been Kurt, I'd know."

Each of the seven remaining colony members concentrated hard, but Dahlia was the first make contact with the closing void that had been left behind by the passing. "Blasco. It is Blasco."

"Are you sure?"

She nodded with absolute certainty. "It's definitely Blasco."

Sada nodded in confirmation. "She's right. I can feel it too. It's Blasco."

The seven all exchanged unhappy glances. The fact that it was Blasco who had been destroyed presented them with a whole collection of highly mixed emotions. Brows furrowed and auras flickered as each of them came to terms with their confused feelings. No one wanted to see another nosferatu die violently, but Blasco, in his blind allegiance to Carfax, had made himself an outcast, and after Renquist's agreement with the voodoo shaman, the entire colony had dedicated itself to his destruction. They could, however, take little consolation in the fact that their dirty work had already been done for them. Two nosferatu had died in a single space of daylight, and whatever human was doing the killing was seemingly determined and resourceful. He or she had crossed the barrier of disbelief and appeared to be extremely well informed about the ways of the New York nosferatu, their habits and their sleeping places.

Once again it was Sada who put the common fear into words. "If the killer has managed to find both Cynara and Blasco, we have to ask ourselves how long it will be before he turns up here."

Renquist sensed that if he didn't step in quickly and restore some measure of confidence, panic was going to start gnawing at whatever sense of organization they had left. "Although we need to be on our guard at all times, I don't think we have too much to fear until the sun comes up. This killer is striking at us during the daylight, when sleep makes us vulnerable. I very much doubt that he will risk confronting us during the night when we are awake, alert, and all our powers are at their most acute. My feeling is that all we can do for the moment is to proceed as we have already agreed. Even though we have to be aware that One Who Knows is out there doing his deadly work, our primary concerns still have to be to move the colony away from New York and to stop Carfax."

Julia stepped forward. "Are you saying that we should just ignore this killer?"

Renquist shook his head. "No, I'm not saying that at all. What I'm saying is that we should each go on with our allotted task and not let this new and dangerous turn of events throw us into confusion. Lupo and I will be out looking for Carfax, and I'm hoping that, since we can assume that Carfax may have been present when Blasco died, our hunt for him may also help turn up this killer. In the meantime, we will go on as planned. Dahlia and Imogene will organize the transfer of the colony. Segal will bring the flight cases up from the cellar in preparation for our final move. Lupo and I will go out into the city, while Julia and Sada coordinate communications from the Residence. We all need to do what we have to do, but we also need to be very, very careful."

With this final urge to caution and call for cohesion, the meeting began to break up, but Renquist noticed that Dahlia was hanging back. "You wanted to say something else?"

"I was wondering if anyone had sensed anything of Carfax." The colony stopped and turned, and Renquist noticed that Dahlia was looking directly at Julia. "I mean, if indeed he was present when Blasco was killed, he is known to the killer, he's certainly alone, and he may well be on the run and under extreme pressure. I would have thought that at least one of us might have sensed something of him. He must be under considerable stress." Now she was looking even more pointedly at Julia.

Julia colored slightly. "I did feel something."

Renquist looked at her sharply. "How is it that you didn't mention it?"

Julia avoided his eyes. "It was so little . . ."

Sada interrupted Julia, her voice was cold and hostile. "Perhaps you had mixed feelings about aiding in the destruction of your creation."

Julia immediately struck a defensive posture. "It wasn't that at all. It was just that I was confused. I wasn't even sure that it was a real impression. It could have merely been a print-through from Blasco."

Renquist moved quickly to head off yet another nosferatu spat. "So tell us what you did sense."

Julia scanned the suspicious faces that now surrounded her and found little sympathy. "I don't know why you're all looking at me like that. Like I said, it was practically nothing, scarcely tangible. I just had this sense of fear and panic and then flight. I also think he might have been hurt, been shot or something."

Imogene sniffed. "That sounds quite tangible to me."

For Renquist, this was actually quite favorable news. If Carfax was injured and running scared, it could well make finding him a good deal easier. Like the others, however, he was suspicious of Julia for holding back on the information. Did she harbor some vestigial loyalty to Carfax, or was it just a piece of petulant payback for the fact that Renquist had exhibited such open distress at the termination of Cynara? "Is that all? Have you told us everything?"

"There is one other thing."

"What's that?"

"I believe Carfax has a vehicle. A car of some kind."

Renquist blinked. "I didn't even know he had a car."

Segal nodded. "He's had it for a while. It's a big old muscle car, a black Firebird with black windows and a red dragon painted on the hood."

Renquist closed his eyes and slowly shook his head. The

world was changing much too fast for him. "I don't suppose you know the license number?"

Segal smiled. "New York custom plates, BAT-666."

Renquist sighed. "You're joking?"

Segal shook his head. "I swear."

Renquist held up his hands. "Okay, okay, we've wasted enough time already. We have much to do, so let's start doing it."

As the colony left the library, Renquist indicated that Segal should wait for a moment. "I know bringing up the flight cases from the cellar may seem like something of a menial task, and you're probably wondering why you aren't going out to hunt Carfax with Lupo and myself."

Segal's face was blank. "I'm sure you have your reasons."

"The truth is that I want someone of great strength here at the Residence in case there's trouble from humans. You understand?"

"I understand perfectly."

"I also want you to keep a close eye on Julia. If she does the slightest thing that doesn't seem right, let me know immediately."

Segal nodded. "I'll be discreet."

Sada leaned around the library door. "There's a human on the telephone who wants to speak to you."

Renquist shook his head. "Not now. Just find out what they want and I'll talk to them later if need be."

"This is a strange one, a female who says her name is Elaine."

Renquist held out his hand for the portable phone. "I'll take it."

McGuire picked up the car phone but hesitated before using it. "I don't see how I can avoid talking to someone."

He and Kelly were sitting side by side in the Chevy. They were parked in a vacant lot near the Brooklyn Bridge and were staring grimly through the windshield at the East River. "If you talk to anyone you'll simply make matters even more complicated."

"So what would you do?"

"I've already told you. All we can do is lay low until dawn, then go to that house downtown and neutralize the rest of the vampires. After that, you can call the authorities."

McGuire looked uneasy. "I don't know. It's all so . . ." He groped to find the words, ". . . fucking unbelievable."

"Believe it."

McGuire shook his head. "I mean, did you see his fucking head? It was turned right around."

Kelly's voice took on an edge of deliberate cruelty. "If you'd listened to me in the first place, Williams might still be alive."

"You think I don't know that?"

"So listen to me now and wait until dawn before you do anything."

McGuire scowled. "It's easy for you to say that. No one knows about you. The entire New York Police Department will be looking for me. My partner's dead, and as far as they're concerned, I'm missing along with the car. For all they know, I could be a hostage. There's probably an APB on the car, and I know for a fact half of the cops on the street will be in a shoot-first-and-talk-about-it-later mood."

"Who would you call?"

"I don't know. Someone else on the squad, someone I can trust."

"You can't tell them what really happened. Not yet."

"You think I'm crazy?" McGuire punched in a number. "Bernstein? Thank God it's you. Yeah, it's me, McGuire. I'm okay, but I need someone to cut me some slack until tomorrow morning." He listened for a moment. "Yeah, I know Williams is dead, but I've got a line on the serial killer. It's . . . well, it's weird and I can't explain until I've got something to show."

He listened again. "Yeah, I can imagine how it is, but I absolutely can't come in right now. Do whatever you can, okay? I'll owe you big time."

McGuire broke the connection and looked at Kelly. "I think this is going to be a long night."

Sada seemed ready to linger in the library, but Renquist indicated that both she and Segal should go about their business. When he was alone he turned his attention to the phone. "This is Renquist."

"Do you remember me?"

"Of course I remember you, Elaine. It hasn't even been twenty-four hours."

"I'm sorry. So much has happened. It's all very confusing. I don't know what to do. After Cynara . . ."

Renquist made his voice as gentle as possible. "Cynara is gone."

"I know. And I've seen the man who killed her."

Renquist felt a hot anger building inside him. "You have?"

"He's a man called Kelly. He's dressed as a priest, a Catholic priest, except I don't think he's a real priest. He may have been a priest once, but now I think he just dresses as one."

"Do you know where he is?"

"It's been a few hours since I saw him, but he was going to a place on Ludlow Street. He had two policemen with him. Except they weren't acting like policemen."

"What do you mean?"

"It's hard to explain. It was just that something wasn't right about the way they related to each other."

"Did you get the names of either of these policemen?"

"No, just Kelly, although I think they were detectives."

"Where were they going on Ludlow Street?"

"I don't know the number, but it was a loft above a music rehearsal studio."

Renquist nodded. "I think I know the place."

"He would be going after the one called Kurt and the other one, his friend . . ."

"The friend's name was Blasco. And he is also gone. I fear Kelly may have been there already."

"I'm sorry."

"Why should you care? You're a human."

"That's the other reason I called you."

"What do you mean?"

"Cynara had started changing me. She had taken me part-way through the ritual. I'd tasted her blood. But then you came and talked to her, and then she made me leave. I'm sorry, Victor. I know you have your own troubles at the moment, but I'm changing. I don't know what's happening to me."

Renquist hadn't realized that Cynara had already begun the transformation of the woman. "What does this change feel like?"

"Sunlight hurts my eyes. My hearing has become uncomfortably acute and my teeth feel like they're moving around in my mouth."

Renquist realized that the woman was well along in the transformation. He wondered why Cynara had halted the process when she did. Had it been that she felt a greater and more urgent loyalty to the colony? Whatever the answer, he felt that he somehow owed it to her to do something for her half-completed creation. "Elaine, listen to me. There's nothing I can do for you right now. The whole colony has to get out of town. You understand what I mean by the colony?"

"Yes, Cynara explained how you lived in groups."

"When the colony is settled, I will call you to me."

"How will I know the call?"

"You'll know the call. I promise."

Lupo held the door as Renquist ducked into the back of the waiting limousine, then got in himself. Renquist leaned forward and spoke to the driver. "Take us to Ludlow and Houston."

Lupo looked at him questioningly. "What's at Ludlow and Houston?"

"Apparently Carfax and Blasco were holed up in a loft on Ludlow. I think it's the one above the rehearsal studio that Carfax used when he had his band."

"Was that the phone call just before we left?"

Renquist sighed. "Is it impossible to keep a secret in this colony?"

Lupo chuckled. "It depends who you are."

Renquist didn't smile. "The woman who called also told me that the human who destroyed both Cynara and Blasco is a priest, or a sometime priest who goes by the name of Kelly."

"New York City has a lot of Kellys."

"This one seems to have a couple of cops who seem to believe him. I'm just hoping they're not the same ones who came to the Residence. If they are, they'll be making all kinds of dangerous connections."

The limo came to a halt near the corner of Houston and Ludlow, double-parked right by Katz's Deli. Renquist lowered the window and peered down the street. A couple of blocks away, he could make out the flashing lights of some kind of police activity. "It looks as though the cops have gotten there before us."

Lupo's face was grim. "If they've found Blasco's body, they'll be sorely confused."

Renquist signalled to the driver. "We're getting out. Find a place to park and wait. We'll be about twenty minutes."

Once the limo had moved off, Lupo glanced at Renquist. "What do you intend doing?"

"I want to have a look around where Blasco was killed."

"How do you intend to deal with the police?"

"We can cloud their minds."

Lupo smiled. "We can do better than that."

"How?"

"Let me do the talking when we get there."

As they came closer, Renquist and Lupo saw that no fewer than five police cars, two crime-scene trucks, and a number of unmarked homicide units were slewed at odd angles, making the street impassable to any other traffic. The whole area was also festooned with the usual complement of blue sawhorses and yellow tape. The emergency lights on the police vehicles slowly revolved, casting lazy washes of colored light, first blue, then red, then white, over the blank staring faces of the humanity who always seemed to assemble in the aftermath of trouble. Most of the uniformed officers seemed to be engaged in keeping the customary scrimmage of reporters, photographers, and local civilian gawkers at a seemly distance. Renquist had never quite understood why humanity had such a need to wait around for so long after a killing, when the excitement was so plainly long over. Human beings appeared to have an almost infinite capacity to turn disaster and death into a bizarre and somber carnival.

Renquist and Lupo had no difficulty making their way through the crowd. They only had to use a small measure of the nosferatu influence and the mass of humans parted in front of them. When they reached the first protective line of New York's finest, Lupo produced a gold badge in a leather slipcase and flashed it at the sergeant in charge of crowd control. "We're from the Mayor's office."

The sergeant took a look at the badge and then quickly ushered them through. Once they were inside, Renquist glanced curiously at Lupo. "Is that badge real?"

Lupo became mildly offended. "Of course it's real."

"How did you get it?"

"Back when he was mayor, Ed Koch gave it to me in return for a favor."

Lupo had to use his badge three more times before they finally made it through to the actual loft where Blasco had died. In contrast with the street outside, the murder site was an area of sinister quiet. The bodies had been removed and the forensic team already had done their job and left. All that really remained was a considerable area of drying bloodstains and chalk outlines delineating where the two bodies had fallen. A solitary female detective was conducting a final check for anything that might have been overlooked. She turned quickly as Renquist and Lupo came through the smashed doorway. "Are you looking for something?"

"We're from the Mayor's office."

"I would have expected you guys earlier, what with all the publicity this case has been getting."

Renquist shrugged. "Better late than never, I guess."

"Well, there isn't much to see anymore. The bodies have been hauled away, the one surviving girl is in Bellevue, quite catatonic, the videotapes have gone for analysis, and the forensic team has been over the place with a fine-tooth comb."

Renquist could guess what the videotapes were, but he wondered who the girls might have been. He assumed they had to be more of Carfax's prisoner victims. He didn't want to give himself away to the police woman by appearing to know too much, but he imagined that even the Mayor's office would have received some kind of preliminary report. Lupo was making his own circuit of the loft. At one point, he stopped and nodded to the larger of the two chalk outlines. "Which one was this?"

The detective looked weary and depressed. "That was Detective Williams. Nobody ought to go that way. I sure hope we get the bastard who did it."

Renquist tried a blind bluff. "Has anything been heard about McGuire?"

The bluff paid off. "There's a rumor going round that he called in to the precinct to say that he was close to the serial killer, but the general opinion is that he saw something up here that pushed him clean over the edge. That he's running round the city, stone crazy and chasing shadows. His car was found, though. Parked in an empty lot near the Brooklyn Bridge."

Renquist thought about this. He suspected that McGuire was far from crazy. He was probably just terrified of trying to tell his superiors the truth about what had happened. He was probably with Kelly, the mysterious vampire killer. They might even try for the Residence when the dawn came. He moved so he was standing by the other, smaller chalk mark. "So this was the other body?"

The police woman looked at him with a good deal of suspicion. "How much do you guys at the mayor's office know about the other body?"

Renquist smiled like a conspirator. "You mean like the wooden stake and the apparent mummification?"

"You know that not even a whisper of that is supposed to get out to the press?"

Renquist nodded solemnly. "Believe me. There's nothing my people would like to see less than this business all over the *Post*. What happened to the weird body?"

"Like I said, it went to the morgue, but I heard there were more agencies fighting over it than the corpse of JFK. Apparently they got Feds down there, and guys up from the Center for Disease Control in Atlanta, professors from Columbia and Princeton, and even the military is trying to get in on the act."

"This is a fucking mess." Renquist spoke directly from the heart. The colony would not only have to get out of New York as quickly as possible, but lay very low for quite a time when they got where they were going.

The police woman nodded. "It's the weirdest thing I've ever come across."

Renquist gently attempted to probe her mind. "What's your name?"

"Smith. Victoria Smith."

As Renquist caressed the surface of Detective Victoria Smith's mind, he encountered a barrier of solidity rare in the mind of a human. It also wasn't that she was trying to keep him out. The barrier was to contain and segregate her own thoughts.

The crime scene had triggered ancient and instinctive knowledge and fear, but Smith was too inculcated in the modern world and the methodology of police work to recognize them for what they were. Firelight night-dreads that went back, via her coded DNA, all the way to her prehistoric ancestors in some mid-European forest, rattled their psychological cages and demanded recognition. Instead of accepting them, however, she simply spooked herself into thinking she was losing her mind in the same way that she imagined McGuire had. She was also disturbed by some of her own responses to the crimes. She was particularly unsure of where revulsion ended and fascination began.

As Renquist sorted through her confusion, the two of them made eye contact. In that instant, something new happened to Detective Smith. Her libido kicked in. In the moment he looked into her eyes, she suddenly and desperately wanted Renquist. He hadn't even had to plant the idea. In fact, the pang of desire was only a very natural clutch for life when surrounded by death, but she became appalled at the impulse, even though under normal conditions she would never have acted on it in a million years. Renquist, however, was gripped by an impulse of his own. Detective Smith could probably use a fast lesson in comparative objectivity and, since it promised to be a long and strenuous night, he also needed to feed. He would not kill her. That would be too much. Indeed, they might both gain something from the mutual experience. He gestured to Lupo. "Watch the stairs for a moment. Make sure no one comes in here for the next five minutes."

"When this is all over, you will remember nothing. Except maybe a trace of the feeling will linger."

Smith's eyes were glazed, and her mouth was slack and hungry. "I don't mind."

"You may feel unaccountably sad for something that might have been, sad in a way that you will never totally understand."

"So?"

"So then go with it."

Renquist put his hands on Detective Smith's shoulders and moved her into a lush and romantic fantasy world created from her own childish dreams. She found herself transported into a magical ballroom where she and the tall, dark man in black who was her partner circled endlessly in stately waltz time on a floor of cobalt-blue mirrored glass. Multicolored lights revolved around them like orbiting stars, and the orchestra swirled and flowed like sounding velvet. Her partner's head inclined and his lips brushed her neck. His breath was warm and scented, masculine, strong, and just a little threatening. The more they circled, the more she melted to him, his strength flowing into her and hers into him. The music grew louder and she was in the grip of a divine dizziness. She seemed to float on the air itself among shadows like a sea of rolling thunderheads, around and around and up and up, like part of an ever-ascending spiral helix. Her feet seemed hardly to make contact with the floor, which was possibly just as well because her legs were so weak that she seriously doubted that they would ever have supported her.

And then she was back in the hellish loft on Ludlow Street and for some inexplicable reason, the rather attractive man from the Mayor's office had turned away and was dabbing at his mouth with a pocket handkerchief. It was a strange gesture that almost bordered on the effeminate. She seem to have misplaced a few seconds in time, and she quickly tried to cover her confusion. "I'm sorry, what were you saying?"

Renquist smiled. "Nothing of any importance."

"I'm sorry. I lost it there for a moment. I don't know what happened. This fucking job is getting to me."

Renquist pointed. "You've got blood on your neck."

Smith put a hand to her throat and then looked at the blood on her fingertips. "How the hell did that happen?"

"This time of year, the big mosquitoes get blown in from Jersey."

Lupo was standing the doorway. He coughed discreetly "I just heard from the office. I think it's urgent."

Renquist moved so he was out of earshot of Detective Smith. He'd given her his handkerchief, and she was still dabbing at the supposed mosquito bite on her neck. "What is it?"

"Ferrari phoned the Residence. He told Dahlia that Carfax had been spotted in some yuppie jazz joint on the Upper East Side. I think we have to go."

The Green Dolphin, on Third Avenue, was filled with the kind of people who had made unreasonable amounts of money out of junk bonds in the late eighties and hadn't had an idea worth a damn since that self-inflated boom, the kind of people who published worthless autobiographies by equally worthless television celebrities, the kind who thought of themselves as hip and progressive but then voted Republican and were forced to work out complex political rationales for their greed and self-interest. The entertainment in the Green Dolphin was provided by a soullessly polite fusion quintet that Renquist would have happily incinerated with a flamethrower, just to allow Charlie Parker to rest in peace. As he and Lupo entered the place, two burly muscle builders flanking the door, who served as the Green Dolphin's bouncers, eyed the nosferatu with considerable suspicion. The mental cacophony created by so many vapid, partially drunk human minds would have made it hard for Renquist to read their individual reactions even if he'd wanted to, but he was fairly confident that they sensed nothing untoward about him and Lupo. Their negative take was merely that the pair, both in dress and manner, were highly atypical of the nightclub's regular clientele.

They eased their way from the entrance deeper into the crowd, moving in the direction of the bar. The interior proved to be a dim confusion of auras and mood lighting. For a brief instant, Renquist caught a flicker of pure and brilliant emerald from the other side of the dance floor. He stiffened and tried to get a fix on its exact location, but it was all too quickly obscured by the backwash of low-key animal excitation that radiated from the mass of dancers in front of the bandstand. He briefly touched Lupo on the arm. He didn't have to say anything. Lupo had seen it too. Without appearing too obvious, they moved determinedly in the direction of where they had spotted the green flash. The flash came again, but now it had moved. This time it came from the far end of the bar by the waitress station. Renquist was now certain it was Carfax. No human had such a purity of aura, or the capacity to will-o'-the-wisp it around a crowded gin joint. He was equally certain that Carfax knew he and Lupo were there and had decided to play with them for as long as he could get away with it. It seemed that the death of Blasco, and even the injuries that he may have sustained at the same time, had taught the young one absolutely nothing. Either he was operating on the assumption that Renquist would never push for a confrontation in the middle of such a mass of humans, or he was just plain crazy. Crazy or not, Carfax clearly hadn't considered that Renquist might have reached the point where he felt that he had so little to lose that it didn't matter if a few humans had their minds blown.

Renquist indicated to Lupo that they should approach the bar from two different directions. Lupo would skirt the outside of the dance floor, while Renquist took the more direct route. No sooner had they parted company than Renquist actually saw Carfax. He was in much the same spot as where the second green flash had originated, standing right beside the waitress station, dressed in a black T-shirt and a burgundy silk jacket, and doing his best to look as though he didn't have a care in the world. He seemed to be in the process of striking up a conversation with two Asian women, but Renquist didn't believe that the direct visual glimpse was any lucky accident. This was confirmed when Carfax deliberately turned his head and winked at his former Master. The gesture was too much for Renquist. Two nosferatu and any number of humans were dead, and this fool still thought that it was nothing more than a huge, if lethal, joke. Renquist angrily projected a pulse of power that instantly cleared a path straight to Carfax through a disoriented crowd that staggered and stumbled, struggling to get away from an unfocused and unspecified fear. Of the humans in the place, the band reacted the most intelligently. As one, they stampeded from the stage, dragging their instruments with them.

"Yynagh cwwnu gatthh!" Renquist's howl of fury was one of the oldest and most foul of nosferatu oaths. Carfax was too uneducated to understand its literal meaning, but the intention would be unmistakable. Still screaming, Renquist lunged through the cleared space. Carfax seemed to have been taken completely by surprise by Renquist's violently decisive move. It was obviously the very last thing that he had expected, and he froze like the proverbial rabbit confronted by the snake, right to the very last instant when Renquist was all but on him. Then his sense of self-preservation kicked in, and he bodily seized one of the Asian women and hurled her at Renquist, at the same time loosing a flash of power that sent every human in the place reeling and even caused Renquist to stagger briefly. By the time that Renquist had disentangled himself from the now hysterical woman, who complicated matters by screaming at the top of her lungs in outraged Japanese, Carfax had sprung up on the top of the bar and was looking round for the easiest route of escape.

Apparently Carfax had reckoned without Lupo, who came out of nowhere like a charging bull and took him down from the knees. The two nosferatu rolled on the floor in front of the bar, like snarling tigers, surrounded by a vortex of snapping, short-circuiting energy. All round the club, lightbulbs and neon tubes began exploding, showering cascades of sparks and broken glass on the now panicking customers and staff. The computerized cash register went haywire, running up tabs of Federal proportions, and an entire shelf of wine glasses spontaneously shattered as the club's sound system first overloaded into pain-threshold feedback that then rapidly climbed, octave by octave, until it threatened the hearing of every human in the place.

It was at this juncture that one of the steroid-pumped bouncers decided to take a hand in the proceedings. The man may have been human and dumb, but his courage was indisputable. As he tried to throw himself on Lupo's back, Renquist was forced to pick him up by the scruff of his neck like a puppy. Before he hurled him across the club, Renquist looked at him with a certain measure of sympathy. "You really don't have a clue what you're dealing with here, do you?"

Renquist threw the bouncer almost off-handedly, but still he flew through the air to land with a crash on the bandstand. Renquist quickly turned to help Lupo, but discovered that while he had been dealing with the bouncer, Carfax had managed to kick himself free of Lupo's grasp and was streaking for the rear of the club. Before Renquist could follow, the second bouncer, again with more bravado than sense, jumped on him. "You people don't learn a damn thing, do you? Can't you grasp the fact that you're dealing with the superhuman?"

He hurled this second human hero hard into the bar. He flopped to the floor and lay strangely, with his head twitching from side to side. Renquist reflected that he might have broken the man's back, but he had no time to worry about the welfare of humans. He was moving to the back of the club after Lupo and Carfax. A rear fire door was open and Renquist could only assume that this must have been the route that they had taken. In a flash, he was in the alley in back of the building, only to be confronted by Lupo limping back looking winded and crestfallen. "I lost him, Don Victor. He was too fast for me. He made it to that car of his and took off. Perhaps I'm getting too old for this high-end physical stuff."

Renquist burst out laughing and, by doing so, vented much of the rage and tension that had been threatening to choke him.

He couldn't help it. Lupo looked so downcast. Lupo, on the other hand, hardly seemed to share his amusement. "I don't see what's so funny, Don Victor. It would seem as though we are now back to square one. I can't think where Carfax might be headed now. He can't have too many hiding places left."

Renquist didn't answer. He was now listening intently. "Do you hear that?"

Lupo frowned. He still seemed deeply offended. "Do you mean the rumble of thunder? There's certainly a storm coming."

Renquist shook his head. "No, no, beneath the thunder. Do you hear drumming?"

Lupo listened carefully. "Yes, I hear it. Like it was coming from somewhere uptown."

Renquist smiled. "I believe it's coming from all over uptown. D'Asson's people are making their contribution. If there's one direction that Carfax won't be heading it's anywhere north of here."

"That still leaves a lot of town to cover."

Renquist nodded. "So let's find the limo and get out of here. I have a feeling the police will now be on their way to the Green Dolphin."

As he spoke, a flash of lightning zagged across the sky. The storm that had been threatening for most of the evening was finally over the city. Again Renquist laughed. Whatever the outcome of this evening, it was already guaranteed to be memorable, perhaps even legendary. They found the limo parked in a side street. In front of the Green Dolphin, police cruisers were starting to arrive with lights flashing and sirens blaring. Renquist wondered what story the humans from the nightclub would have to tell. As he and Lupo again climbed into the long Cadillac, the first heavy drops of rain began to spatter the roof.

McGuire stood at the window staring out at the rain. He and Kelly were holed up in a cheap motel, just the other side of the Holland Tunnel. Kelly hadn't been too keen on the idea of getting out of Manhattan and crossing a state line into the bargain. He had killed two vampires in the space of little more than twelve hours, and he'd been reluctant to leave what he now thought of as the focus of the action. McGuire had insisted, however. He absolutely refused to stay in the city where a chance encounter could mean finding himself forced to explain the day's happenings to everyone from the Commissioner on down, happenings that McGuire hadn't even managed to explain satisfactorily to himself. As he had pointed out before they'd abandoned the Chevy, taken a cab to the other side of the river, and checked into the Hudson Haven Motel: "We also don't have a clue what the vampires may have in mind for us. I imagine they come with a capacity for revenge."

Kelly still didn't see the need to go all the way to the Jersey side of the tunnel. It was all a bit too much like a Bruce Springsteen song, but it was also a point on which McGuire continued to be adamant. It was only later that he finally revealed the reason behind his insistence. "I remembered something from the movies about vampires having a problem with crossing running water."

"That isn't true. It's just a piece of folklore."

They were still in Jersey, though. "Listen, Kelly, you may have done all the reading and shit on these things, but I'm not taking any chances. I'm still having a hard time actually believing what I've seen with my own eyes. So, for the moment, what's good enough for Bela Lugosi is good enough for me."

One of Kelly's very first acts after they had checked into the motel was to uncap a pint of scotch. "Come daylight, it'll be us hunting them again. When the sun is up, we'll go to that cursed house and finish it once and for all."

"And how do you intend to get inside the house? From what I saw, they were able to lock that place down tighter than a bank."

Kelly was getting himself drunk as fast as he could. "So far I've been shown the way, and I don't have any doubt that when the time comes, I'll be shown the way again."

McGuire shook his head in bewildered resignation. "God Almighty."

Kelly smiled sourly and nodded. "Exactly."

So far they had passed the night with Kelly laid out on one of the twin beds, slowly drinking himself into increasingly mystic incoherence, while McGuire paced and stared out of the window between half-hearted attempts to lose himself in TV. On the other side of the river, a jagged bolt of lightning crashed into the city, seeming to strike the Empire State Building, while rolls of thunder banged around the other towers. McGuire glanced back at Kelly. "You ought to take a look at this. It's a hell of a fireworks display."

Kelly craned so he could see out of the window, but didn't bother to move from the bed. By this point, his speech was slurred. "Would that it was the destruction of Sodom and Gomorrah."

McGuire looked disgustedly at his accidental companion and reflected on how much easier his life would have been if he hadn't looked at Escobar's notes and had the bright idea of picking up Kelly for questioning. "You know something, Kelly? You're one sick son of a bitch."

The phone in the limo rang. Renquist stared curiously at it for a moment and then picked it up. "Yes?"

The voice at the other end sounded hesitant and uncertain. "This is Segal."

"Why are you using the telephone?"

"I thought it might afford a greater degree of privacy than broadcasting a direct mental contact."

"You've something to tell me that you don't want overheard."

"That's right."

"Is there a problem?"

"I'm afraid there might be, Don Victor."

"What is it?"

"It's Julia. You remember you asked me to keep an eye on her?"

"Indeed I do."

"Dahlia apparently overheard her in contact with Carfax. It was at a time when she thought everyone else was occupied with their various tasks."

"Contact regarding what?"

"As far as Dahlia could tell, she informed him that you and Lupo were away from the Residence and that he should come there. Dahlia suspects they're setting some kind of trap for you."

"Is Julia aware that you're calling me?"

"I don't think so."

"But you're not a hundred percent certain?"

"No."

"Very well. I think the best thing I can do is to come back there and see what happens next."

He hung up the phone, opened the partition, and spoke to the driver. "You can take us back home now." Finally, he turned to Lupo. "Seemingly Carfax is returning to the Residence. It looks as though he and Julia are in cahoots again."

Lupo's face clouded. "Then we have him."

"I think what we have is a showdown."

Lupo frowned. "You, me, and Segal could take him easily."

"I don't doubt it, but I think this is one battle I have to fight on my own. I'd be obliged if you and Segal would stay out of it."

"You don't owe him that much."

"No, I don't, but perhaps immortality has endowed me with an overdeveloped sense of history."

chapter Nine

A black Pontiac Firebird with a red dragon painted on the hood was parked in front of the Residence. Clearly Carfax was making no secret of the fact that he was there. Renquist let the limousine go, telling the driver that he wouldn't need the car for the rest of the night, then stepped out into the rain. The storm seemed have moved to the south. The lightning now crashed and the thunder rumbled well beyond the towers of the World Trade Center. Renquist smiled grimly at Lupo. "We seem to have the right weather for a life-and-death confrontation."

Lupo in no way shared Renquist's dour humor. "You really insist on handling this on your own?"

"I think it's the only way it can be done."

"Suppose he kills you?"

"That's the chance I'm taking."

"I mean, what do I do if he kills you?"

"In that eventuality, my dear Lupo, you can do what you like to him. It will no longer be my concern."

"What about your sense of history?"

"It will hardly matter if he kills me. History will have already have me recorded as a fool who was slain by an idiot. I will have no way to correct that. I wish you would stop worrying, though, old friend. I have absolutely no intention of allowing Carfax to kill me. You should have a little more faith."

As they entered the Residence, they found that Julia was waiting just inside the front door. "Kurt has returned, Victor."

Renquist nodded. "So I was informed."

"He's in the gallery, he wants to talk to you."

Renquist eyed her coldly. "Rubbish. He wants to kill me."

"I'm not sure about that. Blasco's death has affected him greatly."

"I rather doubt that."

"But you'll talk to him?"

"I'll do whatever is needed."

"You'll have Lupo with you?"

Renquist shook his head. "No, I've already told Lupo that I intend to handle this on my own."

"Kurt is waiting."

Renquist eyes were hard. "He can continue to wait. There's something I want to ask you."

"Which one of you am I betraying this time?"

"You read my mind."

"I suppose that very much depends on who emerges the winner."

"So this is going to be a contest?"

"Could you see it going any other way?"

He looked at her with something close to disgust. "And what are you supposed to be? The fair maiden?"

Before Julia could reply, he moved past her and started up the stairs. Halfway up the first flight, he stopped beside a display of antique weapons that had hung there since the time of Dietrich. After looking them over carefully, he selected a seventeenth-century samurai sword. Lupo grimaced. "Are you sure you want to use that particular blade?"

"Because of its history?"

The sword had the reputation of being what the Japanese had called "evil blade." After a failed power play against their shogun, it had been used by its previous owner when he assisted in the ritual suicides of three of his friends and co-conspirators. After that, he had formally handed it to a fourth knight who had used it on him.

Lupo looked less than happy "It never pays to take chances."

Renquist laughed. "Maybe it's totally appropriate."

Julia started up the stairs after him. "Kurt isn't armed."

"Then I'll have the advantage, won't I?"

Carfax was sitting in the high-backed wing chair that Renquist usually occupied when he used the gallery to meditate. He was still wearing the burgundy silk jacket he'd had on at the Green Dolphin, only at some point between fleeing the nightclub and arriving at the Residence, he appeared to have been soaked to the skin. He looked up as Renquist entered the room. "We did quite a job wrecking that nightclub. I didn't realize you went in for that sort of thing."

"You thought I'd just let you walk away from there?"

"I didn't know what you were going to do. I was intrigued to find out."

"And are you equally intrigued to find out what I'm going to do now?"

"Even more so. I'm also wondering what purpose the sword is supposed to serve. Do you think I'll just sit here and allow you to hack my head off?"

Renquist had yet to draw the sword, and twirled it like a fop's walking cane. "I took it on impulse. I thought it might give me a certain air of authority."

"You thought you'd need it?"

"Not really, but as I said, it was an impulse. I also had the idea that I might allow you to choose the method by which you were terminated. There are much worse ways to take one's leave of this incarnation than simply to kneel down right now and let me strike your head off."

Carfax leaned back in the chair and laughed. "Did you seriously expect me to consider something like that, even for a moment?"

"No, I didn't, but I thought I would give you the chance. A certain logic is at work here."

"Logic?"

Renquist smiled. "Look at it this way. A nosferatu's life can essentially be brought to an end in four ways. The first is decapitation and the removal of the head so healing cannot occur. It has the recommendation of being extremely fast and supposedly painless. The second is the stake through the heart, which I have always considered to be a wretched and somewhat unworthy way to go. I've also always suspected that it wasn't without considerable pain. The third is the fire, which goes without saying must be painful, else why would it have been so popular with the Inquisition? The fourth is the sun, which I can attest from personal experience is not a route that I would choose to make my exit from this plane of existence. Essentially, within a matter of hours—a day or so at the most—you will suffer one of these four fates. I'm offering the one that is generally considered the least painful and the most honorable."

A belligerence came into Carfax's expression and he started to rise from the chair. "The only mistake you're making, Victor, is that I have no intention of dying at all."

Renquist gestured with the still sheathed sword. "Please sit down until I've finished speaking, unless you wish this confrontation to become physical immediately."

Carfax continued to get up from the chair. With a single sweep of his arm, a swashbuckling flourish, and a flash of polished steel, Renquist freed the samurai sword from its scabbard. The scabbard flew across the room and clattered on the floor. Renquist extended his arm straight out so the point of the blade was directly between Carfax's eyes and about two inches in front of his face. "I really would advise you to sit down again, Kurt. You would have to get past the sword to get to me. At best I could blind you. It takes even a nosferatu some hours to regrow a pair of eyeballs."

Carfax stopped, half in and half out of the wing chair, halted by the tip of the sword. The point didn't waver in the slightest, and Carfax half smiled. "Julia believed that it would become physical right from the outset."

Renquist gestured with his free hand. "I think we might both derive a certain satisfaction from disappointing Julia."

Carfax laughed and sank back into the chair. "Julia also believes that she will attach herself to the survivor of this face-off."

Renquist lowered the sword. "Julia's weakness is that she makes a lot calculations that are based on her faith in her own irresistibility."

"You made her."

"Indeed I did."

Carfax looked slowly around the room. Renquist knew he was searching for something he could use to his advantage. "Tell me, Victor, will I be able to make observations like that if I live to be a thousand?"

"You won't live to be a thousand. I've told you that before."

"What makes you so sure that I'm going to die and you're going to live? Faith in your invincibility?"

"One of your problems is that you don't listen. Whether I live through this night or not is quite open to debate. That you will die is virtually a foregone conclusion."

"You mean if I kill you, I will then have Lupo to deal with?"

"Lupo, Dahlia, Segal, and if you get past them there will be the voodoo cultists and the mad priest that finished Cynara and Blasco. I doubt that you even have a refuge to go to when the dawn breaks. You know you can't stay here. You're expelled from the colony, Kurt. The others are going to will you out into the sun if you try and remain here. You're boxed in. Why not take the way out that I'm offering you? You heard those drums beating uptown, Kurt. They were beating for you. One way or another, you're finished."

Even though Carfax did his very best to disguise what he was doing, Renquist sensed a slow build-up of energy in his right hand. He was positioning himself to try something. Renquist pointed with the sword. "Please don't do that; otherwise I will be forced to lop your hand off. I really don't want to see your hand crawling around the floor like the beast with five fingers, trying to reconnect with your arm."

Carfax sullenly let the energy dissipate. "You enjoy having that sword, don't you?"

"Much more than I expected. It really does give me an air of authority, doesn't it?"

"You believe that?"

"You're paying attention and doing what you're told, aren't you? You must admit that's something of a first in our relationship."

"It won't last. Eventually you'll make a slip and I'll have you."

"You're forgetting the other enemy, Kurt."

"What other enemy?"

"Time, Kurt. You're forgetting about time, the nosferatu's oldest enemy. The world turns, Kurt. It will be dawn in just over an hour. Like the song says, 'you don't have time for the waiting game.'"

"In that case . . ." Carfax's right arm shot out like a striking snake. Renquist, taken by surprise, hadn't imagined that the boy had quite such a turn of speed in his bag of tricks. Carfax grasped the blade of the sword, seemingly oblivious to the deep gash that the razor-sharp edge immediately carved in his palm. Purple blood ran back down his wrist as he began to feed energy into the metal, directly up its length and straight into Renquist's hand and arm. The pain was excruciating but Renquist refused to let go his grip. He attempted to start his own counter flow but Carfax had him blocked. Carfax continued to pour on energy and green flame licked up the sword. "Now how do you feel about your symbol of authority, Victor?"

Renquist's hand started to shake. The green flames were all the way up to his elbow. The power overload that Carfax was sending through him would soon start doing organic damage. He couldn't hold on to the hilt of the sword much longer. He could tolerate pain, but deeply ingrained protective instincts would eventually take over and force him to let go his grip. All he could do was to pick the moment, and hope that he could throw Carfax off balance. When he could stand it no longer, he let go and quickly stepped back. As he had expected, Carfax straight away overreached himself. Without rising from the chair, and still holding the sword by the end of the blade, he threw it overarm, straight at Renquist. Renquist's reactions, though, didn't let him down. He dodged to one side and the sword went spinning end over end, swishing past his head with a sound like the rotors of a tiny helicopter. He heard it thud into the wall and quickly turned to look where it had come to rest. The sword, still vibrating, was deeply imbedded in the canvas of the Rembrandt and the wall behind it. It had penetrated the ample stomach of Bent Van Leyden, the subject of the portrait.

Renquist shook his head. "Now *that* is sacrilege."

As he spoke, Carfax was on him, swinging the high-backed chair. Renquist blocked the blow with his forearm. As Renquist angrily hurled the pieces of his favorite chair away from him, Carfax dropped into a half-crouch, ready to spring, looking for the chance and the moment. Renquist delved deep into his reserves of energy. The young one would eventually best him if the conflict was allowed to become nothing more than a simple trial of strength. Renquist had to bring his knowledge and experience to bear. "Shall we stop fooling around and take this seriously?"

Renquist's hands made a fast but complicated pass, locking

both his and Carfax's brain into the same psychic reality, plunging them through space and time into a three-dimensional hallucination of his own creating. The illusion was instant, seamless, and close to perfect. He and Carfax were suddenly back in the white desert of fourteen thousand years ago. Renquist gave silent thanks to Dietrich for supplying him with the raw data from which he had fashioned an imaginary, if alarmingly solid world. He and Carfax were now two huge, armored Original Beings, facing each other in mortal and near-mindless fury. The being that was Carfax, clearly taken by surprise, looked round in amazement. With a guttural, bellowing laugh, the being that was Renquist hurled himself on his opponent.

"Xiizznh ducwm ssoogoz!"

They rolled in the sand in a flurry of snapping fangs and slashing claws. Overhead, the sun was white-hot and the sky a remorseless, burning blue. Carfax was surprised by the illusion and unaccustomed to the new unwieldy body, and Renquist was initially able to gain the upper hand. Renquist had his hands around the Carfax-beast's throat and was attempting to tear its head off, when out of nowhere, two flying discs appeared over the horizon. The combatants quickly separated, each diving for cover as deathrays churned up the sand. Renquist was as stunned as Carfax probably was. The discs were no part of his creation. Could it be that a third party had somehow intervened to prolong the conflict? The only one that Renquist could imagine doing such a thing was Dietrich. Was this one of his abstract moves on the infinite chessboard? And if so, what convoluted strategy was the Old One bringing into play?

While he was still digging himself out of the sand and wondering what the hell was going on, the illusion abruptly changed. Suddenly he and Carfax were two gladiators in a bizarre and ancient arena that stank of blood, death, wild animals, and unwashed humanity. It was nighttime, and the spectacle was illuminated by banks of burning torches. Carfax was scarcely recognizable in partial armor and a bronze helmet with a mask that completely covered his face. In this shift of virtual illusion, Carfax was the one who recovered the faster. He was armed with a small circular shield and a short stabbing sword, and he lunged directly at Renquist. Renquist, who was still wondering who or what was creating these shifts of psychic environment, found himself with a trident and weighted net, a form of single combat that he had never totally understood. As Carfax stabbed at him, he awkwardly swung the net and managed to deflect the thrust, and at the same time, attempted to bring the spear to bear on his opponent. Somewhere beyond the orange light of the smoky torches, an invisible crowd yelled obscenities and derisive comments. Carfax thrust again, and this time he connected, cutting a deep gash in Renquist's upper thigh. Renquist staggered as blood gushed down his leg and the crowd roared. Pain seared through his leg, and he had difficulty standing. Carfax moved forward to administer the coup de grâce.

The illusion abruptly switched again. Now they were two burly cowboys in reeking buckskins, fighting with Bowie knives on the top of a swaying train like something out of a Hollywood western. Renquist had all but come to the conclusion that some incredibly powerful entity was doing little more than playing with them. As he ducked and shuffled on the roof of the swaying railroad car, a thought struck him, its impact of no comfort whatsoever. He had totally taken on trust Dietrich's supposed support. It had never occurred to him that perhaps the Old One was simply indulging his own perverse amusement by shifting two angry nosferatu through time, location, and fantasy. Could it be that, in the place where Dietrich dwelled, the nosferatu capacity for capricious amorality had also been infinitely extended? Was arbitrary betrayal nothing more than an academic exercise for a being in that phase of its immortal span?

Renquist's leg still throbbed with pain. Apparently the injuries sustained in one illusion were carried forward into the next one. With anger mainly generated by the absurdity of the situation, Renquist slashed at Carfax, slicing through his buck-skin shirt and instantly producing a line of blood across the tanned chest.

Mercifully, this illusion lasted only for an instant. As Carfax reeled back from the knife cut, the two of them found themselves momentarily in some Dantean, medieval concept of hell, a cavernous subterranean world of jagged rocks and flaming cascades of lava where, in the guise of two red-skinned, horned and hoofed devils, they grappled in a lake of living fire while tortured souls screamed in everlasting agony all around them. Hell, however, was gone as quickly as the western movie, and they next plunged into the bodies of two huge carnivorous reptiles and the oozing muck of a Mesozoic swamp. The battle continued red in tooth and claw, with thrashing tails and massive bodies crashing through the giant, primitive, fernlike trees and throwing up waves of mud and slime. The first thing Renquist discovered was that the reptile into which he'd now been precipitated was incredibly stupid, and his own intelligence was rapidly sinking into its dull, narrow ferocity. With the remaining echoes of his own personality, he continued to worry at the problem of who or what seemed to be directing the battle and the illusory shifts in era and location. He could hardly believe that this was what Dietrich had meant when he said that his help might come in a way that would be difficult for Renquist to imagine or even recognize. Renquist was certainly having difficulty recognizing any of this as help. The contest was going consistently against him, and his strength was rapidly ebbing. The dinosaur body was covered in bleeding wounds, its vision was blurred, and its breathing labored. His nosferatu power of recovery showed no signs of having been transferred from illusion to illusion. For the first time, Renquist found himself entertaining the idea that he could actually die in this fight. Up to this point, he had only considered his own death as an academic abstract, but now it was a real and frightening possibility. The two lizards had all but fought themselves to a standstill. They both stood, breathing heavily, staring balefully at each other with their small, beady eyes, each waiting for the other to make the next aggressive move. The Carfax reptile slowly swished its huge tail, and the Renquist reptile braced itself for a renewed onslaught. Both reptile and nosferatu consciousness had serious doubts that they would actually survive another bout.

The Carfax reptile let out a threatening hiss, but as it did so, the illusion dissolved, and Carfax and Renquist found themselves back in the Residence gallery. The two of them stood some six feet apart. Their clothes were shredded and their bodies were slick with blood. Indeed, blood seemed to be everywhere. The floor was awash and slippery with it, and it spattered the walls and the paintings. Renquist knew he was close to collapse, but Carfax looked to be in a similar condition. Carfax eyed Renquist with a mixture of awe and exhaustion. "Did you do all that?"

Renquist slowly shook his head. "I couldn't have done that. I don't have the power. Something else has been playing with us."

"Something else?"

"I have no idea."

Carfax leaned forward, hands on his knees, trying to catch his breath. "We have to finish this."

Renquist said nothing. Carfax was right. They had to finish it. No way out was going to present itself, and he was in no way confident that it would be him doing the finishing. Carfax painfully straightened up. With dragging steps, he crossed the gallery and pulled the samurai sword from the Rembrandt. "Now I have the symbol of authority."

Renquist attempted to summon the last traces of his energy, but found he was totally drained. Carfax leaned against the wall for a moment. He too was having difficulty even raising his limbs, but he had the weapon. His words came in a series of short gasps. "I'm going to have your head, Victor. What did you tell me? Decapitation was fast, honorable, and comparatively painless?"

He slowly and experimentally swung the sword, as though the simple effort took all of his strength. "A thousand years is a long time, Victor. Don't you feel that you've had your fair share of mortal life?"

Renquist didn't have strength to reply. Now Carfax had the sword, he could see no way to defend himself. It also didn't seem as though whatever had been plunging them from illusion to illusion was going to intervene in the nick of time and send them to some sliver of illusion where he might find himself with an edge. He was going to have to resign himself to the inevitable. Victor Renquist had, all things considered, enjoyed his long life, both as human and as nosferatu. It was a shame that it had to end at the hands of this stripling who had nothing going for him except resentment and the strength of youth. Carfax started to move towards him. Renquist drew himself up to his full height and squared his shoulders. All he had left was his final dignity. He could at least bow out with grace. Carfax raised the sword. Renquist closed his eyes, but as he did so, the sound of the gallery door opening came from behind him.

"It is dawn, Kurt Carfax. It is time for you to leave this place."

Their mouths opened and the sound that emerged was like a wall of ululating violence and angry compulsion. At the same time, their auras stabbed out like lances of power. Dahlia, Segal, Imogene, Sada, and Lupo, dressed in the ceremonial black capes, stood in a semicircle on the blood-slick floor of the gallery, under the dead eyes of the gore-spattered portraits. Carfax, with his equally bloody body and shredded clothing, clapped his hands over his ears and all but fell to his knees. The samurai sword clattered to the floor. The colony was willing Carfax out of its Residence. He was expelled and he had neglected to leave before the dawn. By nosferatu tradition he now had to leave anyway, irrespective of the fact that such a departure into the sunlight would kill him. The only one not present was Julia, and it wasn't clear whether her absence was out of respect for her onetime relationship with Carfax, or in keeping with another nosferatu tradition that deemed it less than seemly to participate in the destruction of one of your own creations.

The ululation ran up an octave and Carfax began to drag his feet towards the door. The colony opened a path for him. His mind rebelled but his body was no longer his to control. Renquist, equally bloody and tattered, quickly stepped between Carfax and the others. "This isn't right. He defeated me in a fair fight. He was about to kill me and I would have been unable to do anything to stop him."

Dahlia looked at Renquist sternly. "We aren't rescuing you, Victor. So you may as well can the chivalry. This is colony business. It doesn't really involve you at all."

Renquist shook his head. "He bested me. He doesn't deserve to die like this."

Sada was not only stern but also impatient. "Please get out of the way, Victor. This isn't easy and we'd like to get it over with so we can sleep. You two have been going at it for almost and hour and a half and it seemed, at times, like you were going to destroy the entire block."

Imogene was merely cold. "It was fortunate that we had the thunderstorm, otherwise the neighborhood might have been beating on the door with pitchforks and flaming torches."

Dahlia gestured him away. "Please stand aside, Victor, and let us proceed."

Renquist had no will to resist. Despite the display of conspicuous honor, he actually had little inclination to protect Carfax. He looked at him and shrugged, then backed away from the circle leaving his former adversary to his fate. The five remaining members of the colony formally rearranged themselves in a circle behind Carfax. Their auras stabbed out and the ululation started again. Step by step, Carfax was driven towards the door. He clung for a moment to the doorframe, then staggered out of the gallery completely. Renquist heard the hideous singing slowly descending the stairs, and he limpingly followed. He watched from the landing as Carfax was driven all way down to the ground floor. It seemed Julia was to play a part in the destruction after all. Protected by a thick black cape and cowl, she stood behind the front door, ready to open it when the colony finally forced Carfax out and into the light. Renquist was a little surprised that she should be playing such a key role in the lethal ceremony, and he wondered what might have been taking place instead if Carfax had succeeded in decapitating him.

As Carfax was forced on down the hallway, past the grandfather clock, towards Julia and the door, he started pleading. He dropped to his knees, quite literally begging for his life. Again Renquist was surprised. He had expected a little more dignity from the young one. He could surely not have believed that a group of angry nosferatu, in the full flight of a death ceremony, would be swayed or even notice grovelling pleas for mercy and sobbing admissions of fear and the desire to go on living. Struggling every inch of the way, Carfax was forced by the will of the others to crawl backwards on his hands and knees, edging inevitably towards the door and the sun. At the very last minute, Julia swung the door open as fast as she could and, in one final burst of noise, he was hurled bodily out into the daylight.

The rain had stopped, but the streets were still wet and the sky clouded over. Carfax fell down the steps. Smoke was already rising from his body and his flesh had started to blacken. He attempted to drag himself to where the Pontiac was parked, but burning fragments were already falling from him, and he was rapidly losing his human conformation. Flames burst from inside him, and all movement ceased. A sudden puff of pale blue flame leapt upwards and all that remained was a shapeless thing that looked like nothing more than a bundle of charred garbage. A gust of wind scattered flakes of papery ash and, a few minutes later, a street cleaning truck with revolving brushes and jets of spraying water swept away what was left of him.

"It's time we got moving." McGuire did his best to look the other way as Kelly dressed himself. The state of the ex-priest's underwear was close to unnerving, and after spending the night watching the man drink himself unconscious, McGuire had been left in no doubt as to why he had been thrown out of the church. To put it bluntly, Kelly was unpleasant, disgusting, and probably insane, and that fate had compelled McGuire to share a terrible and impossible secret with him was one of the cruelest cosmic jokes he had ever encountered.

"I need more stakes." Kelly was now fussing with the contents of his leather bag.

"We can take care of that on our way back into Manhattan." All McGuire wanted was to get out of the motel room as fast as possible. Being cooped up all night with Kelly had done nothing to improve the atmosphere.

"The stakes are very important."

"Sweet Jesus, all we need is to bust up an old packing case."

"At least the rain has stopped."

"Let's just get moving."

Julia called after Renquist. "Victor, when the sun goes down, I will need to talk to you."

Renquist slowly turned. "Julia, you might be surprised how little we have to talk about."

Before she could say anything, he turned and continued to limp up the stairs. All he could think of was that he needed to clean the blood from his body and then to sleep for as long as was inhumanly possible. Beyond that, he had no inclination to speculate. He knew that the colony was about to relocate. He knew that the killer of Cynara and Blasco was still on the loose, but right at that moment, he was physically and emotionally unable to fight any more battles or solve any more problems. He simply wanted to be left alone.

Fate, however, refused to play along. As he dragged himself towards the top of the stairs, the ancient, grating voice of Dietrich spoke inside his head. "I'm sorry, Victor, you have no choice but to remain awake."

Revolt erupted inside Renquist. "Is that so?"

"The One Who Knows is on his way. I have sensed him. He is currently crossing water, but very soon he will be here."

"And why should I believe you?"

Deitrich grated angrily. "You doubt me?"

"You read me so easily that you already know that. It was you who created those illusions, wasn't it?"

"Of course. Who else do you imagine would have been capable of such a thing? I was very proud of what I created."

"What you created almost killed me."

"You're alive, aren't you?"

"Yes, but . . ."

"If you had fought that young one in real time, you would have been dead in half an hour. With all respect, Victor, you are a thousand years old and he had the edge on you in terms of stamina and strength. Also, if you continued to fight in real time, the two of you would have destroyed the entire Residence, perhaps even a considerable part of neighborhood. Even the leakthrough caused enough commotion."

Renquist had to admit, grudgingly, that there was a certain logic to this. It was so hard to know the intentions of a being that had grown so old and strange. "I suppose so . . ."

"The main purpose of the illusion, of course, was to distract him, so he wasn't aware that the dawn was upon him."

Renquist wasn't sure that he was buying this, even from Dietrich. "That's how it worked out, but are you seriously telling me that you had it all planned in advance?"

"Could you ever believe otherwise? I was your Master once.

Do you not think that I still watch over you?"

"I came within a hairsbreadth of losing my head."

"Isn't that the sweetest way to end a plan? Victory in a hairsbreadth of defeat?

"My view wasn't quite so romantic at the time."

"You should have more faith, Victor. As I said, I still watch over my former pack of snapping cubs."

"This snapping cub is exhausted."

"The One Who Knows is on his way."

Everything in Renquist groaned at this fresh demand. "Even if I accept that, I can't handle it, not straight after Carfax."

"You are the only one who can handle it, Victor."

"What about Lupo? What about the others?"

"They saved you from beheading, didn't they?"

"Yes, but . . ."

"Clean yourself up, rest for a while. You will find the strength. This one is only human."

Renquist knew there was no point in arguing. A nosferatu did what a nosferatu had to do.

Renquist watched on the security monitor as the two humans came down the street. He didn't know if it was just his fancy, but they seemed to be walking extremely slowly, almost trudging, moving like men going to the scaffold. Twice they stopped and spoke to each other, and the conversation hardly looked friendly. It was as though one was much more reluctant that the other, but they were somehow joined by an invisible chain. The reluctant one he recognized immediately. It was McGuire, the police detective, the other, who wore the garb of a priest, was presumably the one called Kelly, the One Who Knew. As far as Renquist could tell, he had everything ready for them. After cleaning himself until no trace of the blood, filth, and taint from the fight with Carfax remained, Renquist had dressed carefully—a ruffled dress shirt in black silk, narrow black silk pants, patent-leather buckled shoes that he hadn't worn in almost a hundred years, and, over it all, a black velvet smoking jacket. Let them at least have the vampire they expected. He drew the line at an opera cape, however. He might play on their fears and cultural dreads, but he wasn't about to act out a bad piece of Hollywood Gothic.

As the two humans approached the door of the Residence, Renquist used the remote function of the building's security system to unlock the front door. Now all they had to do was to push the door and walk in. He decided to ignore the old rhyme about flies and spiders.

McGuire looked up at the building and shivered. The air was still damp and chill after the night of rain. "So this is it?"

Kelly bit his lip and nodded. The morning had brought him a hangover, depression, and considerable lowering of confidence in his mission. A large part of him simply wanted to turn away and hide, and, if he had not had McGuire at his side, he might have done exactly that. Once again, it seemed to be an example of the Almighty leaving him no way out but to forge ahead with his mission. He was denied even the smallest measure of time to recover from the shocks and traumas of the previous day. He simply had to press on into the threatening unknown.

McGuire thrust his hands deep into his pockets, apparently signifying his loathing for the entire situation. He glanced up and down the street to see if he was being observed. McGuire didn't look so good himself. He was unshaven, his eyes were red-rimmed, and his clothes looked as though they'd been slept in—which, indeed, they had. "So how do we get inside?"

"I don't know."

"I thought God was going to show you the way."

"He may yet do that."

McGuire looked up at the surveillance cameras mounted on the wall of the building. "Well, I hope that he does it pretty damn soon, because whoever's inside probably knows we're here."

"It's daylight. They should all be sleeping now."

"You'd better be right. We're staking a great deal on that single fact."

"Is that a pun?"

"Fuck you, Kelly. See if you can find a way through that door."

Kelly scowled at McGuire, walked up the steps of the house, and inspected the front door. McGuire shifted from one foot to the other. "Whatever you do, you'd better make it fast. If we go on hanging around like this, we're going to find ourselves arrested for loitering."

Kelly placed a hand on the door and, to his amazement, he found that it yielded to the lightest pressure. He turned and hissed urgently to McGuire. "The door's not even locked."

"You're putting me on."

Kelly pushed the door again so it was open about six inches. "I told you God would show us a way!"

McGuire face was hard and unhappy. "How certain are you that's the work of God? It looks a hell of a lot like a setup to me."

Kelly pushed the door again and went on pushing until it stood wide open. He waited for a few moments and when no hellish thing sprang out at him, he turned back to McGuire. "So? Do we go inside?"

McGuire sighed. "I guess there's no turning back now."

He stopped before stepping over the threshold, and slid his pistol out of its holster. He gestured to Kelly. "This is your show. You can take the point."

The humans were inside the building. Renquist sat in the library, observing their thoughts and feeling their fear. He had to give them credit, though. Despite being mortally terrified, they pressed on. Before speaking, Renquist adjusted his voice so it could be heard as a soft, compelling whisper everywhere in the building. "Welcome to my house. Although unbidden, you have entered freely and of your own will."

He felt the two humans freeze in horror. Each was almost overwhelmed by a desire to bolt, but both managed to resist and hold their ground. "I am Renquist and I am the Master of this house. I imagine that you are looking for me, so why don't you come to me in my library. Straight down the hall. Follow my voice."

Renquist slowly rose from the his chair as the two men entered the room. "So what is it to be, gentlemen? The wooden stake? Drive it deep into the heart and burn the body? Isn't that the traditional remedy?"

The two men entered nervously. Their fear was obvious to him, but they were doing their human best to disguise the fact that they probably felt they were entering one of the inner circles of Hell. McGuire, the detective, even had a pistol in his hand, held down at his side, partially concealed.

Renquist half smiled. "After all you've been through, you now have nothing to say to me?"

As he spoke, the men's nervousness grew and expanded to a poisonous aura of loathing and fear. Their eyes were still adjusting to the gloom, and they moved with the hesitancy of the partially blind. Renquist's smile broadened. "I really expected more of two intrepid vampire hunters."

The two men seemed uncertain as to what to do next. What had these fools expected to find? The whole colony sleeping, helpless in neat rows of coffins, like some funeral parlor dormitory? As if to confirm Renquist's thoughts, Kelly, the crazy one who had once been a priest, raised his arm with a desperate, dramatic flourish. "Approach us not, foul abomination!"

Renquist shook his head and laughed. "And now they bring out the trinkets, the gewgaws of superstition. This is New York

City at the end of the twentieth century, gentlemen. Are you still unable to separate fact from fancy? Do you expect me to cringe and cover my eyes like some creature on the television late show?"

Renquist took a step forward. Kelly held his ground although obvious terror pulsed through him. "In the name of the Father, the Son, and the Holy Ghost, I order you to stay back."

Renquist halted. Too much pressure too soon might cause Kelly to panic, and panic on the part of either of the humans would add too many random factors to an already perilous situation. Normally he would have predicted no problems in handling two humans, even though it was broad daylight outside, but weakened as he was from the battle with Carfax, he was unwilling to take any chances. "Is that whiskey I smell on your breath?"

A flush of guilt suffused Kelly's aura. Clearly the man continued to feel shame over his drinking. Renquist glanced at McGuire, the policeman. "Did you really think it was a wise move to form an alliance with this drunken buffoon?"

Kelly squared his shoulders and brandished the cross at arm's length, still apparently expecting Renquist to cower away from it. "Look upon the Holy Cross, fiend, and tremble!"

Renquist made a curtly dismissive gesture. "You can put that thing down. It really has no effect."

The ex-priest's lip curled. "You'd like that, wouldn't you? You'd like me to leave myself defenseless." Kelly was also holding an old-fashioned leather bag in his other hand. Renquist was able to read the contents of the case without effort. The club hammer and the sharpened stakes were the source of an excitement that was close to sexual. Kelly couldn't wait to swing the hammer and feel the stake penetrate a body. Renquist looked hard at McGuire. "Your friend wants to kill me. He wants to kill me very badly."

McGuire's expression was guarded. "Do you blame him?"

Renquist raised a questioning eyebrow. "But can you permit him to kill me?" He allowed a little of his influence to come into play. The question was crucial, the start of the essential dividing of the two humans. McGuire didn't answer, and Renquist smiled as he sensed an increase in the policeman's unease. "Wouldn't that be murder, Detective McGuire?"

"I doubt any jury would convict him."

"That's not really the point, is it?"

Kelly glanced quickly at McGuire, as though afraid to take his eyes off Renquist. "Don't listen to him. Remember that he's clever. He's terribly clever."

Renquist had placed the first thin tip of the wedge between Kelly and McGuire. It was his own pointed stake and his task was now to hammer it home. "Think about it, McGuire. You're sworn to uphold the law. Can you really, in good conscience, become an accessory to murder? Can you be a part of what amounts to vigilante justice?"

"Are you really suggesting that I take you in? That I arrest you like any normal criminal?"

"Can you really do anything else?"

Kelly's voice took on a desperate edge. "Don't listen to him. He's the Devil and he'll try to confuse you with a lot of talk."

McGuire was plainly torn. The policeman was wrestling with conflicting emotions. Renquist saw in his memory how he and his partner had wrestled with the same problem when they'd confronted Carfax and Blasco, helpless in the coffins. He and Williams hadn't been quite ready to let Kelly commit something that looked a great deal like cold-blooded murder even if they were convinced the victims were something other than human. "It's a problem, isn't it, Detective McGuire?"

Kelly was now on the very edge of panic. "It's no problem at all. He's just trying to confuse us. Put a half-dozen bullets into him. You saw what happened to the last ones. Bullets will put him down long enough for me to drive a stake into him." He looked at Renquist. "The others of your filthy kind are sleeping, aren't they? You're the only one awake. We only have to get past you, don't we?"

Renquist nodded. "That's right, you only have to get past me, but I think you should know that it will take more than a few 9mm shells to incapacitate me. I am a thousand years old, Kelly, and very resilient."

Renquist saw that Kelly was getting increasingly desperate. His use of Kelly's name had appeared to particularly upset the man. Kelly turned and almost screamed at McGuire. "Shoot him! Shoot him now! He's bluffing. He doesn't want to be shot. He knows it will put him down."

Kelly was right. Renquist didn't want to be shot, and he might possibly be bluffing. In his present condition, he wasn't at all sure if he could take a half-dozen rounds and still keep going, and he wasn't at all anxious to put it to the test. On the other hand, he didn't want to use the influence on McGuire. If, by his own free will, the detective decided not to fire, Renquist knew that he had him. He would be able to turn McGuire on Kelly. It was a calculated risk, but he had to take it.

Again Kelly howled at McGuire. "What are you waiting for? Shoot him!"

McGuire raised the gun, but still Renquist didn't use his power. Seconds passed, and McGuire didn't fire. Renquist stood unmoving. He was becoming more and more convinced that his gamble was going to pay off. McGuire was a policeman, not an executioner. Kelly, on the other hand, was close to losing his mind. "Do it, curse you! Your partner only died because you hesitated!"

This almost tipped McGuire in the other direction. His finger tightened on the trigger. Renquist's voice was soft and calm. "Are you going to kill me, Detective McGuire? Does it seem that I pose an immediate threat to anyone in this room?"

"His kind killed Williams!"

Renquist nodded. "That is true, Detective McGuire. Two of my kind killed your partner. What you or Kelly don't know is that Carfax, the survivor of the pair, died himself just after dawn, just a couple of hours ago. We killed him. Our kind have our own kind of justice."

"Don't listen to him!"

McGuire lowered the pistol slightly. "Is that true?"

Renquist face was solemn. "I swear."

"Don't listen to him!"

McGuire looked at Kelly and shook his head. "It's no good. I can't just shoot him, whatever he is."

Renquist had turned McGuire. Now all he needed to do was to push Kelly fully over the edge. All it took was the slightest nudge. To provide that nudge, he borrowed one of the illusions Dietrich had used on him and Carfax. As far as Kelly's perception was concerned, Renquist's skin turned red, he grew horns, hooves, and a tail, an extra two feet in stature, and had a body covered in the most disgusting, chancrous warts. While McGuire saw Renquist in his earthly form, Kelly was now perceiving him as the standard devil of Christian mythology. The ex-priest turned white. The blood drained from his face. With a howl, he leaped at McGuire. "Give me the gun!"

As Renquist watched with amusement, the two of them grappled for the pistol. Renquist decided it was not only high time to resolve this whole business, but also the perfect opportunity. At a crucial moment, as the gun happened to be pointed directly at Kelly's stomach, he caused McGuire's finger to tighten on the trigger. The gun went off. A look of amazed horror came over Kelly's face as the bullet ripped up through his body. Renquist shut off any contact with the man's mind. He in no way wanted to be a party to Kelly's thrashing, dying madness. Kelly muttered something unintelligible, then slumped forward into McGuire's arms. McGuire carefully lowered him to the ground and felt for a pulse.

"Is he dead?" Renquist already knew the answer, and he only asked to get McGuire's attention.

McGuire nodded and stood up. "Yes, he's dead."

"And you shot him."

"It was an accident."

"He was an extremely unpleasant man."

"He still didn't deserve to die like that."

Renquist shrugged and sat down. He had no time to be dealing with the ramifications of human guilt. "I think we should transact some business, Detective McGuire."

"Business?"

"That's right. Business."

"I don't understand."

"New York has a problem and, as of this moment, you are the only man in the entire city in any position to solve it."

"You mean it has an infestation of vampires?"

"I don't like that word."

" 'Infestation' or 'vampire'?"

"We call ourselves nosferatu."

"It's still an infestation."

"It's also an infestation that everyone in authority will be extremely reluctant to believe in and even more reluctant to admit or reveal to the public."

If McGuire had any reservations about talking a deal with Renquist while Kelly's body lay on the floor between them, still warm and still bleeding, he didn't show it. "What are you suggesting?"

"Most of the city believes that the recent killings are the work of some kind of serial murderer."

"Or murderers."

"I'm afraid you're going to have to make do with just one."

McGuire looked puzzled. "What are you talking about?"

"What this city currently needs is a scapegoat for its killings."

"Or the real perpetrators."

"That would be myself and my companions, and you can't have us. I also believe that you wouldn't really want us. We'd simply create too many complications."

"The killings would have to stop."

Renquist dismissed this as being no problem. "We already have that covered. All of my kind will have left the city within twenty-four hours."

"You want Kelly to be the scapegoat?"

For a human, this one was quite bright. "Who else?"

McGuire shook his head. "I don't know."

"You don't know what?"

"If I could pull off a scam like that."

"He fits the classic serial killer profile. He was a loner, he was a religious fanatic, and he hated women."

"You're forgetting the remains of the two . . ."

McGuire hesitated and Renquist filled in the word from him. "Nosferatu."

"How are they going to be explained away?"

"Those remains will be buried deeper than the alien bodies in Hangar Eighteen freezer chambers. You can tell your superiors the absolute truth if you want to. As long as you give them Kelly as a get-out, they will fall on your neck weeping. Your career will be made. You'll have the power of knowing exactly where the bodies are buried."

"I'm still not sure. I lost a partner in all this. I don't feel right about putting it all down to Kelly."

Renquist was becoming impatient with McGuire's vestigial morality. "You're in this too deep to have any illusions of doing the right thing."

"I just don't feel good about it."

"It hardly matters how you feel."

"I could go ahead and kill you."

Renquist shook his head. "I wouldn't allow that, and even if you did, it wouldn't solve your problem. Also remember that I could much more easily kill you."

McGuire still seemed intent on suffering. "I don't know."

Renquist decided that he'd had enough. He snapped on the influence and McGuire went rigid. "I'm very disappointed in you, McGuire. I attempted to deal with you as an equal, but

I suppose, in the end, all you humans have to be told what to do."

McGuire continued to stand rigid. Renquist spoke slowly and distinctly. "Here are your post-hypnotic instructions. For the next twenty-four hours, you will remember nothing. Once my companions and I have left the city, your memory of all this will return. You will go to your superiors and tell them the whole story. At the same time, you will offer them Kelly as their only possible get-out short of going public with the vampires in Manhattan. If they don't accept that, you're on your own. Do you understand?"

McGuire nodded like a robot. Renquist stood up. "Now go, so I can finally sleep."

McGuire turned and walked stiffly from the library. Once he was out of the Residence, Renquist locked the doors, engaged the alarm systems, and then, close to exhaustion, climbed the stairs to his bedroom.

Epilogue

Deep in the cargo area of Los Angeles International Airport, a truck driver who answered to the name of Kareem looked from the waybill to the seven aluminum flight cases that were being loaded by forklift from the aircraft to the back of the panel truck. He then glanced at the man called Chuck, who had been hired to assist him with the eventual off-loading when they arrived at the actual delivery point. "They look like fucking coffins."

Chuck scratched his ear and took a sip from the bottle of Seven Up that he was holding. "It's probably just because they arrived in the middle of the night."

"You remember the movie *Platoon*?"

"What about it?"

"It's like that scene at the beginning of the movie when the new recruits were arriving in Vietnam, and as they're, like, coming in, the bodies are being flown out in all these hundreds of aluminum coffins."

Chuck shrugged. "It's probably some rock & roll equipment. Someone like Keith Richards moving to L.A., you know what I'm saying?"

"Maybe they're full of coke."

"Maybe we ought to take a look inside."

Kareem shook his head. "I was strictly warned about that. Told we wouldn't get paid, or worse."

"Then they probably *are* full of coke."

When the seventh and last flight case had been placed on the truck, Chuck hauled down the rolling rear door.

"So where are we taking this stuff?"

Kareem walked round to the driver's door. "A big old house in Benedict Canyon. Spooky motherfucker place. All overgrown and surrounded by cypress trees."

"Is this stuff the entire shipment?"

Kareem shook his head. "I heard there might be some other stuff, like furniture, books, paintings, that kind of thing coming in later."

"Will we have to haul them too?"

Kareem shrugged. "Fucked if I know."

He climbed into the truck and started the engine. He waved for Chuck, who was watching a taxiing Federal Express 747, to hurry up and get in. "Yo, homes, let's go! I wanna get this shit done before dawn. I gotta fucking day job to go to."